PROPHECY

Book One of
The Dragonfly Chronicles

ELERI DRAKE

McCollum Creative Endeavors, LLC

McCollum Creative Endeavors
P.O. Box 1712
Apex, NC 27502

Cover design by Najla Qamber
Editing by Melinda DeJongh

Print book ISBN: 978-1-962436-01-4
Manufactured in the United States of America

*First Edition published by The Wild Rose Press under the name Heather McCollum, August 2014
*Second Edition November 2024

For more information about Eleri Drake and Heather McCollum books, please check out her web site.
https://www.heathermccollum.com/eleri-drake/

Eleri Drake Website

CONTENTS

DEDICATION

This book is dedicated to Braden, who has always been my real-life hero.

I love you!

FOREIGN WORDS USED IN PROPHECY

(SCOTS GAELIC AND ROMANY)

àngelas – angel (Romany)

cac – shit (SG)

chiriklò – sparrow (Romany)

daingead – dammit (SG)

duy – mother (Romany)

Meala-naidheachd ort – Congratulations to you (SG)

mo chreach – my rage (SG)

phen – sister (Romany)

seanair – grandfather (SG)

seanmhair – grandmother (SG)

sgian dubh – black handled dagger (SG)

shoshòy – rabbit (Romany)

Tha gaol agam ort – I love you (SG)

Tha thu nad Ghàidheal – You are a Highlander (SG)

Historical Notes

The Romany people, sometimes referred to as Romani, Roma, Gypsies, and Travelers, arrived in England around 1515. They were mistakenly thought to have originated in Egypt because of their darker skin and hair, hence the name Gypsy. The Romany people in England came from continental Europe after an exodus from northern India. They were a nomadic people with strong ties to extended family, culture, and traditions. Misunderstood and often persecuted throughout history, they became an easy target for blame. In order to survive, they traded, took on odd jobs, sold wares and healing cures, and entertained the locals. They often traveled in caravans on the same migratory roads as those on pilgrimages.

Prince Charles Edward Stuart, also known as the Young Pretender and Bonnie Prince Charlie, was the grandson of King James II of England. When his father, James Francis Edward Stuart, fled England under fear of execution, Charles was raised on the European continent in exile. Charles spent most of his life planning to get the English and Scottish throne back for his father. Those supporting his cause were known as Jacobites.

PROLOGUE
ESCAPE

"My wards are weakening!" Serena's mother yelled above the cry of the tempest outside their small cottage. "I must hide you away from here!" Her tone rose and fell against the noise like the voice of a lost person desperate to stay above the crash of waves. Serena had never heard her mother's voice so shaken, and it twisted in her hollow stomach.

Serena's mother was Gilla, Great Wiccan Priestess of the Western Mountains, Keeper of the Earth Mother's magic. Her long braid swayed against her back like a pendulum as she paced across the gray floorboards to the barren hearth.

"How?" Serena asked. Her gaze darted to the rattling door. "With them out there? How?"

The demons flew along the perimeter just outside the standing stones that encircled the cottage, striking wildly at the protection wards her parents had erected with their combined magic. Serena was only nine years old, but she knew that invasion meant death, probably the hideous death her father had endured. They'd found his broken body outside the stones, limp, swollen, bruised. Serena shivered and squeezed the hand of her younger sister.

"Please, Earth Mother, my shields must last!" Gilla shouted at the ceiling.

As if sneering against her prayer, something large dropped on the roof, making all four sisters crouch, covering their heads as loose thatching filtered down.

Gilla pulled a carved oak box from the mantel and turned toward Serena. "Starting with you." Gilla's robes snapped around her as she whisked over to stand before the stone table in the center of the room. The legs of the table anchored into the earth below the house, the floorboards cut and built around them.

"I will send you with my magic," Gilla continued, "all of you." Her gaze slid along her four daughters. "The demons try to steal the threads that hold our lives together in this realm," she said, breathing in shallow gasps. "The threads that I guard inside me." She pressed a fist against her chest.

Serena listened, rapt, ready to follow her mother's instructions. Merewin, the second oldest, stood by her while her twin sisters hugged tightly to each other. A tree beyond the window cracked, falling against the eaves. Serena jumped.

"They have grown strong on your father's life force. But they need my magic strands to remake the world," Gilla said.

With another series of thumps, small bits of dirt and straw sifted down. Serena covered her head and glanced around the once tidy room. *Home.* It had always felt warm, smelling of fresh-baked bread. Now it was ice, a dusty prison surrounded by violence and noise. Serena tried to swallow the dry grit she breathed in and coughed.

"I will send one of my powers with each of you," Gilla said. "The magic the demons need to destroy our world will be all split up, hidden."

Nails scratched at the door, making Kat and Kailin scream. They hid their faces against one another as if trying to hide in their blond tresses. Serena felt Merewin's hand squeeze hers, and they held tightly.

"I need more time," her mother flicked her long fingernails toward the door. Yelps rent the air and coursed off into the shriek of the wind. "They use Druce's magic against his own kin," her mother murmured. Wisps of her hair had come undone from her neat braid, sticking out like hair on a neglected doll.

Gilla glided before Serena with unnatural speed. "You must go now." Wild desperation warred with calm strength behind her mother's red-rimmed eyes. Bits of hay spiked in her hair, dirt marring the smooth skin of her cheek.

"Where, Mama?" Serena asked.

"To when," her mother countered and tugged her forward. Serena squeezed Merewin's hand once more and let go.

"When then?" Serena whispered.

"Each of you goes to a different place."Gilla paused, her eyes scanning her four daughters. "And a different time."

"How?" Merewin, asked.

"Drakkina, the Wiccan priestess, taught me how to thread through the planes of time." Her mother's words spilled over each other in haste.

"But," Serena said, "we won't be together. We'll be with strangers. Away from you, away from our home."

"Eventually you'll find home, find each other."

Large thumps pummeled the roof and then rolled down the slant to hit the ground, squeaking and scurrying for shelter. "Rats." Gilla glanced at the walls as if measuring their strength.

"But how will we find each other?" Serena asked, her voice choking out with the panic constricting her throat. She beckoned Merewin to join her, not ready to let go of her family.

Gilla placed a stone in Serena's palm, pulling her away from Merewin. "You all have my mark upon you, the mark of the priestess, Drakkina." Gilla dropped Serena's hand and lifted the hem of her silver-green robe to show her leg where the brown pattern of a dragonfly lay against her pale skin. Each sister had the dragonfly birthmark somewhere on their body.

"Serena," her mother said and took up her hand that clutched the stone. "You were born first, and you will leave first. The demons will not find you seven-hundred years in the future." Gilla ran her finger along her daughter's firm lips and kissed her cheek.

Serena fell into her mother's arms and squeezed her. She breathed in her mother's summery smell. "I love you, Mama," Serena said, swallowing hard.

"Tha gaol agam ort, Serena." Gilla looked deeply into Serena's face. "You have your father's eyes, so bright, so unique." She breathed deeply.

The shiny red rock nestled into her palm, warming. The rock contained coils of spun fibers wound tightly from the center to the very edges of the stone.

Her mother leaned over it, lips hovering just above its smooth surface. "I freely gift you with my sight. On currents of my blood, on currents of my love, on currents of my fire power given by the Great Earth Mother, send her now within my thread of sight." She then opened her lips and blew gently, so gently.

Serena watched the coils glow softly inside the orb. When her mother's breath ran out, she looked up at Serena. "Deep sight is an immense power. Grow strong so you don't lose yourself in it. Trust your heart. Sight can be biased by your perceptions." Her mother pulled a delicate blue feather from her pocket. She slipped it behind Serena's ear and whispered, "You won't be alone."

Heat grew in the rock until it almost burned the center of Serena's palm and yet there was no pain. The heat spread through her body, and she smelled the sweet summer spice of her mother. "It feels... like I hold a part of you, Mama."

"You do."

The room warped before Serena's eyes as her mother stepped back and turned to Merewin. The room wavered like the end of a dream, bending and fading. The stone's heat spread through the core of her skull and out along the skin of her face. Even her eyes felt hot. She blinked, her empty hand rubbing against the tingling dragonfly birthmark near her navel. Then the heat washed downwards through her stomach, sliding through thigh muscles, past knees to ankles and the very tips of her toes. Serena felt her body melt into liquid or light. Her weightless form watched the world quiver as through a pool of water.

Her body narrowed and lengthened and twisted into a single thread. She felt no pain, just different, fluid. She stretched up through the roof of the house, up through a minute crack in the weakened thatch and out above the howling chaos. She focused on the cottage at the center of the ten soaring stones, watching it shrink as she soared high above the home that had held the love of her family. She would have wept but didn't know if she had tears or even a face.

She shot up through the clouds so that they lay roiling beneath her as the stars glittered above. Long and thin, she twirled and twisted as sun and moon arched over, racing across the sky until they melded into one light, burning, flickering.

Stop! Please stop! It was like being spun in a whirlwind.

Heaviness grasped Serena's essence, pulling her downward through a blue sky, back through the clouds. The earth flew to meet her as her body expanded from the thin thread, tingling and reforming in the air. The stone solidified in her hand once more. A scream pushed out of her as her lungs expanded. "Ahhh!"

Tree limbs brushed her robes, slowing her plunge. Cold water soaked through to her skin as Serena sank, her toes squishing into the bottom muck. She thrust upwards through green pond scum, sputtering and gasping. She flailed about for anything to help her stay afloat and spat out the bitter water. Her hands, one fisted around the stone, churned wildly as long skirts trapped her movements.

A boy's voice called out. "An angel, fallen from the sky. Grab hold," the boy said, and Serena's hand slapped against a rough branch. She grabbed it one-handed, and he dragged her through the water. Reaching the edge, she stepped out, and her knees buckled. The boy turned her over on the muddy bank, concern in his face.

"Help me," she whispered.

"I will," said the boy, and Serena focused on deep brown eyes that smiled down at her. "You are an àngelas, an angel fallen from the sky," he said. His lips formed words in another language, but she understood him. The rock warmed in her hand.

He had shiny dark hair, tanned skin, a firm smile, and a kind heart. She had never seen him before. "You're William Faw," she said.

His eyes widened, somehow understanding her. "You know me?" he asked.

Serena tried to focus again as a loud chirping sound hovered somewhere nearby. "You're to be my brother," she said, and then the pinpricks in her eyes turned everything black.

CHAPTER ONE
THE VOID

13 Years Later - 22 March 1746
Leeds, England

"'Tis time, Serena," William said and nodded toward the bonfires set up for the traveling faire. The flames splashed light and shadows against the gathering crowd. He grinned at her. "The chubs always spend more coin when you dance."

Serena spun, presenting her back to her brother, her dress still undone. "Hook the top." She pulled her loose hair to the side.

"I'm a man now," he said. "I shouldn't be dressing you, even if we are outside. Petra or Duy should help you."

William's fingers touched her skin, and Serena's inhale caught. Cold dread washed down into her stomach as if someone poured a bucket of ice water down her throat. Only her dragonfly birthmark warmed, and she shivered at the contrast. William bled; a slick blackness oozed from his aura. She turned around and stared at him.

"What is it?" he asked, his eyes narrowing. He knew her sensitivity but was still brave enough to touch her, unlike the others in their tribe.

"Let me see your hand, Shoshòy," she said, using his Romany name.

William hesitated but then thrust it forward. Serena didn't have to look at it. She only had to hold it. She clasped it in her naked palm and shivered as the aura bled further into her.

Suspicion, despair, death.

"Àngelas?" he asked.

Serena stared into William's eyes. "Stay away from the fools tonight. It doesn't feel right."

William studied her, but then the playful twinkle flashed through his eyes again. He shrugged. "I'll help tend the fires." He smiled with charm and leaped down from the small porch at the back of their wagon to land with a thump. "Hurry before King Will comes to fetch you himself."

Serena tried to shake the itchy dread that spider-walked just under her skin as she watched her brother trot away. A chirping melody above made her turn, setting the tiny bells around her waist jingling. She smiled at the blue bird, her constant companion. "Sorry, Chiriklò, I need to go," she said, checking the knot on the bright red scarf around her waist. The blue-colored bird sat silhouetted on the branch above her. "I'm to dance tonight."

Serena descended the steps from her family's painted wagon into the shadows under the trees where their caravan camped. She inhaled the early spring air, the smell of unfurled leaves and damp ground calming her, as the bird's thoughts drifted to her. She couldn't read the thoughts of animals, except for those of the blue sparrow that had been with her since arriving to live with the Romany tribe. But Chiriklò's thoughts were pictures instead of words.

Small crowd of men around the central fire. Money coming from pockets. King Will, gathering it. Bottles of spirits being passed around.

She hurried forward, stepping over the large roots snaking along the ground. The growing scents, sounds, and thoughts from the faire pulsed against Serena like the wind before a storm, begging for her attention, but Serena easily thrust them from her. She yanked on her soft leather gloves and wiggled her fingers down into each finger sleeve.

The first knowledge of her great sensitivity had crashed upon her when she'd woken in the Faw camp as Mari, her new mother, or duy, bathed her. Serena discovered that every inch of her skin could read the minds of those she touched. And many thoughts came to her without physical contact. Mari continued to help Serena master her power. Without control, Serena would lose herself to the onslaught around her. *I send you with my gift of sight.* She remembered the words from her birth mother, but was her unnatural ability a gift or a curse?

Serena slowed, stepping between the wagons. She smiled greetings to some of the Roma women nearby as they bustled around to set up tinware and jewelry for sale.

Don't touch me.

What new havoc will she bring?

Shouldn't she be dancing?

She scries the future more than is natural.

Poor King Will.

Their minds tumbled behind polite nods and greetings. Serena shrugged inwardly and blocked their thoughts. Everyone in the tribe saw her as strange, even dangerous. She clutched her arms around herself and turned down another shadow-drenched path toward the glow of the fire.

She didn't belong with normal people. She didn't even look Romany. They were dark of skin with beautiful shiny black hair. Her hair was red. Where their skin tanned under the sun, her paleness burned red. And her eyes... Even without her powers and her strange birthmark, she would always be an outsider. The stone from her mother had helped her understand their language at first, aiding her in learning it incredibly fast. Serena touched the red stone, wrapped in a cord that hung around her neck. But her tribe still only saw her differences.

"Serena," Mari called from near the fire, even though she called out Àngelas in her mind. William had given Serena her Romany name, Àngelas, when he saw her fall like an angel from the sky. Her duy walked toward her through the shadows. Mari's concern penetrated Serena upon contact.

"I'm fine," Serena said. "Just sad for a moment."

Mari rubbed Serena's back and sent soothing thoughts to her. *Àngelas, gift from God, with an amazing power to be cherished, not despised.*

"I know." Serena looked at her mother who hadn't uttered a word out loud. "But still, not normal."

Mari sighed. "You'll find your path, Serena, and you'll follow it to happiness." Mari possessed a small measure of sight as well, but not near to Serena's ability.

Serena's eyes narrowed as she studied her duy. "You've seen this?"

Mari's chin bobbed just enough to be a nod. "'Tis in shadows, of course. There are happy paths and sorrowful paths," she warned.

"But there are happy paths?"

Mari laughed. "Of course, child."

From the distance, Mari and Serena heard a deep beat begin. Pipes, stringed fiddles, and the bass harp joined in to roll together, mixing into a seductive melody. Serena dropped her outer shawl and handed it to Mari.

Mari frowned as she stared up at a little patch of stars shining down through the oaks. "The stars have worried me these last few nights. Be careful, Àngelas. Something dark comes." Serena wanted to tell her about the taint on William's aura, but she'd already missed the first cue. "Later, Duy, we'll talk of the stars." Serena broke away to run in her little leather slippers to the fire.

As Chiriklò had seen, a crowd, mostly of men, gathered around the snapping bonfire that stretched up brightly in dancing shades of crimson light. Members of the tribe, including King Will, held the crowd back from the fire so that Serena could perform around its border. At the edge of the light Serena halted, closed her eyes, and filled her chest with flame-warmed air.

The fire crackled and huffed. Serena drew from the power within the flames. The noise of the people and the press of their thoughts dimmed as she funneled the magic of the fire through her body. She watched the flames flicker through her eyelids.

The thoughts of the crowd became a wall of noise that she held in its place away from her. She balanced it and diminished it until the noise was just part of the wind.

The notes of the flute slowed, and Serena opened her eyes to stare at the flames. They pulsed with the night breeze, powerful and snapping. Like a partner, the flames beckoned her to dance with them. Serena's arms and torso moved in the same fashion. Her head rolled back along her shoulders, her arms extended, offering herself to the heat.

Serena danced, shifting her body with the waves of heat, sometimes facing the blaze, sometimes facing the night chill where the people stood. She didn't see any of them, only the flame. It helped her keep her wall of protection around herself, keeping away the chaos of thoughts.

Serena transitioned with the increasing tempo. Her body answered the music by mimicking its rhythm. Her hair whipped around her shoulders as she turned, her arms languid and graceful. The core of her body warmed with the movement and the thrill of the dance. She held a circle of silence around her where she could breathe, alone within the quiet and peace.

"Bloody drunk fool," Keenan Maclean murmured as he stood vigilant at the fringe of the crowd. His large frame usually relegated him to the back of an audience since at four inches over six feet, he could see above everyone.

He watched his companion, Gerard Grant, who was soaked with royal whisky. The buffoon rammed and tripped his way toward the front row near the fire. As long as Keenan kept his eye on Gerard, he was technically guarding him. He certainly didn't appreciate any type of conversation with the man. If Gerard wasn't so bloody crucial to the Jacobite cause, Keenan would have abandoned him to the Romany faire much earlier. But Gerard Grant secretly supported Prince Charles Edward Stuart, the Young Pretender, making him a covert Jacobite. And he nurtured a warm friendship with England's King George II. Gerard was worth his weight in colonial gold to the Jacobite cause.

Keenan, a loyal Scot down to the marrow of his bones, despised English rule as much as any other Highlander. Having met the untried Prince Charles Stuart, Keenan couldn't support the radical Jacobite cause, either. But his opinion didn't matter since the chief of the Macleans *did* support the Stuart. Sworn to perform his duty to his family, Keenan needed to make certain Gerard made it home tonight and that the contents of his pocket remained intact.

Keenan leaned against the trunk of a wide oak. One last onerous task to perform before heading back at dawn to his beloved Highlands. One more step closer to fulfilling his duty to the prophecy that ruled his existence.

The slow music increased in tempo before the hushed crowd as a performance began. Another man, smelling of turnips and ale, stumbled into him. "Daingead," Keenan cursed beneath his breath, his eyes searching the crowd near Gerard. He should throw the man over his shoulder and carry him out of there before both their pockets were picked clean.

The audience remained motionless, entranced. Even bawdy Gerard studied the performer in stunned silence. Perhaps the dancer had talent. Keenan looked over a sea of heads towards the fire.

A woman moved around the leaping flames. Her hair reflected the red and gold of the fire with such intensity that it seemed to move as a twin flame. She wove her slender arms around her body; white gloves were the only cloth to hide the perfect skin of her limbs. The loose folds of her skirt swirled around her naked calves above delicate leather slippers. Silk swathed her middle, the fabric so thin and supple that it showed her softly rounded stomach as it moved like a wave. The bells sitting low on her waist shook in time with the music as she snapped her hips. Every hill and valley on her body called to Keenan.

Her seductive, half-closed eyes scanned the crowd but didn't connect, as if she saw no one. Lips parted, she whirled with the increased tempo, breasts rising and falling faster with her breath.

Keenan's gaze ran the contours of her face. "Mo bhean," Keenan said in Gaelic. *My woman*. The simple words filled his mind, thrumming through him with the sound of blood rushing in his ears. "Mine," he whispered roughly.

Keenan's thumb rubbed against his other fingers as if feeling her softness. Her skin would feel like the unblemished hide of a doe, tender, soft. "Mo bhean," he said again and took a step forward as if under a spell. Keenan's eyes followed the glimpses of her long bare calves, the taut muscles flashing by as she whipped the layers of skirt back and forth.

Hands fisting against his sides, he shook his head, pushing out the ridiculous urge to hoist her up into his arms and carry her away like a barbarian. As if he were entitled to take her. As if she truly were his partner, his lover, this woman he'd never seen before.

She raised her strong, slender arms up high and rolled her head back, causing fire-colored hair to wash all the way down below her hips. It would run silky in his rough hands and smell of fresh night air and womanly warmth. Keenan felt his loins tighten. Bloody English trews gave him no room to grow.

The woman danced toward the edge where Gerard stood. The bastard leered at her and licked his salivating lips, his hands rising to grab her.

"Move," Keenan demanded, his voice low and threatening as he elbowed through the dense cluster of people.

The dancer whirled away from Gerard's clenching fingers. But it was close, too close.

"Move aside," Keenan repeated.

Angry glares met his chest before climbing up to his fierce expression. The crowd parted. Keenan acknowledged none of them but kept his attention on the dancer as he came alongside Gerard.

"Mmm, she's a luscious tart," Gerard said, his tone garbled. He reached out once more.

It took all of Keenan's strength not to yank Gerard backwards by his collar. Instead, he stepped in front of him, blocking him with his body, his back to the fool.

"Get your arse out of my way, you bloody buffoon," Gerard called from behind him.

Keenan stood right along the perimeter as the dancer moved from side to side a few paces away on the other side of the bonfire. She swung her heavy tresses again, and Keenan could almost feel the fire-warmed silk.

Keenan barely noticed Gerard's attempts to shove him aside. His entire conscious state focused entirely on the sensuous woman who pulsed like a flame, body bending as if an invisible lover swayed her in his arms.

He scratched his hand roughly through his hair. "Insanity," he grumbled, closing his eyes for a long second before opening them again. He could have nothing to do with her. She belonged to the Romany tribe, a wandering people who did not step outside their families. Although... *She looks nothing like a Romany lass.*

As long as the music played, Serena would continue to dance as the flame. She never tired as the serenity of the blazing fire and movement kept the unending thoughts of others away. She heard them only as a whisper, a web of thoughts held out at the edge. She leaned against the web evenly to keep the thoughts from seeping inward, into her circle, and it became as strong as a wall.

As she rounded the fire again, a hole in the wall appeared. *Odd.* Curious, she danced toward it and reached out with her mind. Serena leaned into the hole, her curiosity making her investigate too far. Her mind teetered, throwing her concentration off. Her protective wall shattered. "No!" she whispered frantically, arms flailing as if pushing back from the barrage of thoughts.

Images bludgeoned her. Naked flesh, her naked flesh, pressed from behind, shoved into beds. Her mouth on the men, her lips skimming over sweaty skin.

"No," she gasped as if for air. Quickly she flung hard at the shards of carnal images. She took a wrong step and fell into the void. It caught her.

Serena opened her eyes to stare up at the silent mountain holding her. The man was tall and broad through the shoulders. The light of the fire glowed against his skin, accenting a slash across his left cheek from his ear to his jaw. The scar accentuated the square set of his serious face. His eyes stared back into hers, and they narrowed as if trying to read her.

Read me? Serena gasped as she realized that she couldn't read him. At all. It was as if he were empty, a silence in the noise of thoughts flowing around her.

His arms steadied her as he gazed into her eyes. "Lass?"

Serena was mesmerized. Never had she met someone who was blank to her. Someone with whom she could not read their thoughts, their emotions.

"Are ye hurt?" he asked, his sensual mouth forming the deeply accented words.

Serena glanced at his hands wrapped around her bare upper arms. Nothing, she read nothing from him. Serena snatched off her glove. *His scar.* Scars, chiseled into skin during battle, were extremely powerful. Even her defensive walls couldn't block the gruesome details.

Serena held her breath as she traced her finger down the length of the slightly puckered skin from his ear hidden in waves of dark hair to the rough squareness of his chin. The muscles in his jaw jumped under her touch, but he didn't pull away.

No jolt of battle scenes shot down through her arm and up behind her eyes. No visions of bloodstained iron, muddy grime, and anguished cries of war victims. Just quiet. "I know nothing about you," she whispered. "Are you a... demon?"

CHAPTER TWO

BLOOD ON THE BRIDGE

"A demon?" The man's face relaxed. "Some have called me worse."

Was he serious? Serena couldn't tell. She'd never needed to learn the subtle ways a body moves when it speaks lies or jests, the inflection in a person's tone. She'd always been able to decipher the truth even before a lie was uttered. Now she was lost.

"What are ye called?" he asked, releasing her. The gently rolling brogue reminded her of the mountain people up north on the edge of the sea.

"Serena." What would her name sound like on his tongue?

"Move over, you oaf," said a man from behind who nearly fell trying to push by the giant. "'Tis my turn to meet the lovey," he slurred and leered at Serena.

"Gerard, 'tis time to take ye home, man," said the northerner. She could smell a hint of leather polish coming from him just under the woodsmoke, and she resisted the urge to lean into him.

His drunk companion grabbed Serena's bare hand, and his tongue snaked out to lick a trail of spittle across the underside of her wrist.

Waves of darkness rolled over her: *lust, fear, pain, death.* The ground wobbled as her vision blurred, and she fell toward the void as if it were a safety net.

The northerner caught her against him. "Dammit, Gerard, let her go." He clasped the man's arm, twisting it to yank him away.

"Listen, lovey," Gerard said, dropping her hand to scowl at the tall man before looking back at her with rheumy, bloodshot eyes. "I have more money than this Scottish boor could even dream of having. And I know you Rom ladies like a little coin."

"I don't feel well," she whispered as pinpricks of light sparkled in her vision. The northerner wrapped an arm around her, pulling her to his solid chest to help her walk away. Serena rested in the strange silence that radiated from him. Even without knowing him, she felt safe. *Fool.* Only William and Duy were safe.

"Damn Scot!" Gerard cursed after them. "If you weren't so bloody tall, I'd knock you flat."

The man walked with her away from the fire toward the dark wagons. His gait was steady and confident, as if he didn't worry about tripping on the roots or being waylaid by anyone. He lifted under her enough to keep her moving.

"Let her go, English," Serena heard William call, and she opened her eyes.

"I'm not English, lad."

"Whatever the hell you are, leave her alone," William demanded, and she could feel the angry thoughts from him as he tugged her away from the man. She shivered at the slick inkiness that still surrounded her brother. She glanced over her shoulder back at Gerard as he drank from a tankard. It had something to do with that man.

"He helped me, William." She straightened, studying the northerner who was so blank to her.

"Who are you?" she asked breathlessly. He hadn't answered her question about being a demon.

He stared a moment before speaking, as if weighing whether he should reveal his name. "Keenan Maclean."

"Keenan Maclean," Serena repeated, slowly tasting it and trying to draw any information she could from his name. Pain in her chest reminded her to breathe. "Do you know my thoughts?" she whispered. "What I'm thinking?"

The man's eyes narrowed, his forehead furrowing. This was a look of confusion. Wasn't it? He shook his head. "Nay. Do ye know my thoughts?" he asked and raised an eyebrow. Was that surprise? Maybe jesting?

"No." She frowned.

"And this is troubling?" he asked. His hard eyes searched her face, but a faint grin played on his lips. That was teasing, wasn't it?

William's chest puffed outward. "Thank you, Maclean, for helping my sister. I'll take care of her from here."

Keenan Maclean ran his eyes over William. "She's yer sister?" he asked and looked pointedly between their obvious physical differences. William had darkly tanned skin with nearly black hair where Serena was pale with reddish gold hair.

"Not by blood," Serena said and felt the defensiveness in William. "But by every other way a man could be my brother."

Mari walked around the edge of the wagon. She stopped in front of the stranger and threaded her hand through the crook of her daughter's arm.

To an onlooker it may have looked as if Serena held Mari up, but Serena felt the strength radiating alongside her, allowing her to lean gently into the warmth of her mother.

Mari smiled pleasantly, but Serena felt her senses flow outward toward him, scrutinizing him.

Legs braced apart, he crossed his arms. He wore an outer jacket of deep blue, which came down to his knees. His deeply muscled calves bulged sleekly in the fashionable court hose. The hilt of a short sword flashed inside his jacket against his ribs. He dressed the part of an English courtier, but his hair was his own, natural and dark, not powdered. Although handsome in the courtly attire, he looked too rugged for such finery. His physique and the scar marked him as a warrior.

"Thank you for helping my daughter," Mari said and paused. "Sir?" She reached out to touch his arm, waiting for him to fill in his name.

"No 'sir,' just Keenan Maclean." The warrior tipped his head in response but didn't smile. The firelight flickered shadows across his features, giving him a fierce, dangerous look.

Mari drew her hand back to her skirts. "You dress like the English, but you are not," she said in broken Gaelic. "Tha thu nad Ghàidheal."

"Mistress," Keenan said in English, "'tis dangerous to speak the ancient tongue here. Ye best be careful."

Mari switched to English. "We traveled north, to Scotland, several years ago, near the ocean to the west."

"My home is Kilchurn, on the western coast of Scotland," the man said.

Mari smiled. "Yes, yes, Kilchurn Castle on Loch Awe. I remember your chief well, the proud Angus Maclean. He was quite generous to us and allowed us to entertain. I would have you send him the kind wishes of King Will and the Faw Tribe."

"He is dead," the man said swiftly, his eyes taking in all three of them. Silence followed for several beats.

Mari bowed her head. "I'm sorry for the loss of such a great man." She looked up. "Then I send along the kind wishes to the new chief of the Macleans, who is …?"

"You," Serena said in a near whisper.

The Maclean turned toward the fire and scanned the small crowd. His face caught the glow of orange light on half of his strong features. He half spoke to her and half to the fire. "Nay, Lachlan Maclean is laird there."

Mari's grip on her arm tightened. Surprise and concern radiated from her. Serena never guessed wrong.

Boisterous laughter came from one of the tables set up on the other side of the fire. Keenan reached into his pocket and produced a small bag of coins which he tossed to William.

"For yer trouble," he said and then looked at Serena, "and for yer performance." His gaze met hers one last time and then slid to Mari. "Pardon," he said and bowed, "but I must find my companion."

"Yes," Serena said before she thought better of it. "Find him, he's in need of you." She stood straighter. "I felt death when he touched me."

Mari tugged her, and Serena grimaced, her nose crinkling. *Foolish.* When would she learn not to blurt out what she saw?

Keenan's eyes pivoted toward her. Sharp angles of firelight and moonlight cut across his face, changing his confusion to suspicion. But then without a word he jogged toward the laughter on the other edge of the fire.

One of the older boys stepped around a nearby wagon where men threw dice. "William," Ephram called.

"I have work to do," William said, handing the sack of coins to Mari. "Go inside, Àngelas," he said in his best imitation of King Will and turned to leave.

"William." Serena rested her bare hand on his arm. Her stomach clenched.

"Àngelas?"

She shook her head. "Something feels terribly wrong, dark. I'm afraid for you."

He would take her warning seriously since he knew her powers. Unfortunately, he also knew how she often caused more problems by trying to stop fate.

William's brows gathered, but then he smiled softly at her. "I'll be extra careful tonight. You've already earned enough," he said, nodding to the bag of coins.

With his promise, Serena hoped the sickening in her belly would mellow, but it didn't. He walked toward his friend, a swagger in his step.

Mari waited until they ducked through the door into the tented room of their covered wagon before the questions began to pop quickly into Serena's head. Mari handed her a tin cup of watered-down wine and sat on a tufted chair across from her.

"Keenan Maclean, from Kilchurn," Mari said.

Serena exhaled. "I know, but only because it came from his lips." She took two gulps of the sweet drink and ran fingers over her forehead, rubbing at the ache she felt coming. Pulling the strand of painted glass jewels off over her head, she looked across at the wise eyes that searched her. "I couldn't read his thoughts at all."

"How unusual." Mari stared back and then sipped some of the wine. "But you could?"

Mari tilted her head. "Just some. My gift is not like yours, Àngelas."

"Hmmph, my gift abandoned me."

"Only with him?"

Serena nodded and glanced at the closed door. "Is he dark? Some sort of wizard or demon able to block his thoughts from me?" Demons were very real. She'd heard them pounding on her house in the stone circle in another time. It felt like a nightmare, something not real. But prickles of fear still scattered up her neck to her scalp. Could a demon have found her after all these years?

Mari considered it but then shook her head. "Perhaps some darkness, but not a demon. He...seemed..." She hesitated," sad, I think. I heard the low skirl of their ancient pipes when I touched him."

Serena took a deep breath, her shoulders relaxing. "Why couldn't I hear them?"

Serena felt Mari's concern, but the woman kept her voice light. "I will meditate on it."

Serena sat back against the bedroll and sipped her wine for long minutes while Mari closed her eyes.

The candle flame in the hanging glass lantern flickered, a miniature version of the bonfire Serena had danced around. Usually the flame helped calm her, but not tonight. An itch in her mind tickled at the base of her ears. She scratched at them and pulled the earrings from her lobes. Goosebumps rose on her bare arms, and she rubbed them.

Mari's worry broke through her quiet reflection and into Serena's mind. The middle-aged woman leaned forward to rest hands on her shoulders. "You're uneasy."

"Pain comes," Serena said. "Betrayal, fear."

"You feel this darkness too?"

Serena nodded. "I think it involves the Highlander's companion. The Englishman named Gerard."

Mari pursed her lips for a moment. "Reach out to it, child. Gently so as not to open the gates you hold back. A crack to see the darkness."

"You want me to look?" Serena asked, her eyes widening. How many times had Mari told her to shut her mind or ignore the warnings, to allow fate's song to play out? And now she asked her to seek her magic.

Mari's brow furrowed, and she clenched her calloused hands. "The stars speak to me of treachery." She paused. "This evil stalks us, our family."

"William," Serena whispered. Standing, she grabbed her wool cloak and ducked out the small door. The rhythm of the faire was familiar, normal, as were the muted sounds of the forest around their caravan. She didn't see Keenan Maclean or Gerard. Her eyes moved around the fire. No William either.

Serena washed a cleansing breath through her chest and closed her eyes. The walls she held around herself were hardly a burden to her now after years of training to control what she allowed herself to see. Mari had guided her, with common sense, a duy's love, and the ancient knowledge passed down through her maternal line.

Serena touched the red stone that she wore on a woven silk rope around her neck. It warmed, and she envisioned a stone wall that reached up to the tallest trees and encircled her. The stone sparkled with crystals. Using her internal compass, Serena felt the foreboding like thunder vibrating in the distance.

She imagined a thread flowing from her birthmark near her navel to squeeze through a fissure in the wall. Shooting into the cooling night, her thread darted into shadows, between trees, past the crackling fires of the tribe, past the merriment in the faire's center. Her mind flew, a single thread intent on only one destination: the darkness that itched.

Through zigs and zags, she came upon the bridge that crossed the creek not far from the faire. *Where are you, William?* The trees stood silent in the moon-washed darkness, watching the predator lurking. Serena saw Gerard stumbling, catching himself on the wooden rail. Would he fall in? Was that the darkness? An accidental drowning?

Serena's thread of consciousness hovered over Gerard as the man gurgled and wretched over the side of the brook. Wiping his frothy mouth, he turned to see another man lunge from the shadows. Serena tried to yell a warning, but Gerard's mind was too befuddled to be receptive even if he were sensitive to her power.

The man was larger than Gerard, poorly dressed, a local brute. In one quick movement, he stabbed Gerard through the abdomen. Serena's silent scream was useless. Blood spread like red wine through white linen between his splayed fingers. Gerard sank to his knees, a gurgling sound coming from his opened lips. The rough man looked back over his shoulder and nodded. Serena sent her quivering thread to the other end of the bridge.

A man and woman stood in the shadows, their clothes well cut, costly. "Run! Go back!" she mentally yelled to them. Should she break the thread and run for help? The images were so clear that Serena knew that what she observed was happening now. There was no time to run to them.

Serena watched as the couple came forward. Instead of recoiling from the murderer, the well-dressed man handed the killer a bag and motioned for him to drop the knife near the body. The thug dropped the weapon and hurried off.

Serena watched as the gentleman pulled a rolled paper from Gerard's inner jacket. The petite blond woman tucked it into a small satchel. Anxiety clung to her like a rash from stinging nettles, but purpose held her resolve. The man felt relief and triumph, breathing easier knowing he'd accomplished something great by stealing Gerard's breath and whatever was on the scroll.

To Serena's further horror, William burst from the trees. The man pulled a gun from his tailored jacket.

"No," Serena screamed at William. "No!"

The shot tore through William and shattered Serena's concentration. The scene dissolved, and she fell backwards into the arms of Mari. Chiriklò chirped wildly, fluttering nearby.

"Duy, they've shot Shoshòy," Serena cried and wiped hot tears swelling from her eyes. "Find King Will, I'm going to help him. He's on the bridge." She jumped down from the wagon, nearly twisting her foot in the slippery mud. "Chiriklò, fly to William." The bird shot through the darkness, and Serena ran after him.

CHAPTER THREE
TWISTING DESPERATION

Keenan Maclean knelt over Gerard, loosened the man's cravat, and pressed against his neck. "Bloody hell." He checked Gerard's pockets. *Empty.* "Bloody, foking hell," he cursed and straightened. He'd failed to keep the bastard alive, the only Jacobite supporter that had King George's ear. And the damn letter was missing. How could he have failed so tremendously? He had allowed the dancing woman to distract him from his duty.

A bird screeched near the fallen Roma man at the other end of the bridge. In the moonlight, Keenan watched the tiny bird hop from one end of the man to the other, tilting its head in the disjointed manner birds do.

Padded feet slapped across the boards of the bridge. "Now what?" he grumbled. And there she was, the woman from the faire. She ran to the fallen man and threw herself over him as if she could shield him from the iron shot. But she was too late.

Keenan's frown deepened. Was the man her lover? As she turned the man's face upward, Keenan saw that it was the young man who'd called her his sister. What did he have to do with Gerard's death?

Keenan walked over and knelt next to her. "Serena Faw?"

She wiped her nose against the back of her glove. Tears stained her cheeks. She didn't say anything, barely tearing her gaze from her brother. They worked together to open the man's jacket. Blood seeped from a hole in his shoulder.

"Please help him," she whispered.

The jolt that shot through Keenan was nearly a physical pain, her anguish so raw, her helplessness so devastatingly sincere. All the sorrow in the wretched world seemed reflected in her breathless words. He had felt sorrow before, seen the anguish in the world. But her simple plea tore into him like the sharp teeth of a hellhound.

His eyes stared back into hers, promising more than words could pronounce. "We need to stop the bleeding."

"Yes," she whispered, her face snapping back to where crimson continued to seep from the boy's shoulder. Her hands fluttered above as if she didn't know what to do.

Several Romany men ran up behind them, speaking low in their language. Keenan finished pulling William's jacket carefully from his shoulders. Serena ripped the scarf that was tied to her waist, balled it up and pushed it gently against the hole. From the small amount of blood, Keenan knew that the shot was lodged in the muscle, damming the flow. It must be removed eventually, but right now loss of blood was the first concern.

Serena tied another sash tightly around the wound. Had she saved many from pistol shots? Her gloved hands shook and slipped as she tied the knots. Bright red covered them, and she tried to wipe them on the boards near her.

She swayed slightly on her heels, and Keenan nudged her hands aside. "Let me."

She sat back and pulled off her ruined gloves, tucking them in her waistband. When Keenan finished, he grasped her elbow beneath her cloak to help her stand. She flinched at his touch but didn't pull away.

"Yer brother?" Keenan asked.

She nodded, the light breeze tugging at the curls around her face.

Keenan checked William's pockets, careful not to move him. A few coins tinkled together but nothing more. Keenan looked around and spotted Gerard's coin purse next to William along with a bloodied knife. But the papers were nowhere. What would a Romany lad want with the letter anyway? His people remained wisely apart from politics.

The gun lying near the body must have shot William, but where had Gerard found the gun? It wasn't his. When Gerard had started drinking heavily, Keenan took his firearm from him so he wouldn't shoot anyone or himself. Keenan probably should have let the idiot keep it, another failure on his part.

A pounding crept up the back of his head as he looked between the two men. What an ass he'd been to let his guard down. Without Gerard and his letter, his brother's cause would require months to rebuild. His hard stomach clenched even tighter with shame and disgust at himself until he could taste the bitterness of bile rising up his throat.

"William didn't take his money and didn't kill him," Serena said firmly as she wiped another scarf along her nose.

Keenan threw the purse of coins at her feet as he stood. The loud thump caused a stir amongst the Roma gathered.

Serena spoke to the people around her. "William didn't take the coins. 'Twas the others," she insisted as she waved her hands toward the other end of the bridge, her gaze landing again on Keenan. Frantic appeal bled from her eyes. "The man in the tailored jacket must have thrown the coin purse next to William after he shot him, and the knife, because William saw him and his woman paying off Gerard's murderer, some local ruffian." The words flew desperately out of her. Several from Serena's tribe backed away, disappearing into the shadows.

"What man and woman? What ruffian?" Keenan grabbed her arms.

"Out of the way, you filthy vagabond," a rotund man huffed across the bridge with two others behind him. They held pistols and were sloppily dressed as local authority. The remaining people backed up to allow them into the scene.

The marshal glanced at the bodies. "What crime goes on here?"

"Gerard Grant has been stabbed, killed," Keenan said.

"And my brother has been shot. He's bleeding." Serena pulled away from Keenan to squat back down at William's head. She smoothed his black hair from his face, the love apparent in her touch.

The marshal pointed to the weapons each man had. "Looks like the Rom picked his purse, and they fought. The gentleman was gutted but got off a shot before he died. Thieving Rom." The marshal spat on the ground near William's foot.

"That's not what happened," Serena shouted.

"And how would you know, little miss? Or were you in on it?" The marshal leered at her. "I saw you dance at the gypsy faire. You might not look like them, but you travel with them."

Eyes wide, her hands trembled. She didn't look like someone who would aid her brother in thievery, but times were hard for the poor. Maybe they only meant to take the money, and the boy ended up defending himself. But again, Gerard had nothing to defend himself with. The details didn't make sense. He needed to question Serena about what she saw. But how could she have seen anything if she'd just come upon the scene? Had she been hiding behind the trees?

The marshal motioned to the two soldiers. "Bring the Rom and his woman."

"No." Serena bent down to cradle William's head.

"She's not involved," Keenan said above her. Whether she was or not, he didn't want her dragged off by these leering men.

"And what would you be knowing about this, Scot?" the marshal said with transparent contempt.

Keenan stared at the shoddy man's black eyes. "I know that Gerard Grant is a close friend of the king and was my associate."

The marshal stared hard at him for a long moment and then grunted, turning to his two henchmen. "We'll take the Rom boy to Newgate with the other prisoners next week. For now, lock him up at Leeds Gaol. Leave the woman."

"But he's still bleeding," Serena said as the two gruff men walked toward her.

"He'll probably hang or die of gaol fever anyway," the marshal retorted. "Best let him die tonight."

A shudder ran through the lass. She glared at the men, her lips parting, but then an older Roma man walked across the bridge toward them with a majesty that commanded the others to part. He placed his hand on Serena's shoulder and whispered something to her. She shook her head, but he nodded stiffly. Anguish dampened her face. It was as if her spirit crumpled before him. She turned while the elderly man spoke with authority in Romany to the remaining people. His one arm went out in a gathering gesture.

Two men from the Roma group moved past the guards and picked William up gently. They rested him across the marshal's horse. Keenan watched Serena flinch with each movement of her brother, even though her back remained turned against the scene. It was as if she felt his pain.

Keenan had heard of "The Traveling People" and had even seen some at Kilchurn. Their ways were so different from the ways of the Scottish people that their differences were like magic.

"What should we do with the dead one?" the marshal asked Keenan.

"I'll take care of the body," Keenan answered briskly and looked over at the sprawled figure. Gerard had no loyal family, and he was too dangerous to have many friends. Keenan had found him tolerable as long as he didn't have to spend too much time with him. King George, on the other hand, found him witty and clever. They had become friends, elevating Gerard to worth. But now he was dead, and the letter signed by George describing how he planned to take over Scotland was missing. Keenan's brother, Lachlan, would scream to the rafters in fury.

Keenan swallowed down the tang of regret and wrapped Gerard's body in a fringed blanket he bought hastily from one of the Romany onlookers. His and Gerard's horses were tethered closer to the faire. He watched Serena walk slowly after the marshal's horse, following them into the dark night.

"She's bloody daft," he murmured. She could be seized and raped, or worse.

From the trees came the older woman, Serena's mother. She looked directly at him as she led his and Gerard's horses from the shadows.

"She will need you." The old woman's eyes glistened. "We can do naught for my boy tonight. But you can help them both. Please..." She let the word hang there for a moment and handed the reins to him.

She turned and limped slowly away as if hopelessness tugged at her feet. The elderly man who had spoken with authority wrapped his arm around her, and they walked back under the trees. The others melted into the forest. Keenan noticed Gerard's bag of coins where he had thrown it at Serena's feet. Not one of them had touched it.

Keenan rummaged through Gerard's pockets once more, turning him over this way and that. No letter.

A fierce chirping caught his attention. The little blue sparrow alighted to the ground before him. It took several hops in the direction Serena had walked and then cocked its head back. Then it fluttered up and around him.

"Odd wee thing." He dodged the winged beast. "Are ye ordering me after her?" He had questions to ask, and he wanted to feel her touch him again. He wanted to smell the freshness in her hair. Keenan grunted at the absurdity of his thoughts. "A dead patriot, a missing letter, a ruined mission, and I'm thinking about a lass."

The sparrow chirped loudly as it circled his head. "And I'm taking orders from a bloody bird." He hefted Gerard's body over his shoulder and laid Gerard down into a hidden gully beside the bridge. "Ye won't get any worse than ye are now."

Keenan mounted his chestnut charger and wheeled around. "I'll be back for ye." He left Gerard's horse tied nearby. He'd return to take the body to one of Gerard's associates to bury.

With a slight pressure of his heel, his horse shot off into the darkness. It didn't take long to spot Serena as she jogged along the edge of the road. As his horse thundered closer, she veered into the shadows. At least she knew enough to hide." He slowed his horse. "I'll take ye to Leeds," he called.

After a silent moment, the sound of pebbles sliding heralded her climb up the small bank out from behind the trees. In the moonlight, her tear-washed eyes glinted like glass as she stared at him. Wildly twisting hair draped around her shoulders, nearly to her hips.

"I'll help ye," he said.

She hesitated but then placed her hand in his. He hoisted her up to sit before him and pressed his heels into the side of the horse. She smelled of sweet spices like cinnamon and autumn apples with a hint of wood smoke. Keenan wet his suddenly dry lips, wondering if she'd taste just as good. Her warmth penetrated his chest, coiling down into his body. So soft, so lush, her body moved against him with the rhythm of the horse. He grumbled low and shifted in his saddle as they galloped along the moon-soaked road.

Like most small-town jailhouses, Leeds Gaol looked to be only one level. Its crumbling façade of brick squatted heavily on the small plot of grass, its rear pushed up against the woods. The muted glow of torchlight radiated from the front entrance. All the other windows were dark, but Serena could feel the pain and hopelessness bleeding from the structure, emanating from the occupants.

She flinched as the men dropped William off the horse, feeling the pain his body registered even though his mind was empty with unconsciousness. She breathed deeply and erected her mental wall. She must keep her wits to help him. The heat emanating from the Scottish warrior and the mystery of him was distracting her enough. *Focus.*

Serena slipped haltingly down the side of the horse. Like master, like horse. Huge. She ran over to William and brushed back his hair. He was too pale.

"Ho now. You decided to join the boy?" said the marshal thickly and pulled her up by her bare arm.

I could chain her inside one of the cells, up against the wall, her plump arse bare...

Serena gagged as the man's thoughts slid along her mind. In practiced defense she erected her most impenetrable barriers to muffle the repulsive images. The strain left her flushed and breathless.

"It would be wise for ye to take yer hands off the lass," the warrior said behind her. Even without her senses, Serena heard the thinly veiled threat behind the words.

The marshal snorted and dropped her arm. "No use, girl, your brother is staying the night." The marshal motioned to the men, and they dragged William inside along the stone hallway. Keys jingled as the marshal pulled his dirty hand from his pocket.

The foulness of his breath mixed with the odor of old sweat as he drew close to her. His voice lowered. "Now if you want your brother to have a comfortable stay, say with water and food, we may be able to strike a bargain, my girl." He grinned, showing dark teeth.

Serena fought the revulsion that threatened at the base of her throat. She didn't move away and heard the crunch of boots on pebbles behind them.

"Stay back there, Scot. Me and the lady is having a private discussion." The marshal reached out to grab her arm again. Taking a quick breath, Serena stumbled forward into the rank man.

CHAPTER FOUR
MOLTEN DISTRACTION

The strong hands of the Highlander pulled Serena back quickly, just like she'd hoped. But it had been enough time to find the jingle in the marshal's pocket. Quick hands were something William had taught her as a child. She'd never picked a pocket before, but she'd practiced often with her brother.

"There will be no private discussions with the lady." The Highlander's voice cut through the air with sharp authority.

The marshal shrugged. "Too bad for the boy."

The two men came back out. She needed a distraction, but what would keep the men outside the small jailhouse? Serena tried to breathe evenly to douse the tingling that had started in her arms. The edge of panic made her mind whirl frantically from one idea to the next. She walked haltingly back over to the Highlander's large horse.

Keenan followed. "I'll take ye back to the faire."

She needed his help, but could she trust him? A man she couldn't even read? All her life she'd caught glimpses of thoughts and feelings from people. She learned their secrets without trying, their deepest desires, their hushed sins. Darkness lurked in every person. How could she trust someone she couldn't read at all? Even his expression seemed blank. He moved closer to her, and his fresh smell cleansed her of the marshal's foul scent. Serena drank it in.

"I can't leave William," she said. "He'll die if I don't get him out of there." She searched his veiled face then sighed softly. "You don't believe me, but I know that William did *not* stab your friend. They made it look like he did."

"Ye saw these people?"

"Yes... no... well, in a way I saw them."

"Ye were there, part of the robbery."

"There was no robbery." She shook her head. Her foot stamped on the cooling dirt. "It was a last-minute farce to make it look like one."

"Ye were there then?"

Serena's eyes dropped to the ground. "'Tis hard to explain." She looked up. "I know certain things. I can see them from a distance, sometimes before they happen."

His eyes searched hers, but he didn't ask any questions. Without questions she couldn't defend herself, so she held silent, waiting for him to weigh her words.

William's pain echoed like a dull ache in her mind. She stared up at Keenan Maclean. Let him read the desperation eating her insides hollow. "Help me rescue him. Please."

"In return," he said, studying her, "ye will help me find those who killed Gerard?"

Serena hadn't expected that. She'd seen the man and woman along with the hired murderer. But was that enough to help her find them? She glanced back toward the gaol and then to Keenan. She had no choice. "Once my brother is safe, I will help you."

"A bargain then, 'tis set," he said plainly and glanced around.

The three men still stood outside the jailhouse. "You need to keep them out here," Serena whispered and produced the keys in the folds of her skirts so he could see them.

"Ye're a cutpurse."

"Not before today." She hid the keys in a deep pocket tied around her waist under her petticoat. "Keep them distracted, and I'll go in through the back." There must be a back door. "I'll carry William out and hide in the woods beyond to wait for you."

The Highlander stared, and Serena sighed in frustration. What was he thinking? "Will you come for us?"

"Aye. If ye can't bring him out, hide in the woods. I'll find ye."

Holy God. She hoped he wasn't lying. Could she trust him? She'd never had to trust anyone before, but she didn't have a choice. She must save her brother. William was the only man who looked on her with love and not suspicion.

Serena glanced over her shoulder, speaking softly. "You need to distract them before they go back in—"

She gasped as Keenan pulled her against his solid body. In one swift movement he wound his hands through her long hair and tugged gently to bring her face up to his. His lips descended on hers. At first, her body went limp with shock, but blood thrummed through her veins, heating, melting her along his length as his kiss consumed her. She leaned into him, trusting him to hold her up. The Highlander's hands cupped her face. He slanted her head so that they fit perfectly against one another, their kiss turning wild.

Serena barely noticed the whoops from the three jailors as she struggled to stay afloat under the onslaught of feelings sizzling through her body. Her heart thudded against the bone between her breasts as if beating upon the bars of a cell. The silence in the contact muffled the world around her, and she never wanted to let go.

He released her mouth and ran lips down the naked column of her neck. A tingling spread chill bumps, making her legs wobble. Like a strong drink, the sensation deadened the thoughts and feelings around her until she drowned in peaceful heat.

He branded a path with hot breath back to her face and trailed over to her ear. At the same time, his hands sloped down to her backside, squeezing it, molding it to the evidence that he was just as affected by the kiss as she.

"Now push me away, slap me, and run as if back to the faire." His breath sounded ragged, like her own, and it took several heartbeats for his instructions to register in her bloodless brain. The passionate kiss was the distraction.

William! Pinpricks of her brother's fear and pain shot ice through her, washing a chill through her veins.

Serena yanked her head away from him. "Get off me," she shrieked with real anger, anger for losing herself in the farce. She shoved against his chest with all the embarrassment she felt. The Highlander had befuddled her mind in mere seconds. He released enough to give her access to his face. Serena's slap shattered the hollowness of the night, causing the jailors to double over in raucous laughter. She also kicked the Highlander's shin. He grunted and released her roughly as he rubbed the abused leg.

"Bloody wench," he cursed loudly, and she ran down the road until it turned, her arms pumping.

Serena sucked in air like she was slaking a never-ending thirst. Her slippers pounded the dirt as she ducked off the road, sharp stones bruising the bottoms of her feet. She stopped behind a trio of thick trees and closed her eyes, leaning into them, smelling the moist earthy scent around her to calm down. Her face flushed hot, and she touched her lips. The embrace had been only a diversion, but she'd dived right in. Like some harlot.

Serena rubbed hands down her face and purposely moved her thoughts to William. There would be time for self-flagellation later. When her breathing slowed, she gathered and tied her skirts high so they would stay free of the undergrowth. In silence, she crept light-footed through the trees until she circled around to the back of the gaol. There she watched the silhouetted clouds glide like dark swans on a river, obscuring the glowing moon, and she dashed to the rear of the stone building.

Serena heard a single chirp overhead and saw Chiriklò, more with her mind and ears than with her eyes. The bird darted in and out between the bars of a small window in a door at the back of the prison. Serena grabbed the solid, cold bars, trying to ignore the putrid smell wafting out. She followed the path of the bird with her mind as it moved from cell to cell down the straight inner corridor. Some of the cells were empty. Others were not.

Serena slid her mind past each inhabitant, their resentment, their fear, their pain. One had stolen food for his children, and he worried about them now. One was locked inside for a murder. Bleak desperation clung to two others. At last, she found William. She focused her thin thread of power over him and through him. He was somewhat conscious. Fear and confusion mingled together, accented by sharp stabs of anger and pain.

"I am coming, Shoshòy," she whispered and forced the head of one key into the rough lock. She tried to turn it, but it wouldn't budge. She tried another and another, careful not to let them clink together.

Chiriklò flew back to the window and chirped once. Bawdy laughter from the front of the jailhouse danced back to her on the breeze, twisting her stomach. Finally, the fourth key turned, and the door swung inwards.

The stench of bodily waste and decay slapped against her face. She caught herself on the slime-molded wall, and then hurried ahead. Ignoring the brush of something against her foot, she slipped down the side of the corridor to William's cell. Her senses open, she felt the wavering hope as one of the inmates watched her go by. Would he betray her? Would any of them betray her? None but the one had seen her so far. She moved to the man's cell and tried one of the keys. The lock clicked open.

"Keep silent if you value your life," she whispered and pointed to the back door that still stood ajar. He nodded and crept toward it.

Chiriklò sat above another door. A picture of her opening the man's cell flitted to her. She should open as many cells as she could. With all the prisoners missing, not just William, the tribe wouldn't take the full brunt of suspicion.

The same key turned easily in two other cell doors, releasing the desperate men. She reached William's cell and opened it. Crouching down, she braced her shoulder under his uninjured arm. "Help me, William," she whispered. "Try." She pushed upward, lifting him from the moldy straw.

"Àngelas?" William murmured.

"We need to go." She took as much weight as she could to help him stand, but he was heavy. "Can you walk?"

"Yes." He grimaced. "My shoulder—"

"Shhh."

"Àngelas, I didn't—"

"I know."

She held half his weight as they shuffled along the sticky floor, unable to avoid the foul puddles in the dark. William's weight made her clumsy, and she fell against the stone wall several times. Serena was almost to the end of the corridor when she saw the man in the last cell looking at her through his bars. He was about the age of King Will.

"How about me, lass?" The thick voice held the rolling brogue of a Scotsman. This man had murdered someone, she was certain. She didn't have time to probe more, for reasons or justifications. But he would probably give her away if she left him. Serena pushed the key in and turned it, stumbling again under William's weight.

"William?" she whispered as he grew heavier, making her bend into the wall. Holy Lord, he'd lost consciousness again. How would she ever save him?

CHAPTER FIVE
MISPERCEPTIONS

"William, wake up," Serena whispered, desperation pinching her voice. She couldn't leave him there, and she couldn't drag him out herself.

Serena's burden lightened, and she jerked her head up to meet the dark eyes of the prisoner from the last cell, the one who had murdered someone. He transferred William's weight to his own back. "A kindness for a kindness," he said.

Outside in the moonlight, Serena turned to the prisoner. His fuzzy beard covered much of his face, giving him a rough look in his torn, ragged clothing. The filth layered onto him made him difficult to see, but his eyes reflected the brightness of the moon. There was kindness in them, and she felt the same in his heart.

He shifted William across his back. "Ye won't leave him?"

"He's my brother." She touched William's shoulder where her scarf still held the blood. "He's been shot."

The prisoner nodded and followed her into the woods. She didn't know where to go. It had to be far enough away from Leeds Gaol, but close enough for Keenan Maclean to find them. Her heart thumped wildly. This was a race with no finish line in sight. Her pulse thrummed so loudly that she could hear it. Its tempo propelled her forward on light feet through the night like a doe caught in the scent of the wolf, always looking over her shoulder.

The man bore his burden silently. Only the slight sound of William's toes skimming the leaves could be heard. The man was taller than she had at first estimated. She could smell the pungent odor of unwashed body wafting from him. How long had he been in the gaol? She felt resentment and sorrowful anger from him, but also a glimmer of hope and concern for a woman.

After walking for what felt like half a league, she motioned for the man to put William down next to a fallen log. "Stop to rest."

The prisoner put her brother down and sat on the other side of the log, breathing heavily. "Would ye have any food, lass, or water?"

"I'm sorry, no," she said. Remorse tightened her stomach. "I've known hunger before. 'Tis terrible, but I have nothing with me." The man nodded and leaned back against the log, the sounds of the night weaving in hushed rustles through the forest around them.

Panic hitched in Serena's stomach. *No food. No money. And I've broken the law. If we're caught, we'll both be hanged.*

Although Serena's eyes had adjusted to the darkness, she still didn't know where they were. Which really didn't matter since she had nowhere safe to go. She couldn't return to her tribe with William, not if it would bring the law.

Where was Keenan Maclean? She knew nothing about him except that he'd promised to help her if she would help him. But promises were easy to break and being unable to read his heart and mind made him dangerous. All she could do was trust his words, and words meant very little to Serena.

She shivered, wrapping her arms around herself, wishing she'd brought a warm wrap. The prisoner studied the night sky peeking through the tops of the tall oaks around them. He breathed deeply. "Ahhh, the smell of fresh air." He sighed as if savoring a precious meal. "I must smell worse than a carcass." He smiled in the moonlight. His teeth looked white behind the scruff of beard.

Serena grinned slightly. "You could use a bath, sir."

"Robert is the name, Robert Mackay. And I be thankin' ye, lass, for freeing me from that hellhole. Ye're an angel."

An àngelas? Her breath caught at her Roma name. Perhaps the man was as kind as he seemed despite having killed someone.

"Thank you for carrying my brother. I have naught to pay you with except freedom. You don't need to stay with us."

"Now, lass, what will ye do out here if I don't stay to help?"

The question twisted tightly through her. Serena ran fingers through her hair to rub at the dull ache gathering at the nape of her neck. "I have someone coming," she said and prayed it was true.

"I'll wait with ye."

So they sat in silence with the breeze rustling the leaves overhead. Serena's muscles remained tense as she listened for danger over the even sound of William's breathing. Time ticked by slowly, the heaviness of the dire situation seeming to drag it down as more than an hour passed.

Chiriklò's high-pitched chirping pulled her eyes to the right. Hoofbeats thudded against the road, a drumbeat to the bird's song. Serena reached out to Chiriklò with her mind. He flashed her an image of the Highlander who followed his birdsong through the woods.

Serena sucked in a quick breath as hope opened space within her to inhale.

"Help is coming." She kissed her brother's brow and let her head fall forward, her hair draping them both. A single tear dripped down onto William's pale skin, and Serena wiped it away with her thumb. Help was coming. Keenan Maclean had kept his promise.

⊰⬦⊱

Luck was a fickle matron, but today she smiled on them. Keenan Maclean stood in the crude doorframe of the warm two-room cottage looking out at the slanting rain. Lazy jailors hated to hunt in the rain, and tracks melted into mud. He'd been surprised to find a prisoner, Robert Mackay, helping Serena and her brother in the forest last night. But the prisoner had a sister who was generous, accessible, and knew how to remove a pistol shot. Aye, luck smiled on them.

Keenan's gaze shifted to Serena where she lay in exhausted slumber next to William, a brother who looked nothing like her. Who was this ivory-skinned, auburn-haired Romany woman? Serena Faw was definitely not ordinary. She hadn't complained as they rode and walked through the forest all night. She hadn't shied away from helping Robert's sister remove the shot. *Are you a demon?* That's what she'd asked him. Aye, Serena Faw was unusual.

The lass slept on her back now, one arm flopped over her stomach. He watched the swell of her breasts rise and fall, lips relaxed in slumber, partly open. The kiss at the gaol continued to intrude upon his thoughts. It had been a perfect distraction for the jailors and had given him a topic to discuss with the lusty English bastards while Serena sneaked around back. But the feel of her yielding lips, the press of her warm body against his, haunted him.

Turning, he peered out through the gray sheets of rain. If he were honest, he would admit that he wanted another taste of her, perhaps more than a taste. But what was the point? His life was not his own, nor his heart. The dark prophecy that shaped his every move and strategy owned his life. Keenan ran a hand along an eave, catching the cool rain, letting it run down his bare arm. At present he was too tired to be honest.

Robert Mackay's sister, Gena, placed a hand on his shoulder and whispered, "Go find your rest. Ye will have to move them once the rain stops." She was a stout, older woman with gentle eyes and steady, strong hands, a solid northern widow. The concern for their party etched deep lines in her forehead. "'Tis too easy to find ye here."

"As soon as the rain stops," he said. She nodded and walked to her stool near the fire.

Keenan rotated his shoulders, walking over to the sleeping trio. Lowering, he stretched out onto his side on the blanket next to Serena. She rolled towards him, and he inhaled. He caught her warm scent in his lungs and held it there until he was forced to release it. He rubbed a fist absently over the ache in his chest. Och, she had doe-like skin. He almost reached out to touch it but rubbed a hand over his mouth and jaw instead.

Mo bhean. My woman. The thought echoed inside him, and he snorted softly. *Ridiculous.* He had no woman and never would. He had nothing except duty and honor and death waiting for him.

Serena's lips were so close that he could imagine the warmth of her breath. Even without the Roma coloring, she was exotic. She had an air of secrets, of magic. Pinpricks of warning ran down Keenan's back, cooling the rush of lust her smell roused in him. Magic already played havoc in his life.

Her blue bird flew in through the open door and settled near Serena's shoulder. The strange sight made his breath stick in his chest. What color eyes would Serena have in the sunlight? Forcing himself to inhale, Keenan rolled away from her.

"He must lie still," Serena said, exhaustion like a wet wool blanket over her shoulders.

Keenan, Robert, William, and Serena had departed as soon as the rain had stopped, traveling most of the night, the clouds keeping them in shadows. They'd found shelter at a dilapidated one-room lodge in the woods near the Scottish border.

"The fever has already started," she whispered, looking closely at the redness around the stitched wound in the light from an open window.

"We can't stay long," Keenan said.

She wrapped a clean piece of cloth around the wound in William's shoulder. "How long until we reach your home?"

"With good weather, and few stops, four days."

Four days. Serena cringed, her eyes shutting as she gently shook her head. Brushing back the matted hair from William's forehead, she placed a kiss there, feeling the rising heat. It made her blood rush as if readying her for battle, but how could she fight this?

Robert carried chunks of peat cut from the moors nearby and plunked them into the grimy hearth. "They're damp, so they may only smoke."

Keenan shook his head. "No fire during the daylight. We'd be too easy to spot. When the sun goes down, we can start a fire to cook some meat right before we leave."

Robert walked over to William. "How goes the lad?"

"Lucky to have you cradle him so carefully on your mount," Serena answered. Robert Mackay had turned out to be a blessing. Upon meeting his sister, Serena had picked up on her relief and guilt. Robert had killed an English taxman who'd wanted more from his sister than her money. She lived alone, and Robert had swooped in during the attack and killed the man. He now paid the penalty for saving his only surviving kin. Serena had nearly left him in his cell because of her first impression. Perceptions, even with her powers, could be wrong. Something her duy had tried to teach her.

"He'll rest now. That's all that can be done without more supplies," she said.

Robert patted her shoulder and turned toward a corner of the dirty room. "Time to lower these weary bones to the floor, then."

The man's snore stuttered through the room within minutes. Serena's head ached with worry. She didn't have her mother's herbs to battle fever. Lowering herself next to William, she threaded out a thought toward Mari, telling her they were alive. Serena didn't know if her duy could hear her, but she'd try. She must be worried, both of her children gone.

As the infinite number of hopeless thoughts piled in, Serena felt the weight of a blanket cover her. She looked up in time to watch Keenan walk out the door. She closed her eyes, giving in to the blessed oblivion of sleep, knowing the Scotsman would guard them. He'd come for them in the dark forest, so she trusted him.

Darkness shifted behind Serena's eyes, her mind awakening enough to dream. She was weightless, her body floating through morbid images of the shooting and the dankness of the jailhouse. But then Keenan was there, helping her save William, holding her before him on the horse. She heard Chiriklò's chirping and saw images of their cottage from above. *This is a dream.* She let herself rest within it, surrendering any resistance.

A familiar tug made her turn her face to the northwest. The tug pulled from the dragonfly birthmark near her navel. It had been pulling at her for years to go in that direction. Serena felt it in dreams and sometimes when she was awake, staring off into the woods or sky. Wanderlust, Mari had suggested. It worsened the farther north they traveled and changed to a westward pull as if to some important destination. Now, the thread inside her jerked taut as if someone in the west wound it like a rope from the other end.

Serena's body lifted on the breeze and blew past William and Robert where they lay on the floor. Out the door she moved. 'Twas a dream, so she didn't fight it. Her slippers settled on the soft ground, and she walked among the white birches, over branches, and across a narrow road. She stopped in a clearing of ten ancient stones as if the person who pulled the taut rope stopped winding.

The stones were gray granite with sparkles of white flecked along their rough surfaces. The tops were smoothed, not jagged, as if they'd been cleaved.

Serena turned in the wide circle, spreading arms outward, and tilted her head back. The birthmark tingled against her skin where it sat near her navel. Sun slanted down through a hole at the top of the dense canopy of trees surrounding the stone circle. It fell upon her upturned face, and she squinted at its brightness. The smell of fresh earth after a spring rain surrounded her. The stuttered flight of hundreds of dragonflies darted among the trees towering overhead, and she stared at them in wonder.

"I am here," a woman's smooth voice came from nowhere and everywhere at once, perhaps inside Serena's head; she couldn't tell.

Serena's gaze snapped down out of the trees, meeting a set of pale blue eyes. The woman stood tall, wispy white hair braided. Her robes looked white, but then translucent and then full of every color imaginable as she moved. The many lines etched into her pale skin gave her an ancient and wise look, much like the trees and stones around them. Dragonflies zipped around her head like fairies, creating a living crown.

"Who are you?" Serena asked.

The woman smiled. "I know you well." Her lips didn't move. She spoke to Serena in her mind. "I am Drakkina, and I knew your mother."

"You know Mari?"

"No child, your birth mother, Gilla. And your father, Druce."

"You know my—"

"William will die," Drakkina said inside Serena's head, cutting her off.

The boulder of fear dropped into Serena's stomach so hard that she almost sunk to the ground. She opened her mouth with questions and denials, but the woman held up a deeply lined hand. "William will die unless you give him something now to fight the battle his body has begun. He cannot wait until you reach the Macleans of Kilchurn. The poison creeping within his blood will have spread too far by then."

"Can you help him?"

"I *am* helping him," she spoke wordlessly, a mysterious smile spreading across her thin lips, "by helping you."

"Then tell me. Quickly."

The old woman spoke out loud into the clearing. Her voice sounded older than the voice in Serena's head, but it was the same. "You must seek another, one with great powers to heal."

Holy God! "Can't you show me what to do?"

The woman shook her head. "My powers have faded. You must call upon another. Have patience, Àngelas. I wouldn't have come to you if William's fate were written." The woman winked.

Serena's eyes opened wider, and she barely breathed. How did this crone know her Romany name? And William? *This is a dream,* she reminded herself.

"Close your eyes, child, and ask for the help of a healer," the crone continued. "Call her from your middle, from your mark." Serena lifted a hand to rest on her tingling birthmark, feeling her stomach rise and fall a bit too quickly.

Dream or not, the threat to William was real. She reached out with her mind, past her wall of protection, out into nothingness. "I seek help from a healer. Please."

A distant voice wavered through her plea. Serena clung to it with the tenacity of a sister clinging to the life of her beloved brother. She focused her thread of energy on the far-off voice until she could hear it, almost see it in her mind. She pulled on the rays of red and yellow light until the figure of a young woman came into view.

"I will help ye."

CHAPTER SIX
HEALER IN THE MIST

The woman spoke through the mist that engulfed them. Serena tried to open her eyes to fully see her, but as in many dreams, the vision remained fuzzy. "Tell me the nature of the wound."

"My brother has been shot with a pistol. The ball lay embedded in his shoulder for nearly a day before we removed it. Now a fever threatens him, and yet we must journey for four more days before reaching safety." The unclear vision wavered a moment. "Don't disappear," Serena called.

"I do not understand—piss-tool," came the voice, stronger now.

"He was shot."

"Shot? With an arrow."

Serena shook her head. "It doesn't matter. He has a hole in his shoulder and dirt has tainted him through the wound. We must travel on horseback. What can I do to help him?"

The image cleared briefly, and Serena saw a young woman staring back at her. She looked as confused as Serena felt. She had long flowing hair in a warm shade of brown. Her eyes asked questions, but there wasn't time for them.

A simple dress flowed down her form, and a crown of wildflowers encircled her head. Serena tried to touch on her thoughts, but they were so distant that the words whispered together in a translucent jumble. They stared at one another for a moment before the woman bent to pull up two plants from the ground through the mist.

One plant had white flowers around a yellow button middle. Serena had seen it before.

"Feverfew," Serena said.

The woman smiled. "I call it Fever's Foe for it battles away fever. Boil the leaves in fresh water until the water colors with the juices from the plant. Have your brother drink it, as much as he can."

The woman tilted her head and studied Serena. Then she held out the other plant. "This is burdock. Take the roots and boil them down in water until not quite half the water has boiled away. Make him drink it three or four times a day to cleanse his blood."

Serena nodded.

"Also, pull off the leaves and cover them in a container with spirits, cover tightly and shake every day for a fortnight."

"I don't have a fortnight; we move tonight."

The woman rubbed a slender finger along her head as if to ease an ache. "Then grind the leaves into some spirits and make a paste, strain it through cloth. Drip some of the juice onto the wound to help calm the angry flesh. Ye could also take some of the remaining paste and wrap it on the wound under the bandage. But remember to change it daily or the leaves could add to the festering."

"Feverfew and burdock. I need to find them," Serena said.

"And this," the woman said, the plants dissolving from her hands. She held a small rock that shone in the light with an unusual brilliance. "Use this crystal," she said holding it out as if Serena could reach right over and take it from her.

"How?"

"Place it over his wound. Meditate upon it, channel your powers through it into him."

"Channel my powers?" Serena whispered.

"Aye, I feel," the woman hesitated, tipping her head slightly. "I feel something in ye, something," the woman's eyes narrowed as if trying to see more clearly. "Something like me."

"Thank you," Serena said.

"I am Merewin of Northumbria. Who are ye?" the woman asked as the mist came up again around her. "I know ye."

"Merewin? Wait," Serena called and waved her hands futilely against the fog. "Don't go," she said and pawed at the white diaphanous clouds. "I need the crystal."

A weight clamped down on her shoulders, fingers pushed firmly into skin. She smelled leather and a musky spice. *Keenan?* Her eyes remained closed, as if they were glued shut in deep sleep. He shook her gently, and his large, rough palm slid along her cheek. No one but Mari had ever touched her face. Serena felt a flush run down her neck.

"Wake up, lass."

Serena forced her eyes open, blinking. "Where am I?" she asked, staring into his stormy gray eyes.

"Near the lowlands, still. I think ye were walking in yer sleep."

The Highland burr brought her fully awake, and she glanced around the clearing. The mist, the standing stones, and the two women were gone. The ancient oaks still arched knowingly over her, allowing only a little ray of sun to come down through their branches. Several dragonflies flitted around and shot off into the trees. She tilted her head up, following them.

Serena gasped as Keenan pulled her closer, grasping her chin. He tilted her head so that the rays of light warmed her face, making her blink against the shine.

"Lass, yer eyes…" he hesitated. "They're not a natural color."

Serena pulled her chin from his grasp. "They are unusual, but not unnatural," she snapped and scowled at him.

He stood watching her like she had grown talons and a tail.

"They're mostly blue with some little flecks of red in them," she said waving her hands as if it were trivial. "The colors blend, making them look rather, well, violet." She was used to the strange looks from people over the color of her eyes. Mari said they were beautiful like blue amethyst, but Serena would give just about anything to have brown eyes instead. Although she withstood the scrutiny from most, she didn't want Keenan to think her unnatural.

Keenan reached out and touched her hair where the sun warmed it. "And yer hair…" He swallowed hard. "Yer hair, 'tis as if it flames with fire."

"The sun makes it look redder," Serena said, yanking her hair from his fingers.

"Why did ye come to this clearing?" he said. A strange look deepened the lines in the warrior's face. He looked almost frightened, this mighty man, sword strapped to his broad back and battle muscles.

"I was dreaming of a woman, two of them. One old and one young." She shook her head. "I walk in my slumber at times, especially as I travel north." Serena shrugged. "'Tis one of my…" she hesitated, "oddities." It was the word Mari used with love to explain her differences.

Keenan rubbed his hand through his hair, eyes shuttered, lips tight. "It seems ye have many oddities."

Serena was about to start naming some of *his* oddities, but she couldn't think of any. She glanced down at her feet and gasped. Scattered all around the grove grew clumps of feverfew and burdock. Right in front of her were two bunches in a heap, their exposed roots muddy. The sun sparkled on something among them. Serena bent and fished out the small crystal. Her heart thumped hard in her ears.

"Thank you," she murmured and tucked the crystal in her skirt pocket.

"What is that ye have?"

"'Tis but a rock I found that can help ease William's pain. And these plants, quickly help me harvest some. More of the burdock."

Serena led a frowning Keenan, arms filled with plants, back toward the cottage. His silence felt dark somehow. As if he were suspicious of her like those in her tribe who secretly thought she was a witch.

The sun began its descent as they washed the mud from the plants. "Grind the leaves into a paste with spirits," she whispered to herself to remember everything the dream woman had instructed. Merewin? The name haunted her from long ago, from a nightmare of her childhood.

Robert and Keenan stared at her. She tipped her chin higher. "I need to make a poultice for him and brew some feverfew and burdock for him to drink." She indicated the peat and dry twigs by the hearth. "Can you make a fire now?"

As if Keenan took up all the space and air in the small cottage, Serena had a hard time inhaling fully. Pivoting, he traipsed back outdoors while Robert nodded, and she knelt with the dripping plants, her heart thudding.

"I caught these," Keenan said as he walked back in and handed two hares to Robert. "If ye skin and roast them, I'll rest for a few hours before we ride."

Serena watched the Highlander retreat to a corner. They had placed William in the single cot, so Keenan sat on the floor. He had remained awake all day to guard them and needed to rest.

Serena used the whisky, which Robert's sister had given them, to clean the wound, mixing some with the ground burdock before using it as a poultice. She worked in silence, concentrating on the steps Merewin had given.

"There now," she whispered as she poured small sips of the feverfew and burdock between William's lips. "Drink."

His lips moved, and she inhaled as she saw him swallow. "That's it." She sat back on her heels, glancing at Keenan resting in the corner. He lay with his face to the wall, a mountain of sleeping warrior. Robert turned the skewered rabbits over the flame. No one watched her.

Serena fished out the crystal and laid it on William's cleaned and bandaged wound. She covered it loosely with her hands, closed her eyes, and focused her thoughts into a single thread. Instead of pulling images out, she pushed positive thoughts down the strand and into William.

The crystal warmed against her palm until it burned. Serena pulled back on her thoughts and the crystal cooled. She concentrated again, this time controlling how much light she imagined funneling through the stone into the wound. Would it help? Desperation made her eyes fill with tears, and she squeezed them shut, letting the drops squeeze out to fall.

After long minutes of concentration, a pressure began to fill Serena's forehead. Her limbs ached and seemed to weigh more than they should. Holy Mother Mary, she needed more sleep.

She let the flow of magic die away and tucked the stone into her pocket. Serena surrendered to exhaustion as she lay down next to William's pallet, her eyes moving involuntarily to the mountain in the corner.

The fire snapped behind her, shooting red splashes of light across the back wall. The mountain of sleeping warrior had moved. Firelight and shadow sliced across Keenan's face, his eyes open, unblinking, assessing. Serena's breath hitched in her chest as the warrior stared. How long had he been watching?

CHAPTER SEVEN
WESTWARD KISS

Keenan pushed them hard through two more nights, stopping to rest during the days. The Romany lad seemed to be stable, and Serena continued to pour drinks down him.

She settled to sit across the fire Keenan had built. Thank the bloody Lord, because he needed some distance from her to erase the feel of her soft body pressed into his chest and groin while they rode. The smell of warm spice seemed to drift up from her, as exotic as her people even if she didn't look Romany.

She must be the one. He looked away as the tightness in his chest made it hard to breathe. She was the witch in the prophecy, and he was bringing her home to his brother. *'Tis my duty.*

"With luck we will make it to Loch Awe by mid-morning tomorrow. 'Tis a short ferry ride across to Maclean territory." His words were gruff.

"And your castle is there?" Serena asked. "Somewhere William can heal?"

"Aye," Keenan said, finding himself held by her stare. Was she really a witch? Could she bespell him without him knowing it? Was this why he'd been persuaded to help her? Nay. She'd agreed to help him find Gerard's papers in return. Now that he suspected that she was Lachlan's witch, he must take her to Kilchurn. *Duty is everything.*

"I'll take the first watch," Robert said, propping himself up against a tree.

"I'll sleep next to William," Serena said. The wool blankets Robert's sister had given them were warm and shed water, and Serena curled up in one, throwing the end over her brother.

Keenan watched her curl up next to the young man, and a twinge of jealousy twisted like a serpent in his gut. *Mo chreach.* Keenan surely wasn't jealous of a feverish man with a gunshot wound. She thought of him as a brother, even if they didn't share blood.

Keenan grabbed his own blanket and moved back from the fire to lay on an area of spongy moss. Glancing up, he saw a star streak across the deepening blue of the sky's landscape. His sister said to wish upon every one he saw, but he never had. He laid on the moss and forced his breaths to even out.

Keenan startled awake to the sound of light footsteps on the stone-strewn path next to their crude camp. Dawn was just a dim light hovering along the spine of a mountain range in the east. He turned in time to see Serena disappear into the shadows of the trees that bordered the moors beyond. Perhaps she sought some privacy. But she could get lost on the moors in the darkness or twist her ankle on the spongy peat.

William laid across from the gray circle of their small fire where Serena's blanket remained. Robert slept propped up against a comfortable boulder. He'd fallen asleep and not woken Keenan to watch. Keenan shoved aside his annoyance. After all, the man's sister had proven to be their savior, offering shelter, horses, and supplies.

Neither man stirred as Keenan rose and moved noiselessly past them, past the boulder, past the copse of trees at the edge of the moor. Serena walked slowly several yards ahead of him.

"Serena, where are ye roaming, lass?" he called loud enough that she should have heard him easily above the gentle breeze that skidded across the land. Otherwise, the morning was still. She continued without a backwards glance.

"Ye could fall," he said louder, his voice sounding like a shout in the quiet so pronounced just before dawn. Still, she walked.

He looked behind him at the dawn edging the mountain range. She walked west. She said that she tended to sleepwalk the farther north she traveled. One of her oddities, like having violet eyes and flaming red hair, and an unnatural bird.

In a slow jog across the spongy earth, he passed and turned. She walked on, eyes half open. Her tangled mass of hair caught the glow of sun as it topped the edge of the world behind her. He studied her as she breathed deeply, her lips parted as if she slumbered.

"Serena." He dodged into her path. *Thud*. She'd walked right into his chest. He gripped her shoulders and stooped to stare into her relaxed face, hoping she hadn't damaged her nose. No blood. "Asleep," he murmured and shook her softly, but she didn't wake. He stepped aside, and Serena began to walk again.

Keenan pressed against her straight shoulders, turning her to the left. In her sleep, Serena squared herself to the west and continued. Serena of the Faw Romany tribe contained more mystery than clarity.

Keenan caught up and stepped in front only to have her run into his chest again. 'Twas a wonder she hadn't twisted her ankle on the spongy peat. He took a careful step backwards, and she took one step forward, bumping into him, still asleep. He stooped, his arm going under her legs.

Picking her up, he carried her back to camp. Robert woke up startled to see what must look like two lovers returning from a tryst away from prying eyes and ears.

"She walks west in her sleep," Keenan said without hushing his voice. He shrugged and shook his head. The explanation sounded doubtful to his own ears, and Robert frowned, his brow raising.

Keenan set Serena on her woolen blanket, guiding her down on her side. After a moment, she sat up. Keenan and Robert watched as she rose silently and began to walk once again.

"See, man," Keenan spread his hands wide, palms up. "West, she goes west."

"Bloody odd that," Robert said. And then after a moment, "are ye going to fetch her again?"

Keenan followed her out of the grove of trees. He walked beside her, watching how her feet somehow found the tops of the mossy hillocks so she didn't fall. He dodged before her again. Bowing his head, he looked straight into her face. "Wake, Serena."

She didn't wake. He shook her gently by the shoulders. "Time to head north!" She looked entranced. What would wake her?

He placed one hand on her shoulder, his other tilting her face to him. He studied every detail of her bonny translucent skin, how it lay soft against high cheekbones and a delicate nose, how a sprinkling of freckles dotted the contours. Dark lashes were nearly closed. Parted lips pouted slightly, softly pink and just right for a man's touch.

So he touched, first with his thumb and then with his mouth. He kissed her tentatively, not wanting to startle her. She kissed him back slowly, tilting her face to better meet him. She was warm and supple and beautiful.

His fingers raised to thread through her heavy hair. Soft, so very soft. He wanted to wind it around his fist. Her womanly curves seemed to melt along his length as if they fit perfectly together. His cock rose instantly against the press of his English trews, and fire slid with his blood through his entire body.

Their bodies came together, soft against hard. The thought that she could be the witch of the prophecy didn't matter at the moment. The only thing that mattered was the heat he felt when she slanted her face to deepen the kiss. The spicy warm smell, the taste, the feel of her lush body pressed against him.

Serena stiffened, and he stilled as if caught doing something dishonorable. Keenan broke the kiss and stared into wide violet eyes. Passion lurked in those brilliant, mythical orbs. He rested his hands on her shoulders, willing himself not to look guilty.

"Ye were walking," he said. She blinked, and he touched her cheek. "I—"

Whatever he was going to say halted as she stepped into him, raising onto her toes to meet his lips. The lass molded her body closely, and her mouth opened under his, making him groan softly. He ran hands down to cup her sweetly rounded arse through the layers of filmy skirts. Her hands threaded behind his head, and Keenan's mind turned wild as he scanned the terrain in his memory. There must be a secluded place nearby.

A loud clearing of one's throat dragged Keenan back from the edge of madness. *Bloody Mackay.* He broke off the kiss and set Serena at arm's length. She looked totally befuddled. Had she been kissing him in her sleep?

"Seems ye found a way to wake the lass." Robert chuckled and turned back toward their camp. "I'll start packing up."

Serena looked around. "What happened?"

Daingead. He was such an arse! "Och, but ye walk in your sleep, lass."

"West."

"Aye, west."

"'Tis one of my oddities."

"Ye have quite a few," he said. Maybe she didn't know he'd kissed her.

"So you've pointed out." She frowned. "And kissing someone walking in their sleep?"

Bloody hell. Keenan cleared his throat. "'Tis not something I... do... often or ever, actually."

She tipped her head, studying him, and pulled her bottom lip into her mouth. "Perhaps 'tis a new oddity of yours Keenan Maclean." She didn't look angry, more confused. She touched one finger to her damp lip.

"I suppose so?" he said, but it sounded like a question.

"Good," she said, dropping her finger.

"Good?"

"Yes, good. You need a few oddities, else you'd be dull." She turned to walk back, taking her time to find the right footing.

"Dull?" Keenan ran his hand through his hair. "Oh for a life that is dull." He steadied her as she hopped from hillock to boulder and finally off the spongy moor. How had she managed it so smoothly while she'd been asleep?

"For future reference, lass, is there any other way to wake ye when ye walk in your slumber?"

Serena shrugged. "Mari and William used to tie me down until I woke."

Somehow Keenan found that exceedingly funny, and laughter echoed in the small copse of trees.

They broke through the tree line opposite Loch Awe, and Keenan halted his horse. He looked past the swath of silky red hair resting over Serena's shoulder as she sat before him. Rising above the clear waters was Kilchurn Castle, its hulking form reflected on the smooth surface of the water. Three granite towers rose majestically toward the mountain guarding its back, and white spots of wool grazed along the mountainside. A small village of sturdy cottages popped up along curved lanes before its walls.

He dismounted and stepped back to let her throw a leg over and jump down on her own. After their kiss, he'd tried unsuccessfully to keep some distance between them, but Robert continued to hoist William onto his horse, keeping the lad upright as he rode. It would have seemed odd to force a change in riding partners.

Keenan walked to the edge of the trees and picked some needles from the pine that bordered the water. Breaking the little needles, he held them up to his nose and inhaled the fresh pine scent. The setting sun made the reflection of violet and red-orange all the more brilliant with the dark castle shadowing within it.

"'Tis so beautiful," Serena whispered with awe.

She's so beautiful. Her open admiration of his home only enhanced it.

He breathed out long, hoping to expel the pain in his chest and turned back to the scene before them. "Aye, 'tis a thing of beauty."

They stood, side by side, with the trees at their backs and Kilchurn Castle and the prophecy before them. "Welcome to Kilchurn Castle, Serena." He tore himself from the mesmerizing beauty. "Come. Let's get your brother in a real bed."

As they approached the castle on the one land route, Serena sighed. "More voices," she whispered so low that Keenan barely heard her words. She leaned back into his arms as they swayed with the horse's gait.

It had become comfortable. Even though he knew it was wrong, she fit just right there. His frown deepened and with it, the ache at the back of his head.

The horses plodded over a small wooden bridge and among the houses of the village. The smells of home filled the air: peat smoke from chimneys, tilled earth, sheep dung. The village was modest, but the homes were sturdy and clean, with thatched roofs and mud-caked sides to keep the Highland winds out. The soft glow of cookfires inside gave the small dwellings a cheery look, like a multitude of glowing torches over the surface of land to light their path.

"Hail there, Keenan," Garrett called from beside one cottage.

"Good eve to ye, Garrett," Keenan called back.

Isabell Pritchard came out of the doorway and waved at him. Her two young girls peeked out from her skirts. Keenan nodded at the widow and gave the bashful girls a quick smile. Serena looked over Keenan's shoulder.

"They follow."

"Aye, they rejoice. Their great protector has returned," he said evenly.

A chirping melody floated on the breeze. "Chiriklò," Serena said. The sparrow glided from a barely budding tree. Gasps carried to her on the wind as the bird alighted on her stiff shoulder. Reaching up, Serena let the bird move into the palm of her hand where she cradled it next to her cheek. It twittered softly.

"Are ye not fearful the bird will make a meal for a hawk?" Keenan spoke near her ear as he watched the villagers emerge.

"Chiriklò has been around since I was a little girl. He's not a normal pet. I'd be more afraid for the hawk."

"Another oddity," Keenan said. She lowered the bird to her lap and glanced over her shoulder at him.

"I have quite a few." Serena turned back toward the castle, her back straight.

As she ran her finger down Chiriklò's feathers, Keenan leaned back to her ear. He sought for the right words to warn her. "Ye are welcome to Kilchurn Castle, lass. The people are good souls but curious. Don't take offense."

"I'm used to curiosity from people. I don't look like a typical Roma."

Keenan brushed his chin against her hair. "Lass." He hesitated. "There will be more than just normal curiosity."

Serena shivered before him, turning, lips open in question.

"Hail, Keenan!" Rus, his second-in-command, called out and waved. They stopped before the wooden gate guarded by the familiar iron portcullis that rose to meet the deep azure sky. *Home.* The word settled in his gut, a mixture of anticipation and dread.

His words were spoken low. "Ye see, lass, ye are the savior of our people, the one who will lead us to peace."

CHAPTER EIGHT
ANGEL OR WITCH

Keenan tapped his horse, and they trotted across the planked gateway into the torch-lit bailey.

"What do you mean?" Serena asked, but the shouts of warriors rose around them, and Keenan pulled his horse to a stop before the massive doors leading into the keep.

Men, tall and broad, came running out of a low building off to the side. The double doors of the keep looked as if they belonged to a giant. They towered up into a peaked arch to point toward the darkening sky. The doors swung outward, and a press of more warriors rushed out.

Shouts of "Keenan returns," rang through the air and through Serena's battered mind. Although she was able to block most of the individual thoughts, the hum of emotions washed through her: elation, relief, and something else. Hope.

He's returned.

Finally, I'm ready to spill some English blood.

He'll lead us to victory!

Keenan dismounted amid cheers, and his iron-like hands lifted her before she could swing a leg across. Turning away as soon as he set her on the ground, he spoke to two stable boys. "Take the horses and rub them down well, lads." Serena could just make out, through the crowd of men, Robert Mackay lowering William from his horse.

"The three who journey with me are honored guests," Keenan called out. "The young man has been hurt and needs to rest."

One of the warriors tried to take William from Robert's arms, but Robert shook his head and marched toward the door with his burden. Serena thought she saw William glance around before closing his eyes again. *Fear. Excitement.* She could feel it in her brother even from afar.

"Let me through." She spoke out above the low hum, and several of the men parted to give her room. She ran up and placed a hand on William's head. The fever was nearly gone.

She bent to his ear. "All will be well, Shoshòy. Rest easy." Her closeness and the familiar language comforted him.

She looked at Robert. "Thank you." Robert bobbed his head and continued.

Serena watched him walk up the thick slab steps. It was only then that she noticed the large man standing at the top, illumed from behind by torchlight. His face hid in shadows, but his stance held purpose. She sensed authority around him, an air of importance.

"Come inside," he said to Robert, but continued to watch her. "Ye're welcome to Kilchurn Castle."

Keenan closed his hand around her upper arm and tugged slightly to move them forward. "Lachlan, chief of the Macleans of Kilchurn, please welcome Serena of the Faw Romany tribe into yer home and protection." Keenan's words rang through the hushed courtyard.

If Serena hadn't felt the push of hundreds of curious minds against her back, she'd have thought them alone in such silence. It was as if the Highland wind held its breath while the chief, Keenan's older brother, studied her.

The man was not quite as tall or nearly as broad shouldered as Keenan. He had a handsome face surrounded by brown hair pulled back from his straight, unmarred features. His forehead pinched a bit as if he toiled over some complex problem, and his eyes searched her.

Lachlan extended his hand. Serena took a deep breath and prepared to touch him without her gloves since she'd left them with the horse. She clasped his fingers timidly to allow him to pull her up the remaining steps.

Soft skin, pure and beautiful. Who is she? Is she Keenan's? Romany? She doesn't look Romany.

His thoughts were normal, but something lurked behind them. She sensed fear mixed with frustration so intense that it made her want to scratch at the itch riding up her arms.

"Ye're welcome here, lass," he said, his soft burr like his brother's. He smiled and led her into the cheery interior of the castle's main hall. Serena glanced back to see Keenan watching. Their eyes met and he nodded as if urging her on.

Serena turned back. She coughed and pulled her fingers from Lachlan's grasp to cover her mouth. Breaking the contact helped immensely.

Lachlan stepped away, eyes wide on either side of his aquiline nose. "Do ye have the ague?" he asked. "A disease of the lungs?"

"No, just a bit of dust from the courtyard."

He studied Serena for a long moment. If she coughed again, he considered making her sleep in the barn with the horses. She swallowed against the tickle lurking there.

"Well then," he said, offering his arm again.

The Great Hall was large, with a long table in the middle, laden with food. Most of the men had retreated outdoors, leaving only a few talking heartily in small groups. Tapestries covered several of the stone walls, beautifully woven with colorful battle scenes and victories. One rendition of a beautiful woman caught her attention, for the woman had her coloring down to the deep blue violet of her eyes.

"Sit and fill yer stomachs," Lachlan called out to Keenan, Serena, and Robert, who had just descended from where she assumed William rested.

The fire blazed in a magnificent hearth of stone that had been chiseled to resemble reaching flames on either side. The stone floor was nearly spotless with a few area rugs placed for comfort near sitting areas. The table shone with cleanliness, and the room smelled of dried herbs and flowers. Its cheerfulness did not match the tension she felt.

Keenan strolled over, handing her gloves to her, and turned to talk to his brother. She quickly donned their familiar comfort.

"Tell me brother, what news from Gerard?" Lachlan asked. "Did ye bring the letter?"

"Gerard is dead," Keenan said.

Serena watched cold worry flash across the chief's face. His fear jumped to the surface. "And the letter revealing King George's plans to rape Scotland?" he asked.

"Stolen from his corpse."

"And where were ye when our only hope to unite the clans against the English was thieved?"

Guilt sat heavily in Serena's stomach, which made it impossible to pick up the buttered dark bread. Would Keenan place the blame on her or William? Should she speak up? Before she could utter a word, Keenan sat down next to her and broke off a piece of bread and began to chew. Serena watched as he shrugged his massive shoulders that looked even bigger since they were now contained indoors.

"Lachlan, ye know how hard it was to keep ahold of that slimy bastard. He was always trouble. For all we know, the letter was created as a trap to prove we're Jacobites so the crown can take our lands."

Lachlan plopped down and rested his head in his hands, rubbing as if to chase away some ache. "Keenan, what are we to do now?" He spoke so lowly that only his brother, Serena, and Robert could hear. "We need something to bring the clans together."

Keenan nudged Serena's bread closer, nodding to it. He gulped down some mead before looking at his slumped brother.

"Serena and her brother saw who took the letter, Lachlan. The boy is too weak to travel back, but the lass and I can find them."

This must be what Keenan meant when he said that she was their savior. The letter must be of incredible value.

Lachlan looked up. Although hope emanated from him, his brow furrowed deeper. He frowned nearly as much as Keenan did. She took a bite of the aromatic bread.

"Keenan!" A woman's high-pitched voice echoed through the arched rafters. "Ye've returned." She was tall and slender and rushed down the steps, her skirt pulled up in her haste to reach him. Keenan jumped up and caught her as she hurtled into his arms.

The bread turned to tasteless mush in Serena's mouth, as the lovely woman kissed Keenan's cheeks, his forehead, even the tip of his nose. Keenan wrapped her in a fierce hug and swung her around.

Keenan Maclean had a woman. Serena took a drink of the honey mead. *I have no say in what the man does.* He'd rescued her and William, and that was enough, more than enough. He'd help clear William's name, and she'd help find their letter.

Anger followed the cold path of honey mead down into her stomach. But he'd kissed her, thoroughly, twice. What would the laughing woman behind her think of that?

"Serena." Keenan's voice still held a smile. She turned to face the two radiant people, a tangy aftertaste settling in her tight throat. "I wish to introduce ye to the light of my simple life."

Several warriors behind her snorted, and the lady pinched up her nose good-naturedly at them. Serena stood woodenly.

"This is daughter to the late Angus Maclean, and my beloved sister, Eleanor Maclean. Eleanor, please meet Serena Faw of the Faw Romany tribe."

Eleanor gripped Serena's fingers in warm greeting. "Romany, the Traveling People," she said, and her eyes glittered brilliantly. "I remember them visiting when I was a lass. Papa would proclaim a festival when they came, and we'd dance to lutes and rattles and drums."

Serena stood speechless, still gripping the woman's hand. Slowly her stomach began to unknot. Although the gloves muted the woman's happiness, it radiated up to Serena's rapidly beating heart. She smiled back. "I'm pleased you share the fond memories of my people."

The woman's happiness surrounded her. Eleanor seemed to bring out the smiles from all except Lachlan who still brooded in his chair. She motioned to Serena's seat. "Continue your meal, Lady Faw."

"Please call me Serena."

"As long as ye call me Eleanor. We're too far from court to be curtailed by formality."

Lachlan punched his fist down on the table, making the dishes and Serena jump. "And what the bloody hell will I tell the clan chiefs while ye're away finding the blasted letter that ye were supposed to bring back with ye?" Lachlan shouted at Keenan who had taken a seat at his brother's side. Keenan barely registered the outburst.

"Lachlan yells a lot," Eleanor whispered to Serena. "He's nervous and impatient by nature, but he calms down eventually." She indicated her two brothers. "We're quite different from one another. Lachlan is the eldest and therefore the chief, I was the second born and last came Keenan."

Serena could feel the love the sister had for Keenan without any of her powers. It dripped from her voice, and Serena wondered if she sounded that way when she spoke of William.

"Call the chiefs together and tell them that I," Keenan said and jabbed his finger into his own chest. "I have seen the letter from King George ordering the revocation of their lands, because I have. The English king will give our land to English nobles who have no ties to our homeland because he fears our support of the Jacobite cause. He fears what he cannot control."

Several of the warriors standing nearby muttered curses, and emotions felt hot against Serena's barrier.

Lachlan ran his hands through his hair, making it stand out around his pale face. "Without proof, they won't unite against England. Some even plot secretly with George in order to save their lands. And without the clans united, we won't see James Stuart and his son, Prince Charles, sit on the throne of all Britain."

Keenan lowered his voice, but Serena could still hear. "Remember to consider, brother, that Charles Stuart might not be the best one to lead us."

"Bloody hell. That talk is treason, *Brother*," Lachlan said, stressing the familial title.

Keenan shrugged, unmoved by his brother's theatrics. "All talk is treason to one side or another."

Lachlan moved his hand in the air as if slicing Keenan's words away. "We support the Jacobite cause, any cause to stop the German miscreant from stealing our lands."

Keenan crossed his arms over his chest, his face hard. "There are other ways to secure our lands apart from putting all our trust in the hands of an untried prince who prefers women and drink to battle."

Rage emanated from Lachlan. "Father backed James and his son, and so shall we."

"Father never met the prince as I have," Keenan countered.

Eleanor leaned into Serena. "Old argument. Lachlan won't listen. Let us away to the hearth, else we get an ache in our heads. Ye have the most unusual colored hair for a Roma person," she said, almost touching it but then seeming to rein herself in. Eleanor stood and Serena followed her to the cheery fire lapping up the insides of the huge hearth.

Keenan watched his sister lead Serena away. Had Eleanor noticed the lass's hair and eye color yet? She'd always been obsessed with the legend of his death and the witch that would herald it. Much to their parents' horror, Eleanor studied the Wiccan ways over the years so that she would understand her future sister-in-law. If Serena were the one, Eleanor would discover it. And then what would he do? *I suppose I can die.*

"And what exactly is so blathering funny that ye smile when I rage?" Lachlan accused. "Do ye mock me, brother?"

"Nay, Lachlan." Keenan forced down the rise of temper, held in check through the years. Lachlan was a spoiled child, and retaliating did no good. "I was but contemplating how surprised the clans supporting King George will be when he gifts their lands to English barons," Keenan said smoothly and took a drink of mead while his eyes moved to rest on Serena's back where she stood near the fire.

"Aye," Lachlan said and snorted, his frown relaxing. "If they don't join us, we're all doomed to find English dandies stamping before our gates. But they'd have a bloody battle to broach my walls, eh? What with ye, and yer warriors behind them."

Keenan's brow rose. Lachlan had just complimented him. "They would indeed." He raised his cup in mock cheer. Taking a drink, he let his gaze drift to the hearth.

Serena's hair fell to her waist. Although dirt still clung to her from their trip north, her kindness and beauty shone. Possessing a dancer's grace, her every movement flowed. She accentuated her words with her gloved hands as she spoke, as if part of a dance.

Eleanor said something, and Serena laughed. Keenan's breath caught mid inhalation at the magical transformation her jubilant smile created. In repose the lass was lovely, like a smoothed statue, but in laughter, spirit jumped into her features, bringing them to life.

He took a slow breath and tried to eat more of the venison placed before him instead of staring at her. *Bloody hell.* If she was the witch... Keenan's chest tightened. "Whisky!" he called over his shoulder.

Lachlan laughed. "Spirits for ye, Keenan? Not yer usual drink. Might open a crack in that blasted control ye always keep on yerself."

It was true. Keenan always stayed in control. Whisky reduced reaction time, but right now he needed something to quelch his reaction to this impending explosion. He grunted and took a swallow of the offered drink. The hot trail of liquor snaked down along his throat and into his stomach.

"Serena Faw," Lachlan said, his mouth seeming to taste her name. Keenan doused the image with another drink of the liquid fire while his brother continued. "She's a luscious-looking thing, and nothing like the Roma I've seen before."

Keenan watched his brother's eyes flow over Serena, assessing her, his gaze following the length of hair down her back, the swell of breasts when she turned.

"Aye, very lovely," Lachlan said and wiped the back of his hand across his lip.

Keenan finished his drink in a single gulp. He needed more if he wanted to be numb to his brother's lecherous perusal of Serena.

"Perhaps," Keenan ground out, "ye should go over and acquaint yerself with her."

Lachlan didn't even look at his brother as he rose. "Quite a good idea, Keenan. Always looking out for me," he said, patting his shoulder like he was a faithful hound before walking over to the ladies.

Keenan stood, his body humming for battle. He passed two serving lasses who smiled at him, the twin mountains of their breasts nearly spilling from their bodices. Open invitation danced in their eyes. "I'm weary," he lied as he passed, for every nerve in his taut body buzzed with restless energy.

He strode out into the cool Highland night. Within moments he climbed upon his chestnut war horse and rode through the gates past the sleepy village and out onto the dark moor that stretched for miles.

Keenan's fierce roars filled the quiet spring night as he flew across the darkness, his sword slicing the air. His foe was not one he could chop and fell. His foe was a dark legend that gave the lovely redheaded witch who laughed joyously inside his home to the leader of his clan.

He spit out a curse born of Scots whisky, regret, and resolve to duty, and loosed his horse to ride at will, wild across the moors. Here alone, just man and beast, he could loosen his control. Here, under the cover of darkness, Keenan could rage against his destiny.

CHAPTER NINE
A CRACK OF HOPE

The indoor, hot bath was pure bliss the night before, and now Serena stretched contentedly under the heavy throws on her bed. Pushing up, she noticed a gown draped at the end of the bed. The shade was a medium blue. 'Twas bright, a happy color. "Must be one of Eleanor's." It was certainly more practical than the many layered veils of Serena's dancing costume.

Sunlight filtered through the warped glass in the two windows. "'Tis late." She threw off the borrowed nightdress to slide into a clean shift and tied her stockings with garters. Eleanor had left a pocket for her to tie around her waist to lie under her petticoat. Keenan's sister was both practical and kind.

Serena slipped the strange healing stone in her pocket and centered her mother's red stone she always wore between her breasts.

Standing before the polished glass, she fought to catch the ties of her stays behind her back. "How to tighten these?"

Turning, she strode to the door that was supposed to connect her to William's room. Holding the stays up over her chemise, she worked the latch, peeking through the crack. He looked asleep, but when she pushed open his door farther, he moved his eyes.

"William, can you help me?" she asked.

"Perhaps." He beckoned her inside.

Striding over, she kissed his forehead and looked into his eyes. "No fever, and your eyes are clear. How's your shoulder?"

He lifted it. "Stiff, but it will heal no doubt to your fine talents."

Should she tell him about the old woman and Merewin? It still felt like a dream. But the burdock and feverfew had been real, as well as the healing stone in her pocket.

"When did you start studying the healing arts?" William asked as she turned her back to him. Serena heard him press upright against the back of the bed.

"Desperation brings out unknown skills," she said.

He exhaled as he tugged at the ties. "Once again, I'm dressing you, and 'tis not so easy with a gunshot wound."

"I'm sorry, William, I'll have someone else do up the stays if it pains you."

Rap. Rap.

Serena stood as the door opened inward, and Eleanor stepped inside carrying a tray. The woman gasped, and the tray teetered. "Oh my, excuse me. I meant to bring William some broth."

"I hope there's more than just broth in the kitchens," William called from his position. "A man needs some meat and bread too," he said smiling at his sister's discomfort.

"Good morn, Eleanor," Serena said.

"Good waking, William," Robert Mackay called as he walked in behind Eleanor. Serena's fingers began to turn white as she clutched the undone stays in her fingers. "Excuse me, Serena. I didn't realize ye were unclothed, lass."

"Unclothed?" Keenan's voice came from the corridor. Where she felt the others' surprise and awkwardness at finding her undone in William's room, Serena heard a hint of anger in the rough burr of Keenan's voice. He pushed in past Robert and Eleanor.

"Ye're undressed," Keenan said looking her over from head to toe.

He spoke to her as if she were a naughty child. Her chin tipped upward while she held the stays in place so they wouldn't fall. "Have you ever tried to tie stays behind your back? By yourself?"

He looked between William and her, while Eleanor muffled a chuckle behind her hand. "I've never seen my brother wear a set of stays."

Serena tipped her head to the side as she stared at Keenan. "If you had, you'd know 'tis nearly impossible to get them tied correctly behind the back without help." Serena nodded to William. "He's always been the one to lace them at home if Duy wasn't about."

William rubbed his nose. "I told you we were too old now for me to be dressing you. Making me act your maid," he shook his head, "'tis gotten you into trouble."

"Eleanor," Keenan said firmly, "send up a lady's maid for Mistress Faw."

Mistress Faw? Where was this formality coming from?

"Aye, Keenan," Eleanor said and headed out the door. "And I'll rummage up some meat and bread for our invalid there."

"Invalid?" William grumbled but then called after Eleanor, "many thanks, Lady Eleanor."

Robert cleared his throat. "Good to see ye feeling better, lad. I best check back later," Robert winked at Serena, dissolving her frown.

"I have many thanks to give to you, sir," William called out to Robert as he left. "You and your sister saved me."

Robert poked his head back in the room. "No more than what your sister did for me, lad. And call me Robert."

Keenan couldn't pull his eyes from Serena. Her skin, now clean, glowed rosy. Her eyes flashed indignation, while her hair fell in shining waves that looked like undulating flames. With the road dust washed away, her mane blazed red with gold spun through it.

He clenched his fingers so as not to reach for it. Serena's lips were parted as if waiting to hurl another quip his way, but none came. In her half-dressed state, she looked like a woman who'd just been ravished.

Serena thought of William as a brother, but what did William feel for Serena? "I would have a word alone with yer brother," Keenan said.

A girl peeked around the corner of the door that led to Serena's room. Her cheeks were flushed, and she breathed in and out quickly. "Pardon, but Lady Eleanor sent me right up."

Serena tipped her head toward William. "Don't say anything to upset him."

"I'm not too frail to talk, Serena," William said with a slightly deeper voice. Although the man still looked tired, his coloring and eyes were bright for someone who'd suffered a gunshot. Perhaps Serena had been working magic over him.

She turned to leave, pulling her hair to one side, and Keenan caught a glimpse of the silky nape of her neck above her shift. It was pale and perfect. What would that spot taste like? *Bloody hell.*

Keenan waited until the door clicked shut and turned to the young Roma man. "Do ye love her?" Full frontal assault was how he usually liked to attack.

"Yes," William said.

Not what Keenan was expecting. He studied the man who met his gaze.

William's teasing smile lowered to a serious line. "Serena is my phen, my sister. I love her as such."

Keenan stared at the proud man, weighing his words. There was truth in them. Keenan inhaled fully and dropped into a chair near the bed. "She was found by yer people?"

"She was found by me," William said, his gaze guarded.

Keenan raised an eyebrow. "By ye?"

"She was little, then." William smiled broadly, showing white teeth. "But she sure made a large splash when she dropped into the middle of the pond."

"Middle?"

William nodded.

"Where was she before dropping into the pond?"

William frowned, tipping his head to the side. "Why do you want to know so much about my sister?"

Why indeed? Keenan ignored the first answer that popped into his head. *Because I want to know her thoughts, what makes her smile, what dreams she has for her life.* He thought he'd chased his interest away with whisky and war cries on the moors last night.

Keenan leaned back casually. "Ye were young and perhaps didn't see from where she jumped. Unless she fell from a tree, she couldn't drop into the middle of a pond." He shrugged and looked away. "Ye're still quite young, lad, and probably haven't thought it through."

"Nay." William used his one good arm to push up higher against the headboard. "I saw her fall in the middle, right from out of nowhere. I know what I saw," William said. "She fell from the sky into the pond. Like a fallen àngelas, an angel." The lad held his gaze.

"She is special, yer sister."

William stared back, his lips pinched.

Keenan continued. "She knows how to use magic, doesn't she?"

They stared for a long moment before William spoke. "What do you think, Highlander?"

The door from the corridor creaked, and Eleanor peeked inside. "Meat and bread have come," she said cheerfully, pushing the door wide. "Maddie Grant is with Serena, Keenan." She set the second tray on the other side of the bed and began to fluff pillows and prop up William to eat.

Keenan stood, noticing the faint flush on his sister's cheeks. William's eyes caught hers for a moment. What did that mean? The man couldn't even be a score and ten, and his sister was a year older than he.

Keenan frowned. She'd never married. Even with her beauty and joyous demeanor, no suitor was confident that the prophecy only applied to sons by blood and not sons in marriage. No one wanted to be the second son of Angus Maclean. And so his sweet Eleanor must also suffer loneliness. If she wanted to blush over the Roma lad, let her.

He mumbled a farewell and left the room, with William's words pounding in his head. *What do you think, Highlander?*

"Keenan," his sister's whisper followed him, and he turned to see her shutting William's door.

Eleanor glanced at Serena's door, and then motioned him to follow her downstairs. His sister's delicate hand followed the stones of the wall as they descended. She really was bonny. She should have been married by now, with three bairns toddling about.

When they reached the bottom, Eleanor took his hand and led him to the side behind the stairwell. It was dim there, but he saw emotions cross her face. Hope warred with worry, questions with the firmness of certainty.

"I saw her eyes this morning, in the light of day," she said. "I nearly dropped William's tray." Keenan said nothing, and she continued. "Her eyes are violet, Keenan, and her hair blazes like fire."

"I had noticed."

"Ye'd noticed?" Eleanor said, her voice going up in pitch at the end.

Keenan waited.

"And Robert Mackay talked of this sparrow that follows her. People say it sat on her shoulder as she rode through our gates."

"Aye," he said. "She calls it Chiriklò."

"Chiriklò?"

"Aye, Chiriklò. It means sparrow in Romany."

Eleanor stared at him and then whirled around, took two quick paces and pivoted to pace back. Her hands fluttered in the air. "And ye aren't affected by this? Haven't said anything about it, about these, these…"

"Oddities?" Keenan supplied.

"Aye, oddities," Eleanor said with a frustrated huff and then rested her small hand on his shoulder. "Keenan, she could be the one, the witch."

"At this point, I have little doubt that she is indeed the one," he said plainly.

Eleanor snapped her hand from his shoulder, tapping her finger against her lips. Keenan liked to watch her think. She wasn't only bonny, but clever as well. And sadly, full of hope for him. Hope when there was no hope.

Eleanor lowered her hand. Her small smile worried him. "She didn't seem too taken with our brother last eve," she said.

"Give them a chance," he said gruffly.

"Why?"

Keenan stared at Eleanor. He'd always known that she loved him fiercely and above Lachlan. She'd been trying to discover a way around the prophecy for as long as he could remember, but she'd never actually said anything about manipulating the prophecy in his favor.

"Why give them a chance," she repeated, her voice hushed.

"Why?" he asked back, his gaze connecting with hers.

She looked down and paced within the small alcove. "Aye, Keenan. Why?"

"Because that is how the prophecy goes, Eleanor. I will not steal my brother's wife to save my life."

"But she loves ye," Eleanor said. "'Tis plain to see if ye look."

"What are ye speaking of, Eleanor?" he said. Anger bit into his chest. The hope that Eleanor gave him with false words would only slice through him later with more pain. He shook his head. "There is naught between us."

"Well there's certainly more between the two of ye than between she and Lachlan," Eleanor said. Frantic hope clung to each word.

"That's because we journeyed together, because I helped her and her brother. If Lachlan had done the same, she'd be closer to him."

Eleanor scoffed. "Lachlan help someone other than himself? Not likely."

"Eleanor."

"Ye know I speak the truth, Keenan. I love Lachlan as I must because he's my brother. But he hides himself away, afraid of death. What kind of chief hides away behind his walls, behind his little brother?"

"Enough," Keenan said.

She looked steadily up at him. "I'm not the only one who questions his right to be chief when he hides here behind ye and the walls of Kilchurn." Challenge laced her words.

Keenan's hands tensed on her upper arms, but then relaxed in resignation. Chastising his sister would not make her stop. "I have always accepted my lot. Ye need to also."

She shook her head slowly, firmly. "No, Keenan I do not have to accept anything. Ye're the courageous chief of this clan. Ye saved the witch and brought her here. Ye protect our people with your sword and cleverness. We need ye to bring us to peace. Don't abandon us to Lachlan just because our sire named ye the sacrificial lamb."

"Eleanor, cease," Keenan said low, his tone of warning evident.

She closed her mouth, but her pinched lips gave her a mutinous look.

"I'll protect Lachlan and this clan as I always have. I'll die honorably knowing that I have done my duty." He said the words he'd repeated most of his life, the only words that had brought approval from his parents. It was unthinkable to abandon something he'd been raised to believe ever since he could understand what death meant.

Eleanor's words were soft. "Have ye kissed her?"

The question sliced through him. His answer was traitorous, and he would have denied them if the memories didn't haunt him constantly. He looked away from her and heard her suck in a breath.

Her voice echoed with hope and victory. "Ye have. Ye've kissed her."

"Once, to distract the jailors to save her brother, and once to wake her from some sort of trance."

"Trance?"

"Aye, she walks toward the west in her sleep." He threw his hand out as if it was a trivial thing.

"West?"

"Another oddity." For a brief moment, he almost grinned.

Eleanor smiled, and her eyes shone brightly with youthful enthusiasm. "I'm telling ye, Keenan. She's the one, and we'll soon see that this prophecy did not name ye to be the one to die. Mark my words."

Keenan shook his head. "Eleanor, what am I to do with ye?"

He was about to answer his own question with threats of nunneries and shackles, but a swish of petticoats brushed the stone steps next to them. *Serena.*

CHAPTER TEN
WITCH'S ROOM

"Oh Serena," Eleanor said with a little jump, but she quickly recovered and smiled. "Ye look lovely in that gown."

Serena whirled around, her hand at her chest, her eyes wide. *Thank God.* She must not have heard the treasonous conversation. Keenan led them out of the dim alcove into the Great Hall, where light from the transoms lining the walls brightened everything.

Och, but she was beautiful. Her lips parted, the sides of her hair pulled back into a simple braid of blaze to fall among the gentle waves to her waist. The laced stays and petticoats accentuated her narrow waist, and the color of the blue lamb's wool matched the violet blueness of her eyes.

A matching streak of blue shot across the rafters, diving. Eleanor gasped and Serena laughed lightly as Chiriklò fluttered to her shoulder. Aye, she was the one, and there would be no hiding it today. Once Lachlan—

"Good morn to ye all," Lachlan called as he clipped across the smooth rock floor toward them.

"Good morn, Lachlan," Eleanor replied softly, her eyes darting between Serena and their fast-approaching brother.

Keenan nodded in greeting, but Lachlan's eyes had first gone to the bird perched upon Serena's shoulder, then to her gown. Keenan's gut tightened, and he forced himself to unclench his fist as he watched his brother scrutinize the gown closely along Serena's full bodice.

"Good morn, Mistress Faw. Ye have quite an unusual pet there," Lachlan said, and then he froze.

Keenan could guess his brother's thoughts easily. Lachlan stood in shocked silence, not even breathing. Perhaps he would die on the spot, and this would all be over. The treasonous thought shot a coil of hope through Keenan at the same time it turned his stomach.

"His name is Chiriklò," Serena said. "His color is quite unusual."

Lachlan finally drew in an audible breath. "Aye," he said, his northern accent more pronounced. "Quite unusual, like yer eyes, Mistress Faw," and then almost to himself, "and yer hair blazes like the flame."

Serena's brows pinched, and her gaze swiveled to him as if remembering similar words.

Keenan kept his full attention on the raging that strummed through his muscles and tendons. If he didn't start throwing his sword soon, he'd explode. It was as if things moved in slow motion, but then all at once. Everyone but Keenan began talking.

"They're really just a violet shade of blue," Serena said.

"Aye Lachlan, Serena has violet eyes and blazing hair, and if I'm correct, a fair number of oddities," Eleanor said.

"Oddities?" Serena eyes stilled on Keenan.

"She's the one?" Lachlan said.

"And Keenan brought her safely to us," Eleanor said, folding her hands before her. "As was his duty."

"Brought me to you?" Serena stared at Eleanor before snapping back to Keenan. "What does that mean?"

Keenan released a long breath and shook his head, the same head that now pounded with a need to roar.

"She doesn't know?" Lachlan asked.

"Nay," Eleanor and Keenan said together.

"No!" Serena yelled as Eleanor and Lachlan began babbling. Chiriklò flew to perch somewhere up in the rafters. Serena pressed her palms against her ears and closed her eyes until Lachlan and Eleanor paused.

When silence sat awkwardly between them for several long moments, Serena opened her violet eyes and looked straight at Keenan. He saw understanding there. "Perhaps someone should explain this prophecy to me," she said.

Keenan clenched and unclenched his fists. He breathed evenly, belying the intense need to leave the stifling quarters. "Lass, I told ye as we rode in yesterday," Keenan said somberly. "Ye seem to be the one that our family's prophecy predicts will save our clan and herald in a new era of peace for the Macleans of Kilchurn."

"A prophecy of peace?" Serena asked. "Why does fear surround it?" She glanced at Lachlan then back to Keenan. "What aren't you telling me?"

Keenan returned her gaze. "I have no fear regarding the prophecy," he said hollowly. "Eleanor will explain it further. I must check on the villagers." He turned to leave.

"Keenan." The plea in her voice stopped him mid step. "I am no witch."

He turned back slowly. She looked betrayed, angry, a bit frightened, and all he wanted was to pull her against him, run his hand down her hair and promise her that all would be well. And it would be well, after he died.

"Eleanor will explain, Serena," he said, and blessedly Eleanor chose then to take Serena's gloved hand in hers.

"Come Serena, let's break our fast, and I'll show ye to my work room. Ye may find it as fascinating as I do," Eleanor said, as they approached the long table. Lachlan hastened to catch up to the two ladies while Keenan turned and briskly exited the hall.

He pulled his sword from the scabbard strapped across his back before he reached the bottom of the stone steps. No foes stood in the bailey, only the ones that plagued his traitorous mind, traitorous in the crack of hope that Eleanor had chiseled into him.

———◆○◆———

Eleanor's amazingly strong arm guided Serena through the corridors of the castle. Serena concentrated on putting one foot in front of the other as fury and fear assailed her.

Keenan had known about this prophecy, had realized that she played a part in it, and hadn't mentioned it. Without being able to read his thoughts, she hadn't guessed anything about it.

Serena's chest ached for air, and she forced in a full breath through clenched teeth. She had begun to trust him even though his mind was blank to her. She should have known better. Everyone hid secrets, and she couldn't read his.

Eleanor stopped before a wooden door. Serena sniffed back unbidden tears and caught the aroma of culled grains and spices.

"Several years ago, after our parents died," Eleanor said and produced an iron key, sliding it into the keyhole, "I set up an herb room." She turned it and pushed the door inward.

Inside the cell-like, low-ceilinged room varieties of dried leaves and flowers hung from the rafters. Jars of liquid with dark shapes suspended in them sat on shelves. A large iron cook pot hung in a cold hearth in the corner, and a stout table ran nearly the length of the room. Several books sat open on the table, and more reclined against one another on a tall bookcase. Mortar and pestle, knives, bowls, and filled jars and sacks sat about on shelves. One small window let in a stream of light where dust motes floated about. Although crammed full, the room was tidy, but pungent, making Serena's nose itch.

"I call it an herb room to others, but 'tis really my magic room," Eleanor whispered.

"Your magic room?" Serena sneezed.

"God's blessings," Eleanor said and handed Serena a simple white handkerchief. "Aye, 'tis a magic room that I've created for ye," Eleanor said excitedly and started pointing out the many tinctures and dried herbs she had already prepared.

Serena rubbed her nose with the handkerchief. "For me?" A chill started at the base of her neck, spreading across her stiff shoulders.

"Aye, for the Maclean witch that the prophecy describes." Eleanor beamed with pride.

"But I'm not a witch." Witches worshipped Satan and sacrificed unbaptized babies.

"Ye have magical powers."

Serena pursed her lips together to stifle a sigh. "Perhaps you should tell me about this prophecy."

"The prophecy is a prediction that has come down four generations from a wise woman that my great-great seanmhair, grandmother invited into Kilchurn one dark snowy night."

Eleanor's exuberance dimmed, and she stepped over a bench to sit, waving Serena to take the opposite seat. "My seanmhair worried about her family and asked the wise woman to scry into the future for her."

"What did she see?"

"She saw many things, like births and deaths, battles, and full harvests. And with each part that came true, the final words of the wise woman became more and more real until it became a prophecy."

"Tell me," Serena whispered.

"One day, when the Maclean clan is in its darkest moment, a witch will wed one Maclean son and lead the clan to peace while the other son will defend and die. Lachlan was born seven years before Keenan, so Da and Mother had already decided it was Lachlan who would live by the time Keenan was born." Eleanor nodded. "So Keenan was told that his place in life is to protect his brother and then to die so that his clan will know peace once more."

Serena could hear the words spinning around in Eleanor's mind. Bits of it had played in Lachlan's as well. Serena took slow breaths against her speeding pulse, trying not to choke on the herbs heavy in the air. She cleared her throat. "Does the prophecy specify a time?"

"Nay, just that the witch," Eleanor paused, "has violet eyes." She moved her hand toward Serena's hair, "and red hair." Eleanor's voice dropped. "We've always thought that the prophecy would come true shortly after the witch came, but there's no set time."

Serena covered her mouth with the handkerchief and swallowed hard. She wasn't only a burden on the Highlander because of her brother. She also heralded Keenan's death.

They stared at one another, and Eleanor scooted around the table to sit next to Serena. "This responsibility hasn't been easy for Keenan. Da and Mother..." She sighed. "They didn't seem like they wanted to get attached to Keenan because they knew that he was going to die."

Flashes of Eleanor's memories were filled with cold demands for the younger son to eat with the warriors and family outings with Keenan left behind. Serena felt the pressure of tears build behind her eyes and blinked.

Eleanor placed her hand over hers. "I tried to love him enough for all of us," she shook her head. "But it wasn't from me that he needed acceptance."

"What are the words exactly? Of the prophecy?" Serena asked.

How could a whole clan treat one man like this, raising him to die for them? Keeping him at arm's length, so they wouldn't get attached. *So very cruel!* Her stomach tightened with anger and nausea.

Eleanor stood, pulling a leather-bound book from a shelf. Its cover was inlaid with a beautiful mosaic made with small, polished stones. Eleanor opened right away to a page very familiar to her. Curling marks of faded ink swooped along in even rows.

Serena slid her bare fingers over the words. Dread ran like ants up her arm, and she forced herself not to pull it back. She didn't need to comprehend Gaelic to hear the words, words that had been read and thought by so many people over the years, but Eleanor translated out loud.

> "As the century passes to the
> next, strife with the English
> king boils over. Your son's son
> will join the revolt against the

monarch, but it will be his son that will carry it through to peace. To your son's son will be born two sons, handsome and brawn. When a witch of great power comes with hair ablazin' like fire and violet in her eyes, she will wed the brother destined to bring your clan to peace, a peace to take it into many centuries beyond. The other brother shall defend and die. So say I."

Feelings of hope, worry, and desperate searching rose like waves from the book lying open on the wooden table. The words cut into Serena as if she had read them all these years with all these people. The deepness made them feel real, as if she were a poppet that the fortune teller controlled.

"Close the book," Serena whispered. "Please."

Eleanor clapped the book shut and whisked it off the table. She returned to sit across from Serena and grabbed Serena's bare hand, which sent a jolt of emotion into her.

Serena breathed against the feelings and lifted her gaze to Eleanor's pleading eyes. "He's already accepted his death," Serena said, "but you do not."

Eleanor gave a brief shake of her head without breaking the gaze. "Never have."

"Why not?"

Eleanor sat back, breaking the bond, but Serena already felt the great love between sister and brother.

"I love him, with all my heart, Serena. We are only one year apart. We grew up together, played together, and fought together. But I was treated much differently."

Eleanor stood and walked as if inspecting some of the shelves. "Our mother doted on me and Lachlan, withholding nothing. But with Keenan, she was distant. Our father only praised Keenan in his training, so Keenan made sure that he was always the best. He practiced and trained until he couldn't move. I'd convince Lachlan to help me drag him inside to bed."

Eleanor sat down again. "'Tis not just that I felt pity for him; he wouldn't allow that. His is a life of honor, of duty, and he has never complained."

The rock of anger in Serena's stomach grew sharper with each glimpse she saw through Eleanor of Keenan as a spurned child, his mother turning away from him to usher Lachlan away. "And his parents ended up dying before him," Serena said with a shake of her head.

"And with my parents' deaths, so died Keenan's quest to win their love. Now he just searches to earn respect."

"He wants respect?"

"He grew from a child craving love that never came into a warrior who only wants respect, respect from his clan, from his men, and probably from Lachlan, too."

"And what of Lachlan? Did he try to help?"

Eleanor spoke carefully. "I love Lachlan, as a sister must." She lowered her voice. "But I have never respected someone who allows unfairness to preside without voicing fault." Eleanor kept her face even, but Serena felt the bitterness pour out of her.

Serena sneezed again and barely got the handkerchief up in time. Eleanor rose. "Let's find some fresh air."

The two left the magic room and proceeded out into the bright sunlight. The wind skittered across the ground to run past the edge of Serena's blue gown. She drew in a cleansing breath, filling her chest and pushing out the remnants of musty air. Several men jogged out of the gates in two rows as if running off to train together.

"Lachlan doesn't practice the art of battle like Keenan does?" Serena asked Eleanor.

"Nay. Lachlan knows how to hold a sword but not how to swing one." Eleanor led her to walk the perimeter of the stone wall far from anybody who might overhear.

"Yet he's the leader of your people?"

Eleanor nodded. "Through title, Lachlan is the chief, but 'tis to Keenan that the warriors look for leadership. 'Tis Keenan who trained them, bled with them, healed with them. They swear fealty with words to Lachlan, but they swear fealty with their swords to Keenan."

Chiriklò dove off the bailey wall to land on Serena's shoulder as a group of Macleans escorted a man and a boy inside the gates. The image of a woman, her hands tied behind her back, left in the back of a dim cave, flashed from the mind of the bird into Serena's. She gasped softly as her pulse leaped with horror.

Chiriklò? Who is the woman I see in the cave? Serena said to the bird and then turned to Eleanor. "Who is that man, that boy?"

Keenan stood beside them, his hand resting on his sword as he spoke with the man. The boy stared at the castle steps under his feet.

"I don't know the man, but he wears a tartan with a weave unlike those around here. The boy looks familiar. There are several farmers and shepherds living on the other side of na beanntan," Eleanor said pointing to the mountains rising behind them.

Panic rolled along the thread that Serena focused on the boy. "The boy's name is Jacob, and he's terrified that man will kill his mother who is gagged and bound in a cave nearby."

Eleanor gasped. "By the man?"

Serena nodded.

"Who is he?"

Serena moved the fine invisible thread of sensitivity from the boy, past Keenan who was still a void, to the man who now clasped Keenan's hand and smiled.

Death, hate, vengeance. It twisted into a fuming ball at his center, behind his calm smile, behind the proper words of greeting and story of saving the lad. And it lay coiled to spring as soon as he had a clear shot at Lachlan.

"He wants to kill Lachlan."

"Good Lord, and Keenan will get in the way," Eleanor said.

Serena caught her arm before she could run. "I can help, Eleanor," Serena whispered. "We can't let on that we know anything."

Eleanor sucked in a staggered breath, her eyes wide, but she nodded. Serena looped her arm through hers, and the two of them walked briskly across the bailey and up the steps.

CHAPTER ELEVEN

ONE BLUE ARROW & TWO TAINTED BLADES

Serena kept her pleasant smile in place, the one she wore even when she knew people were suspicious of her. She bent before the boy, touching him gently on the shoulder. "Good day, lad. I am Serena and this is Eleanor, lady of the house. Why don't you step back away from all these gruff-looking warriors with us. I can find you a tart in the kitchens."

"The lad's in my care, and he don't need a tart." The man's face was deeply lined, and his eyes were red from drinking too much last night. She could tell his head pounded, and he fought to hold onto his polite ruse.

Serena tilted her head, willing her heart to slow, and held tight to her false smile. "Every growing lad needs a tart."

"Yes, milady," the boy whispered, blinking rapidly. She could feel him tremble.

The man tried to move around her, but Serena lifted the boy into her arms. The contact sent a jolt of terror and nausea through her, but she kept her smile as she handed the lad to Eleanor.

He tried to reach for the boy, but Serena moved between them. "Uh… his mother was killed," the man said, "and I brought him here to ask the Maclean of Kilchurn for warriors to avenge his mother's death. Until then, he's under my protection. Ye can't take him inside."

"I know why you've come, Fergus Campbell," Serena said.

"I don't know ye?" he sputtered and looked around him. "I'm no bloody Campbell."

Keenan looked back and forth between them, his eyes narrowing, while behind him, Eleanor hurried inside carrying the lad. Serena, Fergus, and Keenan stood in the growing wind at the top of the stone slab steps.

Lachlan appeared in the doorway. "Leave off, Eleanor. I should meet the visitor."

Serena prodded at the warped mind, his plan of attack. He held two dirks tipped with poison. One sang of rage for Lachlan, the other had been dosed as a necessary bloodletting for Keenan. The assassin would strike Keenan first, knowing he was the stronger brother.

Serena's stomach twisted. With a quick inhale, she dragged her toe as she stepped, tripping forward into the Campbell, her quick fingers sliding amongst the folds of his plaid. Careful to grab the handle and not the deadly blade, Serena pulled the dirk out and threw it down the steps.

"Beware," she yelled, her eyes locking with the assassin as she pushed away with all her senses. "The blade is coated with poison."

In a heartbeat, the man yanked her up against his chest, his other blade pointed into her back as he jostled them to the side. Lachlan disappeared, slamming the door. The tip of Keenan's sword stood balanced in the air mere inches from the Campbell's throbbing jugular, just above Serena's head.

"One move, Keenan Maclean, and this poisoned blade slides through her back," he said. "It was meant for a man full-grown, so the poison is strong. She'll die painfully."

"Who are ye?" Keenan asked, his voice solid as twelve-inch ice.

The man yanked Serena with him closer to the wall. The direct contact with such open panic and rage tore at her defenses. He exuded hatred and fear verging on crazed viciousness. His foulness enveloped her body and battered her mind. Standing there locked in his arms, she could hardly feel or sense anything but him.

"I'm Fergus Campbell, and I'm here to kill the chief that supports the Young Pretender, Charles Stuart."

Serena knew all his motives, all his pain. She saw the death of Fergus's mother by his abusive father. She witnessed the crippling of his sister, Jane, and the guilt he felt at having shoved her so hard that she fell in front of the charging horse. Serena saw it all. Fergus's twisted mind, given the seed of hatred and blame from Campbell rumblings, focused on a mission, to right his wrongs, to give his life meaning.

Serena stared into Keenan's unblinking eyes, trying to hold onto the steadiness of the peace she felt when he held her. What she saw there was that Fergus Campbell would die.

Fergus knew it too, but he planned to take her with him. Not because he feared being alone once his spirit leaked away from his body, but because he wanted desperately to make some impact on the world. And at least killing Serena would impact Keenan and Lachlan Maclean.

Serena focused on Keenan's face, the scar running down his cheek that she longed to touch again, the pulse in his neck she wanted to feel beneath her lips. In that moment, she was able to sort through all the jumbled feelings she had about him and his secret.

In the space of a heartbeat, Serena knew that despite it all, she still wanted another kiss from him, to feel his hard body pressed against her. She wanted to live. Even if her death might end the Maclean curse.

Serena sent an image to her sparrow, their connection as true as ever. The bird was never far from her, always a friend and protector. From high above the silent bailey filled with armed Macleans, an angry cry rent the air. Chiriklò dove, an arrow from the clouds. Before Fergus could press the blade against her neck, the sparrow's sharp beak stabbed him directly in his wide-open eye.

He screamed, and the pain crashed into Serena. Her legs buckled. Before she hit the stone step, an iron-like arm pulled her to the right and up against her peaceful void.

The muscles in Keenan's chest moved effortlessly against her, and she heard the sickening suction of his sword pulling free of Fergus's throat. Serena squeezed her eyes closed but felt the tortured mind of Fergus Campbell dim with his life.

God forgive me. I have failed. His last thoughts faded into the ether.

The clang of metal against granite rang through the bailey, and then she felt both of Keenan's arms engulf her in warmth and safety. Her body shook from such sorrow and the darkness of the man's vengeance.

"Serena," Keenan's low voice vibrated through her thoughts, warming her. He peered into her face. "Are ye with me, lass?"

"The boy's mother is alive. Fergus was using Jacob to get close to Lachlan." She swallowed hard. "If the boy didn't cooperate, Fergus would kill his mother. She's tied up at the back of a cave." Serena turned in his arms and scanned the mountain range surrounding them. Using the thread, she closed her eyes and let it roam searching for emotion, for dread and pain. She pointed at one small mountain.

"There, she's there, in a cave. She's hurt." Serena's limbs felt weak, and her head pounded.

"Thomas, gather a rescue party," Keenan said over her.

"How many men?" the guard named Thomas asked.

"Serena," Keenan whispered, "are there more Campbells out there? In the mountains?"

She shook her head where it lolled against his chest. "Not that I've sensed." She took a deep breath.

Keenan nodded. "A party of six."

Chiriklò glided in and landed on Serena's shoulder. He fluttered his wings, spraying her with droplets of water from where he'd washed the blood from him.

"Can yer bird lead them to the cave?"

Serena closed her eyes and sent the image to Chiriklò. "Yes."

Keenan nodded. "Thomas, follow that blue sparrow to the cave."

"Bloody hell," Thomas murmured. "Follow a bird?"

"Aye," Keenan said and carried her into the keep. He held her steady in the sway of his strides.

"Lachlan, get out here," Keenan called, his voice echoing inside. He set Serena in a tall-backed chair near the hearth.

Eleanor took her hand, concern radiating through her. "Lachlan's gone to hide above," she said, annoyance prickling her words.

The lad stood beside her, his eyes filled with tears. "Will they find my ma?"

Serena nodded. "They will. And she'll be so proud of how brave you've been."

Serena took the mug Keenan offered and sipped at the honey mead.

"Fergus Campbell," Keenan said as if searching his memory.

Serena rubbed one hand across her forehead. "He lived a miserable life. His one wish was to do something honorable. The Campbells think Lachlan's support of Prince Charles Edward Stuart will bring more supporters. They fear the prince will control their lands. The Campbells would rather stick with King George, a ruler they know. They think Prince Charles would lead Scotland into more war with England, so Fergus decided to wipe out one of the rallying points."

"He had two blades," Keenan said.

"One was for you. You first, so you couldn't save your brother. The second was for Lachlan."

"Ye knew his plan." Keenan's calm voice belied the tenseness she saw in his clenched jaw. He wasn't as calm as he tried to portray. Maybe she was learning how to decipher some emotions from his face.

"So ye sought the poisoned blades and used yerself as a shield," Keenan said, his eyes staring hard into her own.

She watched his jawline begin to tick. Amazing what one could discern from another without using her powers. He was angry, perhaps furious inside.

"I had to do something," Serena said, breathing deeply to regain her strength.

"I can protect my brother. I have since I could walk," Keenan replied flatly.

Serena looked up at him, her eyes narrowed. "I didn't grab the blade meant for Lachlan," she said and looked back at the cup in her hands. Her hands shook slightly as she lifted it to her parted lips and sipped.

Serena nearly jumped when she felt his thumb touch her cheek. "Ye protected *me*." His words sounded calm, intrigued, so she lifted her gaze. Her breath froze in her throat.

Keenan's eyes held fury, as if all the emotion that he'd kept from his voice pooled into his blue-gray orbs. "Do not do it again."

CHAPTER TWELVE

JOURNEY TO THE KING

Serena swayed with the gentle roll of the horse's gait as they clopped along the misty path against the side of a green mountain. They rode south to find the letter and the true murderer of Gerard Grant as she'd agreed. After the revelation of the Maclean's prophecy, she was glad to be away from Lachlan's constant gaze.

Serena traveled with Keenan and four other Maclean warriors. They were polite but made certain not to touch her. Brodrick, a burly man with reddish hair and a small fuzzy beard, seemed the kindest. He answered her questions about some of the local foliage.

Ewan had a handsome face and quick smile but didn't want to talk to her. He thought her pretty and was embarrassed about the dream he'd had the other night where she'd done things Serena would rather not think about.

Thomas was suspicious of everything she did or said, his blue eyes always darting between Keenan and her. He believed completely in the prophecy that ruled their clan.

Gavin preferred to ride fast, his shoulder-length brown hair flapping behind him as he scouted ahead, his mind focused on possible ambush. They were all fiercely loyal to Keenan.

Their small group had four days' journey back to Leeds and then south to Leicester where King George currently held court at a manor house. Serena hoped that the two richly dressed conspirators who were responsible for Gerard's death would be near the moving court. If they'd ducked out of royal society, they'd be nearly impossible to find.

Serena watched the dawn sparkle across the dewy grass. Her thoughts flipped between William's improving health and Keenan's secrets. They hadn't talked alone since before the prophecy was revealed, and he'd avoided her over the last week since the Campbell incident.

She inhaled deeply, glad to be out in the open away from stares and the bombardment of thoughts. Pushing back the judgements of the four Macleans was easy compared to the questions of so many at Kilchurn. She sighed deeply, letting her breath out over her pursed lips.

Keenan pulled his horse back as the path widened into a narrow cut road. "Ye're frowning. Are ye in need of a rest?"

She stretched in her seat. "No, but I'm bored," she said so that the others riding nearby could hear. She kept her face forward. "No one talks. I miss your sister."

"Aye," Keenan said, a smile curving his mouth. "Eleanor is a whirlwind, but she makes me laugh." He reached over and plucked a small flower petal that had settled in Serena's hair. She held her breath, savoring the closeness Keenan hadn't allowed while they were at Kilchurn.

Thomas snorted. "And that's quite a feat considering how ye brood so much, Keenan. The man's smiling more out here as we travel than I've ever seen him." He turned in his saddle to look at Serena.

Serena didn't need to see the faint tightening of his lips to hear his unspoken suspicions. Thomas, just like the other three Macleans, believed Serena to be Lachlan's soon-to-be wife. Their discomfort every time Keenan paid her attention felt almost like a physical obstacle that she needed to hurdle.

One day finished, three to go, Serena thought as Keenan moved back up to the front of the line. Did he really think she'd marry Lachlan? Not willingly. When she'd confided that to Eleanor, the woman just nodded but inside she'd been full of joy and hope.

They traveled for two more days along the spring roads into England. Each night, the men would take turns following Serena if she began to walk northwest, but Keenan didn't kiss her again. The trees and bushes were flowering, and the woods were alive with the songs of birds and animals awakening. Chiriklò came to Serena after the first day and shared images from above to stave off the torturous boredom.

Serena even caught a comforting thought from Mari during her long hours of silence. The Faw Tribe moved through eastern England and would head back north of Leeds by the next full moon, about two weeks' time. Serena tried to send an image of William healed to Mari but wasn't certain she'd grasp it.

On the third night, they set up camp just north of Leeds in a grove of old oaks and birch. A creek ran nearby for basic washing, and a cave sat empty. Gavin, who worried overmuch about most things, including Keenan's lighter mood around Lachlan's bride, laid Serena's pallet out in the cave. The five Maclean warriors would sleep wrapped in their plaids near the entryway.

Moss grew along the rough walls of the cave, moisture glistening on the contours of the exposed stone. Serena shivered and wrapped the wool blanket, crisscrossed in Maclean red, around her shoulders.

Keenan ducked under the low entry. "Not asleep?"

Serena shook her head. "Soon to be. You're not asleep either?"

"Soon to be," he mimicked.

Serena shivered, and Keenan pulled his wool cape from his broad shoulders and bent forward as he walked to her, sliding it over her back. "Take this. I've an extra blanket with my mount." The warm trapped in the wool penetrated her body immediately, and his masculine scent mingled with the tang of polished leather and fresh air caught in the wool.

"Thank you," she said, and looked down at the layers draping her.

Keenan leaned so close to tie it under her chin that she could hear his breath moving between his lips. "'Tis cold in here without a fire."

"It would be warmer if you slept in here too. More body heat." Serena didn't know what she hoped would happen if he slept near her, but she'd feel warmer. He'd remained near her as they slept around the fire with his men as if he wanted to be the one to grab her if she walked in her sleep. Maybe he wanted to kiss her again.

Keenan's fingers dropped away from the ties. "My men, Serena..." He hesitated. "They believe ye are Lachlan's future bride."

"I know what they think, Keenan."

"Ye can read their thoughts?"

"Yes." She held his gaze.

"But ye haven't touched them."

Serena pulled the long braid that she'd fashioned around to lay over one shoulder. "When the thoughts are strong or when I focus on a person, I can read their thoughts and emotions without touching them."

Keenan sat back on his heels, his gaze cautious. "But not me, ye still can't read my thoughts or emotions, can ye?"

"No."

"Why not?"

"I don't know, but you're the only person I've ever met who's been hidden to me."

"'Tis why I startled ye at the faire." He crouched before her, and she nodded.

"So if ye can read all these thoughts, why didn't ye know about the prophecy when ye met my family?"

Serena scooted back against the wall of the cave, trying to find a comfortable spot where a rock wouldn't grind its way into her spine. "I separate myself from most of the thoughts around me, or else I'd go insane. My duy, my mother, guided me in setting up a wall to protect myself. Behind the wall, the constant chatter is dulled until I barely notice it. Then only strong or threatening emotions catch my attention."

She shrugged. "I don't like to pry. 'Tis like listening to secrets." She looked down at her hands in her lap. "Also thoughts and feelings are raw, without civilized boundaries."

She looked him straight in the eyes. "I also didn't know there was a secret I should be looking for, a secret involving me, a secret that you could have easily told me before we arrived." She'd managed to keep the hurt out of her voice, letting anger tinge her words instead.

Keenan exhaled and then sat, leaning against the wall next to her. "I wasn't certain," he hesitated, and crossed his arms over his chest. "Lachlan had looked for so long; it didn't seem real that the witch of the prophecy could find me in England."

Serena frowned at the word witch.

Keenan's eyes turned to her braid. "When I saw yer hair and eyes in the daylight, I still wasn't convinced. Even when I watched ye perform some ritual over yer brother with that crystal." He shook his head. "Perhaps I didn't want to believe it."

"But when we rode up to Kilchurn, you believed it?"

"Yer bird flew to ye, and I heard the gasps of the people. There was no denying that ye were different. I tried to say something then, but there wasn't time." His eyes searched hers. "I would have prepared ye more but what was there to say?"

"You could have started with, 'Serena, I think you are the witch in a prophecy that says you will marry my brother and lead my clan to peace.'"

"While I die."

Her jaw ached from clenching, and she purposefully relaxed it.

"Would that have helped?" he asked. "Having me say those words before we arrived? Would that have given ye comfort or made the trip easier?" They both knew the answer was no.

"Either way, I don't believe in your prophecy." Serena breathed deeply, the musty smell of the cave catching in her throat. Keenan leaned forward and touched the woven strands of her hair where they lay in the braid.

"A witch of great power comes with hair ablazin' like fire," he quoted.

Serena frowned at him. "Your prophecy may have some ring of truth, but that doesn't prove it will all come to pass."

"Do ye scry into the future, too? Is that how ye saw Gerard's murder? Have ye seen a different outcome for my clan?"

"I don't have far sight, but sometimes I can tell when bad things will happen to someone. 'Tis not exactly the future, because the future can change. 'Tis not set. And that's why I don't believe in your prophecy."

"God sets the future," Keenan stated flatly.

"Some aspects of the future can change," she stated just as firmly. "When I foresee the future, 'tis very hazy, and I often see multiple outcomes. Sometimes when I try to warn away the disaster, I end up making it happen."

Keenan just stared at her.

"Anyway, I felt death on Gerard when he grabbed my arm. A darkness seemed to envelop William when I touched him. Mari encouraged me to concentrate on the darkness."

"Yer mother, she can read people, too?"

Serena shook her head. "She has some powers of perception, but not like mine. My birth mother was a great priestess with immense powers. I suppose one could call her a witch, but she was good, not evil. She gave me her clairvoyance and sent me away."

"Sent ye away?"

"She hid me," Serena said slowly as flashes of memory surfaced. "My sisters and I." She looked down at the blankets. "I have sisters, and they're hidden away too." She frowned.

"Who are ye hiding from?"

"I'm not certain. Something evil. A force." She remembered wind shaking her family cottage, things hitting the roof like hail, and her mother somehow transforming her into something that could escape.

Silence sat between them awkwardly like a third person until Brodrick stuck his head in the entrance of the cave. "Ho now, Keenan. What's taking ye so long in here?" Even though the man's gaze held only mild curiosity, his mind replayed Thomas's opinion that she was seducing their honorable Keenan.

"We're having a conversation," Keenan said.

"A pretty quiet conversation," Brodrick quipped.

"I'll be out before long. Who's on first watch?"

"I am."

"Then go watch." The command was evident in Keenan's voice. Brodrick ducked back out into the darkness.

"So ye focused?" Keenan asked as if not sure of the correct word. "Ye focused on yer brother and ye saw Gerard's murder and William being shot? In yer mind?"

"Yes, and then I ran to him." Serena looked toward the entrance. "Yes, Brodrick?"

The man ducked his face back in. "Och, but I thought ye might want to know yer bird is out here."

"He'll come in if he wants."

Brodrick's mouth screwed up tight before he nodded. His brows raised, and he straightened, striding back out where the wind had picked up.

"What exactly is yer bird?" Keenan asked.

"A blue sparrow."

"What is it to ye?"

"A friend."

Keenan's eyes narrowed. "A friend?" He scratched the shadow of beard along his jaw. "Ye can think to it, and it understands ye?"

Serena nodded. "He's a gift from my birth mother. She didn't want me to be alone." She pulled her knees up under the cape and clasped her arms around them.

Keenan took a deep breath and let it out. Serena held her own breath as his gaze slid down her braid again, but then he rolled back on his toes as if preparing to stand.

"You won't stay with me?" she asked. She trusted him, not his men, which was incredibly strange since she couldn't read his thoughts and intentions. And she couldn't stop remembering how warm his lips were on hers. A flutter, like the rapid beat of Chiriklò's wings, beat inside her stomach.

"Lass," Keenan finished standing, "since ye cannot read my thoughts I best tell ye." His head brushed the roof of the cave, so he bent slightly. "I believe the prophecy is truth and that ye are the witch to lead my clan to peace."

"I agree that I do fit the description," she said, looking up into his eyes.

He didn't move. "And ye will be my brother's wife."

Serena shook her head hard and fast. "It will not happen."

Keenan straightened abruptly and hit his head on the jagged ceiling. "Bloody hell," he cursed, rubbing his scalp as he bent low. "Can ye read possibilities of yer own future, too?"

"No."

"Then how do ye know that ye won't wed Lachlan?"

She would have stood, but both of them debating while bent over would look humorous, and there was nothing humorous about insulting his family. So she sat very straight. "I know because I do not respect him, I don't even like him, and I cannot imagine kissing him, let alone loving him."

A mixture of bewilderment and outrage played across Keenan's strained face, his hands resting on his knees as he bent under the low ceiling. "Ye will learn to love him."

"I won't." She crossed her arms under the blankets.

"Ye will," he retorted, his voice rising slightly as if he commanded an errant squire.

Serena presented her fiercest scowl. "You can tell me what I will and will not do, Keenan Maclean." She drew her hand out and thumped a fingertip to her chest. "But I know I will never love someone who hides behind his brother instead of standing to help defend his clan. And I won't marry where I do not love."

"I was born to protect him, Serena. 'Tis my lot, my destiny."

"What if the fates have something else in mind for you, Keenan? Ever consider that?"

A frustrated noise, somewhere between a snort and a growl, came from Keenan. "Ye've spent too much time with Eleanor."

"She's a clever woman."

He turned and walked, bent over, out of the cave without a word.

Stubborn man. "Hmmph." Serena listened to the men outside the cave settling down around the fire. There wasn't much talk, and soon nocturnal chirps, peeps, and rustling were the only sounds.

She closed her eyes, letting her head rest against the stone wall. For long minutes she concentrated on relaxing each of her muscles and finally leaned over onto the hard floor of the cave. She lay wrapped in the blankets like a caterpillar in its chrysalis. Warm and snug, she tried to keep her mind clear, but Keenan continued to appear riding, smiling at his sister, staring into Serena's eyes with a mix of unconcealable passion and regrettable torture.

"You need to kiss that man," a woman's voice said in the void of Serena's dreamless sleep, making her jerk at the stark sound.

Serena blinked against the thick darkness of the cave and struggled against the blanket to sit up. "Holy Mother Mary," she whispered as she stared across at a white glow in the shape of a woman sitting cross-legged on the floor of the cave.

CHAPTER THIRTEEN

DEMONS AND THE END OF TIME

The spirit looked like the woman from the meadow. *Drakkina.* The name slid across Serena's waking mind. The illumination from her body filled the small cave with light. Several dragonflies flitted around the low ceiling as if searching for an exit.

"Kiss?" was all Serena said instead of a myriad of more important questions.

She nodded. "You must kiss him again, Serena. He wants to kiss you, but his stubborn honor won't let him. 'Tis up to you to," the woman fluttered her fingers outward, "encourage him."

"He *wants* me to kiss him?" she asked. *Holy Mary!*

The woman nodded.

"You can read his thoughts?" Serena asked.

"Not exactly." The woman frowned. "But I've studied him, and I'm certain he wants to kiss you."

"Who are you?" Serena asked and wondered if the Maclean warriors would come running inside at any moment.

"They won't bother us," the woman said. "And you know who I am."

"You just read my thoughts?"

"Yes, yes, I can read yours. Somewhat." She fluttered a hand that looked long and graceful. "What powers I have left are linked to you and your sisters through the mark of your parents." She pointed at Serena's middle.

Serena touched her stomach where the strange birthmark sat near her navel.

"'Tis a dragonfly," Drakkina said and opened her palm up to the ceiling where dragonflies circled. Her lined face held a sheen of youthful vibrancy, and she met Serena's gaze.

"I trained your mother and father in the Wiccan ways. They were masters by the end, but not strong enough to conquer the demons who hunted them."

Serena's throat felt dry and constricted, and she forced a swallow. "I remember," she whispered.

"I was once a master Wiccan priestess until my mortal body withered to dust. What you see is a shadow of my energy held together by what remains of my power."

"Is that why I can't read your mind?" Serena rolled forward onto her knees, closer to the apparition.

Drakkina smiled. "'Tis because I can block you. Perhaps it would be quicker if I did not." Drakkina exhaled long and closed her silvery blue eyes. Images flashed through Serena's mind before she could defend herself.

The end of the ordered world is filled with red: fire, fury, and blood. Tomorrow and yesterday smashing into today. Times crushing in upon one another. Demons, misshapen winged creatures with fangs and talons. Enslaving millions to perform their evil whims under their reconstruction of a timeless existence. Children slaughtered in their innocence for amusement.

Serena paled, her heart leaping into a gallop. "What hell do you show me?" she asked, pressing backwards against the cave wall.

Drakkina smiled but her face held the heaviness of sorrow and regret. "The great oracle in my realm warns me of this outcome. The demons you saw were the same ones who killed your birth parents. To create that hell, they need the powers of both of your parents. They were only able to take Druce's. When they came for Gilla, she gave each of her daughters one of her powers and sent you each through time. Hiding you."

Serena felt an ache in her eyes as a vision of her mother appeared in Drakkina's mind. She was lovely and tall with billowy robes. Her hair had many colors within its pale strands, and she smiled as dragonflies landed on her. But then Drakkina's thoughts turned, darkened, and Serena saw the broken body of her mother upon the stone slab in their home. Her eyes were open and lifeless, her skin gray.

Serena threw up her defenses, but the smell of rotting flesh and the sound of carrion flies remained for several seconds until she could purge them. The demons had killed her after she'd sent her daughters away.

"Are the demons coming for me?" Serena asked. "For my mother's power?"

Several dragonflies alighted on Drakkina's silvery spun hair. "If they knew you were here, but they don't and probably wouldn't waste too much time looking for you anyway."

"They wouldn't?"

Drakkina looked critically at Serena, judging her and possibly finding her lacking. "They know you and your sisters will eventually come to them."

Serena shook her head, rubbing her arms at the chill the grotesque images had spawned. "Tell me more."

"For now 'tis just crucial that you find your mate, your fated life partner."

Serena's brows pinched as she met the spirit's hard stare. "And you believe that Keenan Maclean is that for me?"

Drakkina nodded once and pushed the sleeves up on her tunic, one side at a time. "I am determined to save this chaotic world. Which is why I'm telling you to convince the Highlander that you're his true mate. The bond between true mates makes the magic stronger, and we need strong magic to win over the demons' evil."

"He thinks I should marry his brother."

"Ridiculous," Drakkina said.

"I agree, but there's this prophecy."

Drakkina waved her ringed hand in the air causing several of the dragonflies to buzz up into the ceiling. "Prophecies are often misinterpreted."

"He believes his interpretation is true and won't be swayed." *Good Lord.* There was a mission to save the world, set in motion by her own mother, and she'd already failed.

Drakkina floated to her feet, her diaphanous body shortening proportionally so she could straighten without hitting her head. "Giving up so soon? Very unlike your parents."

Serena's face warmed even though she glared. "I don't know anything about convincing a man to kiss me. Should I just tell him about the demons?"

Drakkina shook her head. "He will think you've dreamt them or are mad." She lifted her fist and began to count off on each extending finger. "Compliment his rugged body. Listen to his words as if they are truly interesting. Use subtle touches at first. His hair, along his face. Then when he starts to look pained, slide your hand up his—"

"I will try on my own, thank you."

Drakkina shrugged and gave her a wink. "Courage is all you need."

Serena was pretty sure she needed more than courage to throw herself at Keenan. "And I only need to get him to kiss me again?"

Drakkina tipped her head side to side and flipped her hands. "That should be enough to nudge things going again," Drakkina said. "The man grows hard under his kilt every time you come near."

"He does?" Serena had witnessed how men and women came together in many minds, but she wasn't sure how accurate the thoughts were. William said to stay out of his thoughts on the subject altogether, and Duy told her it wasn't proper to peek about such things. So she'd had to satisfy her curiosity with those images that bombarded her when she was caught without her defenses.

Drakkina rolled her eyes. "You have no idea of the discomfort you cause him, how every night he strokes himself to release so he can sleep."

A throbbing of heat grew in her pelvis, and Serena blocked her thoughts before the old woman could detect them. "That's not my fault."

Drakkina waved her hand. "Of course not, but he's attracted to you. Just kiss him."

Maybe it was good that Serena was attracted to him too. "If he realizes he loves me, the power from my mother will be safe from the demons? And the world will be safe?"

"For now," Drakkina answered. "Just get him to lose his damn control around you."

Serena's hand went out to the entrance of the cave. "The guards won't leave us alone, and I won't throw myself at him with four other men watching."

Drakkina frowned as if Serena was the one being difficult. "I'll come up with something to keep those men busy tonight," the priestess said. "A storm perhaps."

She glanced at the jumble of blankets around Serena. "You should freshen up a bit." She tossed a ribbon into Serena's lap. "'Twill bring out the blue in your violet eyes." When Serena just looked at it, Drakkina flapped her hand again. "Tame your hair and tie the ribbon in it."

Serena pulled the leather thong off the end of her braid and ran fingers through the tangled mass, tying the ribbon into it.

Drakkina increased the light in the cave. "And pinch your cheeks."

Serena frowned. "If you're trying to build my confidence to seduce a kiss out of this man, you're failing."

"He's your fated mate, Serena. You could have a rat living in that fiery mass and dung on your face, and he would still fall in love with you."

Serena stared with her lips parted. "You're terrible at this."

Drakkina waved off her comment. "Now rest, and you'll wake soon."

Serena snuggled deeper into the warm blankets. Perhaps when she woke, it would be morning, and she would know it was all a dream.

I'm not a dream. Serena heard the voice in her mind. *Kiss him, child, for the greater good.*

Serena pulled the blanket over her. "Get out of my head."

CHAPTER FOURTEEN

TANTALIZING TEMPEST

Keenan balled the rough horse blanket under his head. The firm ground felt good against his back, and the stars watched overhead. It was a perfect night to sleep outside. Why then did the musty confines of the obnoxiously small cave pull at him?

Never had Keenan felt so tempted by a woman, and his cock agreed. He adjusted his ballocks under his kilt. It must be because she was untouchable, unattainable. Serena Faw was the witch of the prophecy; he had no doubt about that. And therefore, she would belong to Lachlan.

Keenan had never envied his brother. Though death followed Keenan through his life, he'd been happy to concede the wedding a witch to his older brother. But that was before Serena's hair had skimmed his hands, before she had slept nuzzled against his chest and then stood awestruck by the sight of his beloved Highlands. That was before she had returned his kiss on the moor. And she'd risked her life to protect his, something no one had ever done, even when he was a child.

Crack!

A bolt of lightning cleaved through the sky, illuminating a bank of clouds moving in. Where the hell had they come from? As if the lightning bolt had sliced through a tin bucket, rain poured down, the wind catching the drops to pelt the men.

Keenan jumped up through the slashing rain to the mouth of Serena's cave. Undisturbed, she slumbered on her side within the folds of the blankets. Her face, lit by the storm, frowned while she mumbled and turned away.

Tingles ran along his arms and legs, all the hairs standing up.

Boom!

White lightning shot down from the sky like Zeus's thunderbolt, splintering a thick oak tree across the clearing. The ground rocked with the force of the explosion and threw Keenan back against the wall of mossy boulders. His men scattered, yelling, but the ringing in Keenan's ears blocked their words.

Crack, crack, creek!

"Watch out," Gavin mouthed the warning as the oak launched its flaming body down toward the cave. It seemed to fall in slow motion as if giving him time to react, the branches clawing toward him.

Keenan hurled himself into the cave just as the top of the massive tree crashed in front of him, its flaming branches scratching the stone on either side of the cave entrance. Greedy fire licked into the opening.

"Use a blanket," Serena yelled, apparently having woken, and tossed him one that had been wrapped around her. Keenan pounded against the tendrils of flame snaking into the cave.

The flames flickered and hissed as the water battled them from outside and Keenan battled them from inside. Small balls of ice danced across the ground beyond, some of them rolling in along the rock floor, sizzling as they hit the hot char. As the last snake of flame flickered out, Keenan backed up into darkness knocking his head on the low ceiling.

"Bloody hell."

"Watch your head."

"Too late. Where are ye?" The brightness of lightning had temporarily blinded him.

"Over here. Against the wall." Her voice beckoned him, like a damn siren.

A flash from outside lit the cave and he glimpsed her sitting, the blanket pooled around her waist. Crouching down, he moved carefully in her direction. He felt predatory as he bent and listened for her movement. Every few seconds the cave lit up followed by a deafening blast of thunder. He lowered himself against the wall.

"'Tis best we stay in here," Keenan said.

"I don't think we have a choice." Her voice seemed small against the gale outside. The next illumination showed the blackened tree branches fully blocking the small entrance.

"Can ye bring on storms, lass?"

Her hair slid against his arm. "No."

"It seems unnatural. The suddenness and strength."

"'Tis not me. I don't have that ability, plus I was asleep when it began."

The storm scattered light around them for several seconds. The smell of burnt wood mixed with the fresh scent of rain penetrating the earth.

"Where are my men?" Keenan crawled over to look around the branches out into the darkness. No souls moved about, only violent tree branches slashing against the hail and rain.

"I'll try to find them," she answered. The next flash showed her face, eyes closed. What was it like to travel into peoples' minds? There was so much darkness in the minds of men: violence, treachery, lust. His chest hardened with an overwhelming need to block those thoughts from her.

Keenan turned away, moving about the tree, breaking off tiny twigs and sweeping up some dry grass he found near the remnants of an old fire near the back. He still had some dry wool and flint in his sporran. He glanced at Serena and saw her eyes closed in calm concentration.

Keenan scratched the steel of his sgian dubh against the flint, catching the sparks in the ball of fine wool in the palm of his hand. The irony of starting a fire after ferociously stomping one out wasn't lost on him. But the wildfire had almost seemed to reach out for them. He shook his bent head. "I need better sleep."

"They found shelter," she said, her voice even. "Gavin and Thomas are together in one cave and Ewan and Brodrick are under a rock outcropping."

A spark caught against the dry wool between his thumbs, and he set it amongst the small dead branches. Keenan blew on the flicker that battled against the dampness until it grew. He sat back on his heels.

"They're tired and wet but safe," she said. "It seems they'll stay the night where they are." The fire glowed against her as it had the first night he'd seen her dancing, a twin to the flame. But instead of half-closed eyes, hers were wide open. She looked vulnerable and luscious at the same time with the blanket wrapped around her hips, her slender arms out to rest on top.

Serena tried to brush her hair aside and caught her hand in it. "Oh." She jerked back as if she'd encountered a serpent.

He crouched before the burgeoning fire. "'Tis but a ribbon."

"Yes, it is, isn't it. I... forgot I tied it in."

Keenan added thin branches until a steady flame filled the cave with orange light. He lowered to sit against the wall across from her, the fire in between.

They sat for long minutes as the world outside raged. He cleared his throat. "Does your tribe move all the time or do ye stay in certain places?"

Serena wrapped a strand of hair around one of her fingers, absently twisting it into a tight coil. He could imagine wrapping her flaming hair around his fist as he held her body before him, entering her from behind. His hands fisted, knuckles pressing into the hard packed floor. *Bloody hell.*

"We winter north of London usually. But when 'tis warm, we move from town to town, running faires and selling tinware and worked leather."

"And ye dance?" Perhaps he shouldn't have started a fire. If he kept thinking such thoughts, she'd see his kilt tent out.

Serena nodded. "And I tell fortunes of course."

"Ye must be very good at it." He tried to keep his tone light, but a groan sat in his chest.

"If I'm too good, we have to move sooner."

"Move sooner?" He tried to focus on her words and not how her lips moved, forming the *O* sounds.

"I used to try to warn people about their upcoming misfortune. But when my predictions came true, it raised questions. Inevitably someone would blame us for the misfortune. Some accused us of causing what I saw. Some just accused me of being in league with Satan."

"Ye *are* a witch," he tried to tease, but Serena frowned. Maybe he should stop talking. And thinking, because his lusty mind kept imagining how soft her skin was under her bodice, how full her breasts were, how her hips curved. He shifted against the hard ground.

"I suppose I am, but I'll only admit that to a Maclean of Kilchurn because there's nothing in your prophecy about needing to burn your witch." Serena turned back to the fire. "And I worship God, not Satan. But my tribe is better off with me gone."

"I don't believe that's true," he said, hating the tinge of sadness in her voice. Without thought, Keenan moved to sit next to her, his long legs extending. He slid a bit of her wool blanket over his lap so she wouldn't see his erection.

She cleared her throat. "So what of your life, Keenan?"

"What do ye mean?"

"It must be difficult thinking you will die to save your clan, your brother."

His brother. Keenan looked at the fire. "My life was probably easier than most."

"Easier?"

"I've always known my purpose. Unlike the men who flounder around wondering what mark they'll make on the world, what purpose their existence is meant to fulfill." He watched the rain slant just beyond the cave mouth. "My duty has been taught to me through word and expression since the day I was born."

She huffed a dark laugh. "We're both trapped. Me in my constant battle to keep out the thoughts of others, and you behind the bars of your prophecy."

Keenan turned back to her and watched the golden light play over her smooth features. The ribbon had fallen from her hair, the braid loosening, and the waves flowed over her shoulder like a twin flame. And just like the fire before them, he felt scorched by her.

Trapped indeed. In this small cave with a beautiful siren who he couldn't stop thinking about. Maybe he should crawl his way out to stand in the cold rain to cool his blood.

"Has your family ever considered that the prophecy is wrong?" Her words were almost the pitch of a song, the words tumbling like angelic notes.

He crossed his arms. "The seer saw many things: alliances, failed crops, and plentiful seasons. She saw remarkable births and bizarre sickness." Keenan spoke slowly to emphasize his point. "Every single predication that the crone foretold has come true. All of them. And this is the last. Her words are true, my fate is to die."

"Perhaps you're the brother to live."

"I believe we've been over that."

"Eleanor read me the prophecy. It doesn't specify which brother."

"Lachlan has never defended a soul, Serena. He made it a point not to learn how to defend. He knows that the brother who defends will die." He shook his head. "Nay, I am the defender."

"I don't believe our fate is written, and neither does your sister." Serena glared at him, her hands clasped into fists in her lap. The woman wore emotions like jewels, the ire in her eyes snapping like sparking diamonds. How magnificent she would look in ecstasy.

The neckline of her blue gown swooped low enough to see the swell of her breasts pushed up by her stays. Her softly translucent skin lay across the contours of her collarbone. He imagined his fingers skimming along that lovely flesh to dip lower into the warmth between her full breasts. The gown curved inward at her waist, a perfect resting place for his hands.

She pulled her hair to one side and re-tied it with the ribbon. She bent her head low to unlace the garters under her knees. The nape of her neck caught Keenan's gaze, that very spot he had glimpsed when she fled William's room, the very spot he longed to taste.

Och, but this was insanity. Keenan glanced at the blocked entrance. Was it too early in the night to start hacking away at the tree with his sword?

"Enough of this dark talk," Serena said with a forced smile that didn't reach her eyes. "Let's talk of happier times. Have you kissed many girls?"

His face snapped to her. Knowing that he would die he'd wasted no time finding pleasure. "Aye," he said, his brows lowering in suspicion.

Her lips tensed into something like a grimace on a carnival mask. "How many?"

Why was she interested? "Dozens." He studied her. The pretty smile she usually wore faltered.

"And ye?" he asked.

"Me?"

"Aye, how many men have ye kissed, Serena?" Keenan rolled onto his feet though he had to remain bent over. He threw more twigs on the fire. *Mo chreach!* He felt like a caged animal.

"'Tis different for women. If I were to kiss *dozens*," she emphasized his word, "I would be considered unclean, a whore perhaps."

"Have ye been kissed by other than me?" he asked. He watched her slender neck as she swallowed. The skin looked soft and pale like the neck of a swan.

She nodded. "I was to be married when I was sixteen," she said. "Mari wanted me to know him better before the vows. He kissed me and... I knew I couldn't marry him."

Keenan sat again and realized he was right before her because the damn cave was too small. "Why?" He reached forward to tug the blanket higher on her, hiding the gentle curves of her breasts. "Did his lustful thoughts worry ye?" Thank the Lord she couldn't read his thoughts, or she'd be the one hacking through the branches to get out of the cave.

She snorted, and he realized that he liked that annoyed little sound. "All men have lustful thoughts," she said. "So do women, by the way." She raised her brows and shifted her shoulders as if purposely making the blanket fall away again. Then she inhaled. "That's not what stopped me from wedding him."

The flames danced as a reflection in her eyes. "What horrid things were lurking in his mind then?" Was he a murderer, thief, or attacker of women?

Her jaw was firm. "He was embarrassed by me, how different I was."

Keenan's mouth opened on a curse. "The bastard."

"If I was... normal, I wouldn't have known."

Keenan shut his mouth and exhaled heavily through his nose. "Perhaps we are alike. Both of us with curses." He fished her hand out amongst the blanket and held it against his palm. At first it felt like a lifeless little bird, unmoving, fragile. Keenan began to rub his thumb along the delicate bones of each digit. She had calluses from hard work, yet her nails were nicely shaped.

"He was a foolish boy. What ye need is a man, Serena. A man who reveres ye for yer uniqueness."

She turned her hand, clasping his. "Keenan, will you kiss me?"

CHAPTER FIFTEEN
KISSES & BETRAYAL

Keenan's heart leaped with hope that he quickly squashed. "What?" *Bloody foking hell.* "I cannot—"

"Just one kiss so I know what 'tis like without being bombarded by emotions and thoughts." She shook her head. "You're the only person I've ever met who I couldn't" she pointed to his head, "read."

"I kissed ye at the gaol and on the moor to wake ye."

She exhaled in a little huff, and her words poured from her like the rain. "On the moor I was barely awake, and at the gaol I was so worried about William, and the thoughts from those horrid men were so loud in my head, I just—"

"Serena..." Her name trailed off from his tongue as she reached forward to smooth what must be grooves across his brow. The touch was firm, but her finger felt tantalizingly good.

Daingead! He grabbed her finger, holding her hand in his as he stared at her. 'Twas like the prophecy gripped his neck from behind as he strained against it.

"Kiss me, Keenan," she whispered.

The tether broke, and he leaned forward. His hand burrowed into her hair, and his lips met hers as his other arm wrapped around her.

A small moan escaped on her breath as he pulled her into his lap. She was a bundle of warm, soft curves and desire.

He felt the ribbon fall to the ground as she pushed her body into his. It was like lightning between them, a sizzling combination of heat and lust shooting through him to combine with Serena's, blocking all coherent thought.

The blanket around her body had fallen, and he lowered her backwards to the ground, leaning over her on his forearms. Drawing back, his gaze raked over her angelic features and half-closed eyes. He could almost feel a magnet pulling them together.

Serena's quick breaths pushed her breasts upward to strain at the blue fabric. He watched with heated inhales as she tugged the laces open, and the swell broke over the edge of her shift. Her pale breasts were free.

He groaned low, his hand sliding against his cock. She reached down his body, but before she could feel his hardness, his hand lifted their bound hands between them, the twining of fingers intimate.

Serena used her free hand to pull him, and he closed the distance. 'Twas as if they clicked into place together, becoming one. Her mouth opened under his kiss. He slanted her face to deepen the kiss, and he cupped her firm breast, the skin so smooth. His thumb rubbed against the tight peak, and she moaned, her legs shifting under her skirts as if she ached as much as he. Keenan imagined her wet and hot for him, and his cock hardened even more.

"Yes, Keenan," she whispered as he pressed himself against her skirts. Her fingernails scratched down his back, and the pleasure pain made him want to ruck up her skirts right there, take her amongst the petticoats, blanket, and stones.

Bloody hell! What was he doing? She was to be—

"Keenan." The ragged passion in her voice threw aside his conscience.

He caught the edge of her petticoat, tugging it upward to reveal the warm skin of her thigh. Keenan looked down at her face as he found her heat, her legs spreading amongst the layers of petticoat. She gasped, moaning as he touched her. With her long, red hair tousled about her face, Serena looked like a sun angel fallen to earth. She felt molten and so ready.

Her eyes were half closed, sultry, bewitching. She wanted him, Keenan, not his cowardly brother. *Mo chreach!* He should stop, but he couldn't.

He kissed her as he rubbed her sensitive nub and worked his fingers inside, his intent filled with raw passion fueled by rage against his future, his assigned duty. Their mouths met in a wild giving, taking, and tasting. He could lose himself in the whirlwind that was Serena, in her wet heat and fragrance.

"I ache for you," she whispered.

Lord, how he knew about aching, about pain. He carried it every day, the physical pain of training hard and the mental pain of knowing his life was meant for one thing only. The prophecy.

The cumbersome, familiar thought weighed down on him like the boulders above. The smell of damp earth, rain, and fire infiltrated his inhale, pushing past the light floral scent from Serena's hair. He pulled back, his gaze taking in the mud and ash around them. He couldn't take Serena here in the dirt. He shouldn't be taking Serena at all.

I'm not taking. She's giving. But he shook off the treasonous thoughts.

Keenan jammed a hand down on his raging cock and released Serena. He rolled to her side, lying on his back to look up at the dark ceiling and exhaled long. He yanked the edge of the blanket, pulling it over Serena where she lay breathing rapidly next to him.

He didn't want to look at her. Her beautiful lush breasts, her skirt rucked up with her legs slightly apart, knowing how ready she was for him. Her own hand had replaced his below. He'd either explode right there or thrust into her first. Lord, help him. He let his breath fill his cheeks and then released it.

"Keenan?" Her voice was sultry, a damn siren. She'd never been pleasured before, and the need to be the one to teach her was nearly overwhelming.

Keenan pulled her toward him so that her head could rest on his bare chest. "This foolish wildness between us... We can't be together, Serena. We can't do what we were doing."

She stiffened, her face rising from his chest. "Because you want to give me to Lachlan."

Nay! He yelled inside. He didn't want that at all. The thought of his brother touching her turned his stomach. But he couldn't admit that, couldn't betray his clan.

In the silence, she pushed away from him, and he heard her quietly lace up her bodice. It would be a bloody long, uncomfortable night, for both of them.

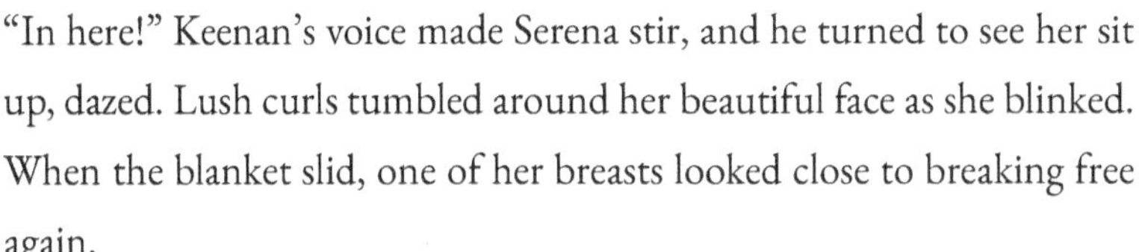

"In here!" Keenan's voice made Serena stir, and he turned to see her sit up, dazed. Lush curls tumbled around her beautiful face as she blinked. When the blanket slid, one of her breasts looked close to breaking free again.

"Serena, yer bodice," Keenan said, keeping his voice low. The lass looked like she'd been tupped. The sight alone made his disgruntled cock rise with foolish hope beneath his kilt.

"Damn tree," Thomas called back, and Keenan shoved forward into the tangle of branches. Maybe if he didn't look at her, his cock would behave.

It took all four Maclean warriors to heave the birch tree sideways. With the unbarred entrance, Keenan plunged out into the morning, free from the cage. "Where the hell have ye been?" Keenan roared at his men.

"We were someplace dry through the storm," Ewan said. "We didn't know ye were trapped."

"Is the witch well?" Thomas asked, looking toward the cave entrance.

"Her name is Serena or Mistress Faw, not witch," Keenan growled and stalked off to find a place to piss, although it would take him some time with his damn erection.

The men had the small, wet campsite packed by the time he returned. Brodrick indicated the cave. "She's still in there preening."

Keenan turned abruptly toward the cave. "I'll check on her." Better to get this over with in a little privacy. He took a deep breath and bent to step into the dark hole.

"God's teeth," Serena said as she bumped into him. "I was just on my way out."

"We need to talk," he said, keeping his voice low. She laid a hand on his arm, causing him to jerk and jam his elbow into the jagged granite wall. "Bloody hell."

"Keenan, last night," she began. "The kiss—"

He tugged her back into the cave, motioning for them both to sit. "Should never have happened, Serena. Not the kiss or the touching or anything. Ye're to be my brother's wife. I took liberties, I—"

"I wanted you to touch me," she said.

He pressed his hand down in the air. "Don't let anyone hear ye."

The daylight infusing the cave showed her pinched lips and narrowed eyes. 'Twas a look of fury, which was far better than one of passion, which would forever be etched on his eyes.

Her lips relaxed, taking on their lush allure. "Keenan," she said. "Surely our reaction last night tells you that I cannot wed Lachlan."

Keenan rubbed the front of his skull with his fingers. "I will never forget yer sweet taste, but lass, it cannot happen again."

"But it must. You don't know what's at stake if we don't... become partners. I didn't believe it, but the ribbon." She fingered the blue bow holding her braid. "And I know you felt things. I felt things."

Keenan's hands fell heavily onto her shoulders. "What's at stake?" It was the easier question.

Serena stared hard into his eyes for a long moment before exhaling. "There's this spirit woman, a priestess who knew my birth parents. Her name is Drakkina, and she came to me."

"She came to ye when?" Keenan glanced around the cave.

Serena scrubbed her palms over her face. "Before when William had his fever and we still had to travel and then last night. She showed me what horrors await the world if we don't... if we aren't together."

"Last night?" Keenan's lips pressed together. "The unnatural storm." *'Twas a trick!*

"She said that we are mates and meant to be together. I asked her of your prophecy, and she doesn't believe it." Her words picked up speed as she continued. "Keenan, she's very wise. She helped me heal William, and she knows things. She says we must be together. For the greater good."

Keenan's face relaxed into the blank stare he'd learned to mask pain. "Did she tell ye to kiss me?"

"Yes, magic between soul mates is stronger. That's what she said."

His hands fisted. "So ye kissed me because she told ye to do it, for the greater good."

Serena swallowed. "This isn't coming out at all right. I wanted to kiss you." She lowered her voice. "She merely encouraged me to act on it."

Her confession rolled like a boulder through his chest.

"But ye kissed me, asked me to touch ye... for the greater good." Where had he heard that before? *Oh, that's right. Throughout my whole life.*

"No," Serena's voice rose.

"It sounds like ye have yer own prophecy controlling ye, Serena. I suppose we do have something in common."

Serena's gaze turned fiery, and her own hands fisted. "I'm not some milksop girl who just kisses a man because someone tells me to."

He was in no mood to listen. "We are both performing a role in our own stories. Performing our role for the sake of the greater good." And yet he'd faltered almost beyond saving. He'd almost thrown away the whole purpose of his damn life.

Keenan turned on his heel and strode out of the cave. "Find yer horse. We have a mission to complete."

DEN OF VIPERS

Serena was given one room at the Red Cloak Inn in Leicester, England while the five Scotsmen had taken the other that was available to rent. A warm bath was sent up by Keenan, and she'd hoped that meant he was softening toward her after three days of near silence between them.

She'd had no idea that Ewan carried a half-made dress of silk mockado velvet tied tightly to the back of his horse during their journey south. Two hired seamstresses had taken a full day to fit and sew the gorgeous green court gown over Serena's form. They'd finished it that morning in time for Serena and Keenan's audience with King George that eve.

The pretty, stout kitchen maid, who was acting as Serena's lady's maid, smiled as Serena turned in a circle.

"Milady, you look utterly lovely. You'll fit right in with the court at Frampton Manor, if you don't mind me saying."

Serena smiled. "I owe it to you, Mistress Winifred, and your plaiting skills." Serena peered into the small glass mirror at the ribbon woven into her hair that matched the emerald-green court gown.

Winifred stopped in front of Serena, hands on hips, and stared at Serena's bare neckline. "Hmm, I hope you aren't chilled this eve, milady. The neckline is quite low."

Serena looked down at the tops of her breasts held up by the tight stays. "I should wear a handkerchief to cover the neckline."

Winifred shook her head. "Not in the evening at court. All the ladies wear their costume without covering up. As if they might fall out bending down."

The maid smiled and patted Serena's sleeve. "You'll do just fine, milady." Winifred's smile made her cheeks round out like small apples, but Serena easily picked up on the envy in her thoughts, and the humorous thought of Serena's breasts popping out in the middle of a dance. But the maid chastised herself mentally for the mean-spirited thought.

"Just in case, you should stay as upright as possible." She demonstrated a curtsey while staying in a vertical position.

"Upright. Yes, of course."

Serena's nerves were on edge from the cave incident and Keenan's silence, and now she must portray a lady before the king of England. Gerard's murders must be caught in order to clear William's name. How she would do that, she hadn't a clue. Even if she found the man and woman, why would anyone believe her?

Serena took two more deep breaths. On the last one she looked down where the rose-hued rings around her nipples teased the satin edging. *No deep breathing either.* She tugged the bodice upward.

Rap! Rap!

With a nod from Serena, Winifred opened the door and then threw it wide to let Keenan and Brodrick enter. "Isn't she a lovely sight?" the maid said with mostly sincere enthusiasm.

Serena turned around to the sour-faced men. She took a deep breath without thinking. Brodrick's eyes dropped to her ample display, and then his face turned several shades of red. *No deep breathing*. Keenan's eyes rested on her chest as well, but instead of looking embarrassed, he looked irritated, even angry.

Serena turned away, making the movement into a circle as if showing the fine ensemble. "They say 'tis the latest fashion."

Brodrick cleared his throat and tugged on his beard. "Ye look very courtly, milady."

"Thank you," Serena said, glancing at Keenan. She stroked down the front of her petticoat. "The fabric is beautiful. Thank you for bringing it down with us. I had no idea Ewan carried it all this way. I'll thank him."

"I'll tell Ewan. Don't bother him about it," Keenan said briskly. He looked stern, serious, as if ready for battle. Did he expect battle this eve?

"Do ye have a cloak?" Keenan asked abruptly. Winifred brought a soft lamb's wool cloak from the bed. "With luck it will be cold in the ballroom," he said and turned.

Damn. He didn't seem any softer toward her.

Whisked through the inn at a breathless pace, Serena's heart trotted as she climbed into a hired carriage. The door clicked shut behind Keenan as he followed her inside and settled himself across from her. Thomas rode above with the driver while Ewan and Brodrick rode their horses alongside. Gavin had already ridden to the manor, sliding in amongst the servants hired for the evening.

The carriage bumped and pitched along the pitted road that was scattered with puddles. Serena concentrated on keeping her seat in the small cabin, one hand gripping the edge of the bench and the other clasping the window casing.

Keenan looked out the glassed window. The moon reflected against his face, accentuating the scar and his ruggedness. He wore English court clothes, perfectly cut to show off his strong body in elegant style. Every part of his grooming, down to his neatly queued hair, made him look the courtly gentleman, proud and serious. But she preferred her Scottish warrior, who smelled of leather, woodsmoke, and Highland wind, the man that used to trust her.

"Keenan," she blurted out. "I'd like to explain about Drakkina and the cave."

Keenan turned his stern, apathetic gaze on her. "What else is there to know? A spirit woman told ye to kiss me, and ye did for the greater good."

The moon flashed through the trees to flicker across Serena's eyes, making it difficult to see his expression. The man was impossibly stubborn. "I didn't kiss you because she told me to," she said, silently adding "you big oaf." "I kissed you because I've wanted to since you saved me from falling at the faire."

Keenan didn't move. Beyond him, the lights of Frampton Manor sparkled against the darkness outside his window.

"When you kissed me on the moors, I wanted more."

His eyes were in shadow, making them even more unreadable.

She ignored his silence and plunged ahead. "But then we were at Kilchurn and you," she took a deep breath, "you gave me up to the prophecy, up to Lachlan." Her gloved fingers rose to the window. "It was as if you had just begun to see me and then you slammed the door."

Silence was broken only by the creak of the wheels and crunch of the gravel.

Serena kept her words even and slow so as not to sound angry, even though she was furious at herself, at him, and mostly at the spirit.

"Drakkina had only just told me that you were my mate before you woke me in the cave. At first, I thought she'd been a dream, and then when I began to think that maybe she was more real than dream, it was... well I," she turned her head away.

"Drakkina's dictate or not, I wanted to kiss you in the cave. 'Twas probably my only chance to catch you alone, and I was running out of time to do it."

When he remained silent, the anger kindling inside her let irritation taint her words. "I seem to remember that you also felt out of time to tell me something before we reached Kilchurn."

Keenan peered through the darkness; his blank stare seemed to weigh her words. Shouts beyond the windows heralded the gates of Frampton Manor. She folded her arms and leaned back into the seat.

"In battle," his muted voice filled the small cabin, "I must trust each of my warriors completely." His mellow tone couldn't conceal the stark undercurrent. "They disclose everything, and I use all their information to best calculate my strategy so we can survive."

"I speak of my heart, and you lecture me on the tactics of war?" Duy would call Serena's tone surly, but so be it. She was surly.

"Life is war, Serena."

They passed through the lit gates into the bailey of the fortified manor house. "And I'm one of your warriors," she mocked.

"The prophecy declares ye as such."

Serena snorted. "You trust that bloody prophecy more than you trust your own instincts, Keenan." Torchlight flashed across his face as they jarred to a halt.

Keenan spoke softly. "There is danger here this eve, so I need ye to be a warrior."

"I know the plan. You've gone over and over it."

"Aye, but can I trust ye?"

Serena leaned forward. "I have bared my soul to you, and I have absolutely no idea what you think about what I said or about me. I think the better question is, can I trust you, Keenan?"

Keenan led Serena up the steps to the entrance of Frampton Manor, her hand resting on his forearm as if attending a royal dinner was something she did every evening. She wore a smile that he knew was false. He never smiled, so he didn't have to pretend that his gut wasn't tormented. It had shifted between twisted steel and heavy granite since their argument in the cave.

And bloody hell, she was right. About him keeping the prophecy a secret until she arrived at Kilchurn. There'd been too much to lose if she'd decided not to accompany him back to his home.

As they entered Frampton Manor, Keenan pulled out the summons that he'd received upon his request. The page took the letter and Serena's cloak, revealing her deeply dipping neckline.

Keenan almost demanded the cloak back, but etiquette and performance were as essential to court as water was to human life. But dammit, the satin edge of her shift under the bodice only drew more attention to the fullness of her breasts, breasts that he would feast upon if given the chance.

Keenan took a deep breath and forced his eyes to roam the landscape of the gilded rooms. In the bloody trews he was forced to wear, he must control his thoughts about her lush form. Englishmen must have small cocks or icy blood else they show their randy selves all the time.

The servant ushered them into the dazzling lit cage of decadence. Several familiar lords and ladies stood about the room in whispering groups. It was a veritable wolves' den of powdered wigs and pompously stuffed costumes. The aroma of stale lamp oil mixed with fragrance to hide the body odor that was so prevalent in the summer warmth. He hated the court, Scottish or English.

Keenan glanced at the statuesque Serena as they approached the makeshift throne where George sat expectantly. Elizabeth Darlington, the king's latest mistress, sat in a high-backed chair next to him. After his wife Catherine died years before, George swore that he'd never marry another, but he took many mistresses.

Serena dipped low into a formal curtsey displaying her cleavage before the monarch's widening gaze. Keenan swallowed his curse and bowed low.

"Your Majesty," the page intoned to their right. "I present Keenan Maclean of Kilchurn and his cousin Serena Mackay of York."

"Rise, rise," George said smiling like a cat about to indulge in fresh cream. He all but licked his puffed-up royal lips. Keenan helped Serena rise. "Come forward, fair lady," the king said. "I don't believe we've met before. I've met your sword-throwing cousin, but I didn't know he had kin so fair."

"Good eve, Keenan," Elizabeth said coyly from her seat. "We didn't know you had relations in England."

Keenan ignored the subtle invitation he read in Elizabeth's voice. A chill of suspicion tore along his muscles, the weight of his hidden dirks ready to be unleashed. Something wasn't as it seemed. Was Serena sensing anything apart from Elizabeth's sexually explicit thoughts? Keenan had danced with Elizabeth at a party in London last year, before her entanglement with George, but nothing had come of it.

"Serena's a distant cousin on my mother's side," he said, his tone as stiff as an icicle.

George stood and walked down the two steps to take Serena's other hand in his. "What a pleasure to have a new face at our little court." He indicated the room. Serena had her gloves on, but Keenan knew she could still touch the king's thoughts and emotions. Hell. Keenan could sense his lascivious meanderings without any magical powers.

Benjamin Frampton stepped out from an arched pair of double doors and nearly trotted to their side. He was a little man, full of overstuffed pride and self-glory. He blended well with the usual courtiers. Frampton's sly eyes slid along Serena's neckline, and Keenan's jaw began to ache.

Frampton turned to him. "So Keenan Maclean, what brings you to English soil?"

Keenan cleared his throat and looked at George. "I bring news of foul play."

"Eh?" Frampton said. George barely took his eyes off Serena to glance at Keenan.

"I regret to inform Yer Majesty that yer friend, Gerard Grant, was murdered near Leeds a little over a fortnight ago."

Silence. George tucked Serena's hand into the crook of his arm. Had he touched her skin? Keenan wasn't sure. Frampton was talking again, but Keenan was trying to hear what the monarch was whispering to Serena.

"'Tis a shame." Frampton *tsk*ed loudly. "I heard a Romany man stabbed him for his money."

"I had his body taken to a local church, awaiting yer instructions," Keenan said to the king.

"He has no family. Just have him buried there," King George said, waving, the lace brushing along the back of his hand as if he had handkerchiefs stuffed up his sleeve. "Have them send the bill to my exchequer."

Serena looked flushed, almost dazed. Probably because George's hand ran up the side of her neck near her ear. Fury roiled within Keenan, his hands fisting. But this was no battlefield where he could lay his enemy open with his blade. This was the court, and the enemy was the damn king.

"Mistress Mackay and I also bring happy tidings of our own," Keenan heard himself say. George raised a furry eyebrow in question. Good, his hand had lowered upon Keenan's words. "Mistress Mackay will not go by her surname much longer. We have wed in the Highland tradition by handfasting."

Serena's glassy eyes blinked several times as she stared back into his own. Keenan walked over and pulled her to his side as George casually disentangled himself from her as was appropriate. Keenan smiled and kissed her forehead. "We will make it official with the kirk as soon as we return to Kilchurn."

Frampton laughed. "I thought you had sworn off the bonds of marriage Maclean. Something terribly romantic about a dark curse or other."

Keenan smirked but smoothed it into a softer grin. "I suppose I was cursed until I found my dear cousin."

Elizabeth sauntered over and placed her hand on George's arm, her smile serpentine. "What happy news."

Serena's weight increased on Keenan's arm. Her pale face slackened, her eyes flickering shut.

"Good Lord, I think she's fainting," Elizabeth said, just as Serena's body began to drop.

Keenan caught her, throwing an arm under her legs to haul her against his chest while the twittering crowd drew closer.

Frampton's wife, Olivia, rushed over. "We have several guest rooms. Take the poor thing to one." She beckoned Keenan to follow, and Brodrick and Thomas flanked him through the twists and turns through the tower house.

Keenan watched Serena's face, her dark lashes against her milk-white skin. She was perfectly chiseled from marble, so cold. Like death.

CHAPTER SEVENTEEN
HAPPY THOUGHTS

"Hold on, lass," Keenan said, pushing through the door that Brodrick had leaped forward to open. He laid Serena on a large bed surrounded by heavy curtains as Olivia Frampton ran off to order some brandy for Serena. Thomas stood guard by the door.

Keenan held two fingers against Serena's swanlike neck. The rapid flutter of her pulse proved she was alive, and he exhaled fully. Women weren't so fragile, were they? But Serena wasn't just any woman. She could be overtaken by the darkness in people.

"Lass," Keenan whispered near Serena's ear. Her breasts swelled as if trying to roll out of the snare of fabric. Keenan's fingers captured the lacy edge of her bodice and tugged upward, something he'd longed to do all night. "Lass, are ye in there?" Had she taken in too much venom surrounded by vipers? From the king's touch? Had she peered into too much darkness and lost herself?

"Brodrick, get over here," Keenan roared.

Brodrick stepped up to the bed, his eyes worried. "I don't know anything about fainting ladies."

Keenan peeled off one of Serena's gloves and shoved it into Brodrick's palm. "Hold it and think of the happiest time of your life."

"Like when I slaughtered that MacCallum from Inverness?"

"Aye. Nay!" Keenan searched Serena's face. "Something happy like that, but nothing bloody, only happy. Like when yer nephew was born, and yer sister was healthy."

"Fine, aye, I'm thinking of it." Brodrick held her hand like it was a dead bird.

"Weave her fingers through yers," Keenan urged.

"What?" Thomas asked, coming closer, horror on his face.

"Do it!" Keenan pushed Brodrick's fingers through hers so there was more contact. He didn't know if that made her readings sharper or not. "And if ye start thinking evil or foul thoughts," Keenan looked Brodrick in the eye with deadly seriousness, "ye could kill her." *And I will kill you.* His gaze spoke the threat even if he didn't voice it.

"Lachlan's witch mustn't die," Thomas said.

Brodrick's eyes grew wide and then closed. "Aye, happy thoughts." He breathed fully, in and out.

Keenan bent to whisper at her ear. "Ye're safe, lass."

Serena's eyes moved behind the delicate veil of her lids. Her lashes flickered against the creaminess of her skin as her eyes opened. "That's it, lass," Keenan said and motioned to Brodrick to break contact.

"Did my thoughts wake her?"

"They helped," Serena murmured and tried to sit up. "I need to build a stronger defense."

"Oh thank the good Lord," Thomas said. "The witch is well."

Keenan sat on the bed, helping her. She leaned into him and smiled softly at Brodrick. "What a beautiful little boy your sister has."

Brodrick's chest puffed up. "He's not so wee anymore. He's going on ten now."

"I'll have to meet him when we return to Kilchurn."

Brodrick nodded, his smile genuine.

Keenan watched the intimate exchange and frowned. He'd always considered it an advantage that Serena couldn't read his thoughts and feelings. But that advantage also prevented their connection, a connection that every other man could form with her. And her bloody bodice had dipped low again.

Keenan's hands balled into fists at his side. "Thomas, return to the ball." Keenan indicated the door. "Tell King George that my wife is fine but needs to rest. I will return soon."

"Yer wife?" Thomas asked, his bushy eyebrows raising over wide eyes.

"Didn't ye hear Keenan in the hall," Brodrick said walking to the door. "Clever too, to keep those royal English claws off her. Probably what made her swoon." Brodrick opened the heavy door, and Thomas stepped out while Gavin, having found them, stepped inside.

"I heard what occurred," Gavin said, his face flushed as if he'd run through the halls looking for them.

Serena pushed upright against the soft tick of goose down. "Keenan, you need to know." She grabbed his fist with both her hands, making warmth flow back through him when just minutes before he'd felt like ice. "King George, he knows that Gerard was a Jacobite. He knows that he stole the letter. George ordered the two I saw to kill Gerard and retrieve the letter." She moved his hand back and forth, her eyes snapping with fury. "Now he's setting a trap so he can arrest you."

Keenan's mind chewed on the information as he stroked her grip with his loose hand.

"Was it George's treachery against us that made ye faint?" Gavin asked, peering at her. It was the closest the man had ever stood to Serena.

"Yes, and no," Serena looked at Keenan. "The king's thoughts were," she hesitated, "carnal, so full of lust, I lost my concentration, and all the other voices in the room began to flood me." Serena huffed with a look of disgust. "I heard so many things."

She glanced at Keenan. "Elizabeth Darlington may be on the king's arm, but she'd rather be in your bed."

Keenan frowned. "I danced with Elizabeth last year, nothing more." George would execute him if he thought he was trying to steal his mistress. "What about the two on the bridge? Did ye sense them in the room?"

Serena nodded. "I think they were there. I only had a glimpse of their thoughts, and they were tangled with the rest, but yes."

"Did they recognize ye?" Keenan asked.

"They didn't see me that day." She inhaled fully, and Keenan heard Gavin suck in a breath as the edge of her bodice slid lower.

Daingead! Keenan yanked a pillow from the other side of the bed and pushed it against Serena's bosom to block the rising swell.

She looked at the pillow and then at him, her brows pinched in question.

"Yer neckline is too low," he said, gesturing to her breasts that were safely tucked behind the goose down rectangle.

Gavin cleared his throat. "When the king was touching ye, he was imagining all sorts of perverted things with ye?"

Serena nodded. "The man has quite an adventurous appetite."

A slight rumble came from Keenan when he exhaled. Serena's face turned to him. "Did you just growl?"

"Exactly how adventurous?" Gavin asked.

Brodrick smacked his arm.

"Ouch!"

"Don't ask her that." Brodrick turned back to her. "Just keep thinking about my wee nephew." He smiled brightly.

Keenan crossed his arms. "Did that change when I announced that we were handfasted?

She met his eyes, and the glow of the firelight brought out the violet in them. "Some," she said. "He thought about eliminating you to get to me. That's when I really understood his trap."

Brodrick mimicked Keenan's cross-armed stance. "What do we do now? If we sneak away, we'll be on the run all the way to the Scottish border."

"And William's name won't be cleared." Determination edged her words.

Keenan walked toward the fire. To outwit a king, and his council, was a tricky endeavor. There were definite advantages to having a witch in the family, and then he felt a rush of guilt over the thought. "I'll tell the king that Gerard was a traitor and Jacobite. That I discovered his treachery but before I could bring charges against him, someone murdered him."

"Not William," Serena said.

"I'll say there was speculation that others were involved, loyal to England. But until we find the two ye saw on the bridge, I won't say more."

"But if there's an appropriate opening to clear William's name, we must try," she said.

If Keenan said too much, his words would sound false. "If appropriate," he said. "First I'll call Lachlan an incompetent leader in his indecision about Charles Stuart," Keenan said.

"Call the prince the Young Pretender," Brodrick said.

"Ye won't call Lachlan a Jacobite?" Gavin asked.

Keenan shook his head. "Better to show him indecisive, which is weaker. I'll claim support of George's right to rule all of Britain and convince him that Lachlan's army is mine to control."

"Best be convincing," Gavin said, his brows furrowed.

Thomas rapped on the door and walked in. "They await yer return with all the speculation ye would see at a cock fight. I wouldn't be surprised if money changed hands within minutes of ye returning."

"Ewan?" Keenan asked.

"Is staying in the kitchens to learn what truths he can from the staff," Thomas said.

Keenan looked at Gavin and Brodrick. "The two of ye, stay with Serena. Make certain no one tries to take her anywhere. If they seize me, get her out of here."

"Seize you?" Serena threw the pillow off her chest and slid from the bed.

All four men sucked in quickly, and she looked down. "Pish," she murmured, anger tinging her voice. She yanked up the bodice. "'Tis the fashion."

Keenan raked his hands through his hair. "Stay in here, Serena." He didn't want anyone salivating over her, especially the bloody king.

CHAPTER EIGHTEEN
A TENUOUS TRUST

Serena listened as Keenan's boots clipped down the corridor, fading into silence. Brodrick and Gavin looked between each other and then both turned to her. The ordeal in the ballroom still weighed against her limbs along with the heaviness of the court dress.

She sighed, sitting back on the bed, hands folding in her lap. "Have I suddenly grown warts?" she asked.

"Nay," Brodrick said. "'Tis just," he hesitated, "ye could really read my thoughts about my nephew and sister?" His words held no judgment, just curiosity.

She'd traveled days with these men and spent two more days cooped up in the inn with them, and this was the closest they'd ever approached her.

"Yes, I could, because I opened myself up to your thoughts. But I don't do that normally," she added quickly. "'Tis rude to eavesdrop."

"So ye don't know what I'm thinking right now?" Gavin asked stepping a bit closer and staring into her eyes, his own eyes buggy like a toad.

"I can tell you are thinking something quite loudly, but unless I open the door to your words, I don't hear them clearly."

"What about that Campbell with the lad back at Kilchurn?" Gavin asked.

"I felt pain coming from him, and darkness," she answered, "so I opened myself up to his thoughts."

"Opened yerself?" Gavin asked.

She looked at the two of them. "Like when you inhale when you enter the kitchens to smell baking bread."

They nodded in unison.

Brodrick stepped to the edge of the bed. His leg leaned along her dress. "But what if I touch yer skin, can ye block that?" He pointed to her gloves in her lap. "Ye wear those all the time."

Serena played with the one that had been removed. "'Tis hard to shield myself when I touch someone skin to skin. And scars are even louder."

"Have ye touched Keenan's scar?" Gavin asked. He too, leaned in.

"I touched his scar the first time we met because I couldn't read anything about him. I'd never met anyone like that before. Even when I try to read his thoughts and emotions, I can't sense anything. Even his scar remains silent."

Brodrick unlaced the ties at his throat and pulled down his shirt partway revealing the puckered line of a scar. "Ye could read this."

"Yes, but I don't want to," she said quickly.

Gavin punched his arm and Brodrick retied the collar. "It wasn't much of anything," Brodrick said, guilt lacing his words.

Serena took a deep breath and rose from the bed. What was going on in the ballroom? She stretched her neck left and right and purposely lowered her tense shoulders, but they seemed to rise on their own accord.

She paced for a long space of time, back and forth across the room in her silk slippers, while the two men just watched her.

"Can ye tell what's going on in the ballroom?" Brodrick whispered.

She stopped, shaking her head. Then continued to pace.

"Are ye reading our minds right now?" Gavin asked.

Again she stopped and shook her head.

Gavin blushed. "Because it isn't right to intrude on a person's—"

"She said she isn't," Brodrick interrupted.

Serena huffed. "Why don't we play a game to keep our minds off our worries."

The two men looked wary. "What type of game?" Gavin asked.

"Gavin, you think of something," she held up her hand, "nothing bad and no," she cleared her throat, "no intimate thoughts, and I'll tell you what I see." She smiled. "Make it hard, something I couldn't possibly know."

Gavin smiled hesitantly. Brodrick waved him away from her and whispered in his ear. Gavin's smile grew, and he returned to her. "Here's something that only Brodrick and I know, none other could have told ye."

Gavin put out his hand, palm up. It was calloused. Serena placed her fingertips lightly on the center of his palm.

She instantly felt embarrassment coming from the man and hoped the memory had nothing to do with him being naked. Serena focused a strand of power into Gavin's rough skin, up under the hair covering his arm, along the muscles, tendons, and vessels running up the back of his neck and into the very core of his brain. All this she covered in the space of two heartbeats without even contemplating how. It was as natural to her as breathing.

And there it was, hidden amongst the questions and slight fear about her abilities. Serena could almost taste the tang of the berries, the flakiness of the crust, just the right amount of spices swirling together into one glorious bite, a bite made even better by the danger. Her mouth began to water, and she swallowed. Her stomach growled audibly through the room. Gavin and Brodrick looked at one another and then back at Serena.

"Excuse me," she apologized, "but I'm near to starving for Nelly's wild strawberry pie." Gavin snatched his hand back.

Serena *tsk*ed. "Stealing the poor lady's pie right off her windowsill."

Brodrick smiled and rubbed his stomach. He was a large man, easily given to bulk, but the constant swordplay in training kept him mostly muscle. "'Tis been nearly a score of years, but I can still taste it."

"Made better by the thrill," she said trying to frown despite the quivering corners of her mouth.

"Och, but we were boys," Gavin defended, his longish hair giving him a roguish look.

Serena shook her head, the happiness of their looting bubbling up inside her even as she rebuked them. They looked between each other in silence, their grins growing until all three erupted in laughter.

Gavin hushed them and pointed toward the door. "Unseen ears may start rumors about our mirth."

Serena put her hand over her mouth. Brodrick nodded but his deep chuckle still punctuated the sudden stillness.

"Brodrick, stuff something in that hole of yers," Gavin said.

"If we only had pie!" Serena said and threw both hands over her mouth as Brodrick guffawed loudly.

"My turn," Brodrick said and grabbed Serena's bare hand. As his fingers wrapped around hers, Serena felt his mirth and acceptance wash through her. Her eyes blinked shut as she savored it.

Brodrick dropped her hand. "I'm sorry, lass. I didn't think. I just grabbed ye and—"

Serena held up her hand to stop him and opened her eyes. Both Gavin and Brodrick peered at her, furrows deep along their foreheads. She smiled. "Thank you, Brodrick." He frowned and looked at Gavin.

Gavin shrugged. "Are ye having a spell again, lass?" Gavin whispered and moved his face just inches from her. "Did Brodrick think something evil into ye?"

"I did no such thing!"

Serena stood up from the edge of the bed. The weight of her exhaustion had melted away with Brodrick's touch. "Nay lass, ye should stay in bed," Gavin urged.

"I'm well, Gavin, even better now that I know," she said, looking at Brodrick, "that Brodrick actually likes me."

Gavin's eyes narrowed, and he turned to Brodrick. "Ye like her? What's that mean?"

Brodrick's astonished face turned red to match the flames dancing in the hearth. He opened his mouth to protest but couldn't seem to find the words. Serena patted the stunned man's arm.

"I mean, that when Brodrick grabbed my hand without thinking first about my powers," she looked at Brodrick, "it meant that you trusted me." She shook her head, her smile fading slightly. "I've never had someone just touch me without fearing me in some way, except for my mother and William."

"Ye mean ye've never had a friend?" Brodrick asked.

Serena shook her head and walked over to the fire. "My tribe has always seen me as strange. I'm pretty certain they're glad I'm gone." She kept the self-pity out of her voice. Serena despised self-pity in others. It was so useless, did nothing to alter their circumstances.

She heard the tread of their boots as they walked over. Hands on her arms turned her around into a bear-like embrace. She knew it was Brodrick even before she looked up. "Well I'm yer friend, lass. Ye've already saved Lachlan and Keenan from the Campbell, and ye've already saved us here in England. Of course, I trust ye."

Not to be outdone, Gavin's large hands on her shoulders pulled Serena around and into his chest. He was big too, but with wiry muscles. "Touch my skin and tell for yerself, Serena. I'm yer friend too." His hug was awkward, but Serena felt his sincerity. She laughed into his barrel chest.

"Do ye not believe me?" Gavin said. "Touch my bare skin."

"Touch ye! What in bloody hell is going on in here!" Keenan's voice was punctuated by the door ricocheting off the wall. It cut through the pleasant waves of trust coming from the two Maclean warriors. Gavin dropped his arms and jumped back from Serena, which nearly knocked her down with the sudden absence of physical support.

"What the hell are ye asking her to do?" Keenan stopped and moved his hand about, "I ordered ye to guard her, not touch her!"

Keenan strode directly toward her, Gavin and Brodrick jumping out of the way. Serena sucked in when he bent, scooping her up. He carried her past an open-mouthed Thomas who stood in the doorway and lowered her back into the bed.

"I didn't mean for her to touch me *that* way," Gavin said.

"'Twas a game," Brodrick said.

"She read that Brodrick was a friend," Gavin said, his words blurting out in rapid fire. "I was just showing her I wanted to be friendly."

Brodrick hit Gavin's arm. "I mean," Gavin said while rubbing his abused arm, "be her friend, just a friend, not *friendly*. Not that way."

"Nothing untoward was going on, Keenan," she said cutting through the noise.

"Friends, huh," Keenan grumbled and kept his glare on his two warriors. Serena held back her smile because they looked like two boys swearing they hadn't stolen a pie from the windowsill.

"While the two of ye were hugging Serena," Thomas said, "Keenan was weaving one hell of a believable lie about his hatred for the Bonnie Prince." All eyes turned to Thomas. "Keenan even said that he had been about to kill Gerard himself when he found him dead."

"What about the letter?" Gavin asked.

"The King asked Keenan if a letter had been found on Gerard and Keenan said that Gerard had bragged about it, which was how Keenan discovered that Gerard was a Jacobite. But after Keenan found Gerard dead, there hadn't been anything in his pockets," Thomas said, a cockeyed grin on his thin lips. "'Twas brilliant."

Keenan's weight sank into the soft tick, making Serena roll into him. "It gave me a plausible way of discovering Gerard's loyalties, and it was partly the truth so the true murderers and King George will think I'm not lying."

"And then," Thomas joined in, "King George said that the letter had been retrieved."

"So it still exists?" Brodrick looked hopeful, and Thomas nodded.

Serena climbed back out of the Keenan-induced gully in the soft bed. "The king admitted that William hadn't killed Gerard?"

Keenan shook his head slightly and looked down. "When I suggested that someone else may have killed Gerard for the letter, Frampton joined in to say that someone may have taken it from Gerard's pocket after the Romany man had killed him for his purse."

Disappointment stabbed through Serena. "Bloody hell," she murmured.

"We're not done here yet, Serena," Brodrick said, his gaze on her.

"Aye," Gavin joined in. "Once we identify the true murderers, perhaps they will admit it."

Serena tried to roll past Keenan to rise, but he wouldn't move. "Why?" she said with annoyance at him. "Why would they when they know the king protects them? William is the perfect innocent to blame."

Rap. Rap.

They all turned to look at the door. Keenan nodded to Thomas who opened it.

A young maid, her brown hair stuffed under a cap, gasped. Eyes going wide, she took in all the men. "Lady Frampton sent me to check in on you, milady. She said you fainted below."

"I'm well. Thank you. Master Keenan was just asking his men to find me an apothecary for some lemon balm tea."

"Oh, Cook has some of that down in the kitchens," she said and waved the men to follow her.

"Go on," Keenan told them, and they filed out the door after the maid, all the while glancing back over their shoulders. Thomas's eyes were suspicious, Gavin looked full of questions, and Brodrick gave Serena a slight nod.

The door closed, and Keenan stood, which allowed her to finally make her way out of the bed. To protect his apparently delicate sensibilities, she lifted her bodice a bit.

"Serena."

She looked up and caught his frown. "Winifred says 'tis the bloody fashion, Keenan."

He waved off her words. "About William."

The anger in her face receded to worry, and he continued. "We will do what we can to save William."

"You have a plan?" Hope sprouted within her.

Keenan nodded. "We'll find the letter, and we'll try to get the murderers to admit their foul play."

She exhaled in frustration. "It won't matter if they admit it. The king commanded it."

Keenan smirked slightly. "He may have commanded it behind closed doors, but if they admit it in public, the king won't support them."

"And what possibly could make them admit such a thing when doing so would mean abandonment by their society and possible imprisonment?"

Keenan shrugged. "Perhaps we can convince them that it would benefit them to show publicly that they are willing to commit murder to help the king's cause?"

A snapping in the fire sparked fiercely, pulling her gaze.

"What the bloody hell?" Keenan said and strode forward, picking up the poker.

The sparks became a familiar voice. "What a stupid plan." Drakkina, the witch from the cave, stepped from the hot air in the hearth. Serena sucked in a breath at the wild tingling along her birthmark and rubbed a hand over her navel.

Keenan dropped the poker and drew a dirk from his jacket.

"Put that away, Keenan Maclean," Drakkina said. "You can't stab me. I'm but made of air."

"You can see her?" Serena asked.

"Aye," he said guardedly while lowering the dirk to his side. "Is she the one who visited ye in the cave?"

Both of them faced the spirit. "Yes," Serena said.

"What do ye want, ghost?" Keenan asked.

She winked one sharp blue eye at him. "You may call me Drakkina, Priestess, or Master if you prefer." She smiled a small mouthful of perfect white teeth. "Although I don't think you have it in you to call anyone master, Keenan Maclean, warrior chief of Kilchurn."

"I'm not the chief of Kilchurn."

"No? Who controls the honed army of warriors from Kilchurn? Lachlan?" She laughed darkly. "I think even with your head clouded by duty, you still see that they follow you, not him."

"Why are you here?" Serena asked, her tone sharp. She didn't trust the dragonfly witch.

"Ah Serena, are you angry with me?" Drakkina asked softly.

Just kiss him. All will fall into place. "You know the answers before I speak them."

Drakkina inclined her head. "I concede the point, young Wiccan." She turned to look pointedly at Keenan. "To answer the tumbling questions behind that blank façade of yours, I did tell her to kiss you, but she responded to your touch out of love for you, not out of duty or purpose."

"Drakkina," Serena said, but the old woman held up a hand to silence her.

"She loves you even if she hasn't identified it yet. And if you'd set aside your imprecise perceptions of what is right and wrong, then you'd realize you love her, too."

She looked between them and frowned. "You are both bumbling fools in your ignorance." She sighed deeply and then waved her hands in dismissal.

"Did ye come to tell us this?" Keenan asked and glanced at Serena.

"Not mostly," Drakkina answered. "I've come to help." She smiled cryptically.

"Help?" Keenan asked dryly.

"First, I wanted to introduce myself to you, Keenan Maclean. And then I will help."

"With what?" Serena's hand crept up the back of Keenan until she had a piece of his rich jacket twisting in her hand.

Drakkina shrugged. "Where I can. Help to find the letter, help to clear your Romany brother's name."

"You can clear William's name?" Serena asked.

"Thank ye, but we don't need yer help," Keenan said at the same time.

Drakkina snorted. "We'll see," she said as her body began to mist away like a wisp of woodsmoke swirled by a light breeze.

CHAPTER NINETEEN
LUCK OR A TRAP?

A light reel moved the courtly dancers about the ballroom as Keenan and Serena stepped under the arched entry flanked by Thomas and Brodrick. Although the spirited notes cast a guileless mood amidst the dainty smiles and appreciative glances between guests, Keenan knew the minds behind the façades often slithered with deception and darkness. He must keep people from touching Serena's bare skin.

Keenan steered them toward the king. "He commanded I bring ye over when ye returned." He'd barely been able to keep the growl out of his voice. "Keep the shawl that the maid found ye in place." At least her gloves nearly reached her elbows.

"You're back on your feet," George said in response to Serena's curtsey. "Good, good. Lady Serena, please rise. I would not be responsible for a repeated fainting spell."

Serena straightened. "Pray, please excuse my earlier fragility. It has been a long journey and the excitement of meeting Your Majesty was too much for me." She spoke with authenticity.

Keenan mentally added actor to Serena's list of attributes.

"You do seem frail, dear," Elizabeth Darlington drawled out. "Those Highland winters just might do you in."

Olivia Frampton tittered nervously and took Serena's forearm. "I'm sure you'll fare quite well up north, Lady Serena. The court can be quite overwhelming when one hasn't been raised within it. Take a turn with me," Olivia said indicating the perimeter of the room. "Tell me about your upbringing. I hear you hail from York?"

Keenan watched them weave a path through the gossipy courtiers, hoping Serena would remember her contrived background.

"I say, she's quite a lovely woman," King George said.

"'Twas what first caught my eye."

"And now that you've handfasted with her, will you truly follow up with a church wedding or has your lust been sated enough that you'll abandon her?" George glanced at Keenan. "I understand that you can leave a handfasted woman after a year and a day if you're not satisfied with her. What a wonderfully barbaric custom."

Frampton hovered nearby, chuckling. The condescending snorts raked against Keenan's temper, making the muscles in his arms bunch. Years of practice hiding his emotions kept his tone level. "We will have the clergy bless the union upon return to Kilchurn."

George's gaze followed Serena.

"Serena is under my protection," Keenan continued, "and I gladly give her the Maclean name. We're tied together until death."

George smiled slyly. "With God's protection that will last longer than the year."

"And a day," Frampton added.

George laughed with gusto.

"I hear there are a number of Scottish clans bending their support to yer highness," Keenan said and took a drink from his wine glass.

George sighed. "Let's talk of lighter things this eve, Maclean. You have a beautiful woman soon to be on your arm again. The food and spirits are a delight."

Frampton puffed up on the compliment.

"Let us talk of Jacobite plots on the morrow and leave tonight open for delights." George smiled at Elizabeth as she moved against his side and linked her arm in his.

Olivia brought Serena back around and Keenan took her arm. "Perhaps we will talk on the morrow," Keenan said. "'Tis only that we cannot tarry long here in Leicester."

"Oh?" George cocked his brow.

"We have vows to say." Keenan pulled Serena within the confines of his frame, trying to discern if she felt weak from her walk amongst the throng.

Benjamin Frampton moved his arms about, showing off his grand ballroom. "We can easily procure a priest and have a grand celebration right here."

Keenan felt Serena's body stiffen although she kept her smile. "We appreciate the generous offer," he said, "but must decline."

Olivia pouted while Elizabeth delivered a look of skeptical elation. She tapped her fan shut with a click.

Keenan kept his gaze on King George. "I've failed yet to present my wife to my brother and chief, Lachlan. As it is, I shouldn't have handfasted without speaking my intent with him first. I wouldn't show further disrespect by wedding officially without his knowledge and consent."

The king raised an eyebrow as if he would argue, but Keenan continued with ease. "I would also appreciate the opportunity to give Lachlan one more chance to join ye in yer quest to unite Britain before

I take his place as chief." He shrugged slightly and tucked Serena's hand in his arm. "After all, he is my brother."

George pursed his pudgy lips. "He has a strong argument, Lady Olivia," he said to the sulking woman across from him.

Olivia's pout broadened into a smile. "Then I will gift you with a wedding costume," she said to Serena.

"Your generosity is too much," Serena murmured.

Olivia waved her free hand. "'Twill be my pleasure. We will clothe you as befitting a friend of the royal court."

Serena nodded and curtsied. "Your graciousness, Lady Frampton, is without bounds. I thank you."

"I'll come with my seamstresses to your room on the morrow," Olivia said.

"At the inn?" Serena asked.

"Heavens, no. You and your Highland chief will stay in your room here at Frampton Manor. I'm sure the King would want you close."

Keenan squeezed her to him. "Don't fret, wife. I had our bags brought to our room." The thought of sharing a room with Serena made his blood flow swiftly, the feel of her skin making his hand tingle. He squeezed it into a tight fist as the bell rang, announcing dinner.

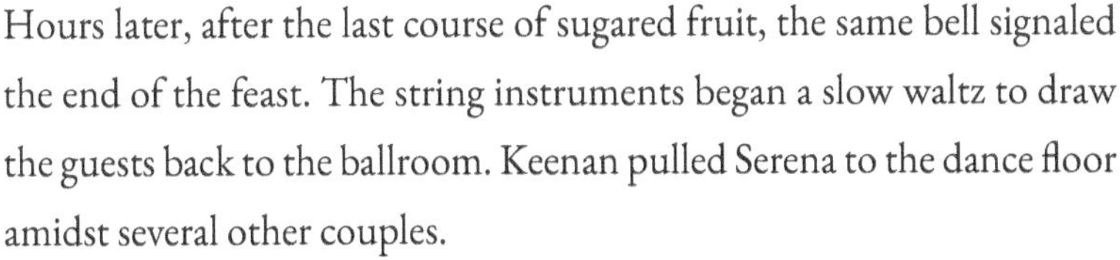

Hours later, after the last course of sugared fruit, the same bell signaled the end of the feast. The string instruments began a slow waltz to draw the guests back to the ballroom. Keenan pulled Serena to the dance floor amidst several other couples.

He bent low to her ear as his hand slid around her waist. The unconcerned touch sent a fluttery sensation through her. "Do ye know the steps, lass?"

"I've been dancing a long time, and not just around a campfire."

Keenan frowned slightly. "But this dance is a bit," he paused, "intimate. Ye've danced it before?"

"I think William would purge his supper if you told him that this dance is intimate, since he was the only man who would dare touch me."

Keenan whisked her into a turn and her dress flared out to the side. Keenan said nothing through several rounds, even though he frowned down at her low decolletage.

As they stepped together once more at the end of one round, Keenan lowered his voice. "Those who were too afraid to touch ye, they were cowards." He shook his head once, a slight movement almost unperceivable. "But I'm glad they never felt the silk in yer hair or the movement of yer form against their bodies." He slid his hand along her waist.

Serena took several shallow breaths without breaking the contact between them. Her heart danced wildly inside causing her chest to swell upwards with each inhale. Keenan glanced down to check her neckline and then back up to her face. Eyes fiercely intense, his tongue touched his bottom lip causing a flush of heat to surge through her. Keenan's thumb grazed her jaw.

"Keenan," Brodrick stepped to their side, shattering the moment. Brodrick spoke close to Keenan's ear. She couldn't hear his words, but she could certainly hear Brodrick's thoughts. *Ewan learned that George keeps his letters in Frampton's study off the library on the east side of the manor.*

Keenan took her arm, and they briskly followed Brodrick off the dance floor. She scanned the room and sucked in her breath so quickly she coughed. "That's them," she whispered, her gaze caught on a couple before the king. "The ones laughing with the king right now. Wearing scarlet."

"Gerard's murderers?" Brodrick asked.

"Ye're certain?" Keenan asked at the same time.

She nodded. "Their faces have haunted me since the faire."

"His name is Cumberland," Keenan said. "Reginald Cumberland." He inhaled. "Let's find the library." Keenan placed Serena back on his arm. "Brodrick, let the others know we might leave swiftly." Brodrick hurried off, and Keenan led her onto the balcony.

"But then we won't be able to make the true murderers confess," Serena pointed out.

Keenan turned to her. "Trust me. I've sworn to help William."

How could she trust him when she couldn't read his thoughts, his emotions?

"Keenan—"

"We're going to the library," he said, sweeping her down to reenter the hall through the far entrance. Several potted trees hid them, and they walked slowly out of the ballroom and down the empty corridor.

"I managed to obtain the plans to this manor." Keenan stopped before the third closed door and pressed the latch. "Locked." He withdrew a ring with three varying keys from a pocket under his plaid. "And keys to all the doors in this house if my contact is to be trusted."

Glancing over her shoulder, she watched the corridor while he worked the keys, gently inserting and turning them until one clicked, and the door swung open. The tang of ink and old pages enveloped the room. Rows of aged tomes were shelved neatly in the glow of a small fire. The door clicked as Keenan shut it behind them. He lit a taper from the small fire in the hearth, and they walked silently through the room to another door in the back corner.

"Is there anyone in there?" Keenan asked.

Serena focused her power through the door but heard nothing. She shook her head.

This door wasn't locked, and they slipped inside. Another hearth fire chased shadows around the snug study. Two windows flanked the massive cherrywood desk. A map of Britain lay unrolled on a second table in the light of the fire. Keenan moved over to it, studying the lines and numbers.

Serena took his taper and padded to the desk. Several piles of papers sat along its perimeter. One semi-rolled letter was placed before the chair as if someone had left it half read. She scanned it quickly down to the signature. George's elegant script marked the bottom.

Mari had taught Serena to read in Romany. Serena had taught herself some English, but George's handwriting was long and fluid, more beautiful than informative.

"Keenan." Her whisper carried in the still room. "There's a letter here from George. I can't make out his handwriting, but it has the feel of something important."

Keenan moved with stealth and tipped her taper closer to the letter. "This is it, the letter outlining his plans to gift land in Scotland to his English Barons." He met her gaze and smiled broadly. "We've found it." His look was pure victory, a man proud of solving a difficult problem.

But then his face darkened in a hundred little ways: his jaw hardened, and little lines furrowed across his forehead. "'Tis too effortless." His words tickled a path down the back of Serena's neck. Keenan peered around the room, into dark corners. "This whole thing," he said. "It was too simple to find. It doesn't feel right."

"The outer door was locked," she whispered.

"An easy lock, and this room was unlocked with fires lit and evidence sitting out in the open. George is more paranoid."

A loud voice from the outer room threw Serena's heart into her throat. "'Tis the king and others," she whispered, feeling the triumph in their thoughts. "'Tis a trap."

Keenan pulled her into his arms, and she gasped. As the study door opened, Keenan's lips descended upon hers. Firmness and purpose, fear and excitement melted together into a rapid pounding of heat flooding through her.

"Aha, we've found Maclean."

Serena clung to Keenan's massive shoulders as he pillaged her mouth. The heat and reined-in power behind the kiss melted all her resolve.

"He's not alone," a woman said.

Serena stiffened and threaded her power toward her. It was the woman from the bridge. Her name was Matilda, and she'd wed Reginald Cumberland last spring in an exorbitant affair.

Keenan pulled back slowly and smoothed Serena's cascading curls along her collarbone. He seemed to be taking all the time in the world. The touch raced through her, battling against the shock of seeing five pairs of eyes on them at the doorway, one pair belonging to the king.

"Pardon us, Your Majesty," Keenan drawled. "We found this cozy room tucked away and succumbed to a quick dalliance."

"You were given a room for that, Maclean," Frampton said sharply. "And the library was locked."

Keenan's brow raised. "Not when I tried it. Ye should have better security when the king is in residence, Frampton."

George stopped before them. Frampton, Gerard's murderers, and Elizabeth Darlington followed him into the small room.

"Just found this study to sate your lust a bit?" George asked. Before Serena could warn Keenan, the king yanked aside Keenan's coat and pulled the rolled scroll from a side pocket.

Serena felt shock, elation, and anger from the onlookers.

"Did this just happen to fall into your coat while you were frolicking?" George unrolled the letter, but he already knew what it was.

"The letter, aye, I saw it just sitting on yer desk," Keenan said calmly. "Where anyone could have taken it." He glowered at Frampton.

"Once again, the outer door was locked," Lord Frampton said, the annoyance within him evident in his voice.

Keenan stared at him until Frampton squirmed, and Keenan turned to the king. "Like I said, someone had already gotten through the lock."

"And you thought you'd help yourself to it," Reginald Cumberland said, his voice the one from Serena's nightmares. Her hands fisted, and she stifled her desire to run at him with punches flying.

Keenan turned back to stare at the man. "Thievery is not one of my vices. Is it one of yers?"

"I'm no thief, and you seem to have been caught red-handed," Cumberland said with conviction. The tension saturated the room and seemed to suck at the momentum of time itself.

Serena kept her protective wall in place, but waves of emotion pushed against it.

"Aye," Keenan admitted easily. "I was coming to destroy the very thing that could rally the Jacobites." Keenan pulled the letter back out of George's hand and strode to the fire.

"What are you doing?" Frampton yelled.

Keenan tossed the parchment into the flames. The fire caught the brittle roll, and long shadows flickered as the fire gorged on the sudden fuel.

He turned back to the stunned audience. "The letter outlining yer plans, Your Highness, would incite the Jacobite army." Keenan shook his head. "The existence of such a letter could be disaster to Yer Majesty's campaign."

Everyone stood still, watching the parchment blacken and shrivel.

Elizabeth was the first to break into the stillness. "I'd say that proves Keenan Maclean is loyal to you, Sire. He just destroyed the very letter a Jacobite could use to incite all of Scotland."

Keenan looked at the king. "Ye think me a Jacobite, Your Highness?"

"I wonder," George answered.

"Your brother is a supporter of the Stuart prince." Frampton said.

"He's never met the lustful upstart," Keenan said. "Untried and unfit to rule anything." There was conviction in his words.

George chuckled low. "I suppose you've escaped the dungeons for now, Maclean."

The dragonfly birthmark on Serena's belly began to warm, and her gaze flicked about the room. It was the same sensation as in the bedchamber earlier. George spoke more with Keenan, but Serena's gaze became transfixed on a misty haze expanding in the corner. Drakkina glided along the floor toward the Duke's wife.

What are you doing? Serena thought.

I'm helping. Serena heard Drakkina's voice clearly in her mind. *Holy Mother Mary!* Serena held her breath while Lady Cumberland spoke quietly to Elizabeth. The men stared at the unrolled map.

Drakkina's cloud-like body hovered next to Cumberland's wife. Drakkina looked at Serena and winked just before the dry mist of her body melted into Lady Cumberland.

The pain in her chest reminded Serena to suck in a breath, and she reached out a thin thread to the woman's mind. Serena instantly felt a tightness throughout Matilda Cumberland, a stunned consciousness shoved aside and muted as if someone literally held her tongue. Serena blinked several times as Drakkina's pale eyes stared out from behind Lady Cumberland's dark orbs. Drakkina had completely invaded the woman.

"I must say," Lady Cumberland's voice filled the room. It was the woman's own voice, but unnatural power pulsed behind the words. "I must say that it is wonderful to be surrounded by those loyal to the crown. The Earl and I are just as loyal to the king as you and your husband are."

"Are you?" Serena said, not sure what else to say. Cumberland looked curiously over his shoulder toward his young wife.

The woman flapped her fan as if hot and smiled wickedly at Serena. "Yes, Reginald is so loyal, Lady Serena, that he paid a local peasant to gut that bastard Jacobite, Gerard Grant."

CHAPTER TWENTY
TWO SOULS, ONE BODY

Everyone turned toward the woman.

Reginald Cumberland's lips tightened into a grim line while Frampton's mouth jerked open in amazement like a trout suffocating on land.

Keenan was the first to speak. "Did ye just say that yer husband, Lord Reginald Cumberland, had Gerard Grant killed out of loyalty to the crown?"

"I certainly did," Matilda said, boasting. "Then we took the king's stolen letter out of his pocket. We were both there to make sure the letter didn't move north into enemy hands." She placed her palm over her heart and bowed her head in a rather disjointed fashion toward the king. "We are proud to serve the court."

"I never ordered such an act," King George said, his words full of bluster. "Gerard Grant was well connected with influential contacts."

"Of course you didn't," Elizabeth Darlington said, patting his arm.

"Of course not," Benjamin Frampton agreed.

Reginald Cumberland turned such a dark shade of purple that Serena wondered if he would have an attack and fall on the floor in convulsions.

"Therefore, the young Romany man, William Faw, didn't commit the crime?" Keenan said, his brows bent as he studied the courtly woman.

Matilda Cumberland clasped her hands in front of her and looked remorseful. "No," she shook her head. "No, the Romany man came upon us while we paid the assassin. My darling Reginald reacted without thinking. I'm afraid he shot the boy."

"The Earl of Cumberland shot an innocent man?" Frampton asked.

Matilda nodded, the feathers in her turban bobbing.

"That will be enough, Matilda!" Cumberland shouted, causing Serena to jump at the impact. The man's panic flew through the air like an arrow, piercing her wall. Serena took two steadying breaths. What would this man do to his wife once Drakkina left her?

"He was a dirty Rom," Cumberland said with a sneer. "He was most likely going to rob us anyway. I shot him in self-defense."

Serena's mouth opened as a nauseating sweep of anger washed through her belly up into her chest. Her eyes were drawn to Keenan's. He stood staring at her, his eyes seeming to will her silence. Serena swallowed down her fury and shut her mouth even as she shouted curses in her head.

Keenan turned back toward Cumberland. "Roma or not, William Faw did not stab Gerard Grant."

"Correct," Matilda called from her place by the gaping and furiously fanning Elizabeth.

"Keep your silence, woman," Cumberland ground out between his pristine, evenly spaced teeth.

King George looked at Keenan. "You knew this William Faw?"

"I traded with the leader of his tribe who is his father. The lad is on the run since he's been wrongly accused of the crime."

"We must do something about that," Matilda said and looked expectantly at her husband. "Or the Romany people might rise up against our great king too."

"Matilda, stop speaking," Cumberland's words sliced across the room.

Serena kept her voice even. "We live in a civilized time where people cannot just go around killing without consequence."

"Very right, milady," King George said and looked to Frampton. "Have word sent to Leeds and surrounding townships that William Faw is cleared of the murder of Gerard Grant. Neither he nor his relations shall be held accountable." King George regarded Keenan. "Do you know his whereabouts?"

"I can carry a letter of innocence to his family," Keenan said. "They may know his whereabouts if he still lives."

The king nodded. "That should take care of this mess then."

Serena couldn't contain her bubble of anger. "And the punishment for Lord Cumberland, for shooting and nearly killing an innocent boy?"

Silence filled the room, but Serena could barely hear it with the emotional noise bombarding her defenses. Suspicion, hatred, unveiled bigotry.

King George cleared his throat. "First, I would like to commend Lady Cumberland for bringing up this injustice. It showed amazing courage. Second, I would say that I appreciate Lord Cumberland's concern over Gerard Grant's betrayal and his courage to act on it." The lady curtsied and Cumberland bowed.

King George turned to Serena. "Cumberland shot William Faw in defense of an attack, imagined or real." The king looked back at Cumberland. "I suggest that you be much more careful in the future."

"I heed your council, Sire," the earl replied smugly. Serena nearly bit her tongue.

King George continued. "However, a man's life has likely been lost and he and his family have lived in fear for these past weeks. I believe you owe them a recompense of two hundred pounds, to be paid to Keenan Maclean to take to the family."

"Two hundred?" Cumberland asked in a flat tone. "I don't have that with me."

"I will loan you the amount. Maclean will be leaving soon," George said. "Does that satisfy Lady Serena?"

The amount was huge and would be celebrated. But was it enough to pay for a man's life? No. But Serena knew the answer that was required. "Yes, Your Majesty. Quite a generous settlement for the injury and accusation." She curtsied and inclined her head.

King George clapped his hands twice, the sound echoing in the room. "Good then, let us go back to the reception. Lord Cumberland, be sure to speak with Lord Frampton on the morrow to arrange your payments to me."

Cumberland didn't say anything but nodded and stalked over to take his wife's arm. Serena watched with fascinated horror as a dry mist wafted its way out of Matilda Cumberland's body. The woman lost her stride and nearly collapsed.

"Oh my, what's happened to me?"

"You've lost your bloody mind," Serena heard Cumberland say with an obvious sneer. Louder he said, "I think 'tis time for you to retire for the evening."

"Yes, yes, I think that might be best," she said simply and let him draw her out of the room. "I feel as if I've been holding my breath." She patted her chest and coughed a bit.

Serena looked at the thin vapor of Drakkina and willed her concern to the crone about Matilda Cumberland's welfare. Drakkina sighed, rolling her eyes, but then she nodded and disappeared.

Keenan took Serena's hand and placed it on his arm. His warm words brushed against her ear as he leaned in. "Ye frown? Everything has worked its way out."

Serena kept her eyes forward and whispered. "Not on its own."

Keenan's breath left her ear as he looked around the room. "The witch? She's here?"

"Not anymore."

It was several hours more of standing, curtseying, and dancing before Serena and Keenan were allowed to leave the ballroom. As they walked across the threshold of their room with Brodrick, Thomas, and Gavin in tow, Serena let out a groan. She yanked off her torturous shoes and dropped them to thud on the floor.

Serena pointed at the offending articles. "Try dancing and walking in those for hours and see if you don't throw them in the fire." She tried to reach her aching foot but couldn't find it under the layers of petticoats.

Brodrick picked one up, examining it. "My shoes are pointy and too tight, but not this tight."

Gavin took it from him, lifting his own foot to measure it by. "Way too tight."

"'Tis a lady's shoe," Thomas said with a sniff. "Of course, it would be too tight for your loaf-like foot."

"Loaf-like? Like a bread loaf?" Gavin asked.

Keenan interrupted. "Find warm beds or bed down in the stables with Ewan," Keenan said.

Gavin chuckled. "Last I saw, Ewan had found a kitchen maid with hair the color of midnight to bed down with."

"And ye will be sleeping where?" Thomas asked Keenan with his usual dose of suspicion. Serena imagined him as a hunched, gray-haired chaperone, ready to swing his walking stick to knock two lovers apart.

"I need to stay in the room for a while so it looks like we're truly handfasted. I'll join ye soon or if the corridor is watched, I'll bunk down near the fire."

The three Macleans shuffled out the door with murmured wishes for good sleep.

The door shut, and Keenan lowered a bracing bar, not trusting the key lock in the door. He walked to the fire to add more kindling. His footsteps clipped over to the bed, and he sat down on the soft tick making Serena roll toward the gully.

"Is she here now?" Keenan's deep timbre pulled tightly at Serena's stomach, making it flip with his nearness.

"The spirit woman?" she asked, pushing herself out of the crater of the bed.

"Aye. Ye said she was in the study, but I couldn't see her."

Serena looked around the room. "I don't sense Drakkina here. Invading Matilda Cumberland's body and making her talk weakened her."

"Drakkina confessed to the murder."

Serena nodded and scooted back into a sitting position against the headboard, which brought her battered feet against Keenan's thigh. "I only hope she helps Matilda now that the woman will have to deal with Cumberland's wrath."

"But the crone isn't here now, ye're sure?"

Serena looked around again, and even reached out a bit with her senses. "I don't feel her presence at all. I would tingle."

"Tingle?" He looked her body over as if he might see an illumination where she tingled.

Serena flushed as she moved a hand to her stomach. "I have a birthmark, strangely shaped like a dragonfly. I've noticed that it warms or tingles, almost like a rash, whenever Drakkina's around."

Keenan looked at her stomach. "I suppose we can add that to your list of oddities."

When he looked up, Serena couldn't help but grin at his serious face. "I suppose so."

"And ye say," he looked again at her stomach, "nary a bit of tingling there right now?"

Oh, there was tingling going on in Serena, but not on her birthmark. She felt heat slide under her skin. "No," she said.

Keenan picked up one of Serena's feet still clad in silky stockings.

"What are you doing?"

He rubbed her foot gently between his two large hands.

"Yer feet are sore," he answered. His knuckles stroked up the middle, giving even pressure along her instep and then to the balls of her foot. The sensations tickled, and she jerked a bit.

"Hold still, lass."

While cupping her heel in one hand, and circling it slowly, his other fingers massaged each of her toes. A cross between a sigh and a groan seeped out of Serena and she closed her eyes at the sensations of achy pleasure rolling up her leg.

"I thought you were accustomed to long nights of dancing."

Serena snorted as she relaxed back into the soft feather down pillows. "I usually dance in soft leather shoes that are flat, not those hard, pinching contraptions."

Keenan continued up her calf to her knee and then took up its abused twin.

"Mmm." Her eyes flitted back open and found Keenan studying her. Her throat clenched, preventing another breath. Serena touched the tip of her tongue to her upper lip. "So," she began and swallowed. She tried to push back up into a more upright position. "Where did you learn to rub legs like this?"

Keenan looked down at his hands. "Mostly on mares after long rides."

"So I'm like a tired mare?" she asked. "Shall I neigh?"

Keenan's grin broke into a full smile. It reached his eyes, making their gray depths sparkle. "I also rubbed Eleanor's feet and calves. They would get sore from chasing after me as a lad."

"You made mischief?" Serena said, trying to keep her moan inside as he rubbed.

"I had an abundance of energy. 'Twas Eleanor's job to follow me."

"Had you no nanny?"

"Nay, the woman responsible for watching us had to keep a constant eye on Lachlan, so nothing would befall him."

"Oh," Serena said, her smile going flat. "And your parents?"

Keenan bent forward to run the flat of his hand up her shin. "They didn't have time to watch after me."

"They ordered Eleanor to do it?" Serena asked.

"She volunteered." His mouth softened. "She raised me, really. Taught me the ways of my world, about the prophecy."

Serena watched him, his head bowed slightly as he worked. "No one else told you about it?"

"Nay, they left it to her. And I wanted to understand why I was treated differently from Lachlan."

"How were you treated differently?"

Keenan stopped rubbing her legs and moved up close to where she sat. He circled his finger in the air. "Turn around and I will endeavor to pull the ribbons and pins from your hair, else ye may never sleep." Serena let her breath out and turned around in the heavy court dress.

With her back to him, Serena could feel his gentle tugs as he began to undo Winifred's beautiful weave. The touch of his fingers in her hair sent chills along Serena's nape. As each curl came down around her waist, he ran his fingers from her scalp to the end to relax the bound curls.

"Once when Lachlan was sixteen, he decided that he'd had enough of playing life safe. At least for the day." His fingers trailed down her shoulders to fan out her hair. "I was nine years old and had been training with the young warriors, eager to show that I could complete my duty for my clan."

Keenan pulled a clip from the top of her head, and a mountain of hair cascaded over her back. He paused for a moment, then cleared his throat and continued.

"Lachlan just wanted to venture outside the walls of Kilchurn, having never been allowed to leave the surrounding village. I pitied his existence more so than mine. His shackles were obvious even to a nine-year-old. So I helped him."

Keenan reached up under her hair and sieved his fingers through the waves to her scalp. She could feel the pins letting go, dropping on the blanket.

"I helped him sneak past the guards, and we ran to the loch. I didn't know that he couldn't swim. I was seven years younger, but I could." Keenan's fingers left her hair, and Serena turned to watch him speak. His features were stiff. "At nine I wasn't as big as he, but I still managed to pull him to shore, thrashing and wailing."

"Brodrick's father found us stretched out in the mud like fish and gave us a ride back to Kilchurn." Keenan didn't say anything for several long moments.

"What happened when you returned?" she whispered.

Keenan stood up from the bed and paced toward the fire. "Lachlan was scolded and sent to bed. A guard followed him for some time after that."

"And you?"

"I was flogged and sent to heal in the stables."

His words were devoid of emotion, no self-pity, no resentment, just words.

"Eleanor tended me and as ye see, I recovered."

"On the outside."

Keenan's large shoulders shrugged. "I learned much that day. I learned my place in the world, the rules of my existence. I learned how lucky I am to have Eleanor."

Serena crossed her arms before her and watched the man prowling through the small room. "This prophecy chained Lachlan to Kilchurn and forced you out to defend yourself and the clan against the world."

A muted sadness dulled his gaze when he looked at her. "It certainly affected our lives."

"Cursed your lives."

Keenan inhaled deeply. "It seems to be dooming our Maclean line. Lachlan waits for his witch. And Eleanor has become an old maid."

"And what of you, Keenan? Will you not wed and have children?"

Keenan shook his head. "I don't want to sire children only to leave them to be raised without a father."

Serena pushed off the bed. "But you don't know when you're supposed to die. Maybe it will be when you're old and gray and ready for a natural death, Keenan."

Keenan frowned at her. "I don't wish for that."

"Why?"

"Because this life is hard enough." He bent to add dry peat to the fire. "To go on alone for so long only to realize at the end that I could have had a life, had children and watched them grow." He shook his head.

Serena rubbed her hands along her cheeks in frustration. "Then find a woman to love. Have children. Watch them grow and love them well."

He looked over his shoulder. "And where do I find a woman who will marry me, knowing I might die at any time?"

"We all could die at any time," she said, frowning. He must be as lonely as she. "You've cut yourself off from the world because you believe it will be soon, but you don't know that." At least she tried to interact with her tribe.

The fire sparked behind him, and he turned to kick some embers back into the hearth.

"What of ye, Serena? Will ye marry if someone asks?"

"I'm not marrying Lachlan, even if he asks," she said. Just the thought of the cowardly man touching her made her stomach churn.

"Love can come after vows are said." Keenan stared hard at her.

Her laugh came like a little choke. "Love won't come without respect."

Keenan set the poker next to the hearth and walked to her. Serena held her breath, hoping he'd pull her into his arms, but he just slid a dagger from his boot. "Sleep with it under yer pillow. I'll return before dawn, so it seems we've slept in here together."

"You're leaving?"

"Don't open the door for anyone but me or one of my men." Keenan picked up her hand and curled her fingers around the hilt of the weapon. His hands were warm and powerful, but she knew they could be gentle and teasing. A spark traveled up her arm from the touch, but then he released her.

She followed him to the door. "What if someone sees you leave?" she asked. "Would a newlywed man stray from his bride so soon?"

Keenan met her gaze. "If someone is about, I'll return."

He turned, but she caught his forearm. It tensed under her hand. "Keenan, I want you to stay."

"Did the witch ask ye to—"

"No." The word slammed out of her. "No," she repeated softer. "I want you to stay. Just me."

He exhaled, his face serious with regret, and Serena's stomach clenched with his obvious answer. His words were low. "Honor is all I have to hold onto in this world, Serena. I can't jeopardize it no matter how tempted I might be." With that he slipped from her grasp and out the door.

CHAPTER TWENTY-ONE
SKIN PALE AS MOONLIGHT

Keenan stood in the dim corridor and willed his blood to slow and his cock to relax to no avail. If she wasn't meant for Lachlan, he'd have kissed her again, touched her again. He flexed his hand as if feeling the silkiness of her hair. Serena smelled of some sweet spice, and her body was made of rolling hills and valleys, warm and inviting.

She knew he might die and didn't seem to care. He would ask her...what? Can I kiss you, lass? Can I kiss every inch of your gloriously fragrant skin? Can I touch you until you thrash and beg for me to thrust into your wet, hot channel? Before he knew it, he'd turned back to the door.

Someone cleared their throat, and Keenan whirled to see Thomas's face in the shadows around the far corner. *Bloody hell.*

"Leaving your young bride so soon," a voice came from the other direction, and Thomas's face disappeared. Keenan turned to find

Benjamin Frampton walking toward him with a glass-globed candle in hand.

"She but needs a drink of sweet wine from the kitchens," Keenan answered smoothly and walked away from the door.

"I'll show you the way, Maclean. My manor house can be quite the labyrinth."

Keenan shortened his step to match the smaller man even though he'd rather stride ahead, leaving him in the shadows. "I'm surprised to find ye still roaming yer halls, Frampton. 'Tis the dead of night."

"One learns more about one's occupants in the dead of night than during the brightness of day." The wily man smiled knowingly at Keenan.

Keenan forced his well-practiced, non-caring smile. "Like the fact that my timid wife needs some wine to relax before a night with her rather new husband."

Frampton laughed quietly and nodded. "Perhaps. But I will keep that in confidence. Wouldn't want to embarrass the lady."

Keenan inclined his head in gratitude. They continued to the kitchen in mild conversation about the success of the reception. Frampton didn't bring up any of King George's plans, and Keenan was in no mood to play spy after his near escape from Serena's chambers. Unfortunately, Frampton continued to follow Keenan back from the kitchens.

As they rounded a bend in the stone corridor, Keenan thought he saw a movement ahead. No doubt Thomas was still there.

"I think I can make it on my own," Keenan said before Serena's door.

"Of course, good eve to you," Frampton said and bowed before rotating on his heel. Keenan watched him turn the corner. Did Frampton wait there in the dark listening for him to enter the room? Keenan had no doubt that the man would love to report to King George that the lady Serena was being neglected by her husband. The royal letch would probably visit her during the night.

That thought twisted in his mind and he pressed against the door. It slid open effortlessly. Daingead! She hadn't barred it.

Keenan stepped into the dim room lit only by the hearth fire. A fresh breeze blew in from an open window as the door clicked closed quietly behind him. Serena hadn't even heard him coming in? Anger licked up inside him, but he kept quiet when he saw her pet bird fluttering on the ledge of the window.

"Thank you, Chiriklò for pulling the laces in the back." Serena's remark was muffled because her face was covered with the white fabric of her shift as she pulled it up over her head. She stood before the fire. "What?" Serena gasped as her head came out of the fabric. She spun around, yanking the ball of linen before her. The blue bird flew off the ledge out into the night.

Serena stood facing him, completely naked but clutching the shift before her. Her hair hung down nearly to her hips, and her long bare legs were slender. Eyes round and fingers clenched, she looked ready to follow her bird out the open window.

Keenan didn't move from his position by the door. His breath lay dormant on an inhalation. His gaze followed the landscape of her hip and the hollow at the base of her neck that he'd been trying to cover all night. But now they were alone. No other man could see the beauty under Serena's clothing.

The fire glow splashed shadows along her where her hair fell in waves, making the red tresses glow golden. *I should turn around.* But his legs were rooted to the floor.

"I didn't expect you to return."

Each breath seemed as if he pulled it from under a heavy stone. He set the wine down on the small table by the door and moved his hand below to adjust himself. Serena's eyes followed. "Ye didn't bar the door, lass. I told ye to bar the door."

"I was going to, but I didn't know if you'd return." She wet her lips, and he nearly groaned. "I was listening with my senses. Thomas was close and Lord Frampton moved off."

"But ye can't hear anything from me."

She shook her head, her shoulders finally lowering as if she relaxed. "Perhaps you should lock the door now," she whispered.

The thought of Thomas waiting around the corner evaporated from Keenan's mind when Serena's fingers opened one by one. He couldn't move, couldn't even blink as the shift she was holding tumbled down her body to the floor. There before him were the soft round globes of her breasts, lifting with her inhale. Her hips were flared and smooth skin, the pale color of moonlight, covered the gentle roundness of her abdomen, leading to the triangle of tawny curls at the crux of her long legs.

Keenan's jaw ached, and he made himself part his lips. They were so dry. He wet his bottom lip with the tip of his tongue. The pressure in his thighs told him just how hard he pushed back against the door where he stood. And his cock had risen immediately, robbing him of coherent thought. It strained to be free of the tight breeches he'd been forced to wear.

The prophecy was no more than a whisper under the deep thud of his pulse. She was exquisite with smooth skin covering supple curves. Her hair draped her shoulders, parted by her breasts, the nipples peaked.

"Do you want me, Keenan Maclean?" Her words were small in the silence, but their impact tore through him.

He wanted to devour her, run his mouth over every inch of her sweet, soft skin, teasing and tasting. His hand settled over his cock that was trying to punch a hole through the fabric. "Aye," he said. A simple word that held so much want.

She was close enough now that he could see her rapid breathing, the flush rising up her collarbone along the soft lines of her neck. Serena touched one of her breasts. Keenan groaned. Passion flared beneath her lashes. The tension in Keenan's body ripped through him as if coiling to attack, and yet he held himself back.

"I know how things work," she said. "But I've never—"

"We will not—"

"But I want to. Badly," she whispered. Her fingers trailed down her abdomen to the curls nestled between her legs, and she touched herself.

His fists clenched until his fingers ached. But he couldn't look away. Was he bespelled? Could the witch of the prophecy do that? And why to him? She was supposed to be for Lachlan, not him. How could he react with such betrayal?

She shook her head. "I won't marry him. I swear I won't."

"Can ye read my mind now?"

"No, I can see it in your face. The weight of remorse you don't need to carry," she said.

Somehow he continued to breathe as the thoughts, the justifications tangled through his mind. What if he was meant to love her before he died? And then after, she could wed Lachlan? What if he was supposed to father the next generation of Macleans through Serena before he died for his duty? Perhaps this was how the prophecy would work. Perhaps he could touch her, could love her. The hope kindled inside him, a straining flame finally released from the glass globe around it.

Keenan took a step away from the wall. Serena's breasts rose and fell on a muted gasp. She lowered her hands and focused on his gaze.

He took another step towards her, his hands releasing out of the fists he'd been clenching. Stopping before her, he inhaled the spicy sweet scent of her. He reached one open palm to skim the softness of her hair, sliding it down its length to where it fell against the curve of her hip. His hand cupped the soft bone beneath her silky skin. *Mine.* The word pierced him once again, like when he'd seen her dance before the fire.

She stepped into him, her naked body molding against his fully clothed one. His hands slid under her hair, down her back to cup her round arse. He groaned, lowering his lips to hers. Her mouth seemed to melt under his, letting him lead the kiss. A small noise came from the back of her throat, and she pressed the crux of her legs against him. His cock throbbed, and he pressed back, only the fabric of his breeches separating their hungry bodies.

His hand rose, sliding up the valley of her waist to rise over one breast. It was full, and when he thrummed the nipple, Serena groaned against his mouth. He kissed a trail along her jaw as she let her head fall back, exposing her slender neck.

At her ear, his whisper came rough and as serious as an oath. "Ye're mine, lass." The words rang through him like a claymore cracking through the ice within his chest.

Bam! Bam! Bam!

The pounding on the door made Serena stiffen, her eyes open wide. "Thomas," she hissed and flew around to the other side of the bed, dropping to the floor, as the door opened.

Keenan turned around, his dirk out in a flash ready to strike.

Thomas stood there, his eyes scanning the room. "Keenan, quickly. Ewan has taken ill in the stables. Ye need to tend him."

"Ballocks," Keenan roared. The suspicious man was obviously trying to stop whatever he thought might be going on in the room. *Fok*. Stop what *was* going on in the room.

Thomas neither advanced nor retreated, his gaze dipping to where Serena rustled with fabric on the other side of the bed. Was she trying to dress on the floor?

The man's gaze returned to Keenan. "I swear, he's sick." Thomas lowered his voice. "And this gives ye a good reason to leave yer wife if someone is listening," he said, emphasizing the improvised role.

Keenan looked over to Serena who rose tentatively from the floor, her shift back over her body, covering that soft, warm skin. Why hadn't he barred the door? But her eyes moved to Thomas, and her cheeks darkened. The man must be thinking something that distressed her.

Keenan shoved Thomas out the door. "Very well," he said, playing his role. "I will see what is wrong with Ewan although I'd much rather spend the night with my wife."

He looked at Serena. "I will return."

"Fare thee well, husband," she called. "Don't be long."

At the door, he paused, looking at her. "Bar the door as soon as I leave."

"I will," she said.

"I'll call to ye through it when I return. Don't open the door unless 'tis I."

She nodded again, and he watched her walk toward it through the crack until it closed all the way. He motioned to Thomas to wait until he heard the bar slip in place. Fire and anger warred with the beginnings of guilt inside Keenan, creating an inferno of fury. Keenan spun on his heel and headed toward the stables. Thomas kept well behind him.

Serena woke groggily from a familiar dream of a cottage surrounded by a circle of tall stones. The smell of fresh-baked bread dissipated from her mind as a tight rapping penetrated the dream-induced peace. She stretched under the heavy blanket, and a glance at the canopy above her reminded her of where she was.

The king's lecherous mind, the letter in the library, getting caught, Drakkina, and then Keenan alone with her in their bedchamber. How he'd touched her, kissed her, whispered to her. Heat and a languid ache slid from Serena's abdomen to the crux between her legs where she'd touched herself in front of him.

Rap. Rap.

"Lady Serena." The voice was insistent through the door. "Are you awake?"

Keenan hadn't returned? Because of his men?

"Who is it?" she asked as she slipped into a chamber robe left in the room by a maid the day before.

"Your hostess." Olivia Frampton laughed. "And a regiment of seamstresses."

Serena quickly pulled the bedding askew on the other side to make it look like she'd slept with a bed partner.

She ran to the door and slid the heavy bar from its holder. Olivia Frampton stood there, grandly dressed in a lovely organdy morning gown, her mousy brown hair piled high on her tiny head. Serena moved aside as the lady's four maids followed her inside with baskets of sewing supplies.

"Sleeping late?" Olivia tittered. She began to order the maids around the room. "It seems we have no time to waste, Serena," Olivia said.

"Your Highlander is eager to be on his way." She lowered her voice to a conspirator level. "I think he's anxious to present you to his brother for his blessing and marry you before God." Olivia smiled. "He wants you bound to him until death, not just a year and a day. I can see it in him when he looks at you."

The woman's sincerity made Serena smile back. Benjamin Frampton may be a pompous windbag, but his wife was genuine.

"We are to leave today then?"

She nodded vigorously while pointing to the dressing table. "Put it there, Estele." Olivia turned back to Serena. "So I've brought this gown," Olivia waved her hand towards one maid who promptly held up a nearly finished dress. "It was to be Miss Wimberley's wedding costume, but the bright blue suits your coloring more, plus 'tis almost finished. We'll just mold it to your lovely young curves, and it will be yours."

Serena was speechless. The gown of blue velvet was richly embroidered with seed pearls and gold thread. Birds flew along the bell of the skirt, and several dragonflies glittered amongst the folds.

Serena sat down numbly on the edge of the bed. "It is exquisite."

Olivia clapped her hands lightly in happiness. "Good, let's get it on you." The woman signaled two of the women to advance upon Serena with a brilliant white shift edged with lace.

They pulled her shift up and off, but before Serena could protest, they threw the new shift over her head and down over her body. Serena ran her hands along the softness of the linen.

"I had a few other womanly items to add to your wardrobe." Olivia indicated the shift. "I hope you don't mind that they were originally intended for another, but there really isn't time to outfit you from bolts of material."

Serena shook her head. "Your graciousness is overwhelming, milady." Serena's words huffed out as another maid wrapped her in stays and pulled the strings behind.

Olivia squeezed one of Serena's hands. The jolt of giddiness from the woman flipped through Serena's stomach. "Now let's have fun."

Over the course of two hours, Serena was fed, washed, prodded, and pinned while Olivia fussed happily. The flitting woman chattered away with her hoard of seamstresses, and Serena played the events of last night over until her head ached.

Keenan Maclean had stared at her naked and had claimed her as his. A flutter of nervous energy tickled inside Serena's stomach at the thought of what would have happened if only they'd been left alone, if only he had returned.

Serena frowned. Could Ewan have really been in peril? What if Keenan acted as if nothing had happened, that he'd never said the words? But he had. *Ye're mine, lass.* She could still hear it.

She thought about his hands on her skin, how he'd cupped her breasts, teasing them. How his mouth had kissed a path to her ear along her neck.

"Oh, it must be getting hot in here. Poor dear, you're flushed," Olivia said and opened the window. "Someone, break down that fire in the hearth."

Holy Mother Mary. Serena shifted so that her legs pressed against the ache between them and tried to think of mundane things like picking wildflowers or saving earthworms that had crawled out into the sun only to get too dry.

A large, shining looking glass was brought in for her to see herself. The dress fit perfectly along the contours of her breasts and waist, and then flared out in the full skirts that fell in a wide bell around her legs. Serena turned before the glass and enjoyed the swish of fabric tickling her ankles. She smiled at Olivia who still prattled happily, completely enthralled with all the details of creating her wedding costume. One she might never have the occasion to wear. King Will would probably sell it once she returned to the tribe. She didn't need something so worldly. The thought dampened Serena's smile.

"Serena, you look lovely," Olivia said, looking at the gown and not Serena's face. "I'm so happy I decided to give the blue costume to you. Your hair stands out even brighter against it." The tiny woman came up to stroke Serena's curls. "Such a brilliant shade of auburn with gold spun within it. Just beautiful. I can see why you don't powder it or wear a wig."

The four maids all nodded their agreement just before the door to the room flew open, causing all four to gasp and spin in a flurry.

"I told ye to bar this door," Keenan strode into the chaos of thread, scraps, and pins. All eyes turned to him, his towering shoulders making him a giant in the suddenly cramped room. He stopped, his eyes resting on Serena as she turned toward him.

Keenan stared, his brow relaxing. "Pardon me. I—"

"Come, Lord Maclean, this is your room after all." Olivia waved him over as the maids giggled and stepped back.

"Turn around for your Highland lord to see you," Olivia urged, and Serena turned her body away from the glass.

Serena curtseyed, and her heart thudded behind the costly fabric and pearls.

"She will make a lovely bride, don't you agree?" Olivia asked.

Serena watched Keenan, but as usual, he was a void to her. Disappointment dropped like pebbles into her chest. He didn't like it.

"Say something," Olivia teased him.

"Aye."

"Aye?" Olivia asked. "That's it." She smiled mischievously. "Why Serena, have you married a blind man?"

Keenan shook his head and nodded to Olivia. "Aye, she will make a lovely bride."

"There now," the older woman clapped her hands together. "You will want to get her properly wed before some other fine young man comes along to steal her."

His face was tight with a look that could almost be pain. Serena's brows pinched together in question, but he turned to Olivia. "I came to tell Serena that we leave within the hour."

"So soon?" Olivia asked but turned immediately to the maids and clapped her hands. We must put it all in a trunk.

His gaze returned to Serena. "We've had a report of the Faw Romany Tribe camping just north of here."

Serena's heart leaped, and tears formed in her eyes. *Duy. You are close.*

"We will visit them to give them the recompense from Cumberland and let them know that William Faw is no longer a fugitive." Keenan turned on his heel and headed for the door.

Serena found her voice. "And how is Ewan?"

Keenan stopped at the door but didn't turn around. "Bad ale perhaps. He will live."

Serena listened as his footfalls grew distant. "Blast," she whispered. Where was the man who'd rubbed her feet and stroked her hair last night? The man who'd claimed her as she stood naked and vulnerable before him? He hid everything behind a brooding frown, and she couldn't read him at all.

Frustration burned a hole inside her, and she rubbed a fist against her stomach.

CHAPTER TWENTY-TWO
CARAVAN HOMECOMING

The tangy scent of rain clung to the unfurled spring leaves as they rode along the narrow path near the Faw encampment. Serena recognized the glimpses of feelings she sensed from her people. A low level, constant awareness and unease ran through her tribe. Like all Traveling People, they worried they'd be harassed and accused when they entered a new territory.

Serena rode her mare silently in the simple gown she'd found on her bed the first morning at Kilchurn. Her pulse sped, and she tried to breathe evenly. Would they be happy about her return? Duy, yes, but not the others. She'd tell them she didn't intend to stay, that she'd promised William to return for him.

Keenan rode beside her, ignoring her like he had all morning. Serena caught him studying her once or twice, but his frown hadn't lessened, as if he was angry with her. Which spurred her own irritation.

"What ails ye, Serena?" Brodrick asked. "Ye should be happy that ye'll see yer clan soon."

Serena felt some guilt resonating from Brodrick and Gavin and a bit of victory from Thomas. Ewan did look pale, so he had been ill. From the others, though, Serena could easily conclude that Ewan's illness had not kept Keenan away all night. Rather the attitudes of his men had bound him to the stables. Had they also talked him into refusing his claim upon her? Did they even know?

She rubbed absently at the back of her head and neck. "I've come down with an ache in my head."

The sound of pots and a murmur of voices mixed with the smell of wood smoke and roasting meat. Serena's stomach rolled with the slow gait of her horse. She took a steadying breath and mentally checked her protective wall.

Keenan pulled his horse back and stopped. He motioned for his men to move on ahead and reached over to squeeze her gloved hand. His voice rolled low in the darkness.

"We've had only silence between us this day. And silence can create strife when none exists."

Keenan's face was softer than it had been before, but his eyes were still distant, devoid of the passion that had strummed through them last night.

"You didn't return," she said.

"I couldn't."

She tipped her head, wishing again she could read even his expression. "Couldn't or decided not to?"

"Keenan," Thomas called from the shadows before them.

Keenan exhaled and started moving again. They walked their horses into the firelight together, and all the normal camp noise ceased. A wildly chirping Chiriklò swooped through the camp and landed on Serena's shoulder.

"Àngelas!" Mari yelled and ran toward Serena's horse. Serena jumped down while Chiriklò flitted to a nearby branch. Mari wrapped arms around her, and the feel of motherly love and acceptance engulfed her like a warm bath. Serena breathed deeply, tears stinging as she held tightly to the shorter woman.

"You've returned, my child," Mari pulled away and touched Serena's cheek. Relief, exhilaration, and celebration raced along the contact. But there was an undercurrent of concern too.

Serena kissed her cheek. "William is alive, and well, Duy."

"Thank the Lord," Mari murmured, kissing a small cross that hung from a chain around her neck.

King Will stepped forward, a kind expression on his usually stoic face. She could feel his happiness to see her. Serena turned and smiled at the stares, ignoring the questions rolling through everyone's minds.

Where has she been?

Why is she dressed like the English?

Does danger follow her?

Where is Shoshòy?

Keenan stepped next to Serena and addressed King Will and Mari at once. "Serena has saved William Faw. He's alive and healing from his wound at Kilchurn Castle in the west of Scotland." A murmur rose within the gathered group.

"We have been to King George's court." Keenan indicated his men and Serena. "Serena risked her life to masquerade as a gentlewoman to prove William's innocence in the death of Gerard Grant." Keenan pulled out a rolled parchment and motioned Gavin to bring forth the small wooden chest off the back of his horse. Keenan unrolled the parchment and read the royal notice.

"And in conclusion, William Faw, of the Faw Romany Tribe, is held innocent in the death of Gerard Grant in the year 1746. Signed George II, King of all Britain."

Keenan handed the letter to King Will and motioned to Gavin. "The man responsible for Gerard Grant's death has been fined two hundred pounds for inflicting worry and grief on the Faw Tribe and for endangering William Faw's life and freedom." Keenan transferred the heavy chest from Gavin to King Will's arms.

Elation rippled through the people. It was hushed in the forest, but they yelled in celebration within their minds. The sum was immense and could buy new caravans to replace the oldest ones. Chickens and a second milk cow. Cloth for new clothes. The list of needs and reasons to hope swirled through the thoughts.

"Serena's courage and cleverness before the king and his court saved William and cleared his name. The Faw Tribe owes her the respect of a warrior, for she is one."

Mari squeezed her arm, and Serena blinked several times to banish the sting in her eyes. Keenan wasn't merely repaying the debt from the duke, he was fostering respect for her, respect from her tribe. Serena nearly lost the battle with tears as the first waves of pride emanated from her adopted father. She'd never sensed them before.

King Will bowed slightly to Keenan with the chest of coins clutched in his arms. "We accept this retribution and will use it to benefit the entire tribe, as William and my daughter would want."

Serena's father looked at her, and she nodded quickly. He quirked his lips into a smile showing the tips of his teeth. He'd never smiled enough to see his teeth before, at least not in her direction. Emotion swelled within her, and she rested her hand against a fast beating heart.

King Will handed the chest to Ephram, who hovered nearby and shot her a smile. King Will clapped his hands. "Let us celebrate!" A cheer rose from the tribe. "Raise the fire, raise the music." King Will looked at Serena. "Will you dance tonight, with the fire?"

Joy made it hard for her to pull in a full breath. "Yes, Papa."

Mari touched Keenan's arm. "Thank you, Highlander. I know you kept my children safe."

Keenan seemed stiff. "'Tis my duty to protect."

A bit of Serena's joy seeped away at his words. She had become his duty too as soon as he had discovered her link to the prophecy. Serena glanced at the other Macleans who'd been given drink and seasoned food. "We'll stay for a while?" she asked.

"Aye," Keenan said.

Mari looked between them. "Of course, you will stay, child. You've come home. You've cleared William's name."

Panic clenched tight in her stomach. Would Keenan and his men ride away tomorrow without her? No, she thought darkly, he wouldn't walk away from her with her tie to his prophecy.

"I must return to Scotland to bring William home," she said.

"We'll speak later about William. Come Àngelas, time to change." Mari led her away, none of the fear inside her showing in her face.

Serena bent over to enter the small space inside the wagon. It had never felt cramped before. But after living under the open sky and in spacious rooms, its tight walls pressed in on her. Serena jostled past the table and bed rolls along the sides of the wagon. She bent her head to miss the lantern and sat on her bunk. Mari pulled out one of Serena's dancing gowns, shaking any wrinkles from the material.

"I didn't have time to prepare it," Mari said snapping the dress harder. "No matter, they look at you not your gown."

"Did you not receive my thoughts that we were near?" Serena asked.

Duy smiled. "I hoped I wasn't imagining it. Then I heard your bird nearby, and I knew." Mari unbuttoned the bodice over Serena's stays. The slight touch of her hands against Serena's skin made Serena twist to look at her. Her duy was excited over something relating to her.

"What is it?" Serena smiled, because Mari was happy about something more than her return and William's health.

"Oh Àngelas, now that you've returned, I have news that should please you."

Serena's brows rose, and she resisted opening herself to Mari's thoughts. It was rude when she was about to tell her.

"We've received news of a young man, Damin Yallow." Duy smiled, her cheeks round like apples. "He is Petra's sister's cousin by marriage."

Serena blinked, the information coiling through her stomach. Mari patted her hand. "King Will has negotiated with his family for your hand in marriage. When you returned to us."

Serena stood, hitting her head on the lamp, and flopped back down. "Duy, you know that I can't marry. I mean, I won't marry someone who can't accept my powers."

Mari smiled enthusiastically. "He'll accept them."

Serena held her breath, trying to keep the alarm at bay while she pulsed a thread through Mari's mind. It was taking too long for her duy to get it all out.

"Damin Yallow was raised by his grandmother, a well-known seer in the Yallow Tribe. She was greatly revered," Mari said and grabbed Serena's clenched hands. "Don't you see, Àngelas? He knows of magic, has lived with it, has loved it in his grandmother. He will respect yours."

Mari nodded sharply to punctuate her point, then sat back with a smug smile. "We didn't know when or even if you'd return, but I urged King Will to move forward once I heard about his background. Damin will be so pleased to know you're home safe."

Serena's probe of Mari's fast-moving mind contained all the details. The Faw Tribe would provide her dowery to the Yellow Tribe. Their encampment was close by, and a runner had been sent to fetch him the moment Serena was spotted returning to camp. Damin Yallow was reputed to be a bit rash but in very good standing in their community, and he was considered handsome.

Serena let out a little groan and buried her face in her open palms.

"Àngelas?"

"No, no," Serena's words were muffled. She felt sweaty and chilled at the same time. She looked up. "I can't marry Damin Yallow. Keenan Maclean has already claimed me."

Mari's eyes widened. "Claimed you? In what way?"

Serena sat up, feeling the judgmental surprise in her mother. "Not with his body." She looked into her mother's eyes. "But with his words." Over the next ten minutes, Serena rattled off every detail she remembered of the last three weeks, alluding to but keeping out the details of the intimate ones. Mari just sat, her hands folded in her lap, silently listening.

"Duy, he claimed me last eve."

Mari's pinched lips opened. "This Drakkina sounds very powerful."

Serena huffed. "Yes, and she says that Keenan and I are destined mates. She foretells a battle against demons in the future, and having Keenan beside me will make me stronger."

Mari lowered her voice. "She could be evil, Serena. Deceiving you."

"But she knows of my parents. She told me of my family, of my sisters."

Mari shook her head slowly. "What if she works to manipulate you?"

"For what purpose?"

Mari shrugged. "Who knows the purpose behind evil?"

Serena thought back on her interactions with the spirit of the great Wiccan priestess. "But she helped me save William. I know he would have died from fever without her interference."

Mari sat for a long moment, and Serena fought against her impatience. "I don't know how the future is supposed to unfold, Àngelas. But I do know that Damin Yallow is handsome and strong and would respect your magic, child." She shook her head. "You would be foolish to reject his offer before meeting him, before touching him to see if his actions are honorable."

"You would have me compare him to Keenan, yet I cannot read if Keenan's actions are honorable."

Mari grabbed Serena's hands in hers. "Àngelas, I want only happiness for you." Her eyes pleaded as well as the flood of hope and worry washing through the contact. "This match with Damin, it sounds like a good one, one that will make you happy through your life. One that will give you children."

Serena shook her head. "But I'm unclean."

Mari sat back on her slippered heels. "You said that he claimed you only with words."

"Yes and no. He's also," Serena stopped and took a deep breath. "He's seen me completely unclothed." Mari sat up straighter. "And he's touched me, my legs, my breasts, my neck, my— "

Mari held up a hand. "Stop."

Serena couldn't help but overhear Mari's mind working through possibilities. Her duy's thoughts nearly screamed. Disappointment, sadness for the loss of such a chance at happiness, worry. What would become of her daughter? No children, no one to love her as a woman should be loved. Serena bowed her head and tried to block the sad thoughts.

Mari clutched Serena's hands. "Don't tell anyone. Only you and I will know."

"And Keenan."

"He doesn't know the ways of our people."

The Romany culture was very strict with regards to seeing and touching women who were not your wife. In some tribes, if a man touched the skirt of a woman who was not his wife, then he was considered unclean and must seek pardon from a council of elders. Serena's encounters with Keenan Maclean would be as damning as if she had lain with him.

"He may not consider himself linked to you," Mari said.

Serena felt her face heat. "He may honor his words."

Mari squeezed her hand. "Think daughter, were his words given while desire numbed his mind? Would he have said just about anything to touch you?"

Serena looked down at her lap, her face so hot it should have melted.

Mari leaned toward her ear. "A man in such a state can barely remember his words, let alone intend to honor them." Her duy ran a hand down her hair and continued in a soothing voice.

"Àngelas, just consider Damin Yallow. Meet him. Give him a chance." Mari cupped her cheek, and Serena looked up into her duy's bright eyes. "I want you to be loved. I want you to have a life next to a man who is worthy of you and your gift."

Serena's words were so soft she almost couldn't hear them herself. "Keenan could give me a happy life."

"Your Highlander speaks of curses and death, not love and children."

Her duy's words were painfully true. When had she heard words of love from Keenan? When had he ever talked of a future? He didn't even think he would father children of his own. He believed that she should marry his brother.

Serena sniffed back the tears that threatened. "I will consider."

⁕

"Here, Keenan," Brodrick said, handing him a tankard of ale. "'Tis a celebration after all." Brodrick ran his hand down his beard as he eyed the small clusters of colorful Romany people.

"If ye keep tugging on that thing, it'll fall off," Thomas said. He turned, scanning the area.

King Will sat near a lantern counting the contents of the chest of gold coins. He was on his third count when Keenan sent Gavin to make sure the man didn't notice a problem.

Gavin walked back to Keenan, shaking his head. "No problem. I just don't think the man's held so much gold before."

"He should put the chest out of sight," Thomas said, glancing around.

"I think the people here are all Faw," Ewan murmured, "not likely to steal their own money."

Ewan smiled at one of the young Faw women. "Perhaps I should mingle with Serena's people a bit, to better understand their customs." He winked and sauntered off in the direction of the colorfully dressed woman. His bowels were apparently feeling better.

Brodrick looked about. "Where did they take Serena?"

Keenan didn't move his eyes from the fire as he took a long pull off his drink and swallowed. "She's still in that wagon." He pointed toward the wagon he'd seen Mari pull her into an hour ago.

Several musicians came forward on the outskirts of the fire glow and began to play a familiar rhythm. Would she dance? Keenan's body grew taut, making him sit straight. Would Serena dance around the bonfire just like that first night weeks ago? She'd mesmerized him. *And I bloody haven't recovered.*

Last night he'd nearly taken her to bed. The feel of her warm, soft curves pressed against his hard body was etched forever into his soul. Thomas had spent an hour reminding him of his duty to Clan Maclean before Keenan's body cooled enough to allow his conscience to control his actions.

In the morning, he'd felt relieved when he'd woken with his men in the barn, until he'd seen Serena's questioning face as she stood before him in the blue gown sculpted to her body. Her disappointment felt like a physical ripping within him.

"That's a fine melody," Brodrick said. "Perhaps a show's about to begin."

Shite. Keenan felt the draw toward Serena merely with the memory spurred by the music. Maybe he should take a long walk in the woods.

"Who are they?" Thomas asked, nodding to two riders who approached King Will. One was older and the other sat straight with energetic youth.

"I think King Will should put his coins away," Gavin said and moved his hand to the hilt of his sword.

The men dismounted, greeting King Will with formal bows before he motioned for them to sit under his open tent. Both visitors were dark of complexion, much like the entire Faw Tribe, except Serena. They must be Romany, perhaps from a neighboring tribe.

The older man did most of the talking while the younger man surveyed the encampment. He looked like he could one day be a decent warrior. His eyes were piercing, searching. As he moved from one end of the lit camp to another, he finally came to Keenan. The two men locked gazes. Keenan felt the man weigh him, judge his capabilities. Keenan shifted his weight into a battle stance, legs apart, arms at his sides, ready to move toward his weapons.

The man spoke without looking away, and King Will glanced over. Keenan nodded once to the Faw patriarch. King Will nodded back and then went on talking to the visitors.

"Thomas," Keenan said evenly, "find out who they are. Quietly." Thomas moved off in the opposite direction. He would skirt the area and try to hear the conversation.

The constant murmur of the small crowd hushed as the rhythm of the music turned more hypnotic, like undulating waves.

"Bloody, look at that," Gavin said in awe, and Keenan's gaze snapped around to see Serena break into the circle of firelight.

CHAPTER TWENTY-THREE

A BATTLE AMONGST KIN

Serena wore the same type of many layered dancing dress she'd worn the night Keenan had met her, but this one shimmered in a shade of blue turned nearly purple by the red glare of the fire.

She stretched her arms over her head, bare except for black gloves that ended at her wrists. The blue silk wrapped around her waist accentuated her trimness and the womanly flare of her hips. The bodice was cut low enough to see her collarbone but not her cleavage. The way the material hugged her breasts was even more enticing than the low necklines that were in courtly fashion.

Her red hair hung in waves, free to dance around her hips as she moved with the beat of the music, her eyes half-closed. Without conscious thought, Keenan moved forward to stand with the others around the perimeter. Would she feel his presence, the void she had felt the first time? The outline of his scar tightened as he remembered how she had run her fingers down it in an attempt to read him. He rubbed his jaw at the ache there.

Serena moved in a gentle undulation, her hips and arms, her torso, her feet dressed in leather slippers. Serena mimicked the flames in time to the melody that surrounded them. He heard the tinkling of small bells tied to a scarf around her tilting hips.

As she disappeared on the far side of the fire, Keenan noticed that Gavin and Brodrick stood next to him, their mouths open like fish thrown ashore. Thomas stood across the fire with much the same expression.

"Sweet Lord Almighty, our Serena can dance," Brodrick said.

"Uh huh," Gavin answered, with the same dimwitted expression.

Keenan's hands clenched into tight fists as he noticed the appreciative looks of the men around him.

The younger Roma visitor stepped forward and caught her hand. No one stopped him. Why didn't they stop him? Keenan shouldered his way through the onlookers. With one quick grasp of the man's hand, Keenan flipped his arm off Serena.

"Don't touch her," Keenan warned.

The man looked mildly amused, but Keenan saw the restrained anger in his eyes. He could fit in nicely with the snakes at court.

"I was introducing myself to King Will's daughter."

"She was in the middle of her dance."

The man smiled. "I could hardly help myself." Then the man said something in Romany, something that made Serena look down at her shoes. Had he offended her?

"I don't speak yer tongue." Keenan began to pull his long sword from the scabbard across his back until the soft touch of Serena's hand on his arm stopped him.

"He didn't offend me, Keenan."

Mari and King Will hurried over. Brodrick and Gavin stopped on either side of Keenan, flanking him. Thomas stood across, his hand on his sword.

Serena spoke. "Keenan Maclean of Kilchurn, this is Damin Yallow of the Yallow Romany Tribe. He is here… on family business."

Damin Yallow's voice was smooth as he spoke in the lyrical Romany language.

"In my land, 'tis rude to speak in a language that isn't understood by everyone present," Keenan said, wishing he could face this man in a battle. The cocky young upstart could use a sound kick in the arse, his face driven into the mud.

Yallow turned his gaze away from Serena to lock with Keenan's. Controlled annoyance lurked there. "Forgive me. My native language flows more easily from me."

"English can be difficult for some," Keenan said.

Yallow frowned at the slight. "So what are you?" He moved his hand in the air as he spoke. "I mean, I know *who* you are, Keenan Maclean of Kilchurn, but what are you to the Faw Tribe?" He inclined his head to Serena. "What are you to Serena Faw?"

Bloody hell, what was he? Keenan's eyes rose directly to Thomas's pinched face. What could he say? What was he to Serena? Was he her friend, her lover, or her soon-to-be brother? Time stood still as he warred with the labels.

"I," he began strong and hesitated. "I helped to save William Faw from the false accusation of murder."

"Serena's brother," Mari supplied.

Yallow nodded. "You are a *friend*," he said stressing the title. "A friend to the Faw Tribe. A friend to Serena."

He was so much more than that. But what could he say here in front of his men, in front of her family? Did they know that he had claimed her? Keenan looked at Serena. She watched him, her eyes glassed over with some emotion he couldn't interpret. She almost seemed to plead with him, but what did she want him to do?

Keenan felt himself nod. "Aye, I'm a friend and protector."

Mari released her breath as she took Serena's arm. "Yes, and a very fine protector at that. He's brought my daughter home to us and has my son safely up in his brother's castle."

"My thanks to you, then," Yallow said. His eyes followed Serena as Mari turned her toward the wagons.

"Good eve, men," Mari called out. Serena looked back at Keenan over her bare shoulder. Were those tears in her eyes? Keenan's chest clenched so tight he thought he might double over. What had just happened? Damin Yallow and King Will walked back to the little pavilion and the rest of the people filtered away, leaving Keenan with his men.

Ewan walked over from the wagons, a scowl on his face. "Roma women only let their husbands touch them," Ewan grumbled at the dumbstruck Macleans. "What's going on here?"

Thomas spoke first. "They only spoke in Romany over there. I couldn't understand a word. They may have been discussing a milk cow if I understood anything."

"I don't like this," Brodrick said low.

Gavin frowned fiercely. "Why do I feel like we were just in a battle?"

Keenan slammed his fist into his other palm. *Crack.* "Because we bloody hell were. And I'm fairly certain that I just lost."

Serena felt the hollowness that a shadow must feel if it had its own consciousness. Her will left her as Mari pulled her along toward a new wagon. Its cheerful yellow and blue paint and carved embellishments would have made her smile if Keenan hadn't just withdrawn his claim on her.

"Àngelas, you'll sleep here tonight. Alone of course." She indicated the door and smiled. "'Tis nice inside, comfortable. Look," Mari said indicating the edges along the wagon, "good sturdy holds for garden boxes. You can have your own."

Serena nodded and ran her hand over the side of the wagon. "My own gardens," she trailed off and turned to Mari. "Wouldn't it be nice, though, to plant seeds in the ground?" Serena indicated the earth around them. Mari looked confused. "There is so much more space."

"But you'd leave them behind when the camp moved."

Serena smiled slightly. "Wouldn't it be nice not to have to move, but to settle and raise vegetables on the land where you live?"

Mari shook her head. "Àngelas, that's not our way. We move on and take what's ours with us."

Serena couldn't explain to her duy her newly recognized feelings. She was only beginning to realize them herself. Perhaps it was all the travel in the last weeks, perhaps it was the nights of luxury in soft, large beds. But the thought of moving on once again with her tribe, or any tribe, made Serena's head ache.

Serna turned back to the wagon. "It looks sturdy enough to hold many garden boxes."

Silence sat between them until Mari's voice broke into Serena's thoughts. *You will be happy.*

Her duy had tears in her eyes despite the smile. Serena had been so wrapped up in her own torment that she almost missed the deep sadness of loss underscoring Mari's hope for her future. Her duy had just found her again, and now she was urging her to move away.

"'Tis still my decision," Serena said.

Mari let go of Serena's arm. "Of course. But please, consider your future." Mari smoothed one of Serena's curls that lay along her shoulder. "Damin is quite handsome."

"I will consider."

Mari seemed satisfied and left Serena standing there in the darkness, its fresh spring smell calming her. She climbed the steps of the wagon that the Yallows had brought with them like a gift to persuade a reluctant bride.

Somewhere off to the right behind the wagon, a stick snapped. *Keenan?* She stepped lightly down to the ground into the twilight. Damin Yallow stood before a tree. Her disappointment was so strong she could taste its bitterness on her tongue.

His hands were in the pockets of his coat, his broad shoulders seemed stiff and higher up than natural. She sensed his nervousness without even trying. "'Tis the wagon we brought, Serena." He nodded to it behind her.

"A pretty color," she said. An ember of anger, infused by her disappointment, grew. "Were you eavesdropping?"

His eyes opened wider. "No. I saw you talking over here near the new wagon, and I came this way as your duy left. I just wished to speak alone with you."

He pulled a hand from his pocket and gestured back toward the fire. "Our introduction was strange, uncomfortable. I meant only to start fresh." He walked forward and bowed gallantly. Upon straightening he found her hands in the folds of her dancing costume. Luckily she still wore her gloves, and she tried to block his feelings, unready to hear them.

"I am honored to meet you, Serena Faw of the Faw Tribe. I am the eldest son of John Yallow, leader of the Yallow Tribe." He spoke in the comfortable smooth flow of the Romany language.

Serena nodded, pulling her hands from his, and leaned against the brightly colored side of the wagon. Damin moved closer. "You know why I've come to visit the Faw Tribe?"

"Yes," Serena said without encouragement. She was tired, tired of pleading in her mind for Keenan to claim her publicly. Not for his brother, but for himself. She was tired of searching for some sign from him that she should risk her heart and go against what her family had clearly laid out for her future.

Damin pulled a long strand of her hair gently between his thumb and forefinger. "I'll officially ask King Will for you in marriage. Tonight."

Serena released her breath and looked up at the handsome, hopeful man. "You don't know what you're asking for." Serena pulled a glove off and touched Damin's bare arm. Steeling herself against the onslaught, she wove a fine thread through him, seeking, discovering who he was. Details that only he would know.

"If you speak of your magic, Serena, I know about it. My grandmother could scry the future and had an unnatural ability to judge people. I loved her, and our tribe revered her wisdom. The Yallows will welcome you."

Strong confident words. Serena nodded. "But do you understand the extent of my magic?"

He looked confused for a moment but then smiled. "I will learn."

Time for his first lesson. Serena smiled back. "Good. I know you speak the truth for I've read it in you."

He raised an eyebrow but smiled encouragingly. Did he believe her when she said she'd read him, or did he think she just played the witch to scare suitors? She sensed it was more the latter, just from his face. When had she begun to read faces, expressions? She never had before. Her chest tightened, and Keenan appeared in her mind, but she quickly squelched the image.

Serena could feel Damin's tamped-down desire for her. But he was honorable and would hold onto his patience.

"You're honorable, Damin." She smiled. "And an excellent judge of horseflesh." He raised both eyebrows, but Serena heard his thoughts through the contact and nodded. "Yes, I could have heard that from King Will, but could my father really know about the foal you brought into the world when you were eight? You were all alone and scared and knew you should find help. But you wanted to be the one to bring the foal into the world. Your pride kept you from running for help even when the mare screamed."

Damin's smile turned stony. "That was a long time ago," he whispered.

"Yes, a very long time ago, but it still haunts you. Rides in your mind whenever you see a mare heavy and about to foal, like the one you rode by early this morn."

Damin stared at her as if she'd grown a hideous wart on her cheek. Serena almost lost her nerve. "I also know that you're excited about this union, for it will elevate you in your father's tribe once you have a wife and children. You intend to get me pregnant as soon as possible."

Damin's face began to harden. Had she pushed too far? "Don't be angry with me for stating the truth," she said.

Damin forced a smile that almost looked real. "Serena, I'm not ang—" he began and stopped. "You would know if I was angry inside, if I lied to protect your feelings."

Serena nodded. "You're beginning to understand, understand that I have more than just a feeling about things. I know things, Damin. I could know all about you, your thoughts, your secret desires, your past, those feelings you keep deep down inside. I could know them all."

He looked at her, tilting his dark head slightly. "You say, *could* know?"

Serena glanced down. "I can block your thoughts and emotions from coming to me. 'Tis harder when I touch your skin without my glove." She flapped the glove she held loosely by her side.

"Is it just your hands that are sensitive?"

"No, my entire body."

"So if we touch skin to skin," he raised an eyebrow, "you won't be able to help but read me, read everything I want to," he hesitated again and cleared his throat a bit. "Everything I want to do to you?"

Serena took a deep breath in and nodded.

He raised both eyebrows and grinned. "That has its advantages."

Serena couldn't help but smile at his reaction. "I suppose it could."

Damin put his hand out to her. "Here, take my hand. I give you permission to walk your way through me. See me for who I am. I have nothing to hide."

Serena laid her hand in his palm. Feelings of worry tangled with excitement. Damin held nothing back. He felt no embarrassment toward her, about her. Only wonder at what Serena could do. Brief images of alliances formed by using her powers, knowing the plans of certain enemies, keeping his tribe safe from trickery and bigotry. These all came along her thread mixed with ideas of dark-haired children running around her skirts.

It was so much that Serena leaned backwards letting the wagon support her. He offered her an honorable life, filled with respect, with the potential for love. She squeezed her eyes shut to keep her emotions inside.

Damin moved much closer in the darkness, so close that he brushed against her body. "Open your eyes," Damin said, his words low and deep in the chilled air. "I want you to see me, Serena Faw, when I first kiss you."

CHAPTER TWENTY-FOUR
STING OF UNREQUITED DESIRE

Damin's lips brushed hers, and a course of desire rushed from him. Serena felt it in her mind, images of how he wished to take her. He would be erotic, gentle, teasing. He tilted her head with his hand so that he could easily slant his mouth against her, deepening the kiss.

Serena felt the hard planks of wood against her back as he leaned his weight into her. She felt the chill of the air around her legs. She felt his hardening jack press against her. She heard Chiriklò chirping somewhere high above. Serena could hear the woods breathing around them as Damin kissed her. Her mind roamed to the scene at the fire and then the lovely wagon she leaned against. What did it look like inside?

She kissed him back. It was pleasant. He seemed quite the expert at kissing. Serena dove into his mind. There were other pretty girls there, lurking in his memory, one in particular still sat heavy near his heart. Kristina.

Serena waited for the stab of jealousy to hit her as Kristina's face surfaced briefly during the kiss. Instead she only felt curiosity. As Damin touched the tip of his tongue to hers, Serena waited for her mind to give way to tumbling heat, but instead she just wondered when she could fit in a breath of air. She must have stiffened because Damin pulled away and smiled at her.

Serena realized that she must have looked stunned because Damin's smile turned cocky. "Forgive me, Serena, for taking such liberties. I lose control around you."

Serena smiled blankly as she worked through the strange kiss. It had been pleasant enough, not forced or awkward. But something was missing, something important. Her smile faltered as she realized that the something missing was Keenan Maclean.

Damin Yallow had everything to offer her, but her heart didn't want it. No fire burned in the kiss, nothing hot and rushing to melt her insides, no throbbing desire in the pit of her stomach and below at her core, making her want to push against him. Instead Serena's stomach tightened into nausea, a sickly feeling.

Damin put his finger under her chin to tilt her face up. "Serena, I didn't mean to upset you." Concern flowed through the touch.

She smiled sadly. "I'm well, Damin. Just overwhelmed."

Male confidence, anticipation, a quickening of his blood. He thought he'd overwhelmed her with passion.

Guilt stabbed at Serena. "Damin, I have much to consider before accepting your offer of marriage. You're a fine man from a respected family. You do me much honor by your interest, but..." Serena shook her head. "I have much to consider."

Damin smiled. "I understand, Serena." He backed up, giving her space. "I know you could read my mind and figure out what my life is like, but let me tell you some things about my tribe, about where you will live. Let us pretend that I must paint a picture instead of you viewing it." He teased her, trying to break the tension.

"I would like that," she said.

Damin stayed close to her as he spoke. Serena let his words flit by. He had a need to talk to her as if she were a normal woman, and she had a need to sort through her emotions. The difference between her lack of reaction to Damin's kiss and the fire that erupted in her during Keenan's was vast. Each time she tried to imagine her life with Damin something unpleasant turned in her stomach, like when a foul smell wafted from a sewer on the breeze.

The children she imagined didn't have dark hair and deep brown eyes. They had blue eyes and light hair. They carried little wooden broadswords and chased sheep on the shores of Loch Awe.

Off to the left, Serena saw a movement of mist among the trees. The birthmark at her navel began to itch, and she rubbed a hand across it while keeping her peripheral focus on the white mist as it coalesced into a ghostly figure. Drakkina's diaphanous image floated close until Serena could make out the pinch of her deep scowl.

"You will love the silver that my friend bends into beautiful jewelry," Damin said.

Serena nodded but then winced as the thoughts of the crone stabbed at her as if she yelled. *What are you doing? Who is this man? Where is the Highlander?*

Serena fortified her wall and sent a quick series of thoughts back to the witch. Thoughts of disappointment at Keenan's refusal to claim her, angry thoughts of appreciation for Damin, mutinous thoughts against Drakkina's interference.

Drakkina crossed her arms over her chest. The shimmering cloud dissipated and then pulled back together.

You are weak, Serena thought.

Images came to her from Drakkina. Images of the Earl of Cumberland yelling at his wife, images of Drakkina forming in the room and scaring the man, images of Drakkina entering him and making him confess publicly so that he couldn't blame Lady Cumberland.

Serena's eyes opened wide.

"Yes, I know the waters in the south can be quite exciting," Damin said, watching her face.

Serena tried to keep her voice interested. "Tell me of the last time you ventured there, Damin. I like to hear the sound of your voice."

He smiled because he also liked the sound of his voice.

Drakkina seemed to stamp her obscured feet in childish rage. *You're encouraging him!*

I must hear him out, Serena defended. *He wants to marry me.*

Drakkina threw up her hands in disgust and turned halfway in a circle before centering back on Serena. *You are meant for Keenan Maclean.*

Serena snorted. *You need to be telling Keenan Maclean that, not me.*

"I know. 'Tis terrible how the English gengas treat us," Damin said, and Serena realized she had snorted out loud.

Drakkina continued to fume so intensely that Serena could see her solidifying and then fading in and out.

What are you doing?

I'm trying to summon enough power to get that ass away from you.

As Damin fell into a comfortable monologue, Drakkina stomped around behind him. She moved her arms this way and that, trying to pull any power she could from the surrounding earth. It was almost comical, and Serena had to watch herself so she didn't smile at an inappropriate time.

"And then we travel up into the Lake Country. 'Tis beautiful there." Damin stopped. "Has the Faw Tribe traveled there?"

Serena moved her eyes back to Damin's and repeated his question in her head. "Um, why yes, we've traveled near the Lake Country, but didn't stay long. It would be nice to spend time there."

Damin continued to talk about a farm where they were welcome. The man seemed to be able to talk forever. How annoying. Damin was unlike Keenan, who barely said more than a few sentences in a single sitting. Which could be annoying in the opposite way.

Drakkina stopped waving, a smile crinkling her eyes. Serena squinted into the dark toward a buzzing sound near her. A bee, perhaps a wasp, and it was furious. As Drakkina waved her misty hand around it, the insect tumbled about, poked and infuriated. Serena leaned away from the tiny ball of rage.

Drakkina pushed the wasp toward Damin.

"Damin," Serena interrupted. "I think that wasp may try to harm you."

Drakkina frowned and continued to disrupt and antagonize the armed creature. The wasp tried to sting Drakkina but couldn't make contact. Damin looked at the insect and shooed it with his hand. "Never mind. 'Tis inconsequential." He turned back to Serena, oblivious to the woman bent on attacking him in the only way available to her.

The wasp picked up Damin's scent as he waved his hand near it, and it changed targets. Drakkina smiled broadly as the pest zipped around Damin. Serena backed away as it buzzed and shot through the air. Damin turned quickly and slapped at the undaunted insect.

"Damin, you best leave. I think 'tis out to sting you."

"Ahhh!" Damin yelped as the wasp delivered its first sting on his hand. And then it dove in toward his face. "Blasted bee!" he swiped in the air as the wasp stung his cheek.

Serena cringed and hoped that he didn't have bad reactions to wasp stings. Drakkina threw back her head and laughed, but the only audible sound was a gust of wind.

"Damin, I'm going inside the wagon now. I don't want it to come after me."

"Go, go, Serena. 'Tis bent on blood," he said. Damin ran toward the fire, his arms circling in wide arcs of defense.

Serena watched Drakkina's image waver. "I don't know if you're for good or evil, Drakkina," she said into the darkness.

Drakkina chuckled and shooed her toward the wagon. "Dream of the Highlander, child." The woman's words floated to her on the gusting wind as the misty form dissolved.

CHAPTER TWENTY-FIVE
ALREADY CLAIMED

"Good, I see you're awake," Mari said as she entered the bridal wagon, holding Serena's beautiful green court costume. "Time to dress."

Serena looked up from the pile of green mockado velvet her duy set in her arms. Perhaps she'd be able to sell the blue one because wearing the wedding costume would be too painful to bear. "You want me to wear my court dress?"

"King Will would like to talk with you. You should look your best." Mari moved her finger in a circle. "Turn and I will pull the stays tight. Your waist is as slender as mine was when I was a bride."

As Mari's fingers brushed against her back, Serena felt her duy's excitement. Serena frowned but let her settle the heavy petticoats over her head to rest on her hips.

"Damin's been to talk to King Will," Serena said.

"Yes, he has." Mari seemed ready to explode with maternal happiness. "He says that you and he seem perfect for each other."

Serena exhaled long, and Mari stopped. Concern coursed through her touch.

Serena draped the white fichu around her neck to cover her swelling neckline. She sat on the edge of the bed. "I don't think I can marry Damin Yallow." Serena stopped. "No, what I mean to say is that, I will not marry Damin Yallow."

Mari flopped down on the chair opposite her and dropped her hands on the tabletop. "But why?"

Serena took a deep breath. "I love Keenan Maclean. And I cannot marry someone else when I love another. It would shame Damin." Mari didn't move. "And I would be miserable." Serena's eyes begged her duy to understand. She was afraid to read her, afraid she wouldn't find the understanding she craved. Instead Serena studied her duy's face. They stared at one another for some time before Mari finally stood. She came over and kissed Serena on the forehead.

"I cannot tell you to marry Damin, but I fear that you're headed for heartbreak, Àngelas. Keenan Maclean is," she hesitated, "he's so different from us, and you can't tell what he's thinking or feeling. You can't be sure of his motives. How can you put your faith in someone when you can't be sure of them?"

"Like every other woman?" Serena asked and smiled timidly. She could feel Mari's reluctance.

Mari patted her shoulder and sighed. "But Damin is perfect for you."

"Damin kissed me last night."

"And?"

"And I felt nothing. How can I marry someone who makes me feel nothing?"

"Love can grow in time."

Irritation surged through Serena at the words that so mimicked Keenan's lectures regarding his brother. Her eyes narrowed. "How can love grow when I feel it for another? Unless my love for Keenan dies, it cannot grow for Damin."

Her angry words caused Mari to sit back. She'd never raised her voice to her duy before. "Forgive me," Serena said. "I'm just tired of people telling me to love someone that I don't." Serena dropped her head into her hands.

She felt her duy's hand touch her hair. "There is more to your journey than you've told me. Who else don't you love, Àngelas?"

"There's a prophecy," Serena shook her head. "Which I don't believe. 'Tis...too much to say."

Serena felt Mari loop a strand of her hair behind her ear. "Ever since William brought you home to us and you became my daughter, I've longed for your happiness, Àngelas. That's all I've ever wanted for you." Serena looked up at the tears resting in her duy's eyes. Mari nodded slowly. "And if you think your happiness lies with Keenan Maclean, then I support your union."

Serena felt her own tears swell in her eyes. "I love you, Duy."

"I love you too, my sweet girl."

Serena squeezed the woman until her duy laughed. When Serena released her, Mari plucked out the fichu, exposing Serena's cleavage.

"If you're out to catch a Highlander, you better show off the prize." Mari stood and slid a hand along the bright yellow molding. "Too bad, 'twas such a lovely wagon." She looked back at Serena. "Hurry now and fortify yourself."

"Did King Will want me to wear this?"

Mari nodded. "He said you should look your best."

Serena laced the snug bodice over her stays. The rich material and emerald color made it beautiful. Serena tried to slow the wild thumping of her heart as she stepped from the wagon out into the bright spring sunshine.

The wagons seemed oddly quiet as people moved about their business in hushed tones. They nodded and smiled at her in her gown, practically bowing. Inside their minds, they had as many questions about the subdued atmosphere as Serena.

Chiriklò chirped from a tall birch, and then glided down to flutter daintily on Serena's gloved hand. She trailed her finger down the sleek blue feathers and flashed the question to her pet. What did her sparrow know?

Images of Damin Yallow talking with his father and King Will came to her in the fragmented bird version Chiriklò used to communicate. All the images were clear to the finest detail, but only viewed rapidly before flitting to other images. Her bird had seen Keenan ride away with Gavin at dawn. One glance around the camp told Serena he hadn't returned. A flapping of panic infiltrated her chest like a trapped bird, but then she saw the other three Macleans talking across the clearing.

Keenan wouldn't leave for Kilchurn without his men, would he? Where had he gone? Chiriklò didn't know the answers.

She stroked his feathers as he hopped up her wrist. King Will saw Serena from across the camp and beckoned her. Chiriklò shot off into the trees. As she walked, most of her tribe set down their tasks and followed until they made a semi-circle behind her as she stood before King Will, John Yallow, and Damin.

Poor Damin! One side of his face was swollen from temple to jawline. "Damin?"

"Bengikanò bee," Damin swore. He called it the devil's bee, but Serena knew who was responsible for the poor man's stings, not a devil but a witch.

"I'm so sorry," Serena pulled her glove off and laid her hand against the side of his face gingerly. His thoughts slid quickly through her touch. She stroked the side of his face, staring into his bloodshot eyes.

Damin Yallow hadn't slept well last night. He'd been up late planning, strategizing with his father, realizing the amazing power he would possess in Serena. Thoughts of her beauty and a happy future as father and husband had given way to thoughts of power and possible riches. He would never lose a negotiation again once Serena could move inside his opponent's mind. He still desired her, but the more he understood her powers the more he realized that he must possess her to use her power.

Serena stepped back. Out of the corner of her eye, she saw the Macleans gather close as King Will spoke in Romany. The whole exchange so far had been in her tribe's native tongue. Serena saw frowns on all three warriors. What must they think of her touching Damin? She purposely kept her wall up. She couldn't become distracted now.

"Serena, my daughter, Damin Yallow of the honorable Yallow Tribe requests to marry you." King Will smiled slowly and turned to the rest of the tribe. "He gives two milk cows and a bull to us for a bride price." The tribe clapped and murmurings ran amongst them. "And I send seven gold coins with Serena for her dowry."

Serena waited until the chatter quieted. She curtsied. With a deep breath, she pronounced her words in firm English. "I am honored that Damin Yallow wishes to wed with me." She saw Damin's father smile. "However, I cannot marry him." A hushed gasp hovered behind her.

"What is this?" King Will said. She could feel his anger buffet her mental wall like an iron mallet.

"I respectfully decline his proposal of marriage."

"Serena, last night *you* kissed *me*," Damin Yallow said in English.

"Damin, you kissed me," she corrected and felt her face flash heat. Maybe it was a good thing Keenan wasn't here. "I'm sorry, but I have decided I cannot marry you." Serena was polite but firm.

"Bring him," King Will raised his voice over the crowd and Ephram led a man into the circle. It was an Anglican priest. King Will turned to Serena. "I have already accepted Damin Yallow's offer on your behalf, and he's paid the fines to Father Kendal for a hasty marriage, today, right now."

Bile rose in Serena's throat. She tried to pull in air, but panic gripped her like a noose. She shook her head. "No, I will not marry Damin Yallow, not now, not ever."

Serena felt Maclean presence behind her. She looked to see Brodrick and Ewan, legs braced as if about to battle. Their hands rested upon the hilts of their swords. Thomas ran for his horse. Brodrick's thick burr rose up in a threatening growl. "If the lass says she will not marry, then she will not marry."

"This is none of your business, gurbeti," Damin said. His black eyes, swollen from the bee, glared at Brodrick.

"Damin, I cannot marry you." Serena looked at King Will where he stood in silent fury. "I have already been claimed by another."

The gasp she heard echoed through her tribe's thoughts.

In the sudden silence, Mari's panic pounded against Serena's wall. Her mother begged her to elaborate, to defend herself. When Serena remained silent, Mari's voice filled the clearing. She spoke in English.

"Claimed with words, just words. My daughter is still a virgin."

Serena felt her cheeks flame even as she stood straight. King Will finally controlled his rage enough to speak. "Claimed by whom?" he said in English and looked to the two scowling Macleans.

Serena raised her eyes to her father's level. "Keenan Maclean claimed me two nights ago." She held her gaze steady, refusing to look toward Damin, while King Will snorted skeptically.

He held out his arms wide. "The Highlander is not even present to support you."

"He didn't know you had my wedding planned for this morning," Serena said.

King Will's eyes snapped. He was not used to defiance. In the Romany culture, the patriarch of the tribe ruled and could only be questioned by another man. The fact that his own daughter disobeyed him in public was a grave insult.

Disdain and controlled fury emanated from King Will. "That he would leave you at all shows that he doesn't hold to this claim, a claim based on words alone."

Brodrick stepped forward. "Keenan is on an errand to cleanse your son's name. He rides to the surrounding authority to show the king's letter freeing William from blame for the murder of Gerard Grant. 'Tis an honorable errand, done to help the Faw family. He left his trusted men to safeguard Serena. He thought she'd be safe amongst her tribe." Although the last was a statement, Brodrick's expression questioned its validity.

King Will regarded the huge warrior with narrowed eyes. Without a word he turned back to Serena. "Come here," he said in Romany.

Serena took two steps closer until the edge of her petticoat nearly touched the toes of King Will's leather boots.

"Àngelas, you will marry Damin Yallow. You will marry him now."

Serena looked to the left, at Damin, his swollen face distorted more by his muted anger. "Forgive me, Damin, but I will not." The silence that followed was so thick with tension that Serena could barely swallow the packed air.

King Will's face turned a blotchy red. With swift power unexpected in one his age, Serena's father grabbed her arm roughly and shook her. Serena heard steel slide free, as she tried to keep her head from snapping off her shoulders.

"Wait! Stop! I say I've been claimed," she hesitated only briefly before plunging ahead. "He's claimed me with more than words alone." King Will pushed her from his grasp as if she were dirty. Serena caught herself and turned to face him. "He's seen me naked, he's," she stopped to take a quick breath, "he's touched me, with his hands, with his mouth."

Serena saw Mari shake her head and close her eyes as if Serena's shame was too much for her to bear. Serena looked away from Mari to Damin. "I may yet be a virgin, but I'm not pure, not pure to wed with you, Damin."

Names like "whore" and "libnì" mixed with pity and fear for her. Serena turned slowly to face the semi-circle. "I'm no whore," she said looking directly at those with the name in their minds and watched their eyes grow wide. "I love Keenan Maclean. I will wed no one, unless 'tis he."

"Unclean!" King Will yelled and pulled her around to face him, his hand raised high to strike.

CHAPTER TWENTY-SIX
MARRY & THEN DIE

Serena braced for pain, her body tense, but Ewan's large hand engulfed King Will's fist, forcing it to his side. Brodrick tugged Serena behind his massive body. Her world tilted, and she grabbed the back of Brodrick's tunic to steady herself.

Serena heard the deadly cocking of flint pistols, and chaos erupted. Ephram centered his pistol on Ewan and another of William's old friends aimed at Brodrick.

Please no! Please no! Serena desperately peeked out from under Brodrick's raised sword arm. She reached under her skirts and pulled free her own dagger, not that it would do much against pistols.

Ewan cursed loudly in Gaelic. Mari wailed in maternal terror. The clergyman dove into the tent while beseeching God. The women screamed and grabbed their children, running toward the safety of the wagons.

Serena turned her back up against Brodrick, her own dagger raised. Her eyes moved across the scattering people of her tribe, their panic, sorrow, and anger pounding in on her. "If you kill these men, you'll bring the whole Maclean Clan down upon the Faw Tribe," Serena yelled.

The leaves quivered along the north path. Chiriklò darted out of the woods, beak closed like an arrow bent on a target. Following out of the dense trees and bushes thundered Keenan's lathered chestnut horse. Keenan's face boiled with war rage. He steered the charger with his legs alone while loosing two drawn daggers into the air. They hit their marks, splintering the shafts of both pistols and scattering their fragments around the two men. A shower of gunpowder covered them like fine ash as they covered their heads and dodged out of the way.

Without fully stopping his horse, Keenan swung down into a run before the last piece of metal thumped to the ground. His long sword sang for blood as he held it out before him ready to strike. Serena pressed backwards as Keenan's back and shoulders blocked her front. She was crammed between him and Brodrick, shielded from any possible threat.

Two more horses thundered into the clearing. Before she could further assess the disaster, Thomas and Gavin flanked her sides, blocking her view completely. Her face was smashed up against Keenan's back, his shoulders so broad above her, his hair loose and windblown. She buried her face in the fresh scent that clung to him and tried to calm her heart.

"Keenan, they'll shoot you." Panic sharpened her voice, making her sound furious. He didn't respond. "I told them I wouldn't marry Damin because you claimed me," she paused, "intimately." She knew the other men could hear her since they stood so close. But she had to warn him. "If they shoot, you'll be the target."

"My death doesn't frighten me," he murmured.

"Well, it scares the bloody hell out of me," she said and thumped his back with a fist.

"Ewan," Keenan yelled. Ewan jogged over and replaced Keenan in front of Serena. She was still surrounded by human shields. She wiggled in the tight space until she turned toward where Damin and King Will had stood before. She peered from under Brodrick's armpit.

Mari was pleading with her father, but King Will didn't seem to be listening. He only stared at Keenan. Turning her eyes slightly, Serena caught sight of Damin, who gripped his bleeding arm where Chiriklò had pecked him. Her pet now sat poised in a branch over the man, and Damin watched the sparrow warily.

The clearing was once again silent. Keenan's voice nearly shook the trees with anger, yet the volume remained controlled. "I leave to clear a Faw's name of murder, only to return to find members of the Faw Romany Tribe ready to murder my men."

"You've dishonored my daughter, Highlander." King Will stood proud, defiant. "I have matched her with a respected man, but she is unclean and cannot wed him."

The clergyman peeked out of the tent cautiously.

"Brodrick, tell me what's gone on here," Keenan said. "Talk fast."

"Serena's father demands she marry Damin Yallow, now, this day. She refused." He stopped and took a breath that he let out in a huff. "She says ye claimed her, with yer words. When her father said yer words didn't matter, Serena told everyone that ye've seen her naked, that," he hesitated. Serena felt him shift his weight from foot to foot. "That ye've touched her. Her father was about to strike her when Ewan and I stepped in."

There hidden by towering Scotsmen, Serena wished with all her heart that the ground would fall away beneath her feet and suck her down. At least Brodrick had omitted her declaration of love.

Damin's voice rang out. "I will wed her anyway."

Narrowing her eyes, Serena threaded her power out towards the man. And there it was. He was desperate to hang on to her, desperate now that he had spent the night developing uses for her magic. But under that desperation was anger. He would punish her for loving Keenan. Serena grasped the dagger tighter.

"I will not wed you, Damin," she yelled back.

King Will looked over at the fortress of Macleans. "I would have my daughter before me."

At some unspoken signal from Keenan, Brodrick stepped aside. Serena straightened to her full height and forced her face into calm seriousness, ignoring the heat consuming her skin. She continued to hold the dagger before her.

King Will took a deep breath. As he released it, Serena felt some of the anger flow out of him and his eyes softened. He spoke in quiet Romany. "Àngelas, I took you into our tribe when you were a young girl. I've raised you to be Romany and have found an honorable man who will care for you despite your strangeness. You would throw that back in my face?"

Serena's eyes turned glassy, but she refused to let the tears escape. How could she make him understand when she didn't understand her feelings herself? She spoke in Romany. "Father, you honor me greatly with this proposal. I am very thankful to you for the years of protection you gave me, the wisdom you taught me, the care you have shown me." She shook her head sadly. "But I cannot wed someone I don't love, someone who wants to use my magic for personal gain."

"There's nothing wrong with marrying to help one's tribe," Damin said.

Serena kept her gaze on her father. "And I will not pledge myself to one man when I love another."

King Will lowered his voice. "What if he cannot love you?"

That was the question that kept Serena's stomach knotted. What if Keenan Maclean couldn't love her, wouldn't allow himself to love her? Was she dooming herself to a loveless life?

Courage. Serena swallowed, continuing to speak in Romany. "Even if he cannot love me, I still love Keenan Maclean. I'll wed no other." Serena kept her focus on her father. Keenan stood unmoving next to her. Did he think her rude for not speaking English? Could he have picked up enough Romany to understand her words? Bloody hell, she hoped not.

Damin stepped forward, still not ready to give up. He sneered and spoke in English. "What does he have to offer for her? I offer two milk cows and a bull as a bride price."

Fury flared inside Serena. "I am not an object to be bought."

"'Tis tradition," Damin's father said, "to honor the bride's tribe."

"I give the Faw Tribe my sword," Keenan said, taking steps, putting him right before her father. Keenan dropped the tip of his sword, clasping the hilt with two hands. Lifting it, his muscles on display through his tunic, he thrust the sword into the dirt. Her father didn't even flinch. His eyes moved over the intricate designs etched into the steel and the small jewels embedded at the ends of the well-worn hilt.

"Keenan, that's yer grandda's sword," Thomas warned behind them.

"'Tis my sword now and freely given. King Will, I believe that the jewels alone will buy your tribe several milk cows and a bull."

Damin's hands fisted at his sides. "I give the Faw Tribe the bridal wagon I brought for Serena."

King Will turned from Damin back to Keenan to see if he would raise the stakes. Serena opened her mouth to argue again that she wasn't something to be bartered for, but Mari squeezed her arm while mentally pleading with her to remain quiet.

"My sword also carries the allegiance of Clan Maclean. Yer tribe would always be welcome on our lands, and ye would have our protection."

"The Yellow Tribe is just as powerful. An alliance with us far surpasses protection from a tribe from leagues away," Damin threw out.

King Will looked back to Keenan. Keenan's voice remained deadly calm, his eyes cold, calculating. "I could continue to match ye object for object, to keep with yer traditions, but I'd rather jump to the end. King Will, in return for Serena, I gift ye back yer son, William."

King Will sucked in through his enlarged nostrils and Mari gasped. "William is no prisoner," he said.

Keenan's words held all the threat of a man determined to win. "With one word from me, yer son is dead. And if I must hold him as ransom for Serena, I will."

It was a bluff, Serena thought. A good one, but Keenan couldn't order William's death. Actually, he could, but he wouldn't. She knew that without reading his mind.

Mari released Serena to grab King Will's arm. Damin opened his mouth, but King Will held up his hand to stop him.

"Keenan Maclean, I accept your terms. I will take your sword and the promise of William's safe return for my daughter."

Keenan nodded, and King Will looked over his shoulder. "Father Kendal."

"Ah, yes, yes, I am here." The nervous priest stepped forward and wiped his hands along the sides of his long vestments.

"There will be a wedding today." King Will said evenly. "For although I accept Keenan Maclean's terms, I won't let my daughter leave with him without his vows before God."

Holy Mother Mary! "Father," Serena said, shaking her head.

King Will stared at Keenan, his stubbornness like a massive boulder. Blood would spill before her father budged on this point. His pride had already taken such a hit. She could feel him mentally digging in his heels.

But she had to try. "Father, you can't expect him to marry me today."

"I expect a lot from the man who takes my daughter," he replied evenly without moving his eyes from Keenan. He didn't even blink. It was a staring contest, like two wolves ready to bite into each other. "Would you demand any less if she was your daughter, Maclean?"

Serena tried to thread her way into Keenan's mind, but it was as if she threaded it through a dark room. He turned to her. His face still looked like a beautifully carved rendition of an ancient warrior as his hair fell haphazardly around his handsome face. But something was different, the ice in his eyes melted as he looked into her own. Was there admiration in the gaze, perhaps encouragement?

Keenan turned back to King Will. "I would kill any man who tried to take my daughter without vows between them. I accept yer terms."

Mari gave a little shriek and wiped at her eyes.

"I but ask for an hour to bathe and talk with my men."

King Will nodded majestically. "Agreed."

Damin Yallow threw his hands up in disgust, turned, and stalked off toward the bridal wagon, his father following.

Mari engulfed Serena in her warm arms. Her duy's lips brushed against her ear. "Oh Àngelas, you wed today." Her duy pulled back to gather the hair from Serena's face and smiled brightly. "My daughter, a wife, married to the man she loves."

Serena leaned into her mother as Keenan walked off toward the stream where her tribe washed. The other Macleans looked between one another, shock marking their faces. Only Brodrick turned to her and winked. Then they all followed after their leader.

Mari ushered Serena to their wagon, sat her down, and pressed a cup of wine into her hands.

"You look pale. Drink," Mari said.

After she'd taken some fortifying sips, Mari wiped Serena's face with cool water and fussed with her hair and ensemble. She looked into Serena's blank face. *What is it, child?*

Serena let out a breath she hadn't realized she held. "What if Keenan can't love me?"

Mari looked at her. "But you love him."

"What if I spend the rest of my life loving someone who doesn't love me in return? How will I ever know for sure if I can't read Keenan?"

Mari squeezed her fingers and smiled grimly. "Love, Àngelas, is a leap of faith." Mari sat on the edge of the bunk, facing her. "You must trust in it for real love to grow. If you think about it, if you loved anyone else, someone you could read, well then it would be cheating, wouldn't it? You'd know for sure if they loved you and there would be no risk, no trust. You'd just know."

Serena looked down at her hands. "What if he chooses the prophecy over me?"

Mari rose and took up a brush, pulling it gently through Serena's hair. Hope pulsed through her. "I have faith it will work out."

Rap. Rap.

Serena's face snapped up. Mari walked over and swung the little door outward. Thomas and Brodrick stood there, Brodrick holding the trunk that held the wedding costume gifted to Serena by Lady Frampton. "Keenan thought ye might want this for the... wedding," Brodrick said while Thomas frowned.

"Thank you." Serena kept her wall up against their thoughts, unwilling to hear the worry about their prophecy.

"We will wait for ye out here and escort ye," Brodrick said.

"I won't take long," Serena said and took the costume from him.

Mari shut the door and smiled at her. "He is thoughtful. 'Tis a good sign."

Serena grabbed onto Mari's hope like a drowning woman in a stormy sea.

Serena inhaled as she opened the door. Luckily it swung outward so her voluminous petticoats didn't block it. The gown was beautiful, and Mari's thoughts painted her like a queen. The blue velvet fell around her in flawless grandeur from a perfectly tailored waist, and the seed pearls speckled it like stars in a night sky. Threads of gold formed dragonflies and birds. It was exquisite, and Serena was glad she could wear something grand before her people after her shameful revelations earlier.

"Ye look beautiful, Serena," Brodrick said as she stepped down and Mari fussed at the ribbons she'd woven into her hair to match.

"Thank you," she said. Thomas said nothing. Did she really want to know what he thought? She sighed inwardly. Leap of faith or not, she must know what Keenan's friends thought.

Serena walked between the two men, listening with her magic as they reviewed Keenan's words when he spoke to them at the stream. Keenan didn't want bloodshed. *This is the best strategy.* Brodrick's thoughts were accepting while Thomas's weighed heavily on him, and one thing Keenan had said ribboned over and over through Thomas's mind like a loop.

I can marry her here and still die while she fulfills the prophecy by marrying Lachlan after my death. The prophecy never states that the witch must be pure, never married before.

Hurt cleaved through Serena as if she'd been shot by a pistol, and she stumbled. Instant tears stabbed behind her eyes as Brodrick turned, and she realized she was holding onto Thomas's arm. The words and Thomas's feelings of distrust, disloyalty, and worry continued to circle in his mind.

"What's wrong, lass?" Brodrick asked.

Serena shook her head unable to speak. What was there to say? She was about to marry a man who planned to die.

As she approached the small tent erected for the ceremony, she fortified herself. Keenan stood there proud and brooding, watching her as she stopped alongside him. No matter what, she couldn't stay with her tribe, not after what she'd revealed, and her father wouldn't let her leave unmarried without bloodshed.

Behind her the busy minds of her tribe whirled about as they watched in silence. In the distance, Damin Yallow's horse dragged away the bridal wagon, its tinkling bells in contrast to the solemn group. Keenan's deep timbre pulled her attention back as he recited his wedding vows. Then she repeated her vows. "Through happiness and sorrow, until death do we part."

She almost laughed. *Until death do we part.* And just when would that be?

CHAPTER TWENTY-SEVEN

BLACKBERRY FORTRESS

Keenan watched Serena impatiently as she hugged her mother. His new bride seemed melancholy despite her fight earlier to claim him. There hadn't been time for Keenan to convince her that marrying him was the best way to get her back to William.

Brodrick came over and thumped him on the back. "Meala-naidheachd ort, Keenan! No bonnier lass lives that I've seen."

Brodrick always had a way of lightening the heaviest atmosphere with his good humor. Keenan grinned slightly. "I have to agree with ye there, but I'll take offense if ye continue to notice her so intensely."

Brodrick laughed and handed him his short sword. "Ye need a second weapon. 'Tis a short sword, but 'tis something."

"Good tidings are in order, Keenan," Gavin said as he walked up. "Any thoughts of how ye'll explain this to Lachlan?"

Brodrick punched Gavin's arm.

"I was just asking." Gavin rubbed the bruised limb.

Keenan looked at Thomas and Ewan who walked up in time to hear the question. "I'll figure out how to tell him on the way home."

He turned toward Serena where she stood near Mari. She looked sad and irritated. Weren't brides supposed to be radiantly happy on their wedding days?

"What did ye say to Serena?" Keenan looked at Thomas. "When ye walked her to the ceremony."

Thomas's brows rose to his hairline. "Nothing."

"I told her she looked bonny," Brodrick said.

Keenan continued to watch Thomas. "Did she touch ye?"

Thomas shook his head.

"Aye she did, Thomas. Remember, she stumbled and caught herself on yer arm. Ye let her hold it the whole way over."

Keenan scrubbed his hands over his face, closed his eyes briefly and glanced back at Serena. He crossed his arms over his chest. "Thomas, what were ye *thinking* when ye walked her over to the ceremony?"

"What?" Thomas stammered. "Ye don't think she read my thoughts, do ye?"

"Of course she did, ye idiot," Brodrick said glowering at Thomas. "She said she could hear strong thoughts without trying." He rolled his eyes into a fierce look.

"I...don't know what I was thinking, probably about traveling home." Thomas turned red through his hasty explanation.

Keenan watched Serena where she sat inside the wedding tent while her parents moved about collecting her few things in a roll of fabric. She was beautiful as usual, her hair woven with ribbons cascading like red gold over her shoulders and breasts. Her delicate features held the mask of serenity, but Keenan knew better. Her spirit looked subdued as it lurked behind those telling violet eyes.

"I want ye all to think happy thoughts, right now," he commanded.

"What?" Ewan and Thomas asked in humorous synchronicity.

"Now."

"What do we think about?" Ewan asked.

"Think about how happy ye are that Serena is my bride." Keenan watched Serena's face and Brodrick followed his gaze. "Think about how beautiful the moors around Kilchurn are. Think about the wonderful Macleans ye will see again soon, whatever. Just think of happy thoughts."

"Ye think she's trying to read our minds right now?" Gavin asked in a whisper.

Keenan almost laughed. "Ye don't need to whisper, man. She can hear ye loud and clear when she concentrates."

Gavin's anxious look spread to each of his men.

Serena frowned, picking at a loose thread on her sleeve.

"Ye all are failing," Keenan said.

"But she said she tries to block thoughts," Thomas said.

Keenan's words came slowly as if educating a group of young lads. "Serena was raised among people who mistrust her. The only comfort she had came from her mother whom she is now leaving, again. She knows ye think she should marry Lachlan, not me. And therefore, once again she is encircled with mistrust."

Keenan looked back at the lovely woman seeming to catch her breath amidst the chaos of packing. "Her only weapon lies in her gift." Keenan's eyes warmed with admiration for the beautiful, strong lass he'd just wed. "She may not wield a sword or shoot a bow, but don't doubt that Serena Maclean is a warrior. She risked her life to save her brother. She saved Lachlan, the boy, and his mother from the Campbell. She masqueraded in court to cleanse her brother's name. She defended herself here this morning. Serena has courage that could match any of ye." Keenan stared his men in their eyes, challenging them to refute his words.

None did.

"So she'll use the only weapon she has when she's threatened. Just as ye would. Just as any warrior would." Keenan nodded to emphasize his point. "Serena Faw is worthy of the Maclean name."

As the point he was making sunk into his men, Keenan watched Serena's face. A slight frown still haunted her lips, but when she opened her gorgeous eyes, there was a light in them, a hint of the spirit that made her so incredibly desirable. And now she was his, and he was hers. His blood thrummed with want, and he had to surreptitiously adjust his cock.

Bloody hell, he was married. He never thought he'd be married, but despite who Serena was, this felt right.

Serena shifted in the seat, sitting taller. Aye, she'd heard his words of her courage through the minds of his men. Keenan's jaw tightened. For the first time he wished that she could spy into his mind instead of depending on those around him to supply her with information. He would just have to tell her, even if talking about emotions was foreign to him.

Thomas's cheeks were ruddy with a flush, but he looked straight into his leader's eyes. "I may have thought about her marrying Lachlan once ye die, like ye said to us at the creek."

Keenan had already guessed as much. He clapped his hand on Thomas's shoulder and walked past him toward the tent. "Next time try not to dwell on my death. It seems to upset the lass."

Keenan strode across to Serena. "Wife, we must leave for Kilchurn." Serena's cheeks reddened at the new title. "Make yer farewells," he said as he hefted her rolled bundle over his shoulder. Keenan turned to King

Will and Mari and gave them a nod. "The Faw Tribe will always be welcome on Maclean land."

King Will bowed his head in reply. "We will travel up into your Highlands this summer. That should give William enough time to recover and continue on with us." King Will's eyes moved to Serena. "And I'll want to see that my daughter is happy with her choice." The hint of threat tinged the old man's voice as his eyes glanced toward Keenan and then back to his daughter.

Serena stood tall before King Will as he placed his hands on her shoulders and leaned forward to kiss her forehead. The old man cupped her face in his wrinkled hands, and they touched foreheads. "You are very brave, my Àngelas." When he released Serena, she smiled fully despite the tears in her eyes.

Mari wrapped her arms around Keenan's torso in a hug. "Care well for my daughter, Highlander," she said smiling. Tears brightened her knowing eyes. She lowered her voice. "Be true to your heart, and don't give into death too easily." She poked him in the chest. "I want grandbabies."

He nodded, the hint of a grin on his lips. "I will try not to die."

"Good, good," Mari said then lowered her voice to a whisper as she turned from him. "Because she will never marry your brother." Keenan watched her walk toward Serena, his insides tight as if he were being pulled between two straining horses. If she did marry Lachlan, Keenan was glad he'd be dead.

Keenan walked to Serena's mare to tie her bundle across its rump. His men led their readied mounts toward him, and he pulled out two of the four scrolls clearing William's name of murder. One he had left with King Will, another he kept for William. He handed the third one to Brodrick and the fourth one to Thomas.

"Brodrick, ye'll ride with Gavin to the north and west. Thomas, ye'll ride with Ewan to the north and east."

"We don't travel directly to Kilchurn?" Ewan asked, his brows pinched.

"Serena and I travel to Kilchurn," Keenan answered. "Ye," he indicated the men as he'd paired them, "ye'll travel to every town on your way to Kilchurn to show the local magistrate that William is innocent." He saw the question in their faces. "The Romany travel, and it would be best for them to have us spread the word before they encounter accusations. That's why King George sent me with four original parchments with his signature."

This excuse was authentic enough that Keenan didn't have to supplement it with the real reason he wanted his men away from Serena. His new bride needed to learn what was in his mind through him, not through the skewed thoughts of their traveling companions. And he wanted to kiss her again.

He turned briskly toward his horse. "We'll greet ye at Kilchurn. Don't tarry. King George is making plans to act against the clans."

Thomas and Ewan took off at once. Brodrick and Gavin walked over to say farewell to Serena. Keenan helped her climb upon her white horse. Colorful rags had been tied to the horse's mane and tail in celebration, making Serena look like a fairy queen in blue velvet riding through the foliage. They rode for over an hour, nearly two, before the shadows began to lengthen.

"The gloaming is upon us. I know a place to shelter for the night," Keenan said.

"Out here?" she asked.

"There's a clearing I've stayed in before, and 'tis quite comfortable. There's spongy moss and a sky of stars above."

Her face relaxed. "I can change into better riding clothes."

Keenan led them off the narrow path into a woods budding with the warmth of the spring evening. "Aye, blackberry bushes, in full fruit as usual," Keenan said to himself, relief relaxing his chest. "Follow me, Serena. Let your horse find her way into the middle."

Keenan disappeared through a curtain of shrubs and trees. The remaining blackberry blossoms flitted up into the air as a funnel of wind whipped them into a dance. They hovered before scattering around the perimeter of the ring of bramble, ash trees, and ancient oaks. The trees reached upward into the deepening blue sky, swaying, their branches filled with newborn leaves, so green and eager.

"'Tis early for blackberries," Serena called from behind and paused. "And the brambles will scratch us."

Keenan broke through the thick foliage into the clearing, hidden in the small unpopulated forest. The first time he'd come across the odd clearing, he'd wondered if it held magic. It certainly looked like a fairy ring the bards liked to sing about.

Tall oaks bent gnarled limbs up into the sky. They formed a nearly perfect circle around the clearing. Low ash trees spread their screening leaves at the height of a man riding a horse. Blackberry bushes billowed up out of the earth, blocking entrance to all but the rabbits that grew fat on the berries, berries that covered the bushes through all four seasons.

Keenan inhaled a full breath of clear air, the hint of pine making it even fresher. Aye, the ring had to be enchanted. He'd stayed nights when enemies hunted him, pressing their way through the foliage but never entering. 'Twas a sanctuary where he could rest or ask the stars about his fate. Serena was the first person he'd ever brought inside.

She dismounted and smoothed her skirts before turning toward him. A gentle wind blew through the clearing, encircling her with blossoms.

"Oh," she said in a hushed tone and raised her arms to allow the fragrant flowers to drift about her as if sniffing a new arrival. Serena blinked several times and let her eyes wander around the darkening area. "By the Earth Mother," she whispered.

"Ye feel it."

Serena nodded. "'Tis like a hum, of energy."

"Are there spirits here then? Anyone speaking to ye, lass?"

Serena shook her head and walked around the mossy ground as the wind gentled. "No other consciousness. It feels like 'tis warded." Serena turned back to him. "I think magic was practiced here at one time, long ago perhaps. Protective magic. Only the residue remains."

"Nothing dark, evil?"

She closed her eyes and opened her arms to the sides as if opening herself up to the air around her. "It feels more like a cloak of protection."

Keenan agreed. In such an unlucky life, finding the clearing had been a bloody miracle. "This place has kept me hidden even with English soldiers searching the woods around it."

A small smile tipped her lips upward, casting a playful look along the planes of her face as the last color of twilight vanished. "Perhaps we should stay here forever then. We're definitely in need of saving," she mused.

Keenan turned to the small ring of stones still at the center of the clearing where he'd left them last fall. "And hide away like rabbits?" The thought soured in his gut. He gathered sticks and crouched to pull some dry wool and peat from his satchel. "Nay, I'm not Lachlan." He cracked the flint and stone together.

She exhaled. "Nay. You're not Lachlan." His brother's name sounded like it might taste bitter on her tongue.

As darkness took over the day, Keenan set a fire with the branches he'd left there a year ago when he'd acted as a spy for the Jacobites. He struck his flint, and the sparks caught on the dry wool Keenan held ready between his fingers. Smoke rose from the small bundle, and he held it to his lips, feeding the fledgling fire with his breath. It grew until he set it amongst the dry twigs on the peat, letting them catch.

Keenan leaned back on his heels, his gaze finding Serena standing on the spongy moss, staring at him, her earlier smile gone. By all that was holy, she was beautiful with her slightly angular features and pert nose, her wide almond-shaped eyes and flowing mane. And they were now wed.

"Will people smell the fire or see it?" She looked about.

He cleared his throat. "The clearing hides anyone within it." He indicated the thick bushes. "And tonight, we are its guests." Keenan threw another peat block on the fire.

It caught greedily, driving back the chill. Light bathed the clearing in a cheery glow and cast an orange and red hue against Serena's already red hair.

They stared across the glow at one another until finally Keenan stood, brushing his hands on the breeches he'd worn on this mission. He grabbed a soft, woolen blanket from his horse, spreading it on an area of spongy moss he'd used before as a bed. Turning, they locked gazes. "Serena, I..." He released a shallow breath, not sure where to start.

She stood opposite, and her words came like the rapid fire of a line of muskets. "We were both desperate to get me away from Damin. Thank you."

"Aye," he said cautiously.

Serena splayed her palms out to catch the first waves of warmth from the fire. Her eyes reflected the flames. "You married me to keep me from marrying another."

"Aye."

"You intend to take me up to your brother so that when you die, I will have to marry him."

"Serena."

Her sharp eyes lifted to his. "Don't deny it, Keenan. I read your plans through your men." She glared, her arms crossing under her luscious breasts, plumping them upward.

"I said that to convince my men to accept my plan quickly. It was a tactical choice that made sense at the time. I had no intention of ye knowing about it."

Her eyes widened.

"A mistake on my part," he admitted. "I knew ye couldn't read my thoughts, but the skewed thoughts of my men were easy to sense."

"So you admit saying that you're bringing me up to Lachlan, so that when you die, I can marry him?"

"Nay, I didn't say all of that. That's what my men inferred. I said that if we wanted to bring ye up to Kilchurn it would be as my wife. The prophecy couldn't come true with ye married to Damin Yallow."

"You never mentioned your death?"

Keenan thought for a moment. He wouldn't start their marriage on lies. "I did say that the prophecy never specified if the witch had been married before and that if I died, the prophecy could still be fulfilled."

Serena's shoulders sagged. "You still intend to die and leave me."

Keenan walked around the fire and caught her shoulders. He stared down at her until Serena raised her gaze back to his, her look guarded.

Damn, he didn't like to speak about himself. It had always garnered pity, something he couldn't stand. "Before I met ye," he said, "all I thought about was staying alive to die."

She tried to look down, but he caught her chin with a finger beneath it. "But now that ye've entered my life, all I've been thinking about is staying alive to live my life, no matter how long or short it is."

Keenan bowed his head lower so that he was closer to her. She smelled of flowers and spice and all the goodness in the world. "I want to live, Serena. I want to father children, I want to be more than a sacrifice for my clan, more than a wall of defense around my brother, more than a noble death as part of an ancient prophecy."

His chest opened at his confession. Here in his magic clearing, he could say all this without his clan and his brother thinking he was dishonorable.

Serena's lips parted, her hands coming up to rest on his chest. The warmth of her palms penetrated the linen of his shirt. "I wish I could read your thoughts," she said.

"Ye don't trust my words?"

She closed her eyes and reopened them. "When I can hear the truths in everyone's mind, not being able to hear yours is... disconcerting. You can lie, and I wouldn't know."

He slid a finger over her cheek to tuck a strand of her luscious red hair behind an ear. "Read the truth in my touch, Serena." He leaned in to kiss her gently even though his pulse jumped. His whole body felt alive and desperate to pull her into his arms. But he wouldn't rush her.

"Please believe me," he continued, "when I tell ye, I didn't marry ye for my clan, and definitely not for my brother. I married ye for me."

"Before you'd said you wouldn't marry, wouldn't want to leave a wife and children." She stared into his eyes.

He'd said that over and over to himself throughout his life, convincing himself that it was better that way. He took her hand. "Someone has helped me consider a different path." He inhaled fully. "I will die one day, as we all. But God willing, I will die after a good dose of living." His lips brushed hers. "I'd like to start living this eve." He waited, barely breathing, for her response.

Her words came strong and sure. "If living involves touching me, all of me, then I heartily agree."

CHAPTER TWENTY-EIGHT
WISHING UPON A STAR

The agreement released a coil he'd felt compressing within him, and Keenan's lips lowered to her parted mouth. So warm, so soft, he nearly melted into her when she slanted her head to deepen the kiss. The immediate wildness of her response surged through him, hardening his cock even more. He twined his fingers through her loose hair. Her tongue slipped through into his mouth, testing while his hand moved down her back to cup her buttocks through the heavy skirts.

Serena shifted against him, her thigh rubbing his cock. He slid his hands in front and unbuttoned her jacket bodice, working it off her shoulders. The bodice was easily peeled away, leaving her in stays over her shift.

"Ye're beautiful," Keenan murmured, combing his fingers through her hair, relishing the softness and working through the little tangles. He watched the slender column of her throat as she swallowed, his gaze moving back up to her eyes. Desire lurked there with a hint of apprehension. He took a deep breath, trying to cool his blood.

Cupping her cheek, he traced his thumb across her soft skin. "Do ye know the way a man and woman come together?"

Her lips pinched for a moment. "I've seen the minds of men. They are explicit."

Bloody hell. It was a testament to her courage that she hadn't run away from him. Men could be violent in their lustful fantasies.

Keenan pulled her close into the warmth of his arms and rested his chin on the softness of her hair. He breathed deeply to calm the rush of his blood. "The minds of men, lass, are rarely accurate when it comes to tupping."

"No thrusting into me against a wall or bending me over until my arse is higher than my head?" She tipped her head to the side. Was she teasing him? He couldn't tell, so he just stared, her words conjuring erotic images of the two of them in his mind.

"Do I not bend my knees to suck your shaft into my mouth, swallowing as much of you as I can? Or let you open my legs so wide that you can see every part of my—"

"Nay," he said, his cock hard as granite now. "Unless ye want to. Only then."

"Why would I want to put my mouth on your jack?" she asked, her voice strong.

He rubbed a hand down his mouth. "Perhaps...," he opened one hand to the side, "I did something like that to ye, and perhaps ye want to... try to give me pleasure that way."

Her brows furrowed. "That is pleasurable? Your mouth on my bower?" She brushed her hand over where he imagined the juncture of her legs lay under her skirt.

"Bower?" he asked.

Her chin raised. "My quim and clitoris. William calls it a Bower of Bliss."

"William told ye that?"

"Of course not. I've heard him laughing with Ephram about women."

"Is that where ye heard the other names of parts?"

"'Tis not like Duy would talk to me about pleasure, but I heard some from the thoughts of newly wedded women in my tribe."

He nodded slowly.

"In women's minds," she continued, "it seems pleasurable to have a man's mouth…" She pointed down, and he couldn't help but smile.

He nodded, and her lips turned upward into a matching smile.

His hand moved down to the bulge jutting upward in the trousers he'd had to wear, and her eyes moved to it. She looked curious, not worried. Her mouth opened as if imagining—

"If ye keep looking at me like that I will spill my seed like a lad seeing his first naked woman," Keenan said, and her eyes snapped back up to his.

"Should I apologize?" she asked, one brow raised.

He laughed and came up to her, pulling her against him. "Nay, Serena. Everything about ye makes heat flow through me."

Her face grew more serious. "I'm feeling quite warm now too."

His hands went to her hair, and he kissed her lips gently, trying to stop the flood of need within him. "Ye trust me, Serena, trust me to make ye feel good?"

"Yes."

He kissed her cheek moving to her ear where he spoke low. "I will make ye thrash in pleasure, lass."

She shivered, and when he came back to her mouth, she kissed him, slanting quickly so that their mouths could open against each other. Like a key clicking in place, something unlocked within Keenan, releasing his shackles against happiness and hope.

Keenan felt bewitched, caught in Serena's spell. She held his breath hostage, but all he needed was her to live. Her curvy form pressed into the contours of his hard body, and she broke the kiss to breathe near his ear. "Love me, Keenan Maclean. Wipe out the lies of other men's minds. Teach me about pleasure. Make me thrash."

Time froze as Keenan pulled back to stare into her violet eyes, into her heart. She trusted him.

A bit of white lace lay against the swell of her pale breasts, and her hands slipped behind her back to tug at the petticoat strings. A billow of cloth settled around Serena as the heavy petticoats landed on the moss at their feet. Undone, the stays loosened, and her gentle sway made them fall down past her hips.

Serena stood in a silky shift, the thin white fabric lying seductively along the hills and valleys of her full breasts, slender waist, and curved hips. Keenan held his breath as she pulled the ties of her sleeves so that they fell with the rest of her costume, leaving her slender shoulders bare except for two thin straps of lace.

The silk ebbed and flowed like a sea of milk across the landscape of her body. She breathed deeply, her full breasts rising and falling, their erect peaks rubbing teasingly against the confines of the shift.

His cock jutted forward, and he adjusted it upward, watching her gaze drop to it and then raise back to his face. She was innocent. He'd known that from the very first kiss before the gaol. But there was a fire of passion inside her.

His blood raced, and his heart battered against his chest. Keenan reached to the back of Serena's head and wound her hair, slowly, reverently. His other drew her even tighter against him, melding them into one. Her softness pressed in brilliant starkness against his own hard muscles. He picked her up, carrying her to the pallet on the soft mound of moss. Several blankets lay nearby to chase the chill once the fire died in the night. He lowered her and pulled his linen shirt over his head, tossing it away.

Serena's eyes washed over his muscles and down his chest, the fire lighting them both in flickering shades of burnished gold. Keenan leaned forward, his arms coming down on either side as he settled beside her. Their kisses moved with the rhythm of their breaths. Her hands roamed his warm skin, her fingers chilled. They stroked lower until she reached his hardness. Keenan groaned, his gaze never leaving Serena's face. Passion overrode any timidity now. He unlaced the ties holding the flap of his trousers together, releasing his erection.

Her gaze slid down the muscles cut into his stomach until it reached his cock. Her perusal shot more heat through him, and he grasped himself, sliding his hand up and down while he worked his trousers down and off, leaving him naked. Her lips parted, and he longed to have her suck him into her mouth, but not at first.

"Ye can touch yerself too," he said. He bent down over her for another kiss then moved over to her ear, touching it teasingly with his hot breath. "'Twill make ye full of wet heat."

"I think I already am," she said, her breath shallow, but her fingers rucked up the front of her shift.

"Perhaps I should check," he murmured, watching her. He shucked his boots and socks.

Her knees raised like two mountains, and little by little she exposed the valley between them. Keenan's eyes traveled up her long legs to the soft amber curls at the juncture. When her fingers found herself, Keenan's inhale caught at the sight of her laid bare to his view. He took in her long red hair spread around her face, her breasts held only by the thinness of her shift, and her spread knees tied with ribbon garters. He'd never seen anything so beautiful, a goddess waiting to be loved before the fire.

He kissed her again to stop from pouncing on her like a randy fool. His lips teased a hot trail along the delicate lines of her neck. He could feel her moving her hand below, her body beginning to mimic the rhythm of mating.

If he looked at her heat, he might just plunge into her, so he kept his gaze on her face. When she thrust her pelvis against his leg, he groaned. "Ye're pushing me near the edge, Serena lass," he rasped.

"I ache inside, Keenan. Touch me there."

She'd untied her shift, and her breasts lay bare. He dropped his mouth to one and rolled the nipple of her other. Serena moaned and he sucked harder, touching his teeth to the hard pearl.

"Oh God, Keenan," she said, rubbing her dampness against his leg, and he slid his hand down to it, touching her heat. She sucked in a breath when he entered her. Her eyes fluttered nearly closed, and she moaned softly while he worked within her, moving between the wet folds against her nub and then inside to a most sensitive spot. She moaned louder and closed her eyes.

"Keep yer eyes open. I want to see yer passion, Serena. I want ye to see me and know who made ye thrash and moan."

Serena's eyes, dark and sultry, opened to watch. Keenan's muscles bunched within him. She was ready, and he could no longer wait to feel himself within her.

"Keenan, please." She was lost in the storm he'd been brewing inside her body. Her skin was flushed and dewy yet also strung as tight as Keenan felt. He moved his mouth down her abdomen, kneeling before her, his long cock straining upright. His fingers worked inside as his tongue flicked across her sensitive nub. She laid flat over the spongy ground.

When she thrust against his mouth, he pressed back, inhaling her musky woman's scent. For long minutes, he played her, loving her with his fingers and mouth. He listened as her breathing increased and her body wound tighter, and he saw her fingers clench the blanket. A deep, resonating sound came up through her to fill the clearing as she moaned, her body contracting in a climax.

In one swift motion, Keenan rose above her, sliding his body along her soft curves. "Serena," he breathed, his biceps framing her face, and thrust inside her at the same time his lips met hers. His tongue moved intimately with hers as he drove through her maiden's barrier, claiming her with his body. She didn't even tense but continued to thrust back even with him fully embedded inside.

Keenan kissed her, and his forehead beaded with sweat as he fought to remain still within her tight passage.

Her eyes opened. "Oh God, keep going."

With a groan, he thrust and withdrew, each time pushing the pleasure higher and higher. She moaned under his weight, meeting him with unexpected strength. Keenan felt her body begin to clench again as his own body neared the precipice.

"Open yer eyes, Serena lass," he ground out while grabbing a length of Maclean plaid lying next to them. He kept their rhythm, his face tight as he wound her hand and his together in the wool.

"Before the stars, within this enchanted place, I claim ye, Serena. I bind ye to me, I bind ye with my body," he growled, circling his hips and grinding into her. She moaned, her eyes closing and then opening. He leaned down to her lips. "And I bind ye with my heart." His breath mingled with hers. "Do ye claim me lass?" he gritted out, his last bit of strength obstructing the tide within his straining body.

"I claim you, Keenan Maclean, I claim you with my body," she said, and Keenan thrust deeply, ripping a moan from her. She grabbed the back of his hair, her nails biting into the sides of his head, and pulled his lips down toward hers. She pierced him with her eyes as her climax began to crest. "I claim you, Keenan Maclean, with my heart," she yelled. All her passion erupted, pouring through her, pulling along his shaft.

Keenan pounded into her, all control gone. He felt her pleasure washing through her as a crashing wave of his own ecstasy toppled over him. His roar thundered through the clearing as he filled her, following her into bliss.

⁘

The blaze behind Keenan relaxed into that of a normal fire, and Serena curled contentedly in his arms. Keenan cocooned them in the blanket on the pallet of moss. Serena nuzzled into the side of him, exhausted. He kissed her forehead, and she sighed in her sleep as if they were just a normal husband and wife.

He felt contentment, her contentment, as if he could read her emotions. How could that be? But he felt the tenderness between her legs and the muted ache of exertion in her limbs. Could he really be picking up on her sensations? He would ask her, but he could also tell she was asleep.

His one free arm pillowed his head as he stared up at the night sky ringed by the trees. Stars glittered in the inky blackness, unblocked by clouds. One star shot across the circle. Keenan followed its wide arc until it disappeared. A shooting star.

Eleanor had told him as a child that he must wish upon every shooting star he witnessed. She said they were magic and would grant him his wish. For decades he'd watched stars trail across the wide skies of Britain but had never once wished upon one, because he didn't know what his wish should be.

Should he wish to defend and die quickly, without prolonged agony? It didn't seem right to wish for death, it went against the warrior in him that battled. Should he wish to live a long life? A life full of missed opportunities, because he refused to fully live knowing that he was meant to die? That would be a torture much worse than death. So instead, he just followed them with his eyes as they shot across the night, watching him, listening perhaps for his wish, a wish that never came. Until tonight.

Serena murmured softly in her sleep, rubbing her leg across his thighs. Keenan pulled her closer and caressed her hair, while his eyes searched the circle above. There, off to the right, another one. His hand stopped in a soft tangle as he watched. The star blazed a trail across his view, its tail so bright it seemed to etch the darkness. And for the first time in his life, there in that magic-filled clearing, Keenan Maclean, second son of the Macleans of Kilchurn, wished upon a shooting star.

CHAPTER TWENTY-NINE
SANCTUARY

"Cac!" Drakkina cursed as she hurled a flash of energy at the brass basin of swirling water, causing it to pitch off the granite slab at the center of ten stone monoliths. The water soaked into the tall grass. Drakkina kicked her hazy foot at a clump of yellow wildflowers. The flowers waved as her foot passed through them.

"Cac! Where are they?" she yelled into the wind whipping through the circle where once Gilla and Druce's house had stood near the western shore of Scotland's Highlands. All that remained was the hearthstone and the stone altar. The altar had once served as their table at the center of their cottage. It was a table built for purpose, built with magic. Drakkina collapsed upon it, resting her cheek against its cool solid structure. At least the magic altar held her form.

Self-pity churned with her frustration. "They married and disappeared," she growled, hating the loss of control.

She looked back down at the tumbled, brass scrying bowl and tapped her gnarled finger on her full lip. "Where could Serena and her mate have gone? The demons?" Drakkina frowned, but then shook her head. "Semiazaz and his pack have no idea in what time she's hidden."

Drakkina slipped her loose indigo veil off her gray hair to fall around her shoulders. "Serena and Keenan are still here somewhere, just hidden from me. Hidden by some other power, not Serena's." There was magic all over the world she could've slipped within, severing Drakkina's link to her.

The sun grew heavy and began to drop toward the horizon. Drakkina could just make out the faint roar of waves hitting the beaches beyond the stones and pines.

She rubbed her hands over her face. "Maybe if I scry the future, I'll see where they'll be." Drakkina focused a thread of energy out of the center of her wrinkled palm toward the abused basin. The bowl teetered in the tall grass, rising to sit once again in the center of the stone slab. She closed her eyes, imagining the small brook not too far from the circle. Once again Drakkina threaded her power to the brook, gathering a fistful of water, pulling it through the trees, past the stones and back to hover over the basin.

As she released the water into the bowl, she leaned back on her wrists. "Don't be so quick this time to knock it over," she chastised herself.

She covered her hair with the thin shawl and peered past the small pool reflecting the deepening sky above. "Show me what's to come," she murmured and threaded her power in an intricate weave above the water. Once the colors lay in a woven pattern hovering in the air, Drakkina lowered her hand, and the blended magic laid onto the surface of the water in the brass basin.

The colors swirled across the slick surface while Drakkina watched, her breath shallow as she waited for the images to coalesce into something meaningful. "Speak to me of Serena and her mate," she whispered, her breath reaching the shadowy surface. "Show me what is to come of them."

Images began to collect on the surface. Serena and Keenan kissing. Drakkina smiled. Then Keenan charging off into a battle, gun smoke, blood curling around his figure as he grimaced in pain. Serena's image appeared, sobbing.

"No, no." Drakkina yelled at the water. "This can't be their future. They're wed now, bound to one another. She loves him, I heard her confess it."

The images swirled apart, melding into others. Serena and Keenan smiled at three grown children who rushed into their arms. Bountiful orchards, fluffy fat sheep. Then the image changed. Serena held a wee baby against her while she cried, clinging to a grave marker. Another man who wore the same colors as Keenan appeared, spitting angry words, then hiding, then charging.

Drakkina covered her eyes with one hand, peeking through the cracks between her fingers. Keenan's image appeared again, throwing himself before the man. Keenan turning from the battlefield, fear changing his face to stone. Serena laying in a pool of blood as it gushed from her belly.

On and on the images swirled under Drakkina's tense stare, her hands moving from her eyes to her forehead to her chin. When the images began to repeat, she took a deep breath in and exhaled, releasing the scrying spell. "'Tis no use. The future's not firmly set. No matter how hard I look, I only see possibilities." And they varied too much to give her any type of relief.

"Goddess help me," she whispered. "What more can I do to force this love between them?" She stretched out a finger with each task. "I threw them together by sending William toward the bridge when Grant was killed. I trapped them in the cave. I cleared up their problem with

William. I chased away that Damin Yallow fool before he could take more than kisses from her. I even altered time so Keenan could reach Serena before her idiot father forced her to marry the other." Drakkina tilted her head to the side. "Which was very tricky."

She floated off the table. "But does anyone care or appreciate my help? Nay," she said, throwing her arms open wide to the surrounding stones.

"Love should be easy enough to orchestrate," she flapped her hands through the air as she frowned. "Get each daughter to find their mates and fall in love," she shrugged. "That's all I have to do." She began to pace through the tall waving grasses. "That and get them here," she glanced around at the clearing. Drakkina tied her cowl under her chin. "Before the demons rip the threads that hold each time in its proper place."

She looked out past the stones again and sighed dramatically. "Get them to love one another?" Drakkina snorted. "I can't even find them."

Serena woke to the heavenly smell of roasting rabbit mixed with campfire and sweet spring air. Her stomach growled, bringing her fully awake. She rolled onto her back and stretched before opening her eyes to blue sky above encircled by soaring green oaks. Memories of the night before ran from her mind down into her body. Her hand moved under the Maclean blanket. She was still naked and tender in all the right places. Serena turned her head toward the fire and smiled.

Keenan wore only his boots and trousers as he crouched, turning the hare over a low smoldering flame. Through the fog of wood smoke, Serena could see his eyes. They held mischief, and yes, happiness. It made him even more handsome.

"Ye're finally awake." Keenan stood up, and Serena let her eyes travel across his naked form. Holy Mother Mary, he was a strong, handsome man with chiseled muscles under a sprinkling of hair across his chest. The trousers sat low on his narrow hips, and she could see the bulge of his jack beneath them.

She rose up on one elbow as she held the blanket against her breasts. She crossed her legs underneath, her hand pressing the ache that flared between them.

"Roast hare and blackberries to break our fast." He kicked at some of the blackened branches to scatter the flame and walked over to her. Serena glanced around for her clothes but didn't see them. Keenan reached under her arms and lifted her up to stand. The morning breeze slid over her skin, making her shiver. He wrapped her in his warm hug while his free hand tucked the blanket around her.

"I overslept."

Keenan used his finger to lift her chin, his eyes sparkling with mischief. "Mmm, ye were up late last eve." He ran a hand across her cheek and into her tangled hair. "Ye have the look of a lass properly tupped."

His smile was contagious and broke away any awkwardness that came from being naked under a blanket with a man outdoors in daylight. "And you," she said, "have the look of a lustful rogue."

"Only with my tantalizing wife."

Wife. She was his wife now, the night making it truly unbreakable. She smiled, and he leaned in to kiss her, unhurried and gentle. It was as if they had all the time in the world to just taste one another, breathe in one another. Awareness crept inside her. He was happy, joyful. She could feel it like a warm ray of sunlight covering her.

"I feel... I think I can read something you're feeling," she said.

He brushed her hair back from her cheek and stared into her eyes. He finally nodded. "I felt something last night. Not thoughts, but sensation or feelings from ye."

She nodded. "Especially when we peaked." Just the word made her core clench as if reliving the explosive pleasure.

His gaze slid past her. "Maybe 'tis this place, its magic."

A gentle breeze cooled Serena's bare backside, and she looked down to find the blanket crumpled at her ankles. Before she could bend to pick it up, Keenan crouched and brought it around her back but pulled her naked front against his body. His chest felt hot against her cool breasts, and she felt his hardened jack press along her belly. Her nipples hardened as he cupped one cheek of her naked backside.

Her fingers dropped down to grasp him, and he groaned.

He rested his forehead against hers, his hand settling on hers before she started to stroke him. "Och Serena, I want ye."

"You have me," she whispered.

"Ye're tender after our adventures last night. I would give ye some time before I plunge into ye again."

"Bloody hell, Keenan," she said, staring up at him. "Just the word plunge has heat pouring through me. Can you feel it?"

"Aye." Keenan smiled broadly. "I'm glad I'm not the only one tortured." He stepped back, settling the blanket around her. "We're also getting a late start this morn."

Serena sat down to pull apart some of the tender meat.

Keenan handed her a cup full of fresh blackberries. "No matter what time of year I come here, the berries are always plump and purple." Keenan popped the berry into his mouth and chewed. He leaned back on his wrists, the muscles in his shoulders cording under his weight. He was so broad and full of strength, yet he hadn't hurt her.

"Ye didn't walk in yer sleep last night," he said.

She looked out at the trees, tilting her head. "I don't feel the pull I usually have, the thread that pulls me west."

He grinned at her. "Perhaps I do, and ye have to hold me down with yer soft naked curves."

Serena threw a blackberry at him, and it broke against his forehead, leaving a purple juice mark. She laughed and leaped up when he threw three back in quick succession. Clutching the blanket, she ran around to the other side of the clearing to catch another handful of berries from the bursting bush. Within minutes the two of them were pocked with sticky sweet juice.

Keenan raised his hands in surrender. "I'm unarmed, lass."

Laughing, Serena threw the few remaining berries into her mouth. She tucked the end of the blanket into the valley of her breasts and walked into his open arms. She licked a purple blotch on the inside of Keenan's bicep. It was sweet and tangy and mixed with the fresh, wind-swept smell that was Keenan.

His laughter stopped as her tongue continued down his arm licking at the little purple marks. She saw another one out of the corner of her eye on his chest. Her lips closed over the sticky juice while her tongue swirled around his smooth skin. She closed her eyes. His skin felt hot and stretched as if over granite. As she moved over to the purple splotch on one of his nipples, she felt his body jerk. Serena swirled her tongue around his nipple until she couldn't taste any remains of blackberry.

"Serena," he gritted out. "Can ye feel what ye're doing to me?"

Oh, she felt it. She trailed licks across to his other nipple, her hands stroking up the sides of Keenan's naked torso. "Can you feel what you're doing to me?" she asked.

"Och but Serena lass…" He trailed off as she licked another purple splotch under the fine sprinkling of hair in the center of his tight chest. She could hear how much he enjoyed her administrations in the rush of his breath and feel it in the hardness of his jack. And she was in control.

Leaning up on her toes to kiss a blackberry mark in the beating hollow of his throat, Serena felt his pulse pound beneath her tongue as she dragged it across the valley.

Keenan's arms encircled, pulling her up against the strength that lay beneath his hot skin. He held her face, tilting it so they could stare into each other's eyes. Untamed heat glazed Keenan's eyes, sending hot giddiness through her. His jaw flexed as if his strong will alone kept him from devouring her in one bite.

As he slanted across her already wet mouth, Serena's last coherent thought was that she had been so wrong. She was not in control of this powerful man. The fire she had kindled began to blaze into something neither of them could stop.

Keenan's lips seared her as he tangled hands through her hair, wrapping it around his fists to hold her captive. She had just baited a lion and was about to be consumed. Keenan left her lips to run his hot mouth down the side of her neck.

Serena exhaled shallow breaths into the soft waves of his dark hair as his mouth claimed one of her breasts. His desire rolled through her, bringing her own senses to a boil. She felt his passion even without her powers, and she climbed to meet it, to embrace it, to build upon it. Yes, she had baited a lion, and he was ready to swallow her, she thought as she sank to her knees before him. Never before had prey looked so forward to being eaten alive.

CHAPTER THIRTY
CALL TO ARMS

Lachlan Maclean paced before the dying flames in the great hearth. He watched the shadows play against the stone walls hung with polished shields, axes, and swords. His father's broadsword, his grandda's shield. They hung there, a place of honor after days of battle. They hung there waiting, waiting for him to take them up. He sighed heartily and took another gulp of the fine mulled wine Eleanor had brought him after the messenger had ridden away.

Lachlan glanced back at the table where several Maclean warriors stood, where the missive lay curled exactly where he'd left it. Eleanor watched him, waiting. His beautiful sister, so lovely and yet no man was brave enough to marry her. He turned his stare to the tapestries overhead, their threads woven and needled to depict great scenes of Macleans defending Kilchurn, Macleans knee-deep in battle defending their family, their people.

Would anyone ever take month after month to needle a depiction of him, Chief Lachlan, son of Angus, into a tapestry? What would it look like? Would it be of him hiding behind the locked doors to his rooms or fleeing down one of the secret passageways dug to evacuate the women and children? Perhaps there would be a magnificent tapestry woven to depict him clutching behind his beautiful sister's skirts.

Lachlan rested his forehead against the back of his hand on the mantel. What to do?

He looked down into the brittle logs, licked black with flame. More likely there would be a tapestry of his brother, Keenan, standing in front of him, his sword raised to protect him, as his duty demanded.

Hamish, his friend from childhood, came to stand beside him at the hearth. "What answer do we send, Lachlan?"

Keeping his forehead against his hand, Lachlan turned his gaze to meet Hamish's stare. "Do we know where my brother is?"

"Nay, but I've sent a scout down our usual route toward England."

"One scout?" They'd never find him.

"Aye, I didn't dare send more in case we need to ride quickly."

Lachlan nodded, rubbing the top of his hair against his hand. He turned his head again so his eyes could study Hamish. What to do? "What say the men?" he said glancing toward the standing warriors on the other side of the room. Keenan was the one who made the battle decisions, especially one this big.

"They are ready to chase the English from our soil and raise Prince Charles to his rightful place." They supported Charles Stuart instead of the English who would take over their whole country, even if Keenan didn't.

"They but wait for Keenan to return to ride," Hamish said.

Lachlan shifted away from the mantel, his spine stiffening. "They but wait for Keenan." Lachlan held his voice down, but softness could not cloak the sharp edge in his tone.

"And yer word, Lachlan. Ye're our chief."

Chief in name only, Lachlan thought.

Hamish waited and cleared his throat. "Chief Maclean, we await yer word."

Lachlan turned and looked out at the rest of the room. "Send word that we arm ourselves to join the call to Drumossie Moor." His voice filled the rafters with its force.

"To Culloden!" the men echoed, raising their swords to stab high into the air that suddenly felt icy against Lachlan's cheeks.

Prickles rose along his arms, but Lachlan ignored them, turning to Hamish. "Send the answer to the MacDonalds that we ride in three days to meet them at Culloden. We'll lay camp on the fifteenth." His stomach thrummed with excitement. He would go to war for Charles Stuart.

"And Keenan?" Hamish asked.

"Keenan can come along if he makes it in time. Otherwise, I'll lead this clan into battle."

Hamish hesitated just long enough for Lachlan to narrow his eyes.

Hamish swallowed and gave a nod. "Aye, chief." He turned on his heel and headed for the door, his men behind him.

Lachlan turned back to the fire as Eleanor came to stand beside him. She placed her soft hand on his rigid shoulder. In that instance, she felt like their mother, ready to caution him.

Lachlan kicked at the logs and several sparks shot out, crackling in the thick silence.

"Very brave, Brother," Eleanor said. "Perhaps foolish, but very brave."

Ire licked up inside Lachlan, mixed with the slight nausea his decision was causing. He shook her hand off and kicked the stone hearth. "Don't pass judgment on my actions, Sister," he hissed before throwing himself into one of the two chairs flanking the fire. He was useless. A useless man.

Eleanor remained standing, hands folded before her. Lachlan looked at his palms. They were supple. He rubbed them together. "They're like a gentlewoman's hands," he said softly.

Eleanor sat next to him and took his hand in hers. She didn't say anything, just ran her fingers along his palm. He hated his hands. "They should be rough, calloused, Eleanor. Not soft like a lady's." He yanked his hand back and leaned forward with his elbows on his knees.

"Dear God, Eleanor, what have I been doing with my life?" The fire cracked and wheezed.

"Hiding," she said simply.

Anger surged through him only to crash down as he recognized the obvious truth. It had been encouraged in every aspect of his life. Be the son who lives, the one to lead the clan to peace. But how could he lead while hiding?

"Hiding," he repeated and scrubbed along his bristled cheeks. "Aye, that I have."

He looked at Eleanor and straightened in the chair. "But I've finally found the witch, so I can stop hiding." The prophecy was coming true. The witch had been found, and he would lead the clan to peace.

Eleanor frowned. "Serena's not here."

"But she was, and she'll return," Lachlan said. Hope grew in his chest, making it feel tight.

"With Keenan?"

"Aye, of course," he began and hesitated, wondering at her question. "Keenan will bring her back." Lachlan's frown increased. "My brother knows his duty."

"And yer duty has always been to hide and yet ye've decided to break free of it."

His sister had a way of twisting a blade that you didn't realize was sticking in your gut. "What do ye hint at, Eleanor. I grow weary of reading behind words."

She narrowed her eyes as if thinking. "How would we all act, who would we all be, if we weren't ruled by the prophecy? Would ye hide here watching yer friends grow in valor and strength? Nay. Would I wither away as an old maid?" She tipped her head to the side and smiled. "Perhaps," she teased. "But perhaps ye would have wed me off long ago so I wouldn't plague ye so."

Lachlan clapped his hand down over hers but did not release his frown. Her words were both terrifying and exhilarating. How would it be to live a free life?

"Would Keenan spend his whole life obsessed with protecting ye, only to die without having ever lived?"

Lachlan watched the tear swelling on the rim of Eleanor's eye break free to race down her cheek. He caught it on his finger. It was a simple drop of water, but it felt heavy with hope and regret and worry about Keenan.

She ignored her tear, continuing. "Or would there be bairns filling the nursery and young lads and lasses laughing through these grand halls, playing out the stories of bravery, stories about two great brothers, strong and cunning." She sat back and looked into the dying fire. "I wonder how different things would be if we'd never heard a single word of our prophecy."

Lachlan let her hand go and looked up again at his father's sword. He'd raised it upon the wall at his da's death. Keenan already had his own sword, from his seanair. That sword on the wall was meant for Lachlan, but it gathered dust.

Lachlan jumped up from the chair. He felt Eleanor's eyes as he picked up a stool from against the wall to move it under the sword. Climbing up, he placed two hands under it, careful not to slice them on the blade. It took a little force to wrench the weapon from its slumber in the hooks. He curled his hands around the smooth leather-wrapped hilt and stepped down. It was heavy and full of responsibility.

Lachlan turned, pointing the sword tip up, feeling his muscles warm at the effort.

Eleanor stood, her smile at odds with the tears running freely down her cheeks. "It looks good in yer hands," she said and sniffed.

Lachlan swung it slowly in a low arc. "Three days, Eleanor. I have three days to learn to swing Da's sword." He was done hiding, done being the Maclean coward. Lachlan Maclean had three days. And he planned to live every minute to its fullest.

CHAPTER THIRTY-ONE
A FRAGILE FUTURE

Keenan walked his horse over to Serena's and mounted. "Don't look so sad, wife. We'll return someday." His words held hope for their future, but something in his tone made it sound more like a goodbye.

"'Tis a special place, Keenan."

He smiled. "For us." He reached out and squeezed her hand before nudging his horse forward out through the thorny bramble.

As they rode out of the dense clearing Serena noticed a shift in the wind. She shivered against it and pulled the blanket closer around her. She sucked in her breath so quickly that Keenan turned in his seat.

"What is it?"

"The pull," she said holding tight to the mane of her horse. "The pull to the west is so great it nearly yanked me from my horse." Serena looked directly west, feeling the tight thread pull sharply from her birthmark. She rubbed her hand across it through the layers of her shift, stays, bodice, and the blanket.

Keenan reined in so that he sat next to her. She met his uneasy gaze. "I feel we must both go west," she said, staring into his eyes, trying to convince him of something she didn't understand. "Like 'tis the most important thing in the world for us to do," she paused. "Together."

Keenan's frown turned in that direction. "A magical pull."

"What do we do?" she asked.

Keenan looked out through the tree line that broke onto rolling hills that would eventually lead them to the sea. He slowly shook his head. "After we return to Kilchurn, then we will see what lies to the west. I must tell Lachlan of the letter being destroyed, and ye must tell William of his freedom."

Serena's stomach quivered, and she took some steadying breaths to focus her shields against the tug. Something or someone was pulling with all their might to bring her, to bring them, west.

Keenan's hand grasped her upper arm, and she opened her eyes. "Do ye need to ride with me?"

Once she fortified the wall around her, Serena felt the nausea abate. "It takes a bit more concentration to prevent me from galloping off in that direction, but I'm well."

Keenan apparently didn't like that answer and swiftly pulled her onto his horse. He leaned back to tether Serena's mount to follow his. "I have no time to be chasing ye across Britain."

Serena's head bumped his chin slightly as she settled against his hard chest. "So you would chase me?" she teased.

His arms came around hers like warm iron. "Ye're mine, in the eyes of the church. With our vows in the clearing, ye're mine before the stars and before God, lass. And I'm yers. Aye, I'd chase ye."

Serena smiled up into his serious eyes. "Then you best chain me to your side tonight else I walk all the way to the sea."

Icy mountain water rushed into a pool below, raising a mist of colors within the secluded glade. Sharp, thin slices of ice jutted out from the high peak where the water crested to fall.

Serena shivered, looking at the freezing majesty of nature before her. She leaned back into the warmth of Keenan's chest as they sat on his horse, staring at the beauty. She felt his arms tighten around her, his breath hot at her ear.

"Ready for a swim?"

Serena twisted in his grasp until she caught his gaze and saw the teasing glint that revealed his jest. "To swim in that would be a wish for death," she retorted with a sarcastic smile.

Keenan's arm extended past her to point at a flat rock on the other side of the pool. "There, the rock bakes with the sun in the summer. A perfect place for a nap." He kissed her ear lightly, causing Serena to tilt her head at the ticklish sensations. "Secluded, warm, rushing water to hide yer lusty screams."

She twisted in the saddle again to look at him. "*My* lusty screams? I remember some ferocious roars that left my ears ringing."

Keenan laughed. "Aye, ye bring it out of me, lass." He kissed her upturned mouth and pulled her slowly in his arms without breaking contact. When he pulled back, Serena saw joy lurking in his eyes, joy to match her own.

Over the last four days, she had watched Keenan transform as they loved one another thoroughly through their journey. Serena had kissed out every last bit of sadness and hopelessness she'd seen haunting him. In their place she found an easy laughter and genuine smile that crinkled the little lines at the corners of his blue-gray eyes. They were beautiful eyes, sparked with life.

"What goes through yer lovely head, lass?"

"I hope our children have your eyes."

For a moment, Keenan's teasing smile faltered, and a slow one of warmth and contentedness replaced it. He spoke low and cupped her cheek with his palm. "Our sons will have my strength and cunning." Serena laughed at his boast. "Our daughters will have yer beauty and bravery."

"And perhaps my magic?"

Keenan frowned briefly before nodding. "If they do ye'll teach them to protect themselves. To use it for good and to not let it rule their lives."

Serena's eyes blurred a bit with unshed tears as she smiled up at Keenan. Here was the man who accepted her for all that she was. Even when they were surrounded by intrigue in the middle of English court, he never asked her to use her powers to discover plots or make mischief to better himself. He'd never tried to manipulate her or anyone else. In fact, he'd never once asked her to read anyone, only to alert them to danger. Keenan Maclean was a good man, the man, she realized, she loved with all her being.

Keenan dismounted and lifted her to the ground. He pulled the blanket from the rolled pallet and spread it for them to eat their evening meal upon.

Serena watched the muscles in his back stretch beneath the thin weave of his shirt. She recalled how she'd come up behind him to run her tongue between his shoulder blades that morning before they left their latest camp. Her sneak attack had delayed them another hour, an hour she wouldn't trade for anything.

She began to unload the satchel of their remaining provisions: cheese and dry bannocks, and a trout that they'd caught that morning in a net Keenan had left across a stream. It would roast up over the fire crispy and hot. 'Twas a good meal for their last night on the journey.

Serena sighed, thinking of their homecoming. Would Kilchurn welcome them? What would Keenan say to Lachlan? How should she act? Several times the conversation had come around to their homecoming, bringing silence between them.

As if sensing the change in her mood, or perhaps reading the tone in her sigh, Keenan looked over his shoulder from where he crouched before a ring of rocks he was placing for a fire. He stood, walking over to sit next to her.

"I've been thinking, Serena, about where we will live." His hand rested over hers.

"Not at Kilchurn?"

Keenan crossed his ankles in a gesture of ease. "We might want a bit more privacy." He smiled wickedly at her and bumped teasingly against her shoulder.

Despite his relaxed impression, Serena could see a small furrow across his brow and felt something like an itch of unease. "Do you think we won't be welcome at Kilchurn?"

Keenan's smile faltered. "'Tis a possibility. The whole clan thinks ye're meant to marry Lachlan, except Eleanor."

The reminder that Keenan's sweet sister wouldn't hate her and Keenan for wedding was a warm balm. Serena lowered her voice so that it was almost inaudible over the rush of falling water. "And do you still believe that I'm meant for Lachlan, Keenan?"

Keenan looked deep into her eyes. She dared not blink for fear of missing some unspoken communication. After a moment, Keenan shook his head slowly. "Nay lass, I feel ye in my bones." He touched her cheek lightly while she held her breath. "I burn for ye." He let out a long sigh, as if he'd been holding his breath all his life. "I don't understand the way of the prophecy, but I know that I'd kill Lachlan myself if he were to try and take ye from me now. Tha gaol agam ort, Serena," he said in thick Gaelic. "I love ye, Serena."

Serena had felt his love in every caress, every kiss, every touch of her hair, but he hadn't said the words. Until now. Tears broke over the edge of her eyes as she leaned forward to kiss him.

"I love you too, Keenan."

Keenan quirked a grin on his face. "So I've heard."

Serena's lips parted, but then she smiled. "Brodrick?"

"Aye, and Ewan."

"'Tis true," she said falling forward into him, knowing that he would catch her. They leaned back together on the blanket to rest in each other's arms.

Later as the sun lowered, they watched the trout roast across some soaked sticks resting on the hot coals. The rushing of the waterfall filled the void of their words, and they were both lost in their thoughts.

Keenan's voice broke into the silence. "There's a vacant cottage on the edge of the village before the castle. 'Tis sound, and I could build onto it."

Serena's heart sped quickly. "A house? Our own house? Where I could raise a small vegetable garden?"

He pressed a soft kiss to her lips and looked into her eyes. "If we are welcome at Kilchurn, aye, then we'll live there. I wouldn't want to stay in the castle, welcome or not. No privacy and the tension may be tiring until Lachlan gets used to the idea of ye being married to me. It took a lifetime for him to find ye, it may take him the rest of his lifetime to give ye up. I wouldn't have us live under that."

Serena placed her palm on his stubbled cheek. "I married a wise man."

Keenan snorted, kissed her palm firmly, and stood up. "For someone so wise, I've never been so unsure of the future in all my life."

"We'll figure it out together." She sighed happily. "And to think, I'll have a house without wheels where I can grow a garden out back."

Keenan's laughter rumbled softly as he poked the fish with the point of his dagger.

"I'll grow herbs in one section," Serena grabbed a small stick and knelt at the edge of the blanket to draw in the dirt. "Cabbages too." Serena talked about vegetable gardens and little fences and a hearth.

Keenan nodded and listened while giving advice. As they talked of their future, Serena felt the heaviness of worry slide from her shoulders. They would be happy. As long as they were together, joy would weave itself through each day of her life. Together, they would face the words and thoughts of betrayal. Together they would love and live. Together.

CHAPTER THIRTY-TWO
CONFESSION

Serena rode her own horse as they skirted the perimeter of Loch Awe. Keenan's warhorse chomped and stamped, longing for Kilchurn's familiar stables. High above, Serena heard Chiriklò chirp as his bright blue body darted from one branch to another. Her pet had been absent during most of their journey, only showing up after they left the waterfall. Serena was thankful for the privacy. Chiriklò's bird's-eye view told her that all four of Keenan's men had returned to Kilchurn earlier that morning.

As they neared the village, Serena longed to reach out mentally to them, and to Lachlan, but she forced herself to erect walls. She must stay strong, and the heavy thoughts and emotions would weaken her.

The wind blew cool as spring's sun tried to thaw the earth. Sheep shuffled together in an undulating clump over the field, and the glassy surface of Loch Awe reflected the waking land. The world hummed, ready to burst with life. Somehow it was oblivious to humanity's fears, anger, and wars.

Serena had learned about Prince Charles Stuart from Keenan on their journey. Keenan completely supported Scotland in its war for independence, but he despised the prince, having spent time with him in France. The Young Pretender, as he was called by loyalists, knew nothing about Scotland and her traditions. He drank hard and wenched hard, sometimes too hard.

Although charismatic with his men, the young prince knew nothing of war, nothing of strategy. Loyal to his clan, Keenan would support his brother's cause, but he put no faith in the prince's leadership.

Before entering the village, Keenan reined in beside Serena, keeping his horse under control with firm but gentle words. He turned to her, his look serious. "Have ye walled yer senses off?" She nodded. "No need to hear the ugliness in peoples' perceptions. They know nothing of us, only the prophecy."

She reached for his fisted hand against his leg. She'd put her gloves on as they neared, but she pulled one off so she could feel his warmth. "And you remember, Keenan, that you've done nothing wrong. Even if I'd never met you, I wouldn't marry Lachlan. I'd only give my heart and loyalty to someone with courage, cleverness, and strength of character." She squeezed his hand.

"Keenan," someone from the village yelled. "Keenan's returned and he's brought her."

Serena pulled her hand back and pulled on her glove. She nudged her horse up alongside his. They would ride into Kilchurn together.

Smiles and greetings surrounded them as they rode to the gates of the castle. Serena didn't see the four Macleans who'd reached Kilchurn before them. She focused ahead as they approached Kilchurn Keep, listening to her horse's hooves squishing in the mud. Chiriklò landed on the blanket tied behind her, tilting his head this way and that.

People gathered behind them and whispers of their thoughts seeped through minute cracks in Serena's walls. It was like a soft hum, a tone of voice and not the words themselves.

There was unease in the hum of the village, a waiting tension among these good people. But as they stepped from their homes to see their arrival, the tension transmuted into anticipation, an ease to their shoulders and a lightness to their worries. As if they all took a collective sigh of relief seeing the witch they thought would lead them to peace.

"Keenan, they don't know yet," Serena said next to him.

He frowned. "Ye're supposed to be protecting yerself from their thoughts."

"I am. But I still feel their underlying emotion."

The wind whipped around Serena's hair, swirling red tendrils up in a small tempest. A murmur rose through the onlookers. She pulled it close to her head, twisting it to behave. The hum of awe and excitement grew. Serena's stomach flipped and twisted into nausea. These people believed in her, believed that she was their savior to bring peace to Kilchurn. They were about to learn that she wouldn't live up to their prophecy.

Would it have been easier to feel their disdain from the very start? Serena swallowed hard and tamped her guilt down into the pit of her belly where she resolved to keep it.

"Ready?" Keenan asked as he stared straight ahead, lifting his hand in greeting to the guards along the walkway above them. They stopped before the tall arching gates, the doors opening.

"Together, then," Serena answered, and they nudged their horses forward in unison, under the walkway, under the arch, into the bailey crowded with warriors.

Serena's eyes scanned the armed men looking for Brodrick, Gavin, perhaps William or Eleanor. She didn't see any of them in the gathering.

As she continued to look across the faces, it took her a moment to realize what she was seeing.

Blood? Dark stains wavered in and out over their cloaks. The tangy stench of sweat and fresh wounds filled her nose. She coughed against it, raising the back of her hand to block the reek. The piercing caw of carrion crows made her tilt her head back to search the blue, empty skies above them. Smoke, she smelled gun smoke too.

"Serena?" Keenan said from his horse, reaching his hand out to steady her on her mount.

She looked back out across the men. "What battle has befallen them," she whispered at the sight of broken and torn limbs, gnarled bones twisted out of their ragged, gray skin. Most of the warriors around her seemed like they should be buried in the ground, not standing before her, hailing Keenan in greeting. They even smiled, their broken faces twisted and pale. Her stomach curled against the sight, and she looked at Keenan. Thankfully he looked normal, but then her powers didn't work on him. If they did, would he match the others? A shudder rippled through her, and she swallowed down the bile rising in her throat.

Keenan nudged his horse closer until they touched. "What do ye see, Serena?"

"They're," she hesitated, pleading with her eyes for him to believe her. "They look dead, Keenan, most of them anyway. Dead as if slaughtered by sword and shot."

Keenan's eyes scanned the crowd. He held his hand up to stop them from advancing.

"All of them?"

His voice held no doubt, no worry about her sanity. He trusted her sight, even though he might not understand it any better than she did. She looked out past him again. For a moment they looked normal, but in a blink, they turned back to grim specters, shot, bloodied, bashed, and crusted with dark blood and smears of mud and ash.

Several women stood in the bailey among them. They looked normal, just curious as they watched. Several older men looked whole and as hardy as they could in their advanced age. Here and there, Serena was able to pick out a man or two that didn't look to have a fatal wound, only a scratch or two.

"Not all, not the women, nor the old men. Some warriors don't look dead, just battered." Serena rubbed her eyes. "Keenan," she mumbled against her hand. "What am I seeing?"

Keenan dismounted, circling his mount quickly to pull her from her horse. "Make way," he said and bent to pick her up in his arms. "Serena feels unwell. Make way."

"Let me walk," Serena said as he shouldered his way through the throng. "I want to walk inside beside you."

He halted, releasing her feet to the stone steps. A warrior stood at the door, holding it open. She knew him from her first visit. Rus was his name. His wife worked in the kitchens and was expecting her first child. Serena let her breath out slowly, thankful that he looked whole, worried but whole.

"Welcome back, milady," he said bowing slightly. He reached out to help her up the steps.

"Don't touch her," Keenan's sharp command was too late as Rus grabbed her arm near her elbow.

As he stood, snatching his hand back, Serena saw the spear tip protruding from his belly, bloodied flesh and muscle caught along the jagged shaft. He warped into a corpse before her eyes, the rancid smell of stomach juices and old blood assailing her. She coughed, covering her mouth, and rushed inside. In the darkened entry Serena pressed herself against the cool plastered stone wall.

Keenan came up before her. "Rus, too?"

All she could do was nod. Words may have brought up her morning meal.

"Deeper breaths, Serena, or ye'll end up heaped on the floor." She forced herself to slow. "That's it, one step at a time. Rebuild that wall of yers to keep them out. I won't let anyone touch ye."

Serena stepped away from the wall. "I'm... ready."

They walked into the Great Hall. The fire blazed hot across the room in the hearth. The tapestries, chairs, and tables all looked as they'd left them. A group of men stood near the far wall under where a sword and shield had hung before. Serena breathed in the warm smell of fresh bread that hung in the air. She imagined her breath moving down into her. As she exhaled, the breath seeped out of her nose into a long thread of power that wrapped around her in circles from head to toe. She drew deeply on an inner core of strength that stemmed from her stomach. Her dragonfly mark began to warm, branding her with tingling heat, hot but not enough to burn.

Some men came forward, and Serena smiled with genuine happiness.

"Brodrick, Gavin, so good to see you here," she said stepping forward as the two men came close. Brodrick opened his arms to embrace her as Keenan stepped between them. Serena ran into his broad back.

"She's not well," Keenan said.

Brodrick peered around Keenan. "She looks healthy enough."

"Aye, she does, but if ye touch her, she may think ye look very unhealthy."

Brodrick frowned in confusion.

"What do ye mean?" Gavin asked.

"Not sure yet," Keenan said cryptically as he watched Lachlan walk over with Thomas and Ewan. "I'll explain later, just don't touch her right now."

"'Tis good to see ye lass," Brodrick said around Keenan. Gavin also smiled at her.

"Does he know?" Keenan asked before his brother could yet hear them. Thomas talked close to Lachlan's ear as they walked slowly.

Gavin shook his head. "Nay."

"Don't forget," Serena said, "we tell him together."

"I don't remember that part, lass," he said with a frown. "This is between me and my brother."

"But I'm part of it, part of your prophecy."

Lachlan had reached them and stopped. Serena turned away from Keenan's frown to look at his brother. Something was different about the man. True, his hair was still shoulder-length brown, his build tall but not filled out like the warriors around them. But there was an air about him, a confidence that hadn't been there when they'd left. And something caught her eye, a sword, strapped to his back. That definitely hadn't been there before.

"Welcome home, Brother," Lachlan said and clapped Keenan on the shoulder. "I see ye've brought the lovely Serena with ye." He turned an awkward smile toward Serena, a smile that seemed at odds with the deep furrows of his brow and circles beneath his eyes.

"I've brought Serena, but, Lachlan, we have much to discuss."

"Talk fast, we have much to *do*," Lachlan answered, stressing the word. "Discussions have ended. We leave on the morrow for Culloden Moor."

"Culloden?" Serena asked.

"Ye plan to go to battle, Lachlan?" Keenan's eyes moved to the sword strapped to Lachlan's back. "With Da's sword?"

"I do," Lachlan answered and turned bright eyes to Serena. "'Tis about time I come out of hiding." He looked back at Keenan. "And we've been called to join the Prince. 'Tis a final blow to drive those English dogs back down into their country."

Keenan shook his head the smallest amount. "Lachlan, I've seen King George's plans for Culloden."

Lachlan's eyes grew round.

"We," Keenan looked first at Serena, and then back to his brother, "saw them at Frampton Manor where George sojourned."

Lachlan's face fell into a frown, reminding Serena of the man they'd left behind. "Ye were close to him and yet he breathes?"

Keenan ignored his bait. "He has nearly nine thousand troops moving that way under the Earl of Cumberland. And there are also some Scots that plan to join him in return for their lands."

Lachlan's face grew red, mottled. "Baa, bloody bastards! 'Tis their betrayal that will defeat us."

Lachlan's words thundered through Serena's ears. That he spoke of Scotsmen and not she and Keenan didn't matter much. She watched Keenan's face, but he gave nothing away.

Keenan kept his voice level, unimpassioned. "Even without the Scots, he has nine thousand troops, well-trained troops. We are no match to that."

"Prince Charles Stuart will outmaneuver Cumberland."

"Ye don't know the prince. I do. He's a grand speaker, a grand talker of dreams and glorious victories. He can rally a group and boil their blood against any army. But nay, Lachlan, he can't outmaneuver Cumberland and his nine thousand soldiers."

Lachlan didn't look at all convinced. "But we have the advantage of prophecy, Keenan. We know that we will come out of this in peace."

Lachlan glanced at Serena. "Ye are the witch of our prophecy, Serena, ye know that. Ye herald the tide of peace for the Macleans at Kilchurn."

Serena felt her heart thump in her chest. "So I've been told, Laird Maclean."

He laughed. "Laird Maclean? Ye have no need to bow to formalities here, Serena. As ye will be part of this family before long. In fact, here before everyone," he began, raising his voice so that the handful of men in the room all could hear.

"Nay, Brother," Keenan said low, but Lachlan talked over him.

Serena spotted Eleanor as she rounded the corner into the Great Hall. Serena kept her eyes locked on Keenan's sister, as if she were a floating branch to hold onto in a rapid river.

"Before God and my family and friends, I make it official and ask Lady Serena to wed with me." Lachlan bowed low and moved to his knee before her. Serena couldn't pull in a full breath. She had to look down at him and away from Eleanor.

"Send me to war with yer kiss and yer vow. Lead this clan to victory against England," Lachlan said.

Time seemed to evade its normal speed as Serena stared at Lachlan bent down, her stomach twisting. She had no idea what to say. For a moment she felt like she sat outside of herself watching the horror unfold, wondering what would happen next, what she would say next. Serena wished she could see ahead so she'd know what words to force from her frozen lips. If it were but a play, and she could see her next line. What would it be?

She must have paused too long for she heard Keenan start to say something, but she couldn't let him stand alone before his brother, before his clan. If she let him answer for her, it would seem that he manipulated all the events in his favor.

Serena held up her hand to Keenan to stop him as her words came forth, loud in the absolute silence of the hall. "Laird Lachlan Maclean, you do me great honor with your request." Serena glanced at the other occupants of the room. The four Macleans who had journeyed with them stood, their legs braced apart, arms crossed. Eleanor stood unmoving by the stairs with William who had descended. Five or six other Maclean warriors, including Rus, had come inside. They all seemed to hold their breaths, waiting on her words. As if those words would decide the fate of their clan at Culloden. Serena swallowed and looked back down to Lachlan.

"Please rise, milord."

Lachlan stood and she began again. "It is a great honor you bestow upon me, but I cannot accept."

Lachlan frowned slightly at her as if humoring her. "On what grounds, milady?"

"On the grounds that I cannot marry where I do not love."

Lachlan smiled. "How young and fresh," he said. "Do not fear, Serena. Love can grow once we're wed. Ye can consider it for the night. 'Tis a good match."

For a brief moment, escape lurked in Serena's mind. She could lie. She could say that she would consider and stop this terrible scene. She could meet with him later, send him a message. Have Keenan talk to him without the eyes of his clan stripping them for all to see.

Serena sighed inside as the weak plan dissolved into an ache at the back of her head. She couldn't retreat, lie out of cowardice. For no matter how she justified the lie, it would still be said out of fear. Serena shook her head. "I cannot love you," she whispered, and then stopped. She wouldn't confess her love for Keenan quietly, she would proclaim it.

Serena took a deep breath. "I cannot love you because I love another, I have wed another."

Several shocked grunts came from across the room, but she ignored them. Eleanor's feminine gasp came from the stairs.

"But," Lachlan's voice shook before he forced enough breath to make the words strong again. "But ye are the witch, the one to bring us to peace. Ye cannot have wed another."

Keenan stepped up next to Serena and took her hand in his. He squeezed it gently but continued to stare at his brother. "Serena and I were married six days ago at the Faw Romany camp near Leicester."

CHAPTER THIRTY-THREE
LOVE OVER SHAME

"Ye married her?" The question hissed from Lachlan, heavy with accusation.

Thomas stepped forward with the other three warriors. "He had no choice. They were going to marry her to a Romany man from another tribe."

Gavin spoke as Thomas paused. "Keenan had to marry her or they wouldn't let her leave to return with us."

Ewan jumped in. "Nothing in the prophecy says that she needs to be a maid. Once Keenan dies, ye can marry her."

"Enough!" Keenan's voice bellowed over Serena's fierce denial, smothering it. "Enough," he repeated.

Lachlan stared at Keenan, his face made of stone. "If ye married her to bring her to me, let us find a man of the kirk to annul the vows, Brother." His words were soft but firm. "Do yer duty, Keenan, and give her to me." Desperation lurked behind his words.

Serena's shock turned to fury. He spoke of her as if she were property, an object to be used, taken, and given. A cloak of protection and nothing more.

Emotion fled Keenan's face as he stared into Lachlan's eyes. A calmness came over him with a look of boredom. Serena only felt the slight clenching of the fist that wrapped around her hand.

"I did more than wed her, Lachlan, I bound her to me in handfasting. I claimed her with my body." The slight edge of challenge sharpened his words, a deadly cold challenge. "She is mine." Keenan used his grasp on Serena's hand to tug her to the side, slightly behind him, shielding her, but she refused to hide. She pressed forward next to Keenan.

A long pause ensued as each brother weighed the other. No one moved. Serena's heart hurt with the weight of the air in the room. The ache at the base of her skull throbbed.

Lachlan's words were low. "Then ye have killed me, *Brother*." He flung the last word as if it were a curse.

"Prophecies are often misinterpreted," Keenan said. His words remained low.

In a burst that made Serena jump, Lachlan whirled around and strode to the hearth. He took a goblet of wine from the mantel and slammed it into the flames. Wine sputtered within the fire, hissing, dissolving quickly in the heat.

The outburst moved each warrior's hand to their hilts. Brodrick, Gavin, Thomas, and Ewan formed a close circle around her, guarding her and Keenan's back. Would civil war break out in this hall, a war between brothers over her?

"No," she yelled and pushed past Keenan toward Lachlan. "He has not killed you, Lachlan. The love that grew between Keenan and me, it was meant to be. Our bond formed on its own, not to spite you, and definitely not to harm you in any way. Your prophecy—"

"Ye know naught of our prophecy, Witch!" Lachlan roared. Serena heard steel slide free behind her.

She continued, undaunted, her heart pounding with her need to end this. "I know you don't want to die, none of us do, but we all do eventually. No prophecy will cause it as none can prevent it."

Lachlan stared at her with a mixture of fury and condemnation. What could she do to stop this? What could she use to squelch the smoldering emotions of betrayal and resentment?

"Use me," she said to Lachlan. "Use my powers to avoid death, death for both of you."

"Serena," Keenan said, but she continued.

"No Keenan, even married to you, I can still read the minds of enemies. I can see probable outcomes. If you two but listen to me, you can both live long lives."

"And continue to hide," Lachlan said, the edge dulled from his voice. He shook his head and looked past Serena to Keenan. "I'm through hiding. I've lived more in these last three days than I have my whole life." He glanced back at her. "I won't hide behind yer skirts." He scoffed. "Let my brother hide behind them."

"I don't hide, Lachlan. I never have." Keenan resheathed his sword. "I only warn ye of a disaster ye are about to walk into."

"I'm going to Culloden, with or without ye," Lachlan said with a wave of dismissal.

Keenan walked close to him. "Serena is seeing things with her magic," he lowered his voice so it wouldn't carry. "She's seeing the slaughter of our men. If ye lead them to Culloden, ye lead them to death."

Lachlan strode to Serena and grabbed her head in his two large hands, one on either side of her face. She gasped at the contact as it crashed through her defenses.

She saw Lachlan's eyes bulging, his lips pulled back in a snarl. But more than the sight of his face, she saw his emotions. His anger, the pain of betrayal, resentment that he'd wasted thirty-seven years not living. "Then see me, Serena Maclean," he spat. "See my future, tell me of my death, a death brought on by ye and my brother."

His face blurred before her, changing. Lachlan's face turned gray, gun smoke char smeared across his brow. Red spread out from his tunic along his chest. The aroma of death filled Serena's nose and slaked against her tongue as if she'd licked the sweat off his skin.

The scream rose up out of her like a frightened bird taking flight, as if she could escape upon it. Lachlan was ripped from her as angry Gaelic curses bellowed up. Serena's gaze wobbled, and then steadied as she tried to center on the moving room. The men shouted and some shoved. Serena watched Eleanor run toward her, William following.

"Serena, come with me. Away from this," Eleanor's soft voice beckoned. Serena tried to focus on her words. She took Eleanor's outstretched hands and looked down at them. Red, warm blood covered Eleanor's hands. So hot, so slippery.

Serena's breath huffed from her like she'd been punched in the stomach. The throbbing at the base of her skull pounded into her as if she were being pummeled from behind. "Eleanor, blood, on your hands, so much blood."

"Whose blood?" she whispered.

"I don't know, but there's so much."

Eleanor's concerned face swam before her.

"Àngelas!" Serena heard William call her from what seemed far away.

The throbbing rose, pounding in time with her aching heart, with each rapid intake of breath. The floor gave way beneath her, and Serena knew she was falling. Falling into blessed darkness, away from the madness. A net of nothingness enveloped her. No thoughts, no anger, no bloody premonitions, just blessed peace wrapped around her limp body. Keenan had caught her.

—◦—

Serena flicked her eyes open, blinking at the piercing glow of the hearth fire. She rolled to her side until her face pressed against a bare, warm chest. With one indrawn breath of leather and some fresh spice mixed with a gentle musk, Serena knew it was Keenan. She sighed into his skin.

"Mmm, ye feel good, lass," Keenan's words rumbled up from the very spot where she lay her cheek. He sat up on an elbow and rolled her flat so he could peer down into her face, searching. Deep lines marked his forehead. "Serena," he touched her forehead at the hairline, tenderly running his fingers across her temple and down along the bone of her jaw. "How do ye feel?"

She smiled gently. "A kiss would help."

His frown relaxed, easing away the lines of worry. Keenan bowed his head and kissed her as if she were a delicate flower he could crush. He pulled back way too soon.

Without opening her eyes Serena said, "nice, but I'd like more." She felt him roll from the bed, and she pushed herself onto an elbow. Keenan walked over to add more peat to the fire. He wore a Maclean plaid draped low over his hips, and she watched the shadows play across the muscles of his bare back.

Her hand moved under her hair to massage the nape of her neck. The pounding had relented but it still felt tender. As she watched his stiff movements, a prickle of unease slid along her skin, making her shiver. Something was wrong.

"Is it late?" she asked glancing toward the covered windows. No light peeked through.

"Nay, but ye slept through dinner," he said and picked up a bowl to bring over to her. He sat down, his hands pushing her hair from her face.

"Really lass, ye are well?"

She nodded as best she could with his two large hands encasing her head.

"Ye screamed downstairs and fainted."

She exhaled. "The images, the smells, they broke through my defense," she hesitated, "when Lachlan grabbed me." Keenan released her face, his one hand fisting as he planted it on the bed next to them.

"He won't touch ye again, Serena. We," he paused, "discussed it, and he will never harm ye in any way again."

"And I fainted?"

He nodded. "Ye said there was blood on Eleanor."

Serena took a deep breath. "Yes, on her hands, but she looked whole to me."

"And others did not?"

Was he asking about Lachlan? "No, some did not. But Eleanor did, just her hands were covered. Perhaps she will help the wounded?"

"Perhaps." He stood and began to pace. She sat cross-legged in the center of the large, curtained bed and watched him. He stopped and turned to her, his eyes deep with emotion. Was it in his eyes, or did she feel the hesitation within him? And something else, guilt.

"Ye know I don't ask lightly for ye to remember such terrible things, nor have I asked ye to use yer powers to my advantage. But the fate of my clan, Serena, the fate of my family," he trailed off. "If there is anything ye could tell me, that ye saw or know that could help them survive, please tell me." From such a large, imposing man whose presence seemed to steal the air from the room, his words were more plea than order.

Serena dropped her chin and closed her eyes while nodding slightly. "Of course, Keenan. I'll help anyway I can." She pushed back to lean against the headboard. In bodily detail, she began to describe what she saw, from the ashen faces to the spear through Rus to Lachlan's bleeding chest.

Sometime during the recounting, Keenan moved to sit next to her, stroking her hand, adding his strength to her.

"Then I saw the blood on Eleanor's hands, and you caught me." Serena leaned closer to him. "I knew you would catch me."

He brushed his lips against hers and pulled back. Sadness weighed heavily in the room, and it made it hard for her to breathe.

"Serena, I need to talk with ye."

Panic curdled up through her stomach like sour milk. She just couldn't handle more upheaval right now. "Keenan, 'tis the end of a very long day. Come to bed, husband. Help me wash the blood from my mind."

Keenan's protest melted on his lips as Serena rose up on her knees to kiss him fully. She ran hands across the firm muscles of his chest, brushing her fingertips back and forth. After a week loving him, she had discovered subtle ways of making Keenan lose his stringent control, and she now understood how taking his jack into her mouth could pleasure her too by watching his control shatter.

She moved her kiss to the edge of his ear, letting her hot breath whisper against him. "Love me, Keenan. I need you tonight." Her lips closed teasingly around his earlobe, her tongue tickling the skin.

For the briefest of moments, she thought he would deny her. Serena threaded fingers through his soft, wavy hair. Keenan closed his eyes, and she ran the tips of her fingers along his temple, following his scar down across his rough jaw. He seemed to hold his breath as if her touch was both pleasure and torture.

When she followed the planes of his body down his muscled stomach to tease along the top of his kilt, Keenan buried his face in her hair. He held her tightly to him as her fingers worked to loosen the material.

Serena changed tactics and slid her hand up under the woolen wrap into the warmth trapped underneath. She found his hard jack easily and wrapped her hand around its length. Keenan growled low against her neck and pulled her hair to the side so he could kiss the nape of her neck, sending streaks of heat racing downward.

"Ye play with fire, lass," he said, his thick brogue muffled against her skin. Serena didn't catch each word, but she caught the warning. In answer she slid her hand up and down along his shaft, running her thumb over the soft skin of the tip.

"I've grown to womanhood dancing around fire," she whispered back.

Keenan growled deeper and pressed her back into the mounds of furs and pillows on the bed. His lips descended on hers, full of purpose, full of desperate passion. Serena poured herself into the kiss, all her worry, her denial, and her trust in him.

She felt him pry her fingers away from him and pull back enough to strip the plaid, leaving him completely bare. The glow of the fire brushed him gold, the shadows outlining every dip and hill of muscle running across her warrior. His eyes locked with hers, intent eyes, hungry eyes, as he pulled the shift up her body, releasing her breasts, and then over her head. The nearly sheer cotton floated to the floor somewhere next to the bed.

Her breasts felt heavy, the nipples chilled, waiting. Serena moved her hands slowly to cup them, lifting them upward so they looked even fuller. She saw his gaze drop to them, and she rolled her nipples between thumb and forefinger. She shifted her legs against his where he kneeled between them. His hungry stare, his bare arousal, and the rolling of her own nipples ignited Serena's body. The flame spread. She tried to keep her eyes open, but they flickered closed as she moaned softly, her fingers still playing with her breasts.

"Och lass, I love to watch ye touch yerself."

And she loved to touch herself, knowing that he watched, as if she were his prey. A tremor of excitement mixed with the flame inside.

Keenan's lips came back to bathe her flushed neck in more heat. His hand replaced her own on her breast, lifting, teasing. The rough contrast of his hand against her skin poured more sensation into her. His lips followed, and the feel of his hot, wet mouth brought her off the bed.

"Keenan," she breathed, her hands running along the broad muscles of his shoulders. "I want to feel you inside me," she said and trailed her fingers down her body to the juncture of her legs. She touched herself, feeling the dampness and heat there.

Keenan groaned as he watched. His large hand spanned the skin across her gently rounded belly, moving lower in long caresses. Keenan met her hand and pushed past it into her channel. Serena grabbed handfuls of blanket on either side of her body as he worked his fingers expertly within her. He rubbed his thumb against her most sensitive spot. "Do ye trust me, Serena?" Her eyes closed. Her breathing rushed out in a pant as she nodded, her head thrown back into the pillow.

"I need to hear ye say it," he said. Serena opened her eyes at the vulnerability she heard and felt from him. "Do ye trust me, Serena?"

Serena stared into his face. Did she trust him? Of all the people in the world, he was the one she could not fully read. Mari had said that love was a leap of faith. To trust someone whom she could not and may never be able to read, that was love.

Serena focused on the stormy gray of his steely orbs. "Keenan, I love you. I could not love without trust."

No single part of his visage changed, but somehow his entire expression did, subtly. The vulnerability turned back to strength, unease turned to conviction. He moved over her body, his face centering on her own as he lowered his lips to hers. His kiss held all the promise of love, of life together, of sincere happiness. Serena felt the tears of joy gathering at the back of her eyes.

She felt his breath warm against her lips. "Aye, I trust and love ye too," he said.

A tear slipped out the edge of her lashes. Keenan caught it with one finger and touched it between his lips. "I would catch all yer tears," he said, "and keep them."

She laughed lightly as more tears trickled out. Keenan ran his hands down her cheeks wiping them all. He kissed her. "No more tears now, lass," he said with a deeply seductive grin. "Since I have yer trust," he said sliding back down her body until he knelt between her thighs. "Trust me to teach ye something ye may like." He grabbed one of her ankles and lifted it up to lay it draped over his shoulder.

Serena watched as he grabbed her other ankle and slid it upward against his other shoulder, making her stomach flutter. She was completely open to him. "What are you doing?"

Keenan moved his hand back to her crux and teased her. "Something ye may like, lass."

Serena palmed her breasts as he lifted her backside up so that he slid inside her with her legs still up in the air on either side of his head. A slow moan escaped her lips as he filled her, stretching her body in the most delicious way.

He groaned as he completely sheathed himself in her slick heat. The comical look of her toes curling around his ears was forgotten as Keenan began to move, hitting parts of her core that sent streaks of sensations ricocheting toward her womb.

"Oh, Keenan," she swallowed between quick breaths as he moved, "that spot."

"Aye," he rasped, "'tis a good spot." Keenan rubbed his length back and forth against the most sensitive ridge inside. Serena's mind whirled into numbness as sensations surged below. The enormous energy ached inside her, building. Her moans became ragged as she drove toward him to meet each of his thrusts. Faster and faster, he rubbed within her.

Serena forced her eyes to stay open so she could watch his powerful warrior's body straining over her, pumping into her. Flesh slapped against damp flesh. Heat enveloped her and Serena continued to pull at her aching breasts. Keenan growled above her as he watched. He reached down to the vee between her legs to rub his callused thumb against her sensitive nub. The incredible friction shot the ache higher within Serena.

"Keenan," she yelled as the eruption shattered her. The rolling waves of ecstasy pulsed through and around Serena, gripping her, splitting her. Keenan's roar echoed her own as he poured himself into her quivering body.

He continued to pound into her until the last shudders of sensation began to ebb. Keenan turned his shoulders so her feet could fall to either side of him, and he pulled Serena against him on the bed.

Serena laid her hand against his heart and felt the same pounding rhythm pulsing in him to match her own heartbeats. Keenan's arms surrounded her, his heartbeat against her cheek, and his legs lay entwined with her own. She breathed in the combined scent of their love, somehow feeling his physical satisfaction that mirrored her own. She still couldn't read his thoughts, but there was a physical connection between them, strong and pulsing with their shared release.

"Mmm," she said against his skin. "I definitely like playing with fire."

CHAPTER THIRTY-FOUR
TO CULLODEN

"Serena, lass, wake up." Keenan's voice rippled the dark warm pool of her exhausted sleep. Serena rolled away, grasping for the mental comfort of rejuvenating oblivion.

"I must go, and I won't leave without kissing ye."

Serena's eyes blinked open, and she rolled toward Keenan. He was fully dressed, dressed in the rugged clothes of a warrior as he sat beside her on the large bed. "Where?" she asked, pushing up and hugging the blankets over her naked breasts. "Where are you going?"

A determined glint to his eyes made her stomach roll, and she pushed up onto her knees, letting the blanket fall away. "No, Keenan," she said shaking her head. "You can't go with them to Culloden." Fear contracted all the muscles of her body.

"Serena," he soothed, pulling the blanket up around her shoulders. "I must. How could I stay behind when my entire clan goes to fight for their freedom?"

"But you don't support Prince Charles."

"Nay, but I support Lachlan and my clan. If he's foolish enough to go, I must go too."

She threw her legs over the side of the bed. Serena ignored the wobbling in her muscles as she wrapped the warm blanket around her body. This is what he wanted to talk about last night. He wanted to tell her he was leaving. "You're going to defend him," the words spat from her mouth with panicky venom.

"If I must," Keenan answered. "But I also go to lead my men." He came around and took her hands. "Serena," his words were gentle but firm. "I trained those men. I can't abandon them now to my brother's strategies; he has none. They truly will be slaughtered if I don't guide them through this."

"But," she glanced around desperately. "But there are others who could lead, others you have trained."

He shook his head, adjusting a strap that crisscrossed against his chest.

Angry tears sat unshed in her eyes, blurring her sight until she blinked them away. "Keenan, I saw so much of that slaughter yesterday. Please," she pulled on his hands, "do not go. We are supposed to be together, the house in the village, the vegetable garden, the years of living and loving. Keenan I trusted you to stay with me."

Keenan's face hardened, his gaze boring into hers. "Would ye have me stay here, hiding while my clan goes off to war? Ye could never love a coward."

"You wouldn't be a coward."

"To my clan, I would. To myself, I would," Keenan led her back to the bed and pressed her gently to sit on the edge. "Serena, every one of my men is leaving a wife or their family. I'm just one of them, one husband who must do my job in keeping this clan safe. Doing my part to push back against English invasion."

She shook her head, sickly worry and angry betrayal heating her cheeks and words. "But you are not just one of them." Serena tried to keep from yelling. "The prophecy marks you for death, Keenan."

"And yer sight marks most of them for death," he pointed out.

Serena jumped up. "But they don't know that. I'll go down there and tell them all what I see, then they'll stay home."

"Nay," his voice warned. "Don't put the fear of death in them. It will crumble their will."

"But it will stop them from going."

Keenan shook his head. "It won't. They'll still go, for not to go would make them cowards, afraid of death like Lachlan has been his whole life. For those ye scare into staying, ye will dishonor. For those who still go, ye will kill their confidence. 'Tis what feeds their strength. Confidence and courage will carry them through this battle. Without them, they have no chance at all."

Serena fell into a seat before the cold hearth, and Keenan knelt before her. "Lass, every wife must wish her husband farewell to battles."

"Not every husband has convinced himself he will die defending his clan," she whispered, knowing that she would never be able to break what Keenan had believed his whole life.

He shook his head and tilted her chin up to meet his gaze. "I no longer live, waiting for the prophecy to come true. I don't live for my death," he said. "My life changed when I realized that I love ye, Serena." He took her hands in his. "Back in our clearing under that night sky, for the first time in my life, I wished upon a shooting star, because I finally have something I desperately want. Ye, Serena. I wished to live my life with ye, a long life. That wish won't change no matter what enemy I face." He squeezed her hands as if trying to press his reasons inside her. "Before, I never cared if I returned from a battle. Now I know I must."

Keenan pulled a soft cloth from his belt and wiped away the one tear that had broken free. Serena took a deep breath past the ache in her chest, and Keenan stood, pulling her up and wrapping his strong arms around her. Serena clung, rubbed her face into him, and breathed his scent. She felt his hands play through her hair and the ache in his own chest, the guilt for leaving her.

"I won't hide up here while you ride away," she said. "I won't play the coward, either." Serena felt his chin graze her head as he nodded.

"You could never play the coward, my lovely warrior." He kissed her hair, then pulled away slightly, pulling a dagger from his boot. The light caught the glint of the sharp blade. Intricate knots twined together along the silver length up into the cross hilt. "It was my mother's, gifted to me to help me defend, to help me fulfill my obligations." He looked at it and turned its hilt to Serena. "Ye'll be safe here, but I want ye to keep it with ye." She slid it from his hand.

A quarter hour later, Serena flew down the winding stairs into the Great Hall, her skirts nearly tripping her. The empty stone room felt like a tomb in its silence. She wrapped her wool cloak tightly around her shoulders and pushed out through the oaken doors. Eleanor stood next to Robert Mackay and William on the steps leading into the bailey.

William. She hadn't even greeted him yet. She ran to him, and his arms went instantly around her, hugging her close. "I love him, William. I love Keenan."

William pulled back and bent to touch her forehead with his. "I know, Àngelas, and we will wait here together for his return."

Serena looked out across the Maclean warriors standing in orderly groups within the bailey. Keenan walked amongst them, issuing orders, inspecting weapons, horses, and wagons.

Eleanor looped her arm through hers. "He's made sure that the Macleans have their own supplies. He doesn't trust the prince to bring enough food for his troops."

Serena felt numb, but it had little to do with the morning chill as she focused on Keenan, his tall figure walking with confidence and strength among his men. He knew what he was doing. He'd trained his whole life to lead armies, giving them the best chance of survival.

Perhaps with his decision to go his men wouldn't look so bloody to her. Serena turned her attention to some of the troops and thinned her defenses, spying as if through her fingers to see their futures. She spotted Rus. The spear still poked out gruesomely from his gut. Serena caught her breath, and Eleanor pulled her up against her.

"I'm well," Serena lied as she slammed the layer of protection back in place. She had to be strong, as strong as the men before her and the women and children huddled within the walls placing bits of ribbon and spring flowers in the tunics of their husbands, brothers, sons, and fathers. The mood was somber as if she'd already told them of their fates.

Keenan spotted her and weaved through the soldiers to her side. Serena forced a stiff smile. Shoulders back, chin held even, eyes blinked clear of any moisture. Keenan walked straight up to her, and she pulled the blue ribbon holding her hair. She tied it tightly to a strap that ran above his heart.

"Fare thee well, Keenan," her voice rang out in the hushed air. "Come home to me." He pulled her into his embrace with such emotion that tears welled in her eyes. His warm lips moved against hers for an intimate moment before he pulled away. The angry cries of crows overhead fell across the bailey as a brisk morning wind whipped hair around her head, sending its ends flapping like a flag. Keenan captured the errant strands in his leather-clad hand.

"Trust me, Serena. I will do everything I can to be with ye again." He waited for her nod before he turned away and jogged back to Thomas and Ewan.

Lachlan sat mounted near the gates. His eyes met Serena's, and he nodded. She nodded back. Fury no longer contorted his face, only determination.

"Serena," Brodrick's voice caught her attention as he and Gavin strode closer. They were suited like the others.

"Brodrick, Gavin, find your mounts," she said softly.

"Keenan just asked us to remain here and secure yer safety, milady," Gavin said.

Panic gripped the inside of Serena's stomach, coming out as anger. "No." She grasped Brodrick's tunic as if to shake him. "You are going today."

"Milady?"

Serena wrapped her hand around Brodrick's bare forearm where his tunic cinched up. *Disappointment. Impotence. Reluctance to stay behind.* The panic in her stomach relaxed slightly. "You have to go, Brodrick, you and Gavin." She looked at Gavin. "William and Robert will watch Eleanor and me. But you two must go."

"Keenan worries about ye," Gavin said.

Serena looked past the two warriors and watched Keenan's back as he rode out of the bailey onto the road leading through the village. In orderly fashion the Maclean warriors followed, some on horseback, some on foot. Wagons of supplies lumbered through the gates with men sitting three across the back, their legs dangling. Creaking, clopping, words of farewell, and prayers made up the cacophony of the leaving.

Brodrick was shaking his head. "We'll stay to guard ye."

Serena studied his eyes, her brow rising. "Brodrick," determination kept her voice firm. "Who will guard Keenan?" The two warriors looked at one another, and then back to her. "With your prophecy," she said, "no one will guard Keenan's back. They will all guard Lachlan thinking that he's the one to survive, not Keenan. Who will guard Keenan's back?"

Brodrick kept her stare for a long moment. He frowned deeply, his lips pinching hard together, and then he slowly nodded. "Alright." He turned on the stairs.

"What are ye doing?" Gavin asked, his wide gaze following him.

Brodrick looked back at Serena. "I'm going to aid the Maclean who has wed the witch, who with him will bring peace to our clan."

Serena's heart clenched with hope, and she brought her fist up to rest over it as she nodded to Brodrick. He believed the prophecy could mean Keenan lived and Lachlan died.

Gavin looked between them and let out a loud huff. "They left us but one horse." Gavin jogged after Brodrick to his large horse.

"Fare thee well," Serena called as she and Eleanor waved to the two men. The horse snorted and trotted through the gate, the two warriors, pushed up against each other on his back, following the Maclean army.

As the gateman rotated the gears to lower the heavy iron bars, Serena pushed her hand into her pocket where Merewin's healing crystal sat with a bit of the Maclean plaid. The scrap of fabric was part of the blanket Keenan had used to handfast them in the clearing. In the privacy of her pocket, she wound it around her fingers.

Eleanor hugged Serena's shoulders. "Trust in him, Serena. Ye'll be together again."

Serena nodded. "Yes, we will." She turned to go inside, her next words caught within a gust of wind. "In this life or in death. We'll be together again." The thought of their bond transcending this physical plane gave her strength.

CHAPTER THIRTY-FIVE
TRICKERY MOST BLOODY

Drakkina stood in a pentagon scratched into the top layer of meadow, her arms stretched above her head. Dragonflies flitted about her, landing and shooting off in a dance. Her voice rose through the sun-filled circle within the ancient soaring rocks. "I call out to the fire of the sun." She tilted her face up to catch the heat of the glowing orb directly above her.

She spread her feet apart in a *V* amongst the wildflowers that stood still, absolutely still as if listening to her words. "I call out to the earth that circles life through its layers, to the rocks that support us upon their shoulders."

She moved her arms, rotating them, her wide sleeves like wings. "I call to the air that surrounds us and its wind that cleanses all who are strong enough to withstand it." A great breeze rose up in a swirl, bending the wildflowers, their lives dependent on their slender, flexible stems.

Drakkina's aged fingers pointed toward the western shore. "I call to the water that gives life to this world."

Drakkina closed her eyes and raised her hands upward again until they pointed in line with the fierce sun overhead. "I need your strengths, the power from each element. Fill me up, gift me with your strength as I gift you with a sacrifice of my blood." Drakkina drew her nail across her palm, her magic easily cutting into her own misty flesh. Red blood swelled along the line, and she held it over the center of the pentagon. Drops of her blood—misty, half-real blood—dripped onto the scuffed dirt and scattered flowers.

A howl resonated through Drakkina's ears as the wind whipped up and wove through the tall stones. The heads of each wildflower bowed down flat as if in worship. Drakkina held her arms open wide. Her long white hair whipped around with her flowing robes. The heat branded her skin, scorching with its intensity.

Drakkina smiled, her eyes closed to the onslaught of power. She listened as the stones resonated with wild magic, bouncing off each of the ten sarsens where they stood guarding the sacred circle. The power poured into Drakkina, fighting against her indrawn breath, squeezing her as if there was no room left in the circle for her ephemeral body.

Drakkina forced a breath down into her aching chest. "Yes," she screamed above the cacophony of swirling, vibrating chords of sound. "Bring me your power. Death stalks Serena and her mate. I need your power to bring her here to safety. It must be done."

With her last word, Drakkina's eyes snapped open to the blinding light of magic glowing in the circle. She pulled the threads as if winding them into a tight ball above the center of the pentagon. It was not physical but mental strength, strength that came with centuries of training and honing her skills that wound the threads of elemental magic into her.

The light hit the center of her palms first, the burning tight against her skin. She pulled then, from her center. Slowly the hot light bore down through Drakkina, sliding between the temporal imprint of her ribs and spine, flicking along the vessels and arteries, pumping the magic through her entire body.

She lowered her arms and breathed deeply, studying her misty body. It looked solid, to the point that her legs almost blocked the sight of the wildflowers behind them.

"Thank you," she whispered and wrapped arms around her once tired body that now resonated with youth and energy. "I will use your gift wisely." The breeze swayed the flower heads and rippled through the trees outside the circle. The dragonflies zipped down as one body to engulf Drakkina. She turned toward the east with determination.

"Deny me now, Serena. I dare you." Drakkina held her hands out in that direction and felt currents of power gathering through her. "Come to me, Serena. Come. And bring your Highlander with you."

The sun hid behind gathering clouds as Serena walked the edges of the bailey, speaking in soothing tones to the women and children of the departed warriors. It had been a day and a half since the men had left. Even though the threat to Kilchurn was minimal, many of the families had come to stay within its walls. Serena and Eleanor opened the castle to all who could fit as if they were under siege. The close proximity to the anxious people pummeled Serena with emotional energy. She was becoming mentally exhausted at holding the voices and unease at bay.

Serena ducked through the doorway and stepped past several playing children on her way into the Great Hall. A fire blazed in the hearth, but the quiet room still felt cold. She clipped over in the boots Eleanor had given her to sit next to her and William at the long table that still held a platter of bannocks.

Robert Mackay stood from his seat near the fire. "I'm off to make the rounds."

"Thank you, Robert." She smiled with as much hope as she could muster. He nodded and turned toward the door.

"I'm tired," Serena said softly.

William took a drink of mead, swallowed, and turned his face to her. "No doubt the press of so much unease," he said glancing toward the entryway where several mothers spoke with their children in hushed tones. They were all quietly waiting. For something. News of the battle wouldn't come for days, but it seemed life had stuttered to a halt as the men marched away.

Eleanor leaned toward them. "'Tis as if they know the battle will not go well."

"I said nothing," Serena said.

Eleanor squeezed Serena's hand. "I know, but we often underestimate the power of intuition in women."

"I'm going to lay down for a bit," Serena said and rose from her seat.

"Excellent idea," William said.

"When I come back down, we must come up with a rotating plan to keep the fields and livestock tended."

"I'll organize a fulling party," Eleanor said. "We have some woolen cloth to make impervious to rain."

Serena crept up the steps, her mind and heart twisting and tumbling with worry that she kept trying to push down. Otherwise she would crumble, succumbing to the despair of losing him as if he were already dead.

Serena leaned into the roughness of the wall to pull in a fortifying breath. "He plans to return to me," she whispered. "He's been training his whole life for war." Keenan was the strongest, most skilled warrior she'd ever seen. The thought helped her breath even out.

She hadn't replaced her gloves after eating, and she ran her hands along the wall as she continued up the steps. Serena stopped in mid step as a spark of power surged up her fingertip as she grazed one of the chiseled mason's marks.

Yanking back her hand, she bent to look closer at the outline. The mark was shaped like a dragonfly and hummed with energy. The image coalesced into that of a real dragonfly. She blinked to clear her tired eyes. Had the membranous wings really lifted from the rigid rock? She reached out to hover her palm just above the image.

Tingling warmth pulled at her. It didn't burn but felt comforting, alluring. Slowly she lowered her hand until it came in contact with the stone mark. Need shot through the touch, up her arm, spreading down to her heart and up into her mind. Need to move, to move west.

"I must go," Serena said to the stone, answering its spell with a whisper. The power urged her to go, but her rational mind questioned how. The gates were lowered, only opened for needs, not desires.

Follow the marks. The words echoed in her mind as if someone had spoken them aloud.

Serena's birthmark tingled where it lay etched in her skin. Glancing again at the rock, her eyes turned downward, down each narrow step, knowing without being shown where the next dragonfly mark was chiseled as if it glowed against the gray. She took several steps down, turning with the winding staircase until she found the next. Sliding her hand along its shape, she once again knew where to find the next dragonfly mark lower still.

A mist flooded her mind, warm and calm like in a pleasant dream. *So tired.* Serena's legs continued to follow mark after mark. Was Drakkina summoning her? It mattered little because there was no resisting the pull. Her mind fogged over, and her vision dimmed as if she truly were asleep.

Time flitted and compressed as through a dream. It seemed only a blink before Serena opened her eyes with the bite of wind as she walked sedately through the back gardens. Her feet carried her toward the next dragonfly mark in the castle wall near a newly tilled plot for herbs.

Serena watched detached as her fingertip touched the center of the last dragonfly. As she depressed the small stone in the middle of the carving, a hiss of wind blew through the widening crack that meandered subtly down the wall. Serena shoved against the stone and the seemingly unmovable blocks of granite swung outward.

"Serena!" She heard her name called as if from far away. "Serena, what are ye doing?" Eleanor's voice called to her as Serena slipped through the slender opening, ducking to fit under the mass of the huge wall above her.

"Stop, Serena, wait!"

She wanted to reply, turn to Eleanor and assure her that all was well, but she couldn't turn. One foot in front of the other, Serena walked west toward a tree where a horse stood. Where had the horse come from? What was Eleanor saying behind her?

Another wave of need washed through her, dissolving the questions like honey stirred in hot water. Serena notched her leather boot in the stirrup and hoisted herself into the saddle.

Something tugged at her skirts, but she barely noticed. *So tired.* Serena leaned over the strong neck of the horse to rest. She felt the beast's strength, its blood throbbing beneath its skin. She heard her own steady breathing as darkness swirled around her. The horse's body warmed her, and she belatedly realized that she was cold without her cloak.

A frantic voice, so small, pulled at her consciousness. It was engulfed by the sound of her breathing. "Nay, Serena, don't go." It sounded like Eleanor's voice. Why was Eleanor there? Serena couldn't remember. "Please climb down."

Serena could no more climb down than she could fly. She was stuck in place, lying across her horse, waiting for something to happen. Serena felt the side of the horse dip. The rocking righted itself and another warmth fell across her back, hugging her.

Eleanor's muted voice cut through the fog in Serena's ear. "If ye're going somewhere, I'm going with ye, Sister."

The horse shot off into the woods behind Kilchurn. Eleanor's cloak surrounded Serena from behind as her friend wrapped it around them both.

Eleanor's fear soaked into Serena. "Where are we going?" Eleanor asked. "Why don't ye answer me?"

Serena dragged her hand along her thigh, backward. Finding her friend's hand, she clasped it, squeezing. Eleanor squeezed back tightly and leaned against Serena's back as the horse sped along through the woods, somehow knowing exactly where to go.

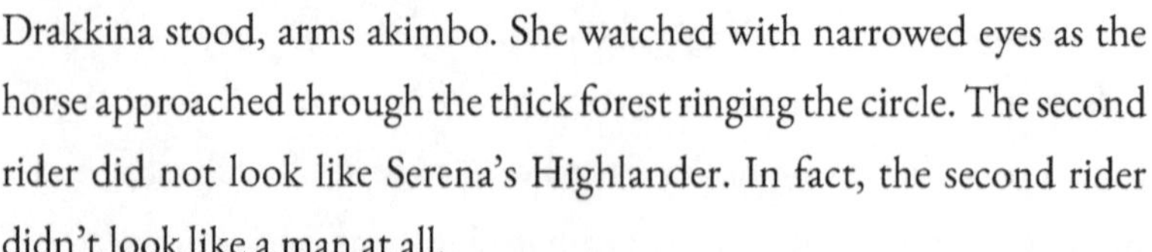

Drakkina stood, arms akimbo. She watched with narrowed eyes as the horse approached through the thick forest ringing the circle. The second rider did not look like Serena's Highlander. In fact, the second rider didn't look like a man at all.

Cac! She didn't bring the Highlander! Keenan Maclean was still out there, somewhere unsafe at a time when Drakkina felt death hovering near Serena and him. That's why it was imperative they both come to the circle, where she could protect them. Instead, Gilla's daughter brought a woman.

"Who are you?" Drakkina's frustration poured acid into her words. Serena and the woman sat up as if they were one. Serena blinked from the spell and the other woman stared with wide eyes.

"Me?" the woman asked stupidly.

Drakkina threw her hands out toward Serena. "I know who she is. Who are you, and why aren't you Keenan Maclean?"

Serena shook her head as if clearing it, her hands rising to slide across her eyes. "She's Keenan's sister, Eleanor. Have I been asleep? On a horse?"

"Where is Keenan Maclean?" Drakkina yelled, stamping her foot.

"Is she...?" Eleanor clung to Serena. "I think I can see through her."

"Despite her temper, I think she means well," Serena said to Eleanor.

The two women slid off the labored horse. Drakkina flicked her fingers at the beast, and it walked out of the circle toward a creek for water and grass. Drakkina tried to ignore the gnawing of anger and fear within her. She lowered her voice, but the terseness could not be filtered out completely. "Again, where is Keenan Maclean, Serena, your mate? I need to protect you both."

"Can you protect him?" Serena asked, regaining her alertness. She hurried over to Drakkina while Eleanor stayed near the outer edge of the circle.

"I can protect him in this stone circle, which is why I've called you here. Why didn't you bring him?"

"He left for Culloden before you called me."

"No! The fool!" Drakkina turned, hands on her hips. Panic raced through her as her eyes flew from stone to stone. Her blood pumped hard in her nearly solid veins. She hadn't felt so alive in centuries, nor so scared. If the Highlander died, Serena wouldn't have her destined mate. What would that do to her chances of winning in the final battle with the demons in the future? Each daughter must come to the battle with their mates beside them. She knew the instructions from her oracle. And she was failing with the very first one.

"Can you bring him here, Drakkina, save him?" Serena asked, hope making her words tumble out. Gilla's daughter suffered.

"Can I bring him here?" she repeated Serena's question and tapped a finger against her lips. "I thought I was," she said absently. "He doesn't have my mark to pull him to me like you do."

"Perhaps he won't die at Culloden," Keenan's sister spoke up. "He could come home."

Drakkina drilled into the woman with her fierce glare. "Death stalks all the Macleans, I feel it, I know it. And Culloden will be a disaster for all of Scotland."

The woman paled and placed a hand along her throat.

Drakkina's eyes shifted back to Serena. "He loves you. Why would he leave you?"

"He said he had to fight with his men. Had to lead them so Lachlan wouldn't march them foolishly to their deaths."

"Culloden is certain death," Drakkina mumbled darkly.

Tears swelled out of Serena's violet eyes, and she wiped them away, her lips tight with anger. "I trusted him. Trusted the plans I had for our life together. Children, vegetable gardens." She took two deep breaths as Eleanor came close to hug her. "What if he chooses to die instead, to be the sacrifice he's been taught to be? What if our love is not enough to pull him from that path?"

"He's chosen to live," Eleanor said. "He will lead his men and defend, but now he will also try to live."

Drakkina rubbed deeply lined hands across her face. She had died centuries ago and yet she couldn't rest, couldn't go beyond into oblivion. She had to save this mess of a world, and even though she couldn't fully enjoy the pleasures of the earth any longer, she was tied to it. And she wasn't giving up when she'd just started.

Drakkina sniffed the afternoon air. The dark calm before death stunk of anxious men and dirt and hot raging blood. The wind was full of it. "Perhaps he didn't love you as we thought," Drakkina said and dipped her finger into the glassy surface of her oracle. Serena had apparently pleaded with the man to stay with her.

Serena straightened away from Eleanor. "He loves me as I love him. I feel it in him still as he struggles," she said, closing her eyes and turning east toward Culloden.

Drakkina's finger froze, and she turned sharp eyes to Serena. "You can read him?" He was meant to be her mate. Her powers shouldn't work on him.

Serena shook her head. "No, not read really." She stared out toward the distance as if spying him there on the edge of battle. "But I feel his emotions. We formed some sort of connection between us when we lay together under the stars in a magical clearing surrounded by blackberries."

"Magical clearing?" Drakkina asked. "What magical clearing?" No wonder Serena had seemed lost to her for a time.

"It was in England."

Drakkina held tight fists against her mouth as she thought and then dropped them. "Keenan Maclean feels your emotions too?" Drakkina slid away from the table and walked closer to Serena.

"Yes. We handfasted in the clearing, and I felt his love, his commitment, and I trusted those feelings."

"What do you feel now?" she asked.

Serena turned toward the southeast and closed her eyes, taking three deep breaths. Her eyes squeezed tight as if pushing back tears she refused to let fall. "He feels irritated, angry over foolishness perhaps. Determination." She opened her damp eyes. "And he's hungry."

Drakkina's mind whirled. "He can feel your emotions too?"

"He's said as much, after the clearing."

"And physical sensations?"

"I don't know, but I think so. Like I said, he's hungry."

"Then pull him here! Think that he must come, that he must leave."

"Would that work?" Eleanor asked.

Serena looked at the pebbled ground and then met Drakkina's gaze again. "I already asked him to stay back, but he feels he must go with his men, his clan. He thinks I'm safe at Kilchurn, and he must help save those who aren't. He is a warrior and leader of men." Serena's voice had grown steady with conviction.

Drakkina frowned at her resolve, but the thought echoed in her mind. *Safe, the Highlander thinks she's safe.* "What if you aren't safe? You can pull him away from battle."

Serena shook her head. "I won't lie to him."

Drakkina narrowed her eyes. "You don't understand, child. I need you both alive, the whole bloody world needs you both alive. Good bloody hell! Everyone in the past and future needs you both alive."

Serena faced her. "You're right Drakkina, I don't understand. I don't understand how you know that, where you come by that information. I know that the world has a strange way of continuing on and that prophecies are unreliable. You say you were my mother's mentor, but I don't really know you at all. I can't trust you."

Drakkina's heart pounded, at least she thought it was her heart, or where her heart should be if she still had one. She flapped her hands out around her. "There's no time for that, woman! Try to call him away from Culloden. Now!"

Eleanor stepped before Serena. "Try it, Serena. Maybe he will come."

Serena shook her head and slid the dagger from its sheath tied in the folds of her gown. "He left me this," she said and handed it to Eleanor, "and his trusted men. I'm not in danger, and I won't lie."

Drakkina focused on the blade. "Peril, real life peril. He'd feel it. By the Earth Mother, let him trust it," Drakkina whispered the prayer and rushed toward Eleanor.

Drakkina concentrated on the bits of energy comprising her form, turning them translucent until she was nothing more than mist again. With a surge, Drakkina squeezed between the particles that held together Eleanor's body until she completely joined with the stunned woman like she had with Matilda Cumberland and then her husband. Eleanor's consciousness gagged against the intrusion, but Drakkina blocked it out, focusing her energy on moving Eleanor's limbs like a puppeteer.

Had Serena seen her squeeze into Eleanor? Could she read her intent? Eleanor still held the dagger, and Drakkina raised it high.

"Forgive me," she said through Eleanor's tight voice as she plunged the silver blade downward. The blade sliced into the flesh above Serena's right breast. Down through muscle, between bone until the hilt lay flat against her skin.

CHAPTER THIRTY-SIX
WAR &
HOPELESSNESS

Keenan watched Lachlan slump down against a boulder in the misting rain. Keenan raised his arm, a signal to his men to halt their march. They had made it to the moor, but darkness was beginning to fall, and Lachlan didn't seem like he planned to stand again soon. His brother looked up at the gray gloom around them.

"Mo chreach!" Lachlan cursed into the rain.

"Take yer rest men," Keenan called. "Disperse rations." The Maclean warriors pulled the supply wagon near a copse of scraggly trees. Rus unloaded wrapped cheese, cured meats, and bannocks. Keenan sat next to his miserable brother and handed him a lump of cheese and strips of venison.

"We don't have to continue with this foolishness," Keenan said chewing hard on the meat's tough edge.

Lachlan stared out across the vastness of Culloden Moor. Off in the distance smoke snaked up through the tree line. Those would be King

George's men, under the command of the vicious Earl of Cumberland. Scouts reported nearly nine thousand English, Irish, and supportive Scots, just like Keenan had seen on the English king's map.

"I don't care what Murray and the Prince think, I've met Reginald Cumberland," Keenan said. Most recently at Frampton Manor where he'd been forced to hand over gold to pay the Faw Tribe. "There's no way he's letting his troops drink themselves into oblivion in honor of his birthday; not before the start of a battle." Lord Murray, the commander over Prince Charles Stuart's army, had convinced the prince that they should cross the moor during the night and attack the drunken English troops.

The troop of two hundred Macleans had traveled for a day and a half to reach the muddy hills of peat and bog across from Cumberland's massive troops. There were Scots spread out around the perimeter of the moor, waiting for the signal from the Stuart prince and Lord Murray to attack. They had arrived an hour ago to a haphazard band of close to five thousand Scots, no provisions, no organization. Just like Keenan had anticipated.

Keenan swallowed down some cheese and then chewed his oat cake. At least his men had food and blankets. Most of the other troops were becoming weak from hunger, cold, and exhaustion.

In Lachlan's silence, Keenan's thoughts drifted to Serena. He'd made the only promise he could, to try to survive while still leading his men. Deep in his gut, Keenan felt his nerves tightening. Fear? Never before had he worried over the start of a battle, but never before had he actually cared about living through one.

"Ye love her." Bouncing sleet muffled Lachlan's voice.

Keenan threw his blanket over both of their heads so that they sat in a small cave together, upper arms touching.

They both knew he spoke of Serena. "Aye, I love her."

Lachlan nodded, his head knocking the covering. He turned dark eyes toward Keenan. "When did ye fall in love with her?"

Keenan remembered her cool fingers as they traced his scar the night they met and then the kiss on the moor. Keenan met Lachlan's eyes. "Before I knew who she was."

Lachlan peered intently at him and exhaled slowly. He turned back to the darkening moor. "If King George walked up to us right now," Lachlan said, "to strike me down." He wiped the freezing water that ran down from his eyebrows with his hand. "Would ye step before me, Keenan? Would ye defend me, Little Brother?"

"Aye, I would," Keenan answered without hesitation.

Lachlan's eyes measured his words. "Why?"

It was a valid question. Why not let Lachlan die so Keenan could become the brother who lived? He already had the witch, why not abandon Lachlan now to the prophecy as Keenan had been abandoned by almost everyone since birth?

Keenan rubbed his dirty hands along his own wet, mud-smeared face. "Because ye're my brother. Even if I don't believe in yer prince, Lachlan, I do understand what loyalty is."

Lachlan stared, his face relaxing until the hint of a grin crept along his lips. He looked back out to the slowing rain. "This is miserable business."

"Aye, bloody miserable business," Keenan agreed. The rain and sleet ebbed. "I'm going to go check on the horses. We need every beast in this battle." Already, Brodrick's horse had disappeared after bringing those two fools.

Keenan threw off the blanket and stood to shake the water from his hair. He straightened out his large frame, stretching his back when suddenly white-hot pain shot through his chest. He doubled over with a huffing sound and fell against Lachlan.

Lachlan struggled under his mass. "Keenan?"

Keenan grabbed the right side of his chest. Had he been shot? It felt more like a blade.

"We're under attack!" Lachlan yelled. Men scrambled everywhere, grabbing swords and shields as they ran toward the two brothers.

Keenan held his chest, searching his bleached tunic. No blood poured from him, but the feeling had knocked him down, a searing burn into his flesh.

His face paled. *Serena!* Could it be her pain he felt?

Keenan caught his breath as men gathered around them, torches glowing in the gloom. His mind tumbled as he rubbed his chest. "I'm not hit," Keenan said.

"But ye crumpled," Lachlan insisted.

Brodrick pushed his way through the crowd, Gavin behind him. "Ye left Serena at Kilchurn?" Keenan asked.

"Aye," Brodrick said.

"She made us go," Gavin said.

"And she was well?"

"Hale and hearty," Brodrick said. "Determined to try to keep ye safe."

Keenan leaned forward, propped against his knees as feelings thundered through him. *Shock, pain.* Never before had he felt such a connection with Serena. *Resentment, remorse.* Each dark color of emotion bled over him, coating him in her unfiltered anguish. Sorrow and finally acceptance.

Acceptance? Of what? Dying? It was the last emotion that gave him the strength to decide.

"Serena's been stabbed," Keenan said. "Here." He rubbed his still aching pectoral.

"How do ye know this?" Lachlan asked, examining the spot.

"We're connected somehow," Keenan shook his head, his eyes traveling to the tethered horses.

"Are ye leaving us?" Rus called out as the large group of men watched.

Keenan barely noticed Brodrick and Gavin climbing together on another horse as Ewan and Thomas took Ewan's mount. Keenan looked back at Lachlan, standing there alone, against a backdrop of Culloden Moor. What a bloody horrible choice to make, between his clan and Serena. Guilt pulled at him, at his honor before the eyes of his men. These were men he'd trained, men who depended upon him. How could he leave them to his brother's leadership?

Keenan came close to Lachlan. "I tell ye brother, this scheme is doomed. Like I said, the Stuart prince's strategy won't work. We don't need Serena's warning to know the outcome of this. Come away now. We'll pick a different battle with the English."

Lachlan shook his head. "I can't leave," his words were low, only for Keenan. "'Tis the first time I've felt their respect," he said glancing past Keenan's shoulder toward the expectant men. "I can't play the coward anymore, Keenan. It will kill me."

"But ye'll die here."

Lachlan smiled grimly. "Perhaps, but 'tis also the first time I will truly live."

"But the men."

"I'll put Rus in charge of our strategy." Lachlan nodded. "Ye trust him. And ye've told me of Serena's warnings. I'll tell them all and let them protect themselves as best they can from what she saw. Or they can go."

"They won't," Keenan said shaking his head. The pain in his chest felt so fresh that he looked down to see if blood pooled between his feet. But there was only mud and trampled grass.

"Perhaps," Lachlan grabbed Keenan's shoulders in his hands and shook him slightly. "But ye, Brother, ye must go. If she dies, so does the prophecy and our chance for peace. Ye must keep our witch alive."

"Lachlan... Brother—"

"Nay, Keenan." He nodded, using his father's favorite utterance. "'Tis yer duty." Lachlan's eyes warmed with a hint of a smile. "Yer heart was never for Da's cause because ye don't respect the Prince. Finally, yer heart is for something."

Lachlan raised his voice so all could hear. "Go to her, save our witch, Keenan. Without her alive we have no chance for peace. Ye must go to save our clan. I know ye will do yer duty."

Air wheezed out of Serena's stunned lips. Drakkina drew out of Eleanor's body, rematerializing next to Serena.

"Quickly, bring her to the stone table," Drakkina demanded.

Eleanor looked down at her shaking hands. "What have I done?"

"You've done nothing!" yelled Drakkina as she frantically tried to catch Serena's wilting body, but the woman's form fell right through her own, onto her side, crushing the wildflowers. Serena's low moan squeezed inside Drakkina's chest. "What have I done?" Drakkina breathed softly and turned her fury on Eleanor.

"Move!" Drakkina ran over to Eleanor, waving her arms in the air before her face. "Pick her up and place her on the stone table while I call her sister here to save her."

"Her sister?" Eleanor said, her eyes wild.

"Move!"

Eleanor snapped into action, heaving Serena up and wrestling her as gingerly as possible onto the stone table.

"I must keep her on her side," Eleanor said with a sob. "The blade protrudes from her back." Eleanor pulled her hands away from the wound. Serena's blood flowed down her palms, staining the edges of her sleeves at the wrist. "It was her blood she saw, her own blood. Oh dear God."

Drakkina ignored her and looked around the stones. "Chiriklò come to me," she called, and the blue bird screeched loudly as it wove in and out of the stones around the circle. Drakkina knew it had been close, never far from Gilla's girl. It flew to perch on Serena, chirping and squawking.

"No time to panic, and I don't have eyes to peck out." Drakkina threw her arms in a southeast direction. "Go to him. Find Keenan Maclean and lead him here over the bridges I'm weaving." Drakkina closed her eyes and pictured the lands between them, mountains, lochs, moors until she reached Culloden in her mind. She pulled upon the magic thick within her. The power threaded out, bending the miles, folding them into short lengths. She did it as quickly as she could.

"Go," she ordered the bird and heard its small wings stretch as it soared. "Go fast," she said as she wove a second thread around the first, pinching together the layers of time that lay across the land. Each moment in time was in itself complete, held apart from every other instance in time. But Drakkina's magic, much like the magic the demons desired, could collapse those layers, shortening time, bringing it together like a folded blanket. It should shorten Keenan's journey from days to perhaps an hour. If he came.

Eleanor cried as she dabbed at Serena's pale face. Keenan's sister looked up at Drakkina with hatred seeping out with her tears. "Ye've murdered her, demon, witch, whatever monster ye are." She spat in her direction and returned to croon over Serena.

"The pain will bring him here," Drakkina said defensively. An uneasy tightness formed in Drakkina's stomach as she looked at Gilla's eldest, her chest growing red with blood.

"It will bring him to her corpse," Eleanor yelled.

"Not with Merewin helping us." Drakkina turned toward the northeast and spread her hands wide. She wove another thread with her diminishing powers, a thread back through time and forward through space to another dragonfly birthmark, on Gilla's second-eldest daughter.

"Merewin, I have need of your magic," Drakkina called into the air. "Merewin, I need you now to save your sister." The silence twisted in Drakkina. What if she couldn't call the healer? She should have called her first. *Fool!* "Merewin!"

"Calm yerself, old crone," a sassy female voice answered. "I'm here."

Drakkina sucked in a calming breath and lowered her shaking arms. A misty figure stood near the inside edge of the stones. She was faint, much too faint.

Drakkina closed her eyes and focused a portion of her magic on the stones, pulling on their strength from the earth beneath them. The air began to hum as the stones pulled more power up through the earth. The wildflowers wilted, adding their life force. When Drakkina opened her eyes, Merewin stood solid within the circle. Mist moved outside the stones, as if the circle sat apart from the current time, but also within it.

Merewin, tall like her father, slender like her mother, had long wavy brown hair and snapping green eyes. And they narrowed as she took in the scene before her.

"What has happened?"

"She's your sister, Serena," Drakkina answered as Merewin ran across the circle.

"I know who she is. What's happened?" Merewin shoved Eleanor aside and glanced at her bloody hands.

"The woman didn't harm her," Drakkina said. "She can help you where I cannot." Drakkina showed how her hands passed right through Serena's arm.

Merewin tore strips from Serena's petticoat and wadded it against the small tip of blade sticking out from her back. Serena's chest rose in short shallow breaths as Merewin laid her ear against her breast.

"A lung is punctured; I hear the wheeze."

"You can heal her," Drakkina said.

"Aye, I can," Merewin said tersely, "but I'd still like to know what happened."

"Later." Drakkina ignored the piercing eyes of Eleanor and watched Merewin pull several stones from a bag tied to her waist. Some were polished, some rough. Merewin carefully rolled Serena to her back, the padding preventing the blade from moving. She gave several jagged crystals to Eleanor.

"Lay the clear quartz along her stomach up her sides near the wound." Merewin held up a smoky, smooth crystal. "My rutile quartz will ease her breathing and lesson her shock." She laid it against the hilt still buried in Serena's chest. Drakkina recognized jade stones that Merewin placed in each of Serena's palms, curling her fingers around them.

Merewin closed her eyes and moved her hands gracefully over the stones. Drakkina stared, trying to see the intricate web of healing threads that Merewin wove. *Fascinating.*

The power to heal was one Drakkina had never mastered, but this young woman held complete control of the power. She used the stones to help her focus the intricate energies required.

Drakkina looked at the dagger hilt. "Shouldn't we remove it?"

Merewin didn't open her eyes, and a frown creased her flawless brow. "Nay, not until I'm certain."

"Certain?"

Merewin lowered her arms and touched several of the stones. She bent low to Serena's face and brushed back her hair. "Why don't ye warm from my magic, Sister?"

"What?" Drakkina squawked. She clasped her misty hands.

Merewin didn't rise but turned her face to Drakkina. "My magic isn't working on her." She turned back and kissed Serena's forehead.

"Sister, open your eyes, see me."

Serena's eyes flickered. Merewin smiled. "There now. Ye must open to my power, else I cannot help ye."

"What do you mean, you can't help her?" Drakkina demanded.

Merewin pulled back, still smiling at Serena. "I can only heal those who want to be healed."

Drakkina wafted over to Serena and looked down at her. "Serena, let your sister heal you. He's coming. I know he is. Trust him to come to you."

Serena's eyes had lost any type of focus. "If he's to die, then so will I."

"No!" Drakkina wailed as she yanked her shawl off her head and threw it on the shriveled wildflowers. "You are not to die. Even if he does, you cannot die. Stop dying this instant."

Merewin looked at Drakkina like she'd gone mad. Perhaps she had. The tightness in her chest moved behind her eyes. She wouldn't cry. It was weakness to cry, and she was the powerful Drakkina.

Merewin turned back to Eleanor, and the two of them began to pack around the wounds. Merewin dabbed drops of liquid on Serena's pulse points and dropped several drops between her parted lips. "This is Apophyllite gem essence," she said to Eleanor. "It fights off hopelessness."

CHAPTER THIRTY-SEVEN
STRENGTH OF SISTERS

Voices wavered in and out. Serena felt the cool weight of stones along her body. A wet rag wiped at her mouth. "Serena, you must want to live for my magic to work on you. Do you not want to live?"

Serena squeezed her eyes and managed to flick them open. Large eyes framed by long lashes stared into her own. Serena was mesmerized by the warm green orbs.

"I remember you." Serena coughed, and pain made sparks form behind her eyes.

The woman ran her hand through Serena's hair, brushing it back from her face. She smiled. "I'm Merewin. We've met before, though at the time I thought it a dream."

Serena watched her lovely full lips. Soft golden-brown hair framed a heart-shaped face. "I'm your sister," Merewin said. "Our mother sent us away, hid us. Do ye remember?"

Serena caught glimpses of a girl laughing as they danced in and out of the large stones around their cottage.

"I remember." Serena pulled in a shallow breath, but her chest screamed with pain.

Merewin smiled broadly. "I do too." Merewin squeezed her hand, but it felt like she was wearing thick mittens.

"I'm cold," Serena said and coughed. The taste of iron lay across her tongue.

Eleanor came into view, her eyes red with tears. She rubbed Serena's mouth then placed her cloak over Serena below the dagger. "Serena, ye have to live. I wasn't the one to strike ye."

"I know."

"And I didn't want to strike you, Serena," Drakkina's loud voice came from nowhere and everywhere at once.

"This is your doing?" Merewin snapped.

Drakkina's misty form hovered over Serena, making her gasp, which led to another cough. Concern, self-righteous defensiveness, and panic floated with the priestess. "Listen to me, Serena," Drakkina's voice spoke into her mind. "It was the only way to make him leave the battle. He must have felt the attack through your bond with him." The image wavered slightly. "He'll be here soon. Don't die, child. It was never my intent to harm you mortally."

"Perhaps it would be easier to die," Serena murmured. Life was so hard. She'd been fighting for normalcy her entire life, and she would never truly know it. Her magic would always single her out, and without Keenan she'd never know love.

"Serena," Merewin snapped, blocking Drakkina's floating form. Merewin's eyes were as firm as her hand that squeezed Serena's useless fingers. "Ye must not be my sister, born of Gilla's blood." Serena watched her beautiful, storm-filled face. "No daughter of Gilla would give up so easily."

"I am sorry to meet you so late," Serena said.

Merewin ignored her words. "Do ye remember our mother, Gilla?"

"She was beautiful and hummed all the time."

Merewin's face tightened, a sad smile on her lips. "I'd forgotten that. Aye, she hummed." She leaned closer to Serena. "Mama fought for us, to save us, leaving herself helpless to the demons."

"Demons?" Eleanor asked.

"Yes, demons!" Drakkina shouted. "If you only knew how important this is!"

Merewin held Serena's hand. "She didn't give up even when they killed Papa. She fought until the end. Don't make her sacrifice in vain, Serena. Mama died for us." She shook her head, soft brown curls falling over her shoulder as she looked down over Serena.

"Ye're a warrior, Serena," Eleanor said, squeezing her other hand. "Keenan told me that. Ye saved William, ye saved that boy and his mother from the Campbell. Brodrick said ye stood up to yer whole tribe. Ye even lied to King George."

Serena looked first at Eleanor and then Merewin. "Mama was a warrior." The ring of trees above came more into focus.

Merewin nodded, tears glistening in her once again soft eyes. "She fought for us all."

"She fought for this world," Drakkina added hovering nearby.

Anger added to Serena's clarity, and she breathed fully in through her nose. She would live, if only to learn a way to slap the crone.

"If you live, I'll let you slap me," Drakkina said.

Eleanor gasped. "The stones are glowing!"

Serena felt Merewin's strong hands touch her skin. The cool fingers warmed, and a heat spread out, connecting stone to stone along Serena's numb body. A sizzle stroked through her, making Serena gasp. Flesh and muscle tugged together, closing across the stab wounds inside and out. It hurt and itched and burned.

Merewin stood, eyes closed, forehead furrowed, hands sliding along Serena's body.

"Woman," Merewin said to Eleanor. "When I say, pull out the knife in the same slant that it entered."

Eleanor bit her bottom lip and nodded while she wrapped her hands around the hilt. She bent, studying the slant of the blade.

"Now!" Merewin yelled and pain ripped through Serena as the blade yanked free, stealing her breath. Merewin covered the hole with both of her hands, and the sharp pain dulled, blending away like a smudge wiped with a wet cloth. Merewin's magic crept along Serena's limbs. Serena could follow it with her mind, noting how the numb areas awoke, first to pain, then to discomfort until the injuries dissolved.

Serena struggled onto her elbows, the stickiness of the drying blood around the hole in her bodice the only evidence of the wound.

"Holy Mother Mary," Eleanor gasped and helped Serena sit. Stones rolled to the table and into the grass.

Merewin opened her eyes. "You are healed, Sister," Merewin said, fading as she gathered the rocks about her. The vibrancy she'd emanated before had dulled, the lines of her face sharper as if she'd been drained.

"Thank you," Serena said, trying to grab her hand, but Merewin was already gone. Serena slid off the stone slab, feeling strong. "Eleanor, where's our horse?"

"Where are you going?" Drakkina said.

Serena pivoted, piercing the witch with a harsh stare. "To help my husband."

"No!" Drakkina shouted. "Stay in the circle where 'tis safe."

"Safe?" Serena yelled.

"You and your mate are in terrible danger. 'Tis safer here than anywhere else in this world."

"You want me to hide," Serena said and shook her head. "Damn all the prophecies and warnings of this world! I'm going to Keenan's side, and we'll meet fate together!"

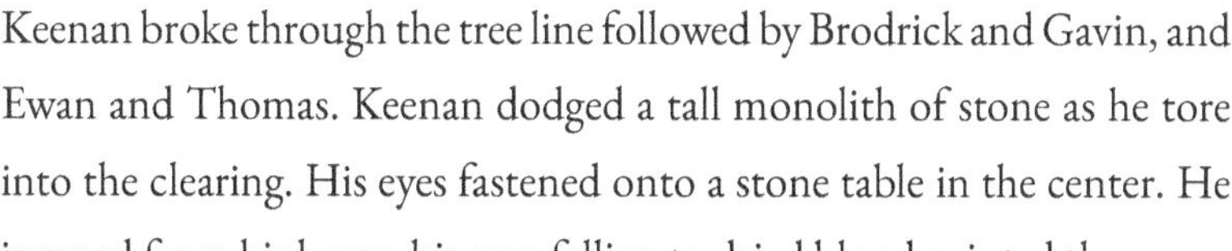

Keenan broke through the tree line followed by Brodrick and Gavin, and Ewan and Thomas. Keenan dodged a tall monolith of stone as he tore into the clearing. His eyes fastened onto a stone table in the center. He jumped from his horse, his gaze falling to dried blood painted there.

He turned. "Serena!"

"She's not here now." The spirit's voice wafted to him on a breeze as she materialized.

Hot fury whipped through him. Without breaking stride, he pulled a dirk and hurled it toward the witch. A startled look crossed the wrinkled face as the blade cut through her vapor to clang unheeded against one of the stones behind her.

"Sometimes 'tis good to be nothing but mist," she said, floating nearer.

"Where is she? What have ye done, old witch?"

"Hold your blade and your temper, Highlander," Drakkina admonished and pulled back the stray curls of white hair that tossed wildly about her face. Her eyes narrowed but flushed cheeks and rapid movements gave her a flustered, anxious look. "Your wife is whole and well."

"Even though ye stabbed her."

"You know?"

"I felt it!"

"Then you know she's headed for your battle?"

"Nay!" Keenan roared.

Drakkina stared, resigned. "I couldn't stop her."

"The battle," Ewan said. "She goes alone." His face mirrored the horror pinching at Keenan's features.

"With the other woman, your sister," Drakkina said.

Keenan turned, slamming his fist down on the bloody granite.

Drakkina pointed in the direction from which he'd ridden. "I brought you here over my temporal bridges. Serena travels back over them."

"Then we return over them," Thomas said pulling his horse forward. After the ride over whatever temporal bridges were, his men hadn't even questioned him about the misty spirit.

Keenan looked to the blue bird circling the stones. The wee beast brought them there. "He knows the way back."

"Stay," Drakkina said, her voice trembling. Keenan looked at her. She seemed suddenly old, tired, as worn as an ancient hag. "Once she sees you aren't there, she'll return. She will always return to the west." The hag dripped resignation as if she already knew his answer.

"We go," Brodrick said.

Thomas climbed onto his horse. "The prophecy says that she will lead us to peace. The prophecy—"

"Is no more!" Keenan's roar filled the stone circle, vibrating off the tall monoliths to tremble through the gathered men. "I ride to save Serena, not the witch." His eyes narrowed with challenge as he looked at his faithful men. "I ride because I will it. I ride because I love her."

Power and strength flowed through Keenan's body as he shed the shackles of the prophecy. Energy like he'd never felt before rushed in his blood. He breathed in, filling his lungs as if for the first time. No longer would he try to decipher the words, the plan for his life. Only he and God could control his future.

"The prophecy has damned my life, damned the lives of my family," he said, and turned his horse in a tight circle. "No more."

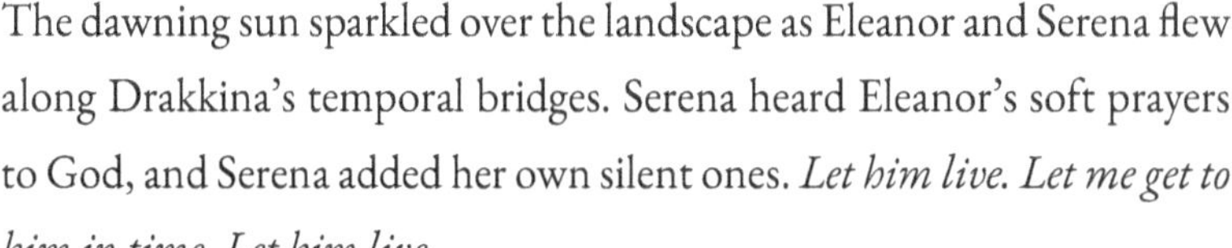

The dawning sun sparkled over the landscape as Eleanor and Serena flew along Drakkina's temporal bridges. Serena heard Eleanor's soft prayers to God, and Serena added her own silent ones. *Let him live. Let me get to him in time. Let him live.*

Up ahead a patch of air quivered. "Hold on!" Serena yelled as they plunged off the end of the bridge onto normal ground with too much momentum. The horse screeched, tripping over the land, as Serena and Eleanor clung around the beast's middle. Somehow, he kept his feet under him, his gallop slowing until he stopped. The horse trembled as much as his riders.

They dismounted, and Eleanor threw her arms around Serena. "Dearest Lord, I never want to get on a horse again," she said into Serena's hair.

Serena hugged her back. Feelings of thanksgiving eclipsed the fear and worry that Serena felt twining around Eleanor's heart. There was also the white brilliance of hope within her, glowing softly, hope and trust in Serena. It funneled through Serena, making her even stronger.

She glanced around and tugged Eleanor to follow her toward voices ahead. They ducked under heavy pine branches, and she pushed one aside, careful not to let it hit Eleanor, and walked out of the trees. Serena came out onto the edge of a bank facing a boggy moor that stretched far before them: Drumossie Moor, better known as Culloden. Eleanor stepped up beside her and gasped as she squeezed the feeling out of Serena's hand with both of hers.

Men in tattered plaids walked back across the moor toward them, some limping, some walking with their heads down, some crawling.

"Is it over?" Eleanor asked.

Serena shook her head while her eyes searched for one tall figure that should stand out from the crowd. "No, too many of them are still alive for it to be over."

"They look like they've been to battle," Eleanor said. She sucked in breath and pointed. "That's Lachlan! And John and Angus!" Eleanor cupped her hands around her eyes to see against the sun that was three quarters up to its zenith. "And Hamish, Lan, and Fergus." Her head turned to scan the crowd. "But where is...?"

"He's not here," Serena said, her voice numb.

"He must be here. Keenan wouldn't leave his men."

Serena looked at Eleanor. "He felt my wound."

Eleanor's eyes turned to her and then glanced behind them toward the temporal bridge. "Ye think he—"

"Fell for the trick," Serena finished the sentence. What had Drakkina done? She'd taken Keenan away when his clan, his family, needed him most. But hadn't that been what Serena had asked of him earlier? She swallowed down the bitterness of guilt as if it were moldering fruit.

"It wasn't a trick," Eleanor countered. "Ye were stabbed."

"I let my weakness, my doubt in Keenan…" Serena swallowed back her tears. "I should have read Drakkina, known what she planned—"

"Serena, nay," Eleanor said.

"Would the Macleans be crawling back across a moor if Keenan had been here to lead them?"

Eleanor didn't say anything as the two looked back out over the moving ground. Lachlan had made it halfway across the field when Prince Charles rode out on a white horse, his orders blowing away from the women on the wind. Eleanor and Serena clung to one another as they watched the men turn back around and form lines.

"Holy Sweet Mary, Mother of God," Eleanor prayed out loud. "Save our men."

Save our men. Serena added her own prayer. When had these Macleans become her men? It didn't matter, they were. *Save them.* Serena thought of the wives and children she'd left at Kilchurn. Their hearts full of hope and fear.

"Look," Serena said and pointed to the line of red-coated men at the far end. They marched as a united front, perfect precision, row upon row. "There are so many."

Both women jumped as a volley of British gunfire popped in the distance, slicing through the first line of Jacobites.

"Nay!" Eleanor yelled as a second volley exploded. Dust and gunfire smoke billowed upward toward a clearing sky. The deep boom of a cannon followed. Clumps of peat and men flew into the air where the cannon hit. Their mangled mass of broken bodies twisted in the smoke and mud.

Serena scanned the field. She caught a glimpse of the cockaded bonnet of the prince, retreating from the slaughter. In an instant their proud leader was gone, his leadership shot out from under him. She steeled herself against the onslaught of emotion. The Scottish fought mostly with swords, scythes, and axes, which did little against the British artillery.

"I have to help him," Eleanor said and stepped off the bank, her boots churning down the steep slope, kicking rocks loose.

"Eleanor!" she yelled.

Eleanor looked back for a moment at Serena, her face red and washed with tears. "He's dying out there." She ran onto the moor.

Lachlan stood, blood on his hands as he grabbed his thigh. He'd been shot in the leg. He must have heard Eleanor's cry because he turned to watch her run to him. They were too far away for Serena to hear, but she could see Eleanor pull Lachlan's arm, trying to persuade him from the field. Cannons boomed, echoed by screams and thumps of debris and bodies. Guns popped continuously. The resonance of guttural war cries lay like deep water over the moor, flooding, smothering, drowning.

Serena couldn't breathe. Her overlapping hands pressed hard against her chest as she heard the popping of another deadly round of gunfire. Lachlan must have heard it too because he threw Eleanor to the mud and covered her with his body.

"No!" Serena screamed. "Eleanor! Lachlan!" Serena jumped up and down, her fingers curling and uncurling at her sides. She took a step toward the edge of the moor and looked around for something physical that she could use for a shield. There was nothing but rocks and...

"Keenan?"

CHAPTER THIRTY-EIGHT
PROPHECY FULFILLED

Keenan pulled his horse up quick so as not to plunge down the hill. The horse neighed, its eyes wide with terror from another run along the warped bridges. Keenan spotted Serena and something tight uncoiled in his chest, something that allowed him to breathe again.

"Keenan!" she cried, and he jumped down, pulling her into his heaving chest, engulfing her. She felt strong and sturdy.

"Are ye hurt?" he asked, holding her to look at her chest. "I felt it, and ye're covered in blood."

"I'm well. 'Twas Drakkina, but..." She threw her arm out to the battlefield.

His eyes lifted over her head, and he stiffened at the sight of men crawling in the mud, bleeding and dying across the moor.

Serena pushed against his chest. "Eleanor, Lachlan." Serena's words seemed to garble together. "Lachlan threw himself on Eleanor! She ran out to pull him off the field. He's shot and..."

Her words hit him like a mace, kicking him into motion. "Brodrick, Gavin," Keenan said as he grabbed his shield from his horse. "Guard her until I return."

Keenan plunged down the hill, rocks and dirt scattering under his heels as momentum enhanced his swiftness, and he used his honed balance to keep himself upright. He held his sword in his right hand, his shield in the other. Thomas and Ewan flanked him. Energy and intent billowed up into him. His muscles flexed as his legs leapt across the soggy moor toward his brother's body.

He and his two men crouched down under their shields as a barrage of gunfire rained down on them. Ewan grunted. Keenan looked to his left to see his friend wipe a fresh swell of blood from his leg.

"'Tis nothing," the warrior said and the three rushed forward through the smoke, dodging British and Scottish artillery.

They ran low to the ground, bent over as they hurdled fallen Highlanders and pools of fetid water tinged red with blood. Men shouted, grunted, screamed. Cannons boomed and shook the warped earth beneath Keenan's boots. Smoke, mud, and the tang of blood burned inside his nose. War, full-on dirty war, what he'd been trained for, what he'd practiced all his life. Keenan's voice carried above the noise, out across the moor. "Lachlan! Eleanor!"

"Keenan! Help!" Eleanor's frightened cry sent another surge of ruthless energy tearing through him. Raw need gave him inhuman strength as he lifted Lachlan off his sister. Blood seeped through Lachlan's shirt near his shoulder and dripped from a wound in his leg.

Thomas took the unconscious Lachlan while Ewan took both shields.

Keenan hoisted Eleanor against him, his arm under her knees, his shield draped over his back. He ran, his legs churning as if he climbed a steep incline, dodging bodies and sword blades, leaping over ditches and death. Eleanor clung to him as if she were a wee lass, his dear sweet sister who'd always stood strong in support of him, who'd showed him what love was when there wasn't any to be found.

Keenan's eyes focused on the lone woman standing tall on the rise. Serena's red hair tossed wildly around her shoulders with the wind, blazing like a flame in the noon sun. Her hands pressed out before her as if feeling along a wall, violet eyes closed, forehead furrowed. The guttural growls of warriors pierced by screams of agony and death beat at his back as he tore across the mottled land toward his love and toward their life together.

Half the hill came down under his heels as he climbed the bank.

"Ewan's been shot too," Keenan yelled, and Brodrick helped the man up the slope.

Serena opened her eyes and grabbed Keenan's arm. "He watched you. He's coming."

His gaze washed over her, not understanding, but feeling the panic race through her. "Who?"

"I threaded through them all to find their leader," Serena said breathlessly. Keenan set Eleanor down on a wet boulder.

"Lord Cumberland." Serena shook his arm. "He saw you run here." She looked into Keenan's eyes. "He's still furious about having to pay our tribe. His mind and heart are blackness." She shook her head. "All he wants is death, Keenan. He's consumed with it, and he's determined to slice you down."

Keenan wrapped her against him and turned to scan out at the field. A contingent of horses moved across the moor. Their British riders sliced and chopped at the exhausted Scottish warriors. Cumberland rode in the middle of them, protected from most of the danger. Serena pulled away to check on Eleanor and the barely breathing Lachlan.

"He will die," Thomas said sitting near Lachlan while Brodrick wrapped a sash around Ewan's leg. "Just like the prophecy said."

Tears streamed down Eleanor's face. "He was defending me." Eleanor looked up at Keenan. "He was defending me and now he will die and ye will lead the clan, just like the prophecy said."

The anguish in his sister's words cut through Keenan. "The prophecy is dead," he said. "We follow no prophecy."

Serena fished out something from her pocket and placed it on Lachlan's chest near the worst of his seeping wounds.

She looked up at Keenan. "Then let's really be rid of it." She placed her hands over the wound and closed her eyes. A labored breath rattled past Lachlan's bloodied lips and then he lay still.

"Nay," Eleanor whispered on a sob as Lachlan released his last breath and died.

Serena continued to breathe, eyes squeezed shut, lips pursed tight. "Not yet, Lachlan."

"Not yet, Brother," Keenan murmured in the stillness and dropped to clasp his brother's hand.

"Cumberland's nearly upon us," Ewan said, trying to stand with his leg tied.

Keenan turned back to the field. Cumberland and his men were close enough for Keenan to make out the commander's sneer. His beady black eyes searched him out. The man must also blame Keenan for his wife's confession.

"Surround them," Keenan said with a glance at Lachlan, Eleanor, and Serena. "Let nothing reach them."

Keenan felt a hum in the ground beneath his feet, as if Serena pulled magic from it. Lachlan's body twitched.

"The bastards come," Ewan said, anticipation lacing his words as he balanced on one foot. Thomas held his shield and sword ready, Brodrick coming to his side.

Cumberland and his men left their horses at the bottom of the steep embankment and charged up, swords flashing, curses flying. Thomas and Brodrick met them at the ridge, striking two down while the others scrambled up.

British steel struck Highland iron as Cumberland's soldiers attacked, trying to hack through the circle around Lachlan, Eleanor, and Serena. Keenan's blade sang, and his warrior's blood ran fiercely through him as he moved through the familiar motions with deadly grace. His breathing followed the cadence of his heartbeat as he clashed and defended over and over until the red coats lay scattered haphazardly across the ground. Now only Cumberland and his standard-bearer stood. Cumberland brandished his sword, his narrow eyes hard and venomous.

"Strike at me, and ye'll join yer men," Keenan said, his stance casual.

"You are a traitor, Maclean, and will die a traitor's death."

"I protect my clan, Cumberland. I stand for what is mine."

"Against King George," Cumberland said.

"I stand against no man save my enemy."

"You support the Pretender Prince Charles."

There was movement behind Keenan and Eleanor gasped.

"*I* support Prince Charles Stuart," Lachlan said. "Not Keenan."

Keenan didn't move his eyes from his adversary, but relief twined with surprise within him.

Lachlan's voice was weak, but he was conscious, alive. "Keenan has tried to convince me to place my loyalty elsewhere," Lachlan said. "He is not loyal to the Prince."

"Then stand down," Cumberland spoke directly to Keenan, his eyes never wavering.

"He will strike," Serena said.

"No doubt," Keenan said more to Cumberland than to Serena. "I won't stand down until I know my family is safe."

"I know your family's prophecy, Maclean. Isn't it your duty to come meet me here and die?" He grinned and spit on the dirt. "You Highlanders are all about duty."

"No prophecy rules my actions, Cumberland," Keenan said, his voice lethal and calm. "If ye think I'll die by yer blade, then come meet me." Keenan took a step toward the earl and sliced his sword through the crisp air in a fluid figure eight.

Reginald Cumberland's eyes opened a hint larger.

Keenan took another step closer to the hedging man. The standard-bearer retreated several paces. "I don't fear death, and I don't welcome it." Keenan arched his sword in another fluid movement, the blade literally singing as the wind whistled by. His eyes hardened, his body on the verge of elegant violence. "Death," he said with menacing softness, "I defeat it."

Keenan stood, his sword arm ready, waiting for Cumberland's response. The sun caught his blade, and Keenan angled it slightly so that the sun shone into the leader's eyes.

The earl squinted. "Tread carefully, Maclean." Cumberland lowered his sword. He glanced at Lachlan somewhere behind Keenan. "And your brother is a traitor. The king will deal with him." Cumberland backed slowly from the scene, arguing with the standard-bearer to leave the bodies of their soldiers.

Keenan turned to find Eleanor helping Lachlan to sit. "Good God," Lachlan said and ran a hand down his face. The gray pallor of death had receded.

"She did it," Eleanor said, tears running down her cheeks while she smiled.

Serena sat next to Lachlan, her faced drained of color. Keenan knelt before her, pulling her to him. She came weakly, and he cradled her, willing strength into her.

Lachlan looked at Serena. "Will she recover?"

Brodrick handed Keenan a blanket, which he put around her, trapping their combined body heat underneath. "We've defeated death more times than I wish to count today," Keenan said and kissed the top of Serena's head. "She's a warrior and will recover."

She tipped her face up to him in the shadow of the blanket, and he saw her smile. The movement untwisted the worry within him.

"I love you, Keenan."

He leaned in, kissing her lips gently. "I love ye, lass. And I will always battle to come home to ye."

Horns sounded. Runners from the Scottish commander, Lord Murray, rode through calling a retreat. The battle was over in little more than an hour.

Kilchurn Castle loomed majestically ahead of them. Sheep roamed the hillside. Chiriklò twittered with two robins in budding trees that flanked the path. Serena and Keenan walked hand in hand after visiting several of the soldiers at their homes. Spring bloomed around them as the warm breeze cleansed the air and earth. It had been a fortnight since they'd returned from Culloden, and tales of the battle had followed.

Culloden had been a massacre. One thousand Highlanders had given their lives to only three hundred-sixty-four of Cumberland's men. Thanks, though, to Keenan's training and Serena's magic, all the Macleans had been saved. Cumberland's campaign to kill all Scots earned him the name The Butcher. He continued his killing rampage, murdering the injured and Scottish innocents in his way, for days after the battle. His savagery disgraced the British army and his own reputation.

"I'd have gutted the man if I'd known." Kennan had said upon reading the report.

Rus jogged up and fell in line with them as they walked toward Kilchurn. "He's gone."

"I know," Keenan said. "He bade us farewell at dawn." A second chance at life, Lachlan had called it. Wanted to make his own adventures, and no arguing would stop him. Lachlan had left with several loyal young warriors to travel south to pay their respects to the Faw Tribe.

From there Lachlan hoped to journey to Ireland or the Colonies. He was being hunted by the English as a leader of the Jacobite cause.

A letter under royal seal had arrived the night before from King George himself. Apparently, the standard-bearer had spoken up on Keenan's behalf. Maclean lands would belong to the clan as long as Lachlan no longer led them.

Keenan laced his fingers through Serena's, remaining silent. She still couldn't read his thoughts, but the tightness of unease filtered to her through their bond.

"Eleanor is starting a tapestry to capture the battle with Lachlan at the head of the Maclean regiment," Serena stated.

"He would like that," Keenan answered. They walked on together in silence.

She was halfway through the small village before the eerie quiet caught at her busy mind. Windows stood empty, doors closed.

"Rus," Keenan said firmly as they neared the gatehouse. "I need to talk with ye and Brodrick. With Lachlan gone, we need new leadership."

Rus nodded. "Aye, we have some things we'd like to discuss with ye, too," he said, his voice stern. They strode through the deserted bailey. Only the gateman stood watch and waved. Up the steps, Rus reached the top and pushed open the arching oak doors, letting Serena and Keenan walk into the entry.

After the bright sun, the total blackness of the corridor blinded Serena. She smelled spring wildflowers, brought in by Eleanor no doubt, and fresh-baked bread for the afternoon meal.

As the narrow corridor opened into the Great Hall, Keenan stopped abruptly, halting Serena with him. She blinked twice, astonished. The entire room, from the winding tower steps to the space before the hearth, to the tops of the long tables, was filled with Clan Maclean, silently waiting. Women, children in their arms, stood next to their returned husbands. Mothers, fathers, old and young alike.

Brodrick's thick voice filled the air above the packed humanity before them. "Let it be known that on this day in the year of our Lord, seventeen hundred and forty-six, that Keenan Maclean is proclaimed The Maclean, Chief of the Macleans of Kilchurn." Without words, each man in the room slid his sword free, filling the room with the slicing sound of steel. All tips pointed upward to the rafters.

Thomas stepped forward next to Brodrick. "And let it be known that on this same day, we welcome Serena of the Faw Tribe with our gratitude and hearts to walk beside our laird."

Gavin stepped up next to Thomas. "So that they both shall lead Clan Maclean to peace."

Rus jumped up on the bench near them. "So say I," he yelled raising the tip of his sword even higher in the air.

"So say I," Robert Mackay called from the back of the room.

"So say I," yelled Ewan at the same time as two other men whom Serena had healed along the Inverness road leading from Culloden.

"So say I," Eleanor called out raising her clasped hands in the air where she stood close to William.

Then the hall exploded in an uneven chorus of shouts, three simple words that rippled through Serena. "So say I!"

In the deafening thunder of acceptance, Serena let Keenan pull her to the table. He lifted her up next to Brodrick and jumped up himself.

Looking down at her, Keenan smiled into Serena's eyes. She nodded briefly, and he turned out to the throng of people.

The room hushed. Keenan's sword slid free, and he raised it overhead. With his other hand, he grabbed Serena's and raised up their clasped hands between them.

"So say I," Keenan's voice boomed through the room.

"So say I," Serena followed as she smiled broadly at the sea of faces.

Again the room erupted, and Serena laughed, unable to keep the happiness inside. Keenan lowered his arms, sheathed his sword, and pulled Serena into his embrace. He looked deeply into her eyes. "Welcome home, lass." He paused and smiled. "I think if we start tomorrow, there'll still be time for yer vegetable garden."

Smiling, Serena leaned into him. Their kiss, full of hope and love, consumed them as the celebration continued.

Continue with Book #2 of the Dragonfly Chronicles as Merewin travels back to the 10th century only to be captured and taken to Denmark to heal a Viking leader's ill son. Merewin has been gifted with the power to heal, but hearts can only be healed by love. MAGICK is a classic Enemies to Lovers tale full of adventure, strong female characters, and love in the time of Vikings.

Magick

https://www.heathermccollum.com/book/magick/

Be the first to know when Eleri Drake has a new cover reveal, release, sale, or giveaway! New subscribers receive a free e- copy of THE BEAST OF AROS CASTLE!

Sign up for my once-a-month newsletter at:

https://www.heathermccollum.com/about/newsletter

Newsletter

Did you love Keenan and Serena's adventure? If you did, **please leave a review where you purchased this book** and let others know about it. In the vast ocean of publishing, please help this guppy find the people who love her stories. **Thank you!** *Eleri*

About the Author

Eleri Drake is the penname of Heather McCollum, a *USA Today* and *Publishers Weekly* bestselling author of Scottish historical romance. Books written under the pseudonym Eleri Drake contain fantasy elements to make the adventure and passion even more fun.

Growing up, Eleri/Heather dreamed of fairies and magic. She would swim in her family swimming pool with her legs together, hoping they'd fuse, and she'd turn into a mermaid. Her favorite television show was *Bewitched* where she wished to be Tabitha, the playful, trouble-making little witch child. Now she can funnel all her whimsy into these romantasies set back in time.

Social Media Links for Eleri Drake

Follow me for book info and writer-life fun!
Just use the QR code below (through the camera on your cell
phone) to link to my social media apps. Let's stay in touch!

OTHER SERIES BY HEATHER MCCOLLUM

HIGHLAND HEARTS

First Book – Captured Heart
Enemies to Lovers

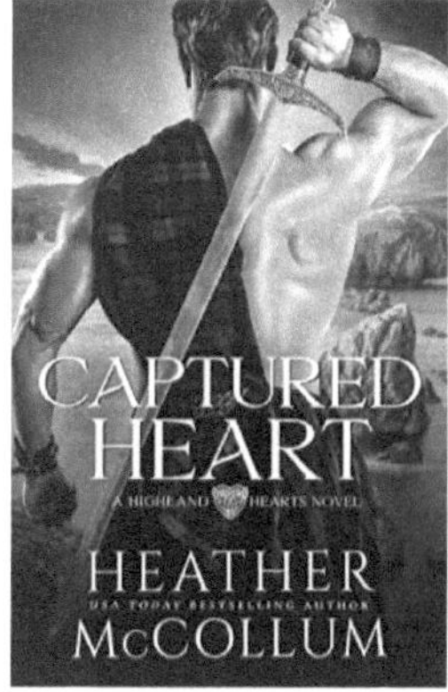

Captured Heart

Set in the early 16th century Highlands. A Scottish Historical Romance series, spanning generations, with a touch of magic. The women in the Macbain Clan have the power to heal, a "gift" that gets passed down through family lines. Those with the gift must evade witch hunters and deal with suspicion. They harness herbal lore and learn to use their magic to help those they love.

HIGHLAND ISLES

First Book – The Beast of Aros Castle
Marriage of Convenience

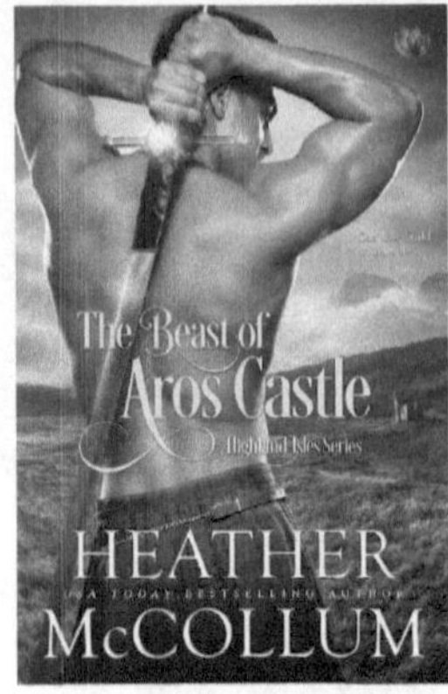

The Beast of Aros Castle

Set in the mid-16th century on the western isles off Scotland. Fun banter and laugh-out-loud adventures with the broody chiefs of the clans and the feisty women who find their way into their lives. Mysteries and secrets abound!

THE CAMPBELLS

First Book – The Scottish Rogue
Enemies to Lovers

The Scottish Rogue

Set in the 17th century in Scotland. Two English sisters journey to Scotland to start a school for the local people in a castle that their brother bought (or so he thought). They quickly realize that on top of learning to read, cipher numbers, and serve tea, the girls need to learn how to defend themselves against both Scottish and English villains. The school becomes a self-defense school, and the pupils are called the Roses (beautiful but with dangerous thorns).

SONS OF SINCLAIR

First Book – Highland Conquest
Enemies to Lovers

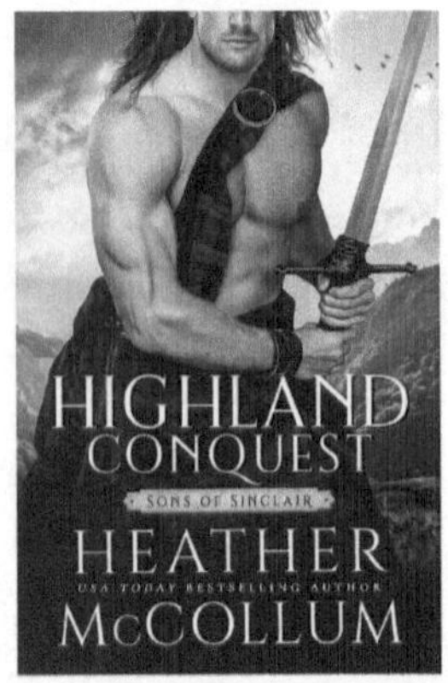

Highland Conquest

Set in the late 16th century northern Scotland. Four brothers were raised by a mad, war-loving father to be the biblical four horsemen of the apocalypse. They are mere flesh and bone, but they were raised to be Conquest, War, Judgement, and Death. Learning to love, the most powerful prize of all, challenges all their beliefs.

BROTHERS OF WOLF ISLE

First Book – The Highlander's Unexpected Proposal
Marriage of Convenience

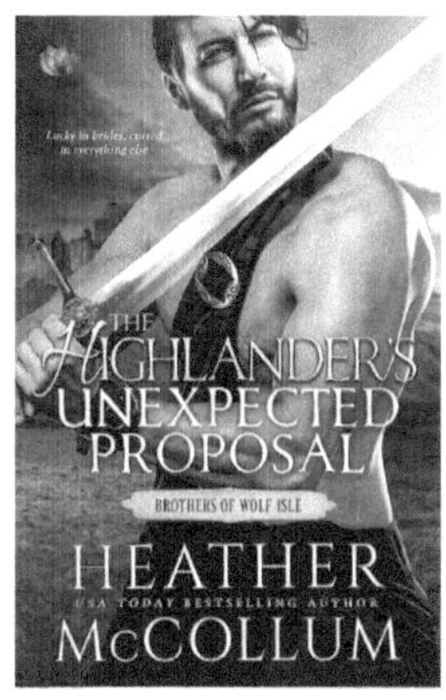

The Highlander's
Unexpected Proposal

Set in the 16th century off the west coast of Scotland. Five brothers are trying to rebuild their clan on their ancestral isle, but the isle is said to be cursed. To break the curse, they must learn truths about love. The original idea for this series was loosely based on the musical *Seven Brides for Seven Brothers*.

THE QUEEN'S HIGHLANDERS

First Book – The Highlander & the Queen's Sacrifice
Secrets, Body Guard, Tudor

The Highlander & the
Queen's Sacrifice

Set in 16th century London at Queen Elizabeth's court.
Three of the queen's ladies get mixed up with visiting
Highlanders to expose assassination plots. Poisoned
gowns, a chastity belt, and masquerade fun!

BROTHERHOOD OF SOLWAY MOSS

First Book – The Highlander's Wild Flame
Enemies to Lovers

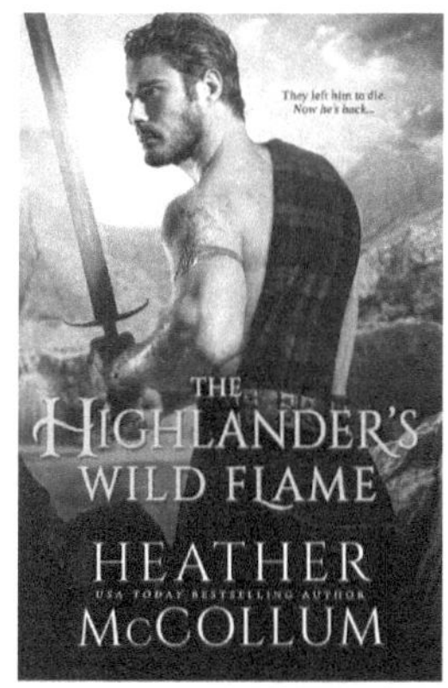

The Highlander's
Wild Flame

Set in the mid 16th century Highlands. Four Highlanders, who were raised as enemies, escape an English dungeon by working together. When they return to the Isle of Skye, they pledge to convince their feuding families to unite to strengthen Scotland. Alliances are only as strong as the emotions behind them, love being the most powerful. Strong women and a witch work to bring elements of fire, air, water, and earth together to strengthen their isle.

Rohaise the Red (novella ghost story)

Rohaise the Red
Novella Ghost Story

Based on a true haunting in Scotland.

The troubled spirit's name is Rohaise, and her yearning to live once again is fierce, fierce enough to kill for love and freedom.

ACKNOWLEDGMENTS

Thank you, dear readers, for trying out my new writing sub-genre! Your support means the world to me.

Also, thank you to my wonderful editor, Melinda DeJongh. Her eye for detail has helped me polish this tale.

At the end of each of my books, I ask that you, my awesome readers, please remind yourselves of the whispered symptoms of ovarian cancer. I am now a thirteen-year survivor, one of the lucky ones. Please don't rely on luck. If you experience any of these symptoms consistently for three weeks or more, go see your GYN.

- Bloating

- Eating less and feeling full faster

- Abdominal pain

- Trouble with your bladder

Other symptoms may include indigestion, back pain, pain with intercourse, constipation, fatigue, and menstrual irregularities.